A HOLLAND AND A FIGHTER

LORI L. OTTO

A Holland and a Fighter

Lori L. Otto Publications

Visit our website at: www.loriotto.com

First Edition: June 2019

Printed in the United States of America

🌸 Created with Vellum

*to you, the most devoted of readers,
especially the Holland Bubble*

CHAPTER 1

PART I - LIVVY

*W*aiting inside the lobby, I closely inspect the painting featured behind the concierge desk. With a critical eye, I see things I could have done differently. I never used to pick apart my work when I was painting regularly. Once I finished a project, I'd move on to the next and leave all the past ones where they shone best: in lobbies, bedrooms, museums, on the sides of 40-story buildings, wherever. Now, though, I'm my worst critic.

This one needs more paint. More *blue* paint. Maybe *green*, too. *Damn it.*

"Mrs. Scott, your car is here."

Not lingering on what I can't change, I smile at Leon and walk out the door he holds open for me. "Thank you, sir. I hope you have a great afternoon."

"You have fun with the ladies," he responds, having heard my plans when I asked him to arrange the ride for me.

I stop walking and turn around. "Bridesmaid dress shopping... like this?" I motion to my expanded figure, which feels five times larger than it likely is. "I'll do my best."

"You look lovely."

"Jon probably paid you to say that."

"I won't say," the concierge teases. I laugh as I make my way to the town car. Instead of taking the backseat that's being offered, I point to the front. One of our regular drivers, Norman, quickly opens the other door for me.

"Thank you. You don't mind a little company, do you?" I ask him.

"I never mind the company of a pretty lady."

After he shuts the door, I mumble to myself. "Jon paid *all* of them."

Norman buckles his seatbelt and checks all the mirrors before pulling away from the curb. "Mrs. Scott—"

"Livvy," I correct him, as I do every time he drives me anywhere.

"Livvy, where are we off to today?"

"Prune," I say. "First Street between—"

"Between First and Second Avenues," he says with one raised eyebrow. "You have reservations? Oh," he chuckles. "Who am I talking to?"

I smile and nod. "It's *Coley's* lunch. She dines where she wants and covers her bases."

"So, she does."

"It's a side-effect of dating my brother," I clarify. I don't know if Coley would lead such a structured life without being engaged to Trey. "Now be honest, Norman. You've known me for a few years. I need the truth."

"You know I hate these questions, Livvy."

"Suck it up. Does this dress make me look fat?"

My driver glances over at me quickly, then back at the road. I can see the blush on his face, and I laugh at his discomfort. There's only one answer to the question, and I can't be mad at *him* for it.

"Now, Livvy, if you're trying to hide your pregnancy, I will honestly tell you that your dress does not do the trick. I can see your bump."

"Not trying to hide the pregnancy. That cat's been out of the bag for a few weeks. So, I look fat, huh?"

"You can tell you're with child, sweetheart. *Fat* and *with child* are two distinct and separate things. You are glowing today, and that dress looks delightful on you. And I haven't seen Jon in weeks, so no, ma'am, he did *not* pay me to say such a thing. I'm a free thinker."

"Mm-hmm," I say, side-eyeing him. "But you're also married. You know the rules."

"I do know the rules."

"A-ha!"

"That doesn't change my opinions."

"All right. I'll quit harassing you."

"Thank you," he says with an exaggerated sigh of relief.

We chat about his wife and grandkids the rest of the way to the restaurant. While I have a history of letting myself out of cars, I don't mind the assistance of a sturdy man when I have to get up from the lower seats.

"Will you need a return ride?"

"I think Coley will make arrangements for all of us. I have no idea where all we have to go. Should be an exhausting day, for sure."

"Tell her hello."

"I will. Be safe."

I have to walk about 30 feet to the entrance of the restaurant. On the way, I hear a handful of people shouting adoring praise about my baby bump. They're still yelling at Livvy *Holland*, though. It doesn't matter that I've been married to Jon for nearly 10 years. I'll never shed the Holland moniker—not that I mind. I love my family and I proudly wear the name my parents gave me.

Jon minds, though. When he's with me, he'll normally shout his last name for principle's sake. It's always funny when Dad's around, too.

"Sister Scott!" I grin when I hear Shea's voice, looking around from the foyer of Prune. I nod at the hostess and make my way to my sister-in-law.

"Sister Scott!" I say to her on my way to the table reserved for us in the small restaurant. She pushes herself up cautiously to give me a hug. The embrace is weak, and our hugs are destined to get worse and worse as the weeks go by.

We stand side-by-side and compare bellies. "I'm winning!" she exclaims, clapping.

"Yeah, you keep cheering about your bigger baby and remember how that thing has to make its entrance into this world, yeah?" I tease her.

"Stop scaring me!" She backhands my upper arm before we both ease into the booth.

"You're fine. I'm just carrying Auggie differently, that's all."

She starts laughing. "You have got to stop calling him that."

I grin widely. "I just can't. I'm falling in love with it."

"There's no way Jon's going to let you call him that."

"All men want a namesake, right? I'm just trying to figure out what to call little Jonathan Augustus Scott the second. Why not Auggie?"

"Why not Jon? Jonny? Nathan? Gus? Junior? Hell, call him Flip or Sam or Harry, but by God, don't call him Auggie. Kids will tease him relentlessly."

"My girls are already going to get him acclimated to the teasing. They're calling him *Froggie*."

Shea chokes on her drink. I give her a minute to recover. "They are not."

"Edie even made him a little cross-stitch of a frog. My grandmother's teaching her."

"Oh my god. You can't encourage this!" She's still giggling.

"I know. But it's so fun to watch Jon get all red and squirmy."

"Did people call him Auggie when he was little?"

"I don't think he was very open with his *full* name. You know what their childhood was like. That would require people to pay attention... there wasn't a whole lot of that going around."

"I know," she says.

As if reading each other's minds, we both check our watches at the same time.

"Where is she?" Shea asks. "She's always Little Miss Prompt."

"Right?!" I shake my head. "She did have to pick up her Maid of Honor first. Maybe Stella's pokey or something."

"Maybe."

"Should we look for her?" I ask, pulling out my phone and scrolling for the friend locater app.

"Give her a few minutes."

I nod. "How's Will?" I ask her.

"My husband is sexy as ever," she says with a glint in her eye.

"Shut up, he will never be as sexy as mine."

"Girl, I got the sexiest of all the Scott brothers, and you know it."

I huff aloud at her proclamation. "I don't think so."

"Really? When's the last time you got any play? Huh?"

"Now, you know that's not fair, Shea."

"I told you."

"Sexy and sex have nothing to do with one another!" I argue.

"The hell they don't! Every. Damn. Day."

"Still?" I whisper in moderate shock. "I mean, whatever. Jon and I are fine."

"How long has it been?"

"How many months along am I?" Shea already knows the answer to my question and just likes to rub it in. "It's not Jon's fault."

She smiles, and I might detect a tinge of empathy in that grin. *Maybe.*

"Auggie the Cockblocker," she says.

I nod my head. "Auggie the Cockblocker. He's killed my sex drive. This *boy-child* has killed my sex drive! The girls were the total opposite. I was just like you once..."

"How funny is that? What do you think it means for your kids?"

"I don't want to think about that. My kids are little babies who are never growing up."

"Your girls are seven and eight—and they both have birthdays right around the corner."

"They were just babies yesterday," I say, pouting.

"They're darlings."

"Willow's a darling. Edie's a hellion. Whatever. I love them both."

"Of course, my goddaughter is a little darling."

"She gets it from you..."

"Whatever. Will is the sweetest..." She gets a faraway look as her thoughts linger.

"C'mon, Shea. Which one is he? Sexiest or sweetest, because you can't have it both ways."

"Oh, yes I can. I *do*."

"Fine. One-hundred percent, your husband takes after Jon, though. And I'm tired of arguing with you about this," I say with finality.

"Fine," she concedes. "Let's talk about godparents. Did you two ever make a decision?"

With my first two children, the circumstances in our lives led to easy choices. With Edie, our firstborn, it was always going to be my uncle, Matty. I mean, from when I was a teenager, I knew I'd pick him for a godfather for my future child, way before I even knew if I'd have children. He's just *that guy* that I knew I'd always want in my kid's life. And Jon felt the same. My uncle had always been our champion... he kept our secrets and made arrangements for us to be together when my parents never would have allowed it. I guess Matty knew the eventuality of our marriage... of our happily ever after... of our eternity together.

Edie loves Uncle Matty and his husband, Nolan. For almost nine years, Jon and I lived across the hall from them, so they kind of helped us raise both of the girls. It was the perfect arrangement—one I'm grateful for. I'll forever be indebted to them for all they've done for us, although I think my uncle feels the same way. He'd always wanted kids; the closest he got was being a step-parent to Nolan's children, but they were teenagers by the time he came into their lives.

Matty, both girls and I all *sobbed* the day we moved out of our loft three months ago. Full-on, runny-nose, went-through-an-entire-box-and-a-half-of-tissues *sobbed*.

We still go visit a few times a week.

As for Willow, who came a very short time after her big sister, Jon and Will were coming off a rough year in their relationship. It took Will going away on tour with his band for Jon to realize what a stand-up guy his younger brother truly was. I always knew. But while he was gone, Jon came to his senses, and used the godfather invitation as an olive branch. Will was honored.

He'd just met Shea, and we didn't know her well, but after only a short time with her, we knew what Will knew: that he'd be a fool not to keep her around forever, and that she'd be a wonderful addition to our family. Fortunately, Shea took a chance on our crazy brood, moving from Minneapolis into the glaring spotlight we live under in Manhattan.

Willow adores them both.

"Yes," I answer her. "We are going with... Trey as the godfather..." I pause, heightening the suspense and trying to read her reaction. She's a blank slate as I announce my little brother's name. "Your poker face is good," I comment.

"Go on!"

"And Max for the other godfather."

"Really!?"

"Yes." I shrug my shoulders, admitting that our indecision got the best of us.

The decision came down to a choice between my brother, Trey, and Coley—who's still running way later than usual—or Jon and Will's youngest brother, Max, and his longtime boyfriend, Callen. It was a source of legitimate tension in our new home in the Flatiron district—like we were choosing sides or picking who was the better brother. I *hated* it. Jon *hated* it. Trey and Max, best friends since they were six, thought it was a dumb topic of contention and kept telling us to flip a coin.

I was *not* going to flip a coin for a godparent.

Not that we're religious or something. Sure, it's a sentimental title, but that's just it. It's all about the sentiment, and that means a lot to me.

"We haven't told them yet, but I figure those two are always going to be close anyway. They can share a kid if we're gone, right?"

"I mean, I can't bear the thought of that, Liv," Shea says, putting her hand on mine, "but absolutely. Sometimes I think Max and Trey are soulmates in their own right. Just on the friendship level. You know?"

"No, I know," I say, nodding. "I've never held onto a friend that long."

"Well, you have me now, Sister Scott," she says, "and I'm not going anywhere."

"Good. You can be my, uh... *friendmate?*"

"Oh, no, Livvy. That's all wrong. Umm... *soulfriend?*" She looks wary as she laughs, realizing how much worse that sounds.

"But is it racist if I say that?" I ask her playfully as I touch her mocha skin. She nods her head vigorously. "See, I thought so. But I'm *so* calling you that from now on."

"Please don't call me that," she says, chuckling harder.

"I won't because I don't want to lose the only *soulfriend* I have."

"Why do I say words before my brain processes things?" Shea asks.

"It's one of the things I love about you!"

"So back to Max and Trey. Both, huh? Sure you don't want to hold off for baby number four?"

"That baby doesn't exist. *Won't* exist," I vow. "Four children are excessive! This is the family we wanted, honestly. Jon has always loved having two siblings. And I love having a little brother. Best of both worlds. No room for baby four... so *snip snip* is gonna happen," I tell her.

"To Jon?"

"We've talked about it."

"I guess it's best that way, because you're going to be Charlie's godparents, so should something happen to Will and me—"

"Can't-happen-won't-happen," I say, shaking my head at what's one of the worst thoughts my mind can conjure. Losing Will or Shea would devastate me, Jon—my entire family.

"Should that happen," she continues, "we're going to give you that excessive family you never wanted."

My eyes water involuntarily. "Just to put your mind at ease, Charlie would never be considered excessive to us. I've already told you; Jon and I will help you and Will whenever you need us. *However* you need us. He's already as much my family as my own kids. Just like you're my sister like Trey's my brother... this body's not giving birth to any more babies, but the Scott and Holland families can never be too big."

My best friend wipes her eyes. "Thank you. But nothing bad is ever happening to us."

"Never," I assure her, finally seeing Coley come in the front door. "And soon-to-be Sister Holland has finally arrived!" I shout a little louder than I probably should have.

"Girl, you know people are going to think we are the worst damn nuns Manhattan has ever seen," Shea says as she lays her hand flat on her belly.

"And we would be—with our sexy husbands," I say with a wink.

"The worst!" she agrees and laughs as we stand to greet my brother's fiancée.

"How are my favorite goddesses?" Coley asks, looking as beautiful as ever with her flowing blonde hair and naturally bronzed skin. As I give her a hug, I can see two patches of freckles on either side of her nose.

"Fat and happy," I respond.

"Times two," Shea tacks on, embracing her.

"Do you remember Stella? She was at the engagement party."

"Of course, I remember. Good to see you."

"Oh, my gosh!" she exclaims, looking between me and Shea hurriedly. "Who's due first?"

"I am," I tell her. "Early September."

"Mid-September," my sister-in-law states.

"Planned?" Coley's Maid of Honor asks.

"The babies? Yes. The timing? Well... we wanted to raise babies together, but we had no idea we'd actually be able to conceive so closely to one another. We both started trying around the same time, and I guess we're both equally fertile. I kind of knew I was," I admit. "It was super easy with the girls, too."

"Sorry we're so late," Coley says, finally settling into the booth with us. "Believe it or not, it was my fault. Joel has a catering event and needed some extra serving bowls, so I went and picked up some for him. We got caught in traffic because I apparently got some cab driver who just moved to the States last week or something."

"You took a cab?"

She nods her head.

"Does Trey know you took a cab?"

"Your brother is not the boss of me," she says, waving me off.

"Don't you literally *call* him 'boss?'" Shea asks her.

I laugh as my brother's fiancée rolls her eyes. "Habit from college. It's just cute now."

"You can't take cabs, Coles," I tell her. "You just can't."

"We're not getting into that right now. My day," she pronounces. I smile and agree with her. "I've decided on what you all are wearing to our wedding, and that's why we're all here!"

"You're both going to love it," Stella says.

"I hope it's stretchy fabric, because Lord knows what this body is going to look like in December," Shea says. "I know Liv has no trouble losing baby weight, but... I've already got curves she doesn't have."

"I had no trouble losing it eight years ago," I correct her. "I'm in my mid-thirties now. The game has changed."

"Let me show you Stella's first," Coley says. "Everyone has a different color." She opens up her bridal notebook that she started last summer and turns to a section toward the middle. Shifting the book, she points to a gorgeous formal gown.

"Red?" I ask her.

"Red, yes. But just hers." She flips the page to swatches of fabric in six different colors. "You two get first choice of your colors. Everything will be custom made. And all the décor will match. Bouquets, flowers in your hair, jewels, shoes."

"It's beautiful. So colorful."

"Looks very Coleyesque," Shea says.

"What is Trey wearing?"

"They'll all wear dark-dark gray suits, and if I can get Trey to wear a tie," Coley begins, "it'll be white, like my dress. The rest of the groomsmen will wear the pepper green color—their ties and vests, too. Doesn't it complement the other colors well?"

My stomach does a little flip of excitement for her, knowing she's going to have the wedding of her dreams. They've been engaged for nearly four years, and it took about three of those years for my brother to convince her to let our family pay for the ceremony and reception. It's the only thing that makes sense, but she never wanted it to seem like she was taking advantage of our wealth.

Anyone who's known Coley for more than ten minutes would know that she's just not that type of person. She's the type of person who deserves wonderful things in her life. And people. I couldn't be happier that my brother fell in love with her.

"So? Where are our dresses?" I ask her.

She has this funny look of self-satisfaction on her face. I turn the page in her book, only to find it blank.

"We just have to go see them?" Shea asks.

Coley shakes her head. "I'm going to let you pick. We're going to try on all styles of dresses today—anything you like, anything that's flattering, and it has to make you feel beautiful. That's all."

My jaw drops. My sister-in-law looks at me in confusion, as if she heard Coley wrong. "What's the rub here, Sister Holland?"

"What? I just want you both to have a fabulous time at my wedding. Stella picked out hers. We want you to do the same... and then we have something else planned for you."

"There *is* a rub," I say skeptically.

"Ha!" Coley says. "Like, literally," she giggles. "You know that spa a few blocks away from your apartments? We're all going there for massages. They apparently do the best prenatal massages in the Flatiron District, and I thought you two would love that."

"You're doing this wrong, you know, Coles? We're supposed to do stuff for the bride," I tell her.

"Well, when we set the date, we didn't expect to have two preggo bridesmaids in the mix... and you're family, so I can't very well make you guys work and do shit for me in your fragile states," she jokes.

"Fragile, my ass," Shea says.

"Right?" I laugh. "I swear we will pull our weight, regardless of the fact that we have two little boys tagging along everywhere."

"And we'll have three months post-pregnancy before your wedding. Your bachelorette party will be legendary," Shea says. "All I'm going to say is you've never been there before."

"Do I need my passport?" Coley asks, her eyes wide. Stella looks away, as if she may tell our secret by continuing to engage in the conversation.

"Don't know, Coles," Shea says. "You'll just have to wait and see."

CHAPTER 2

*W*ondering what my second daughter is doing, I look back from her closet to find her lying on her stomach on the floor, propped up on her elbows, reading one of the twenty books she had sprawled out around her when I'd walked in five minutes ago.

"Wils, I told you to choose three books to take with you tonight, not to start reading one."

"I have to read them to see if I want to take them, Mama."

"You look at the cover and the back to see what they're about. That's how you pick what to take. Otherwise you're just... reading it *now*."

"I'm not hurting anyone," she says softly.

"No, but Daddy and I have somewhere to be later, and we don't want to be late. Did you want to help me pick out your clothes for this weekend?"

"I don't care."

"I don't care," I mimic quietly to myself, plucking a few pairs of cute leggings and some *non*-coordinating tops. Willow has a style of her own. I've learned it by now. Just as long as things don't look like they go together, she'll wear them. It's not *today's* fashion, but I like to think my youngest daughter is just ahead of her time. She's beautiful in anything she wears.

Edie, on the other hand, will likely be a clothing designer when she grows up. She has an eye for trends and can spot the latest styles before I even see them coming. The tabloids love to feature her for what she's wearing, and at this age, she loves it. Jon and I hate it, and we're hoping she grows out of it soon. Edie used to tease Willow relentlessly about her clothes until the younger sister showed no sign of caring about the teasing, and Edie lost interest. Now, if anyone messes with Willow, Edie puts an end to it right away.

Jon says both girls take after me: Edie with her sense of style and Willow with her self-confidence. I like the thought of that.

"What shoes are we wearing? Did your uncles tell you what they had planned for you this weekend?"

"Who knows, with those two?" she says. I laugh at her seven-year-old wisdom, which isn't off the mark at all. Max and Callen are very fly-by-the-seats-of-their-pants kinds of guys. It's all Max, really. I think Callen has general plans for things, but it's up to Max whether they follow any of them.

"I'm going to pack some sneakers since you're wearing those." She doesn't look back but acknowledges me by wiggling her Mary Jane-laden feet. "Preference on socks?"

"The ones with the smiling rainbows." Her response was immediate. "Since I'm going to see them."

"Umm... I think they know you're okay with their relationship, sweetie," I tell her, looking at her strangely.

"Oh, I know. But every time I wear them, they buy me something cool. It's sort of a deal we have."

"What?"

"Edie, too. I bet she's taking hers. They tucked a note in the socks when they gave them to us."

I drop the socks in her suitcase and go next door to Edie's room where Jon is helping her pack. It's strategic, because he's a much better negotiator than I am when it comes to her. "Is Edie taking any socks?"

"Yeah. She wants to take these," he says, holding up her pair of rainbow-striped knee highs. I huff and turn to my oldest child. "Edie, hon, please show me the outfit you're wearing with those."

"I don't think we've packed it yet."

"We've packed all of your outfits, bunny," Jon says. "We agreed on them all, remember?"

"Why are you taking these socks, little miss?"

"Because they buy us presents when we wear them," she says meekly.

"Did you know about this?" I ask Jon, laughing. He starts chuckling, too.

"It doesn't surprise me, but no. It's anything goes with those two. He knows our kids are influencers, I guess."

"Max and Callen are influencers," I counter.

"Not to tweens."

"You know what? I'm changing," I tell Jon.

"What?"

"I'm changing. You know that ugly rainbow Christmas cardigan I bought two years ago for that party? I'm putting that on and I'm letting those boys buy me a present. Mama wants a diamond bracelet."

"I'll buy you a diamond bracelet," he laughs.

"It's the principle!" I say, walking away.

"We're gonna be late!" he shouts after me as I go to our room down the hall.

"Principle!"

"Is Willow packed?"

"Yes. She just needs some undies and she has to decide on her books!" I holler.

After pulling on the oversized sweater and checking my hair and makeup once more, I return to Willow's bedroom, where the rest of my family is gathered with all their things.

"Nice, baby," Jon says, nodding. "That'll photograph great on the red carpet."

"Right?"

"No."

"I'll take it off before we get there." He quirks his brow and smiles, lifting only one side of his lip. "Don't get any ideas. It's just a cardigan," I say, patting the bump that's hidden from view by the monstrous rainbow addition to my outfit.

He nods and rolls his eyes. "The tabloids are gonna love this."

"I know," I giggle. "They'll be wondering about this for weeks."

"Can I tell them why, Mama?" Edie asks.

"No," Jon and I both say sternly, in unison.

"We don't talk to them, Edie," he says. "Ever. You don't stop for them.

You don't pose for them. You don't take things from them. You don't go anywhere with them. And you do not ever talk to them. Understood?"

"Oh my god, Daddy, yes!" she says, exasperated. She's heard it a million times. "I was kidding."

"Then *ha ha*, bunny... but still, no," he says, tugging on a strand of her hair. "Are you girls ready? Wils?" he says, kicking her foot to get her attention.

"Two more sentences."

"Nope," he says, bending over, picking her up and swinging her around three times.

"Daddy! I lost my place!" she squeals through her laughter.

"You'll find it again," he says. "These three?" He plucks three random books out of the pile—not even the one she'd been reading.

"Yes, Daddy," she answers, taking the handle of her luggage.

I love how they love their daddy.

*L*ike they always do, Max and Callen greet us just as we arrive. Our families have made a habit of sharing our locations, so we always know where everyone is, to make sure everyone's safe. It's a precaution we feel we need to take, and none of us have ever abused anyone's privacy.

"What the fuck, Liv," Max says quietly in my ear when he hugs me, and it's not so much a question as it is a murmur of disgust at my outfit.

"What, this old thing?" I ask, ushering the girls into the lobby of the building on 5th Avenue while Jon and Callen get the girls' luggage and pillows.

"Why in the world are you wearing that?"

"I heard from two little birdies that you guys give presents for rainbow accessories..."

"Little *yappy* birdies, huh?" he says as he glares at my daughters, who are both giggling next to him. "I have never heard of such an arrangement. Callen, Liv thinks we give presents to our guests when they wear rainbows."

"I'm offended by that suggestion," Callen deadpans. "Livvy want an Altoid?" He produces a tin from his pocket and pops it open.

"You jerk," I say, pushing his arm away. "What sorts of things do you get them?"

"Nothing," Max answers, shaking his head vigorously. "Never. I've never seen a rainbow in my life. I'm colorblind, in fact. Are you wearing colors?"

The girls are in stitches now.

"Books," Willow finally says.

"Lip gloss," Edie answers. "But just the shiny kind. And barrettes."

"And here I was blaming my mother for those," I admit. "As long as it's not candy or some shit like that."

Both of my daughters immediately hold out their hands, palms up. "Jon?"

"*I* didn't say it," he says.

"My handbag is in the car."

He hands them each a dollar. "Mama's sorry," he says.

"Sorry, girls. Don't say words like Mama says."

"At least we reward them for, you know, doing something good... and not for *your* bad behavior," Max says. "What kind of mother are you?"

"Shut up before I have to pay them more, okay, Uncle Max?" I take off the sweater under the cover of their lobby. "Can you hang on to that for me?" I ask Callen. "I don't want to have to worry about that all night."

"I cannot promise we will hang on to it. We may burn it in some sort of cleansing ritual. We had about an hour to fill in our busy weekend *schedge*, right, Max?"

"It's the perfect activity. We'll do it on the roof."

"Yay!" both of the girls exclaim.

"No fire, guys," Jon says. "I can never tell when your crazy ideas may take a turn for reality, buddy," he says to his brother. "And don't let them climb on the edge of the roof, okay? Don't make me worry about that."

"Don't worry about that," Callen says. "I've got that fear. They won't even get near it."

"Thank you."

"You guys have fun at the premiere. Make sure you record the movie on your phone for me," Max says.

"Nope," Jon responds, not missing a beat. "Thanks for watching them this weekend. You know how to reach us if there are any problems."

"We know, we know. Matty's across the hall, and Jack and Emi are on standby. We know the drill."

"Jack and Emi will be available after seven," Jon says.

"Really?" I ask, surprised.

"They said they were going to dinner."

"I don't remember that," I tell him. He shrugs.

"You be good boys," I say to Max and Callen. Turning my attention to my daughters, I smile. "Be sweet, girls." I lean over and exchange kisses with them both. Jon follows me and tells them goodbye, getting big hugs from each of them. "We'll call you in the morning."

"Good bye, you two!" Max shouts, waving as if we're leaving forever. The girls are laughing again at his antics. "And Liv, check your hair."

"Aurgh," I grumble, wanting to give him the bird but catching myself before I do. "Bye."

"Good thing you love him," Jon says as we climb into the awaiting car.

"I know. If he wasn't so damn loveable, I would hate that little asshole. You know, it's funny. When I look at my brother, I see a full-grown man. He's a Columbia grad. He's going to Harvard Law. He's, like, eight feet taller than me," I exaggerate. "And when I look at yours, he's still that mouthy, six-year-old kid. Why is that? They're the same age."

"Technically, Max is older," Jon corrects me. I glare at him. "He's just always going to be a kid at heart. And that's why we love him."

I lean into my husband, letting him put his arm around me. "I know. I wouldn't have it any other way."

"Are you excited about this movie? They say it's Philip Winthrop's breakout role."

"They do," I say. "And he's going to be there."

"On the red carpet."

"Maybe right behind us... who knows?"

"What if he asks, 'Mrs. Scott, will you come home with me?'"

"You already know he's on my list, Jon."

"Don't break my heart, Liv."

"Don't ask me those questions! Plus, maybe he'll bring CiCi Chapman. She's on your list, so..."

"I would never," he says.

"I would never, either," I tell him. "You're crazy to think otherwise. Philip's just, you know... super-hot. So what?"

Jon removes his arm from my shoulder to make his hands into a heart, which he then proceeds to break into two halves.

"Uhhh... that doesn't mean you're not, Mr. Sensitive! You're the sexiest man I know."

"Because you don't actually *know* Philip yet. Semantics."

"No. *Not* semantics. You're being ridiculous. Is my hair messed up?" I ask him.

He fixes a few strands in the front, then shakes his head. I kiss him once before applying more lipstick.

"Hey, did you know Coley took a cab the other day?" I segue poorly.

"What? Really?"

"Yeah, to our little spa day."

"Does Trey know?"

"I'm sure he doesn't. I didn't tell him. I don't want her to think I'm a snitch."

"Is that why you're telling me?"

"Well, I mean, I told her she can't take them... but she didn't seem to take me seriously." The fact of the matter is, we've had to keep our circle of trust very small in recent years as my family's wealth has continued to grow. The Hollands have been the wealthiest family in the country for a decade, and Dad's investments are never bad. Jon and I make good money—him in architecture, and me in fine art. Sometimes, we even work together, and those projects are even more financially lucrative. Will has two prodigious and successful careers: he's notable in the science community, but he's rich and famous in the music world. Callen's family is also incredibly well-off, and Max was the recipient of a very public, high-dollar donation for saving the lives of many people last inauguration day. The concentration of this much wealth makes each and every one of us a target. We'd received threats before.

"I'll talk to him. It's for her own safety."

"Thank you."

"We've arrived," our driver announces as we pull up to the classy Trevena Theatre.

The flashbulbs are immediate as we get out of the car. We don't often do red carpet events, but when Jon found out that Philip Winthrop was going to be at this one, he decided to surprise me.

We pose for a few photo ops, but neither of us answer any questions, even the innocuous ones. We just smile and move along. Jon nudges me at one point and signals to an elevated platform where the star of the film is doing an interview for a cable entertainment channel.

"Yep. He's just as handsome in real life," I comment, not allowing my eyes to linger. My cheeks flush hot, though, and Jon notices and laughs.

As he ushers me inside, he leans in and whispers into my ear. "See, my hope for tonight is that there will be some really steamy sex scene with him, and that it'll get you all revved up or something." He's smiling and has those little wrinkles around his eyes to let me know he's kidding, but I know there's some underlying truth there. I feign a smile and look to the front of the theater, waiting for the movie to start, now feeling sad and guilty and a little angry.

He points out different celebrities every now and then, but finally, the lights dim, and I'm relieved that I can relax the muscles in my face. My real emotions surface, and my eyes swell with tears.

I thought he was just taking me out on a nice date, but he really is just hoping to get laid tonight... and, yet again, I'll get to disappoint him, which I never, ever want to do.

He's always understanding about it—he is. He never pressures me, but I've been with him long enough to know his wants and needs, and four months without sex is not something I ever dreamed would happen to us. We've always been very intimate with one another—for as long as I can remember. When I was pregnant with the girls, my sex drive was even more out-of-control, which Jon, of course, loved. With this boy, though, I've craved Jon's attention and affection—the handholding and cuddles and kisses—but nothing more. My doctor says it happens sometimes. It's a hormonal thing. We shouldn't worry.

But right now, as I sit in this theater, unable to get lost in a movie starring a gorgeous man while I sit next to the love of my life, I worry.

I start crying. In the middle of this comedy, I start crying uncontrollably.

"Baby, what is it?"

"Can we go?"

"Of course," Jon says, but I'm already nearly out of our row. "What's wrong?" he asks when we get outside of the viewing room. He's got his arm around me and is trying to shield me from on-lookers.

"Just call our car please."

"I've already texted him, Liv. He'll be there by the time we hit the end of the carpet."

"I don't want to go out there, Jon," I cry harder.

He wipes my eyes with his thumbs and reaches into his jacket to pull out his sunglasses, putting them on me. "It's okay. You can just look down and hold my hand. We'll go quickly."

I nod, sniffling, trying to breathe and calm myself. "Let's go."

The incessant flashing begins again, as do the questions—this time louder, more unscripted and invasive. They can tell I've been crying, and everyone wants to know what's wrong. It's the longest fifteen seconds of my life.

In the car, Jon asks the same questions.

"When we get home," I finally say, my throat tight. I keep his sunglasses on the whole time.

I can tell he knows it's something he did by his silence; by his distance when we walk into our home together.

"We were supposed to go out for dinner, too," he says, trying to cut through the tension. He loosens his tie. "Want me to order in?"

"I'm not hungry."

"You will be," he says. I take off his shades and look at him severely. "I can make us something later, though."

I go upstairs to our bedroom and shut the door before he can follow me in. I want to get out of the fancy dress and wash my face. I want a few moments to myself.

Once undressed, I decide to take a lavender-scented bubble bath to soothe my frayed nerves. I know being this upset isn't good for the baby. After sliding into the hot water, I close my eyes and hear his voice again.

My hope for tonight is that there will be some really steamy sex scene with him, and that it'll get you all revved up.

Am I being too sensitive? Of course, I am, but I know my feelings are still valid. I try to get my mind off of it by thinking of my girls. Maybe I'll call them once I'm out of the bath and see if they're having fun. They'll center me and remind me that my place here as a mother is just as important as my identity as a wife.

Jon knocks softly on the door. "Liv, I have some sparkling water for you. Can I bring it in?"

"Sure," I tell him, getting choked up at the mere thought of seeing him again. It's not rational. Nothing's rational when my hormones are like this.

He sets down a champagne glass on the rim of the tub, filled with bubbly liquid and raspberries at the bottom. I smile a little at his thoughtful extra gesture. He hangs up his coat and tie in the adjoining walk-in closet, and then takes a seat on my small vanity stool, which he pulls up next to me. "Lay it on me. What did I do?"

"Do you think I already don't feel bad enough that we haven't had sex in months? Do you think I need little reminders?"

"No, Li–"

"And honestly, Jon, for you to think any other man would somehow *get me off* over the valiant efforts of my own husband–do you think I'm that fickle? Or inconstant? My god!"

"I was jus–"

"I know you have needs, Jon, and I'm so sorry that I'm failing you as a wife right now, but I'm doing the best I can and I feel like I've always been so good to you and that, like, it's not my fault. The doctor said it's not my fault! I'm not choosing to not want to be, you know... sexual with you. I want us to be back in that place, but nothing's going on down there for me. I just... don't... want it. I've never not wanted it, but this pregnanc–"

He pushes off the stool and surprises me with his lips on mine. His arm is in the bathwater with me to steady himself, even though he's still got his dress shirt on. "Will you shut up for a second?" He says as he looks into my eyes.

"You acted like Philip Winthrop was your key to getting laid," I whine.

"I was kidding, Livvy. It was a stupid joke, that's all. I'm sorry I said it, but I meant absolutely nothing by it."

"I hate that I disappoint you. I hate that it's something you think about."

"Well, shit, baby... I miss you, yes. I think about you making love to me often, but I've never once been disappointed. Do you know how lucky I've felt for the last... what, twenty years of my life? Most men don't get a woman like you. I am *grateful* for you."

"You're just saying that because I'm in the bathtub, crying."

"No, I'm not. Scoot over," he says, only kicking off his shoes before welcoming himself into the large bathtub next to me, fully clothed.

"You have lost your mind," I tell him, only managing a slight chuckle.

He puts his arm around me. "Olivia, all I care about right now is that you take care of yourself and that little guy in there." His hand rests on my belly, and I put mine on top of his. Our fingers weave together.

"Our little Auggie," I add.

"Oh my god, no." He laughs and kisses my forehead. "But you just need to do those two things. I can even manage the girls for the next few months."

"I've got the girls," I vow. "I can't paint. The smell makes me nauseous, so you've got to make the money."

"You know we're fine on the money. We could both retire tomorrow, if we wanted."

"You know we're never going to retire."

"I'm well aware. Retiring is for people who hate their jobs," he says.

"Retiring is for people who *have* jobs. We have *passions*."

"We have life," he adds.

"We do. A great life."

"The best. I am the luckiest man, Liv. Ever. And don't you ever doubt how I feel about you."

"So," I say, hesitant, "you really didn't get tickets for me to see Philip Winthrop in hopes of me getting turned on by him?"

"You want to know why I got us tickets for this?"

"Why?"

"To make sure we had plans you wouldn't want to get out of. I can barely get you to leave our home since we moved in here."

"Well? Can you blame me? You built us paradise... in the middle of the Flatiron District. We have everything we need here, and we're close to our best friends."

"I'm glad you love it here."

"I do." I squeeze his hand tightly. "Wait, why'd you want me to leave it then?"

"Because I've been working on something for you and I needed to get it in here—to surprise you."

"Really?" I look up at him, feeling guilty again. "Did I ruin that surprise, too?"

He kisses me again. "Nope. It's waiting in the other room. I'm going to dry off, get changed, and let you finish bathing. Then we can go have a look."

"Okay." He slowly gets out of the tub, his wet clothes weighing him down. "And Jon?"

"Yeah?"

"I love you. And thank you."

"I love you, too."

Feeling better, I hurry and finish my bath, then put on some lounge pants and a loose-fitting t-shirt. Jon is similarly dressed and waiting for me on the bed. I finish my last bit of water and place the glass on the nightstand. "Ready?" he asks.

"Ready. I love your surprises."

"I do have the best surprises."

I clap my hands in anticipation and follow him out of our bedroom and down the hall. We pass the girls' bedrooms and the small, open library. We're heading toward the nursery.

"You did something for Auggie?"

"I... did something for the baby," he corrects me, refusing to call him by the nickname. Before we go in the room, he grabs a box of tissues from the bookshelf and hands them to me.

"Oh, man. It's that good?"

"Yeah, I think so," he says.

"Shit," I mumble, but smile, preparing myself for the best—and worst.

He holds my free hand in his before opening the door and looks me directly in the eyes. "I feel the need to prepare you a little."

"I'm worried now."

"It's a bassinet," he says softly. My heart sinks and my eyes water. He nods, and his lips break out into a smile. "I finished it." He says it in a whisper. I'm crying and my arms are around him before we even go inside the room. He holds me tightly, dragging his hands slowly up and down my back. "Shhh," he says soothingly. "It's okay."

"I can't go in," I tell him.

"It's beautiful, baby. So, so beautiful."

"I miss him so much." The words barely come out of my tightened throat.

I was six weeks along when we decided to tell my father I was pregnant—my biological father, Isaiah. He'd had a minor heart attack in October, and his health hadn't improved much since. It was as if his spirit had been broken—he'd lost interest in his sculpting and he was depressed, feeling his life was coming to an end.

Jon and I thought the news of another grandchild might give him something to look forward to. After all, he loved Edie and Willow, and was always happy when they came to see him. He had been so good with them as babies, too. When we told him, it was just what he needed. The life came back into his eyes and he started taking care of himself again. Everything was on track.

And then, at the end of February, we got a call from the hospital in Hartford. He'd had another heart attack while working in his shop. A neighbor heard a commotion and came to his aid immediately. We made it to the hospital just in time to say goodbye. He didn't recover from his second episode. It was devastating.

When we went to his shop, we found out he was in the early stages of building a bassinet for the baby. He had beautiful, elaborate drafts of it sketched out on his worktable. The wood was purchased. He had cut the first few pieces. And that was it.

Years ago, he'd made a sweet little coat rack for Edie, and a toybox for Willow. In addition to the fact that our third child would never meet my biological father, I was heartbroken that little Auggie would never have anything specially-made by his Pop.

I wipe my eyes with a couple tissues and reach for the door handle, leading the way into the room. The sight of the small, walnut cradle takes my breath away. "Ohhh... it's even more beautiful than I could have imagined it, Jon."

"Isaiah had everything designed and detailed to the last letter, Liv. I stayed true to it all. Even down to the finish. I had to get some help from an expert a few times, but... I think it came out like he wanted it."

"Oh, yes. It's perfect." I run my hand across every inch of its smooth wood.

"You won't find a nick or a splinter anywhere. I've sanded the hell out of that thing."

"And when he grows out of it, he can put toys in it, or use it as a laundry hamper..." I say, thinking of how our son can get use out of it for years to come.

"And he can use it for his children, and they can use it for theirs. This is going to last for generations, baby. Isaiah designed his work to last," he says.

"He'll never be forgotten."

"Never. He's made his mark, for sure."

I admire the bedding tied with cute bows to the sculpted, vertical slats. "Who did this?"

"Your grandmother. She made a few different covers. And they'll wash nicely, she said," he tells me with a laugh. "They go over this padding here, see?"

"Not too cushioned. It's perfect. I just can't believe you did all of this," I say, looking up at him.

"I couldn't imagine not seeing that project through, Liv. He would have wanted our son to have that. It's what had inspired him to keep going," Jon says, his eyes watering. "I couldn't let him down."

I pull his head to mine for a soft, sweet kiss. "Thank you," I whisper to him.

"You're welcome," he says, leaning in again. When his lips touch mine this time, I don't want them to leave. I put my hand on his neck and hold him close, deepening the kiss. His hands caress my cheeks. I take a few steps backwards until I feel the wall behind me. Because Jon's being cautious, not knowing what I want, he leaves a gap between us.

For the first time in months, though, I don't want that gap. I want to feel him against me. My hands move quickly to his waistline, and I pull him so his body is flush with mine. They venture beneath his clothes, touching the bare skin of his ass.

"Mmm," he grunts into my mouth. "What's going on?" he quickly asks as he takes a breath.

"I'm not asking questions," I tell him. "I want it, so we're doing it."

"Really?" he asks, pulling away in shock.

I nod.

"This isn't because—" He stops asking when I push his pants and underwear to the floor. "No?"

I shake my head and take off my shirt. His head moves immediately to my breasts. "Oh, wow." He sucks harder than I'm used to, but it feels amazing. "Do the other side."

"Fuck, yes, I'll do the other side," he says, pulling me to my knees. When we're on the floor, I start touching him gently, palming him and tugging and feeling him grow in my hands. It's fantastic. "Are we doing this here?"

"Absolutely," I tell him. He looks around and grabs a few of the baby comforters we'd already collected and lays them on the floor. I carefully ease back onto them as he rips off his shirt. "Take my pants off for me, okay?"

"My pleasure." I'm naked in no time, and his full weight is on my body seconds later as his lips and tongue play with mine.

"I love how you feel on me," I tell him.

"I love how I feel in you," he says. "Are we ready for that?"

"Maybe a little more..." I say, and he's moving down my body and then kissing me between my legs. "Oh, yeah. A little more of... oh, yeahhhh. Of that. Yeah. Oh, god, yeah. Ohh..." I can feel myself beginning to orgasm, but before I do, I fist his hair to get his attention. "Come back on top of me."

"Are we ready?"

"I'm so ready."

"Oh, god," he says, positioning himself. He lets out a huge sigh as he presses into me. The expression on his face is one of relief and sheer delight. "Oh, baby."

I smile and welcome him, getting lost in the intimate moment with the best husband a woman could ever ask for.

"So, I guess we'll wash up these blankets," I say to Jon as we both stare up at the ceiling of the nursery. His hand is clasping mine tightly.

"We should have turned on the ceiling fan first."

"So sweaty," I say.

"I'm too tired to get up," he responds. "We'll cool off eventually, yeah?"

"Where's your phone? You have that app that controls the thermostat. You can crank it down to, like, fifty."

"My pants don't have pockets."

"So sad."

"That fan has a remote, though," Jon suggests.

"Where is it?"

"In that drawer by your foot."

"You mean by *your* foot."

"I mean, technically," he says lazily, "but it's also by your foot."

I *kick* him with that foot, then cross both my legs over his body. He starts laughing. "Now you're just making us both hotter."

"Fine," I say, finally getting on my hands and knees to find the remote. Jon's right behind me, though, and on top of me. "What are you doing?"

"I can't look at you naked like that and not attack," he responds, kissing my neck.

"Now I'm super-hot," I tell him, nudging him off of me and handing him the remote.

"Hot *and* sexy."

"Not what I meant."

"But it's the truth." He clicks the fan on high and we both lie back down on the floor. "Was that, like, amazing sex, or has it just been four months?"

"It was amazing. And it's been four months."

"Just checking." He props himself up on his elbow and lightly draws circles around my navel. "You know, this was not even in the general vicinity of responses I thought I'd get for this bassinet tonight, but thank you."

"I didn't think I'd want this for another five... six... who knows how many months? So, thank *you*. It's funny what turns a girl on, huh?" I tease him. "Husbands doing the sweetest, most unexpected, non-sexual things. I guess that's my aphrodisiac."

He smiles and questions me softly. "Who knew?" He kisses my hand, and then my cheek. "Aren't you getting hungry yet?"

"I'm starving. The *baby's* starving. We're both kind of wondering why you aren't feeding us."

"Hey now... what are you hungry for?"

"I... kind of want a burger."

"A burger? You want me to fix you one?" I shake my head. "You want to order in?"

"I don't want to wait. Can't we just go pick up something?" I ask him.

"You really want to go out like this?"

"I was thinking maybe we'd put our PJs back on... maybe our hoodies. I can borrow your shades again."

"It's dark."

"Don't care."

"Sounds good," he says, not arguing. "Meet you downstairs in five?"

"I'll be there." We kiss once more before he helps me up and hands me my clothes. I go to the master bathroom to clean up and make myself a little more presentable, but I don't intend to give anyone a good photograph tonight. I'll just keep my head down the entire time.

Jon's wearing his ten-year-old Columbia baseball cap when I get downstairs. He looks so cute and boyish when he wears that; it reminds me of when we were much younger. He looks like high school Jon, like the one that asked me out for the first time when I was fifteen and he was seventeen. On my tiptoes, I deliver to him another kiss. I feel like I've fallen in love with him all over again tonight.

"Did I already tell you how lucky I am to be with you?" he asks.

"Will you still be saying that at two in the morning when I'm nudging you to get me some Tums?" I ask him.

"It will be tinged with sarcasm, but yeah." He tosses his keys in the air once and catches them, setting the alarm and opening the door to the apartment for me.

I notice he slipped on his jeans. "Should I put on actual pants or something?" I ask him, suddenly having second—*rational*—thoughts about my lounge pants.

"Nope. Normal people do this every day. We're just ordering burgers, running in, picking them up and leaving. Why can't we be normal for a night?" he poses the question to me.

"The Scotts go normal... I like that," I tell him.

"The car should be ready when we get downstairs," he tells me, holding his hand out for me. Butterflies blossom in my belly. "Did you just blush, Liv?"

I shrug my shoulders. "This is... fun. I just feel so... happy."

In the elevator, he envelops me in a hug. "This *is* fun."

Once we're in Jon's SUV and hidden by his tinted windows, I pull out his phone and find the menu for the place with the best burgers in the city—he's the keeper of all the bookmarks to our favorite places. "Wow, they have a bunch of new things since we last did this."

"It's been years, Liv," he laughs. "I hope they'll still serve us."

"We tip very well," I remind him. Their food caters toward an adult crowd, so it's not someplace we take the girls. When we normally get nights alone, we go out to nicer, sit-down restaurants—places where we can carry on a conversation with one another.

"Think they'll make them to go?"

"We'll tip even better. I'll call them."

"I'm thinking you should have worn jeans..."

"The high's wearing off from earlier, huh?" I ask him, pinching his forearm and laughing.

"See if they'll bring it to the hostess stand," he whispers as I wait for someone to answer.

"Thank you for calling Raoul's. How may I serve you?"

"Hi. This is Livvy Holland," I say, earning a poke in my side from my husband for using my maiden name. It's the one that gets the impossible done in this town, though. *Scott* can open many doors. *Holland* gets us the red-carpet treatment.

"Yes, Ms. Holland, what can I do for you this evening?"

"My husband and I have had a crazy night, and we were just wondering if there was any way we could get a couple of your burgers. It's, like, the only thing I'm craving..." I say.

"Oh. Ummm. Let me ask the chef," she says.

"We'll pay whatever," I tell her before she slips away.

I link my fingers with Jon's while I wait for an answer. He holds on to me tightly.

"Ms. Holland? The chef says we can prepare burgers and fries for you and your husband. How would you like them cooked?"

"Oh, thank you so much!" I gush. "Both medium rare with everything on them. And could you have them ready at the hostess stand? We've been working in the nursery tonight, and we're not really dressed to make an entrance, if you know what I mean."

"Of course, Ms. Holland. We'll have them ready in fifteen minutes."

"We'll be there. Thank you!"

"*Working* in the nursery, huh?" he asks.

"Sounded better than screwing, right?" I make a production out of sliding his phone into the pocket of his tight-fitting jeans.

"A little more to the left," he suggests.

"Yeah, yeah..." On my phone, I shoot a quick text to Shea.

Me: *Guess who got some...*

I wait for a response, but by the time we get to the restaurant, I still haven't heard anything back from her. If I know her and Will, she's probably *getting some*, too. Still... she should be celebrating this with me! It's been months! Auggie the Cockblocker took a night off!

"Ready?" Jon asks.

"Do I have to?" He nods his head, but I already knew the answer. It's not safe for me to idly sit in a car late at night in SoHo, just like it's not safe for Coley to take taxis by herself. They're easy opportunities for bad things to happen. The words originally came from my father but have since been echoed by all the men in our family.

There are times when I miss the freedom, but I would never give up my life with my family, and especially my life with Jon. Not for anything in the world.

People are excited to see us out in public. Many of them are yelling my name, but I keep my head bowed down, not wanting to be in any pictures tonight, and I know that's the only reason they're calling me. Fortunately for us, they're just average New Yorkers. No paparazzi tonight. That's one good thing about going somewhere we don't normally visit—none of the vultures are waiting on the off-chance they may catch a glimpse of us.

Jon makes quick work of the transaction. I don't even watch him pay because I know he'll tip them very well. When we met, he was very frugal with his money. After growing up without any, I couldn't blame him. But since realizing what we make and what we stand to inherit someday, and knowing that both of his brothers are taken care of, too, he is good about taking care of people who take care of us.

And trust me, getting us these burgers is truly taking care of me tonight.

"I cannot wait to eat this," I tell him when we settle back into the car.

"Mrs. Scott?" he says abruptly.

"I will, though! Don't worry. I wasn't going to start now!"

He shoves his phone in my face before we pull away. "Can you tell me why Will is sending me sexually suggestive emojis right now? With confetti and champagne?"

"I mean," I say, grinning, "what's sexually suggestive about an eggplant? And a peach?" I ask innocently.

"There's a rocket and a tunnel, too, ma'am," he says, mockingly annoyed. I scroll though no less than twenty texts from his brother—half dirty, half congratulatory—all very *Will*.

"I just have no idea."

"You told Shea."

"I haven't seen Shea!" I argue.

"Does your phone have an eggplant and peach on it?"

"Absolutely not! When Shea and I talk food, we spell it out. She's a chef. She's wordy like that."

"Stop playing coy. What'd you tell her?"

"I just told her to guess... who... *gotsome*," I say quickly.

"Got some?" he asks. "That's how you talk about it? What are you, 13?"

"It's been awhile, okay?" I laugh.

"I got some," he says, mimicking my voice.

"Oh my god. But wait! Don't get onto me about telling Shea. It's obvious you've told your brother you *haven't been getting any* by his response to you."

"Brothers talk! Whatever! It's a guy thing!" he counters.

"Well, so do sisters."

CHAPTER 3

*W*ill hands me a book as I sit at a small table in the book store. I take one look at the cover.

"Nope," I say, handing it back to him.

"By what criteria?" my brother-in-law asks me.

"It's written by a Ph.D. *You* could have written this. I hear how you talk about the universe, and I can't understand you. My daughter's not going to understand this book, and I refuse to let another of your birthday presents to her sit and gather dust until she's in high school."

"This is fucking censorship," he mutters under his breath, but not softly enough to be out of earshot of Willow. She clears her throat loudly from the seat next to me, *not* looking up from another book she'd already picked out for herself. Her hand is raised and pointed at her uncle.

"That's six dollars already, buddy," I tell him. "We've only been together for forty-five minutes."

"I believe you've contributed two to the bucket today, so don't act like your shit don't stink," he says. "God damn it!" He laughs, handing her three dollars.

"Now I think you're just doing this to give her cash."

"Maybe I am."

"Then just give her the cash and stop being a bad influence on my baby girl."

"Uncle Will's never a bad influence on me, Mama," she says, straightening the gaudy plastic 'Birthday Girl' tiara he'd bought for her to wear. Edie's had been much more classic when he took her on the town a few weeks ago. "I know what words I'm allowed to say. Don't worry. He told me I can't say them until I'm 13."

I look up at him seriously. "He said that, huh?"

"Mm-hmm!" she responds brightly.

"He lies," I tell her. "You know what happens if you do—all that swear money comes back to me and Daddy."

"When can I say them?"

"When you're 18," I answer, "and *never* in Granddaddy and Memi's presence. You got that?"

"Were you 18?" she asks me.

"I sure was," I fib, squinting at Will to make sure he doesn't give me away. He doesn't really know one way or the other anyway. I doubt I cursed around him at that age.

"Here." He hands me another book. The cover's cute and colorful. The illustrations are actually paintings, which are a plus, of course. The text is easy to read but introduces some complex topics. It's the perfect thing to bring about conversations between Willow and Will about his area of expertise.

"You did it. You finally found something."

"It's too young for her. She'll read it in a day and then want more."

"No, you'll read it *to* her in a day, get excited and want to tell her more. There's a difference. This is something I want you to let her read to you. I want you to let her ask you questions. And I want you to stop, slow down, and speak to her on her level. She's interested, Will. I get that. But I'm afraid if you keep going over her head, you're going to scare her off. You think I wouldn't be proud to have an astronaut for a daughter?" I ask him. We both look at her.

Her face beams, and she nods her head. Since she was four, it's been her dream to go to space, and it's all Will's fault. Now, when the day finally comes when I have to say goodbye to my daughter on a launch pad, I just may kill my brother-in-law for his influence on her, but I'll be beaming with pride for her with every strike of my fist to her uncle and godfather.

But the thought of her that far away from me scares me to death. Fortunately, I know I have years to get used to that idea.

"I'm getting her this and a more advanced one," he says. "This one." It looks like a text book, and I shake my head. "Liv, it's my present to her, and you're not stopping me."

"That's why I'm with you. To stop you from a, overspending, and b, from getting her things she can't use!"

"I didn't overspend last year! I stayed within the budget you gave me."

"And then Shea turned around and bought her that necklace with the Saturn pendant."

"I had nothing to do with that. She did it on her own."

I nod my head, acknowledging what he's saying. I gave them each a budget this year, something I'd never had to do before. Standing up, I pull him away from Willow but keep my eye on her. "When Charlie's born, and we all start spoiling him, you'll understand why we do this. They can't expect to have everything handed to them. We have to be able to give them things to work for."

"I get that. I do. But she is hungry for this knowledge, and I'm going to feed it to her. Sorry, Liv. If you want me to buy used books for her, I will."

I crinkle my nose and go back to my daughter, standing behind her. "I don't like the smell."

He rolls his eyes at me. "Thought so. Hey, Dubskie." He takes the tome over to my daughter. "Check this out." She's startled by the weight of it dropping on the table in front of her, but she recovers coolly and opens the large book with authority, determined to prove me wrong. I can see it in her face. "What's that word?" he asks, leaning over her.

"Co..." She pauses. "Co-ro-na-graph."

"Very good. You sounded that out nicely. Now what is it?"

"Will, come on, she's seven!"

"I'll be eight in a few days!" she argues.

"Eight, fine! God... seriously, Will." I start to take the book away, but Willow puts her palms down and holds on, looking up at me.

"It's something that blocks the sun's rays from the surface."

"What?" I ask her.

"Why?" Will asks.

"So you can see its corona."

"Which is..."

"The outermost part of the sun!" she says, as if we all know these things. I'm sure I learned it at some point, but many, many other facts have taken residence in my brain since then.

"And have you seen a coronagraph before?" Will asks.

"You have one at your work. In the observatory!"

He grins, looking at me with a smirk. "Yes, I do. Now, do you want this book?"

"Please?" she begs.

"Fine," I concede. "It's in the budget?"

"You're not my wife. I'll get her what I want," he mouths off. "And you're wrong about me; *you're* the one who made her interested in the universe."

"How so?" I ask, holding her hand as he takes all the books and carries them to the register.

"You gave her the middle name Skye. She's been fascinated with the sky since she learned her full name and you know it. It has nothing to do with me. I just facilitate her lessons and make sure she has the *right* answers to her questions."

"And you love every second of it," I remind him.

"Of course, I do. I can only hope Charlie shares her passion in astronomy."

"Uncle Will?" she asks.

"Yes?"

"Are you going to stop spending time with me when your baby comes?" Willow is suddenly sullen, genuinely sad.

"What?" We step aside and let other people pass us in the line. I take the books so he can give her a big hug. "Dubskie, no!" he says, adamant. "He's going to need me sometimes, but I will still make time for my nieces. Once your little brother is here, and Charlie is here, I have a feeling you're going to be seeing a whole lot more of me and your aunt. You can mark my words."

"I have a feeling he's right," I assure her.

"Excuse me. Will?" a woman says to get his attention. She's standing in between another woman and a man. They're probably all in their twenties. People had been staring at us all afternoon, but no one had had the nerve to approach us until now. As I look around, other people are watching the interaction.

"Yes?" He smiles graciously, standing up straight. Willow assumes a position behind her uncle's leg, holding on to his jeans. He has his hand on her back, comforting her. She's been shy with strangers since she was a toddler, and always prefers to stay close to the men of the family if there's one around.

"Can I have your autograph?" She tries to hand him a Sharpie and a special edition vinyl of the latest album he contributed his guitar skills to.

"And can we get a picture?" the guy asks, already poised to take one.

"Listen, what are your names?" Will says, his hands making their way into his pockets—a deliberate move.

The woman speaks again. "I'm Jennifer. This is my friend, Jennifer, too, and he's Richard."

"Jennifer, Jennifer two... Richard, it's really nice to meet you," he says, charming as ever. "I'm really flattered, and I appreciate your support and enthusiasm, but I'm just out shopping with my niece and sister-in-law." He nods to me, and I wave.

"I know! It's Livvy Holland!"

"Scott," he corrects them. I nod to say hello.

"I'm trying to make this day about the birthday girl," he continues, looking behind him at Willow, "and I don't want to make this day about me. Hope you understand and respect when I politely decline autographs and pictures today."

"She's so cute!" the second Jennifer says.

"That's so sweet, of course," the first Jennifer chimes in. "I'm sorry for bothering you."

"It's no bother. Thanks," Will says. The lingering crowd begins to disperse, but a few start snapping pictures before leaving. "None of the little one, please."

All the phones drop at his request. He waves, and we return to the checkout line.

"You handled that nicely," I tell him, patting him on the back.

"Not my first circus," he says, nudging me. "So, Dubskie, where are we going after this? Cupcakes? That crazy doughnut place you like?"

"I want astronaut ice cream!" she exclaims.

Will and I both shake our heads as he pays for the books. "Dubs, you hated it last time."

"I loved it!" she says, not remembering the experience clearly like we do.

"You took two bites and wanted to wash it down with water. You don't remember that?" he asks her.

"No. I want it, Uncle Will. Please?"

The eyes. She uses her puppy dog eyes on Will. He looks over at me. "We'll go there first and just stop for actual ice cream on the way back to your place. Okay?"

"Yay!" Willow says, skipping beside me.

"Well, now we have to," I respond. "And can you tell me why you're calling my daughter 'Dubskie?'"

She grins. "It's my aviator call sign."

"Oh, it is?"

"When I become a pilot, I'll have to have one."

Like Maverick and Goose. "Sweetie, you're not joining the military."

"But I have to learn to fly!" she says.

"You can do that without joining the military."

"But I want to go to NASA!"

"You can do that, too, without the military."

"But... I like my call sign," she says with a pouty lip. "Uncle Will gave it to me."

"And what exactly does it mean?"

"She said," Will begins, "that when she becomes an astronaut, she wants to go by W. Skye Scott—again with the Skye," he says as an aside to me. "So... Dub is from the W. The rest is self-explanatory, really."

I smile at them both. "That's actually very cute."

"Captain W. Skye Scott," Willow says.

"Commander," Will corrects her, helping her into the awaiting town car.

*A*n hour and a half later, the car drops Willow and me off at our building. Will lets her have one of her books early but keeps the others to wrap for her actual party. When we get up to the 55th floor, Jon is waiting at the door for us.

"Daddy! Look what I got!" Jon wipes his hands on a dishtowel before taking the items our youngest daughter hands him.

"*I Am Stardust,*" he says, reading the cover, "and half-eaten freeze-dried ice cream."

"That's for you," she says.

"Yum," he says sarcastically, giving me a kiss on the way in. "Did you have fun? By the looks of your hair, you did." Her long hair, whipped around by the wind, is now intermingled with the cheap tiara. I hope it's not knotted in there.

"We did. He bought me books and took me for ice cream, and we went to the park and I made 17 dollars!"

"Willow!" I say through gritted teeth, admonishing her for telling on her uncle—and me.

"Seven*teen?*

"It was your brother," I say, shrugging.

"Mama paid me six."

"He's a bad influence. Linguistically. You know this."

"I worry about his own children."

"Charlie may be a free-thinker. Maybe he'll be the one to make everyone realize words are words," I say, rolling my eyes.

"You're starting to sound like Coley," Jon says. Our soon-to-be-sister-in-law poet has always been an advocate for the importance and equality of all words. *'They all have their time and place,'* she always says.

"She's a smart woman."

"Are you ladies hungry?" he asks. "Or did you spoil your appetites on this god forsaken, sorry-excuse for a treat?"

"I didn't eat anything, so *this* lady and tiny gentleman are starving."

"Uncle Will just bought me a big sundae shake with a little cupcake through the straw!" She puts her hand on her tummy. "I can't eat *anything* more *now!* Maybe later, Daddy."

"I worry about his own children," Jon says again, looking at his watch to denote the time of day that his brother chose to feed our daughter dessert—right smack in the middle of dinner time. "And *you* didn't stop him," he whispers to me, touching me lightly on the nose.

"It's for her birthday..." I say weakly. "Where's Eeds?"

"Painting upstairs... so you may want to hang out down here for a while. I told her she had to stop at dinner time."

"The watercolors don't bother me," I tell him, linking my elbow through his. "Now, what can I do to help get dinner ready?"

CHAPTER 4

My mom thumbs through a magazine in the chair next to the hospital bed, being far more patient than I am today. She'd probably be less patient if she had to wear nothing more than a thin sheet in this freezing cold room.

"Remind me to bring a blanket next time," I say softly.

"Does that mean I get to come again?"

"You can always come, Mom."

"It's the first time you've asked."

"Well, the invitation's always there."

Jon is putting in extra hours at work in an effort to complete a major city project two months ahead of schedule, so he'll be able to take time off when the baby comes. As one of the senior partners, he doesn't have to go into the office much anyway, and could take whatever time off he wanted, but this particular project is a renovation of the city block of his childhood apartment building, so it holds some personal significance to him. He came to the last sonogram, and every single one I had with the girls, so he's not really missing much. I'll take him pictures; that's what he asked for.

"Do you think Dad's doing okay with the girls?" I ask her.

"I'm sure he's fine. He's probably prepping the homemade mac and cheese right this very second."

"Should I call him and check?"

"Liv, would you please just relax and enjoy this time with Auggie?"

I grin when she calls him that. "Auggie doesn't do a whole lot yet, Mom. He's growing hair now... I hope. I figure it's best if I just let him do his thing."

"He hasn't moved yet?"

"Barely," I tell her. "Nothing anyone else could feel."

"Maybe you should ask Dr. Northam about that."

"Maybe you shouldn't make me worry, Mom. He's fine."

"I'm sure he's fine, Liv. And the sonogram will tell us that."

Both of the girls were very active by now. Jon had been able to feel slight movements with both of them by this time in their pregnancies if he was patient enough. But nothing about this pregnancy is like theirs, so I've stopped comparing them at this point.

"Livvy," Dr. Northam says, finally coming into the room. "I am so sorry we're running late today."

"It's not a problem," I say, smiling politely. "It's just really cold in here."

"Jody," she says to the ultrasound technician, "can you grab a blanket for Mrs. Scott before we begin?"

"Of course." She reaches into a cabinet three feet away, then places the fleece over my torso.

"Thank you so much."

"You look flushed today, Livvy. Are you feeling okay?"

"I'm fine," I tell her. She rolls a device over and puts my arm in the cuff. I stay still while it takes my vitals, watching Jody as she gets ready to do the sonogram.

"Your blood pressure is 150 over 97, sweetie," the doctor tells me.

"Okay."

"Liv, that's high," Mom says.

"Are you sure you're feeling alright? Nothing's stressing you out?"

"I mean... I was cold, and you guys were running a little late is all. I'm sure it's nothing."

"And she hasn't been able to paint," my mother adds. "The smell makes her nauseous."

"That's true," I admit. "That centers me, and I don't have that right now. So maybe I'm just a little anxious because I can't do that... and I want to.

"I've tried other outlets–drawing, watercolors–but nothing quite fills the void of painting my murals. I did sketch one out a few nights ago–one for Charlie's nursery. I think I'll actually have time to paint it after Auggie's born, but before Charlie's born–you know, as long as the nausea is gone."

"Slow down, Livvy," Mom says. "You're putting far too much pressure on yourself."

Dr. Northam is flipping through my files. "I'm looking back at your pregnancy with Willow. I remember the paints made you sick then, too. But we didn't have any problems with your blood pressure then. Nothing at all."

"It's nothing *now*. I'll meditate or something when I get home."

"Dr. Northam," my mother interrupts. "I think it might be worth mentioning that Livvy's biological father had two heart episodes in the last year. He passed away in February from the second one." I look down and twist my wedding ring around my finger, feeling the hole in my heart that he left when he died. "Just something you should probably add to her medical history."

"I'm so sorry to hear that, Livvy," she says, taking my right hand into hers. "That must have been hard." I shake my head, hoping we can start the ultrasound soon. It breaks my heart to think of what little time I got with my father on this planet. He didn't know who I was until I was 21, and we didn't really begin to have a relationship until five years later.

So, nine years. I got nine years with him. I'm grateful those nine years were when his granddaughters were here, and that he had a chance to know them. He loved them so much. I'm crying before I can stop myself.

"I'm sorry, sweetie," Mom says, handing me a tissue. "I just felt like she needed all the information."

"I know, Mom. I'm fine."

"I need you all to keep an eye on the blood pressure. You can buy a device to measure it."

"We'll get one on the way home," my mother vows.

"One-twenty over 80 is ideal," the doctor says. "If you're not seeing it closer to that range in a couple of days, I want you to call me."

"Okay," I say, wiping my eyes.

"Now. Who wants to see this little boy?"

"We both do," I tell her assuredly. "And Jon wants pictures."

"Has he warmed up to 'Auggie' yet?"

"Oh, hell, no. It's just going to have to catch on at home... or he'll have to wear earplugs all the time." The doctor laughs.

I inhale sharply at the cold gel on my belly but am quickly distracted by the image on the display next to me. "There he is, Mom. There's your first grandson."

"Ooohhh," she sighs, gripping my hand. "Look at him!"

"His heartbeat is strong," Jody says. "It looks like he's waving at you."

"Hi, Auggie," I say softly. "We see you in there."

After reviewing the ultrasound, they tell me he's still progressing normally.

"Now, Livvy, have you had any headaches or light sensitivity lately?"

"No."

"Has your vision been okay?"

"It's been fine. I'm feeling fine."

"Okay. Before you leave, I'm going to give you a kit to take home," she says. "I want you to collect some urine samples."

"Fun... what are we testing for?"

"We're looking for protein."

"Preeclampsia," my mother says.

"You're definitely not a high-risk candidate, Livvy," Dr. Northam explains. "We just don't want to take any chances with this precious baby, do we?"

"Of course not."

I settle into my favorite side of the sofa recliner in the media room at my parent's house after dumping my bag and the large, plastic container and instructions outside the door to the guest room–my old bedroom. With my phone in hand, I start to compose a text to Shea, but think better of it. I'd rather talk to her in person, and maybe after her next visit to the doctor. After all, I'm trying not to worry–I don't need *her* to worry... then there's no peace between the two of us.

"Give me that phone," my mother says, handing me a teacup on a saucer.

"Mom..."

"This is the plan. You're going to spend the next six hours over here doing whatever relaxes you. But I know messing around on your phone isn't going to help you. WebMD'ing everything the doctor's office just talked to us about isn't going to ease your mind... so let's spend the next six hours doing something you love. Do you want to read? Watch some old reruns? Nap? Draw? Take a walk? I'm at your disposal. I'll be at your beck and call. Here," she says, giving me one of the remote baby monitors. "If you need something while I'm upstairs, just call out for me."

"Oh, you're gonna regret this," I tease her.

"My sweet daughter wouldn't take advantage of me," she says, patting me on the knee. "Would you like a blanket?"

"That soft quilt that Grandma Hennigan made would be awesome. And maybe one of those foam pillows?" I ask.

She goes into the other bedroom and grabs both, tucking them around me as if I were on my death bed. "How about some music?"

"How about you fix yourself some chai and bring that box in here that I saw in the guest room?" I suggest instead. "Were those Trey's baby things?"

"They were," she says, smiling wide. "Wouldn't you rather some alone time to calm your nerves?"

I shake my head. "I'd rather hang out with my mom. You calm my nerves."

"Awww. You didn't always think that."

"Well, you didn't always *do* that... but now, it's always nice to be around you. I really appreciate how... calming you are."

"Thank you, Livvy," she says, and I see her eyes get misty as she walks past me to the other room. I take a sip of the chamomile tea and breathe in its aroma.

Mom sets the box in front of us on the coffee table and settles closely next to me with her own blanket. She takes out a handful of items and places them into her lap. "This is what we brought Trey home from the hospital in. Do you remember that?"

"Only from the pictures. That thing swallowed him whole." I pick up the tiny blue outfit that says it's for newborns, but he was a preemie, and the smallest clothes didn't fit him until he was a few months old. "He lived as a burrito for weeks, if I remember correctly."

She laughs. "He did. Your dad could swaddle him like no other. Mine always came loose, but anytime Jacks wrapped Trey up, he'd never come free unless we untucked the blanket ourselves. And he would sleep so well like that, too."

"Trey or Daddy?"

"Both of them." She smiles. "That little burrito would be centered on Jacks' chest. I'd tuck a blanket around them both just to make sure Trey wouldn't fall."

"Look at this silly baseball jersey!" I say, picking up a very small red, white and blue shirt with HOLLAND on the back in proportionately tiny letters. It has been perfectly preserved, wrapped in paper inside a sealed bag.

"My brother bought him that. He was certain he'd be a baseball star."

"And there's a hat!" I say, giggling. "It's like it was never worn."

"It never was. He was too small when we got it, so we put it away... and then when I found it again, he'd already outgrown it. You should take it for Auggie."

"Oh! But it's Trey's, I shouldn't do that. You should save it for his son. He'll have the Holland kid, anyway," I say, shrugging.

"Auggie is every bit a Holland, Livvy," she says, surprised.

"I just meant his last name, Mom. That's all I meant by it. Auggie's a *Scott*, and Jon won't have you forget it."

"Nor should he. We should get one made for him then—don't you think?" Her eyes are wide with excitement. "Or what about a little onesie sleeper that looks like a baseball outfit with his name embroidered on it?"

"That would be so cute!"

"We should put Auggie," she whispers, almost deviously.

"Oh... you know I want to so badly! But how about SCOTT on the back and AUGGIE in cursive on the front?"

"Perfect," Mom says. "And what number should he be?"

"I think... like, 3, right? He's the third kid."

"This is going to be so cute! I cannot wait. I know a woman on the hospital volunteer board who can do this for us."

I smile at her before taking another item from the box. It's an unremarkable set of blue overalls with a snail on them. "Why'd you keep these?"

"Trey took his first step in those."

"I love that you kept them for that reason..."

"Here are the socks that he was wearing, too," she says.

"I wonder if Simone had a box of my stuff like this," I ponder aloud, referring to my biological mother.

"I used to think about that all the time. I'm sure she did. All moms keep certain things that are special to them. I know you and Jon aren't big on keeping a ton of their physical things, but I love the fact that you have so much audio and video and pictures of the girls as they were growing. You'll never forget how Edie babbled to herself as she played, or how Willow whimpered when you left her room at night. Those sounds are so beautiful."

I nod my head. "Jon and I go back and listen to them every few months. They're simply precious to us. And now, we have recordings of them reading books, or trying to explain their logic about the things around them. What a wonderful world we'll have to look back on when we're your age."

"I'm not that old."

"I never said you were." I kiss her on the cheek. "I love you, Mom."

She brushes my long hair out of my face. "I love you, too, sweetie."

"What if the tests come back positive?" I ask her, leaning my head against the back of the sofa. She mimics my position.

"Then you have more days like this one, sweetie. They'll probably change your diet. Maybe put you on medication. It's not something you need to worry about this afternoon, though. No worries right now. Calm space." She nods her head, trying to get me to play along. "Clear your mind."

"It's hard."

"I know."

"You worried a lot with Trey... how'd you get your mind off of things?"

"I talked to you. I thought about things from my past. I imagined how our future would be, after he was born. I enjoyed the positivity your father brought with him every time he walked in a room. His smile would lift my spirits. He has the power to take away all my worries. He always did. He still does," she tells me. "And tonight, when I tell him about this, he'll reassure me that everything will be fine. If you need that, he'll do the same for you."

"Then forgive me when I call," I tell her, laughing.

"I know Jon eases your fears." I nod in agreement. "You're going to be just fine. Auggie's going to be great. I just sense he's going to be your little troublemaker. Maybe he's just giving you warning signs now," she teases. "You've had it easy with the girls."

"I already have a little troublemaker. Her name is Edie Sienna. I believe you've met her?"

"Edie's a little angel. You have no idea what a troublemaker is—just wait until she's a teenager."

"Isn't she?" I joke with her. "Sometimes it feels that way."

"I don't think Edie's any more difficult than other children."

"She can be a challenge," I say, "but she was more of a handful when she used to tease Willow so much; they're so close in age it was almost too much to handle at once."

"They could have been twins," she reminds me. "Think of what Grandma Holland went through with Jacks and Kelly. Or Steven and Kaydra, with Stevie and Daniel."

"Oh, god. I couldn't handle Stevie and Daniel for an hour. I remember that time when you and Dad were watching them for the weekend."

"They were in their terrible twos for about six years." We both chuckle at the truth in that. "They turned out okay."

"A lot of discipline happened in that house, though. More than Jon and I have had to dole out."

"If Auggie requires it, you'll adapt."

I wonder to myself who will play bad cop to our little boy. I can't help but picture our son as Daddy's shadow. I've always envisioned them being very close—likely having a deeper bond than Jon has with the girls. It's not that he's always wanted a boy, or that he doesn't love his daughters with all his heart. It's just that I feel like he's already raised two boys with his brothers and did such an amazing job with them both that he was made to have a son of his own.

But I know his brothers didn't turn out the way they did by Jon going easy on them. *So, I'll be the good cop.* I like that role.

*A*fter Mom heats up some lunch for me, I take a nap—a *long* and restful nap. When I awaken, I remember no dreams, and am shocked to see the time on the small clock and to hear my husband outside the guest bedroom door, talking softly with my mother. They both sound serious, and I can only imagine the conversation they're having. I wish I could hear them better.

A lump grows in my throat. The last thing I want is for Jon to worry about me or the baby. I need for him to be strong for me because I already feel unsteady and unnerved again.

When I get up to the door, I press my ear against it.

My mom is talking. "...and when he got the chicken pox, we had no idea about Livvy. The doctors asked if she'd had them before, and we didn't know. She hadn't gotten them while we'd known her, but it was possible she'd had them earlier. She couldn't remember.

"She treated her brother like he had the plague."

"Oh, I remember," Jon said. "I definitely remember her coming to art class one day with a face mask on. She had colored–"

"Colored on it with pencils, yes! I remember! Those beautiful flowers," my mother laughs.

"She kept it on for the first five minutes of class. She was waiting for me to ask her why she was wearing it, as if I didn't notice it on her or something. But hell, in my mind, I didn't want to catch what *she* had!"

I sigh, relieved, and finally open the door. I can hear my heart racing in my ear, though, and worry what that says about my blood pressure. I can't let things like this get to me.

"There she is," Jon says, looking back at me. "Did you enjoy your day of leisure?"

"Did Mom tell you what's going on?" I ask him.

"She did." He picks up the test kit from the floor. "We've got our work cut out for us tomorrow."

"There's no *we* in that, buddy."

"Not yet," he says, laughing at his joke. "*Wee*? Get it?"

"Oh, you're so stupid sometimes," I say, giggling with him as he pulls me into his lap. "Where's the monitor, Mom? I want to test."

She goes upstairs quickly and brings back the blood pressure tester that we'd bought at the drug store. I put it on my wrist and start it up, holding it over my heart and telling Jon to sit very still. When it's finished, he reads off the results.

"One-forty-seven over 93." He sighs. "That's high. You just woke up, baby."

"I was anxious," I tell him. "Worried that you guys were out here worrying."

"Okay," he says, shifting me so he can look into my eyes. "There are things I can't stop you from worrying about, but worrying about me worrying? I draw the line there. That's ridiculous."

"He's right, Livvy," Mom says. "You need to minimize the things that stress you out, and we're going to be strong for you. We'll bring the faith that things will be okay. Don't worry about us. Okay?"

I hesitate before answering but realize they're right. "I know."

"Good," Jon says. "Now let's go relieve your dad of babysitting duties. You feel up to rejoining your family?"

"Of course," I say. "I want to see my girls." I get up and hug my mother tightly. "Thank you for everything today. I needed it. All of it."

"I enjoyed spending time with you. And I'll probably join you both for the next ultrasound, if you don't mind. I loved seeing Auggie on that screen!"

"His name isn't Auggie, Em." Jon's gathering up my things but stops long enough to glare at my mother with a playful smile. "You've got to think of something else. Just... Jonny is... bearable. No one calls me that anymore."

That statement hits both me and my mother hard, but I know he didn't intend for it to sound as harsh as it did. He's dealt with his mother's passing, but it was such a shock to all of us that it's still hard to accept that she's gone sometimes.

"Come give me a hug," Mom tells him.

He drops everything and willingly accepts it. "I love you, Em." He used to call her 'Mom' often but hasn't called her that since Margie died. I think it's just too hard for him and he doesn't want his mother to think he's replaced her.

"I love you, too, Jon. Take care of our girls."

"*My* girls," he says, always his comeback when either of my parents give him these instructions.

"We are our own women," I've begun saying back, to make our ulti-mate independence clear, "but I'm happily married to you." We always kiss, just to know where we stand; to reassure the other that the love and passion haven't died.

"Call me tomorrow, Livvy," Mom says, watching us get into Jon's car. A few photographers are across the street taking pictures. My mother is quick to hurry inside once we pull away from the curb.

CHAPTER 5

*K*nock knock knock.

The door swings wide open, and a shirtless Max stands facing me. "I did not expect you."

I look beyond him at the mess in the loft that used to be mine. My brother-in-law takes a step closer to me and pulls the door nearly closed to block my view.

"No, sir," I say. "I am the landlord here. Let me in."

"You said you wouldn't pull shit like this, Liv."

"And you said you'd keep it clean."

"No, I said I'd clean up for your visits," he corrects me. "You're not supposed to show up unannounced. Callen! Livvy's here!"

"Bullshit!" I hear him yell from another part of the apartment.

"I'm not fucking with you!" Max shouts back.

"Will you please keep it down? My girls are right across the hall."

"Shoulda called and warned us."

"What, you'd install a censor into your brain?" I ask him sarcastically, finally pushing my way in. "Callen! I hope you're dressed because I'm in the loft!" Catching a whiff of something, I walk quickly to the back living area. "What. In. The. Hell?"

"Shoulda called us, Liv," Max reiterates from behind me as Callen almost manages to hide a turquoise bong from me. The windows are open on the north side, so he must have been trying to air out the place.

"You guys are getting *high* in here?"

Glancing back and forth between the two of them, I only get a shrug from Callen.

"Are you not sure?" I ask him sarcastically.

"Are you mad?" Max asks.

"I'm shocked!" I shake my head, trying to understand. "When did this start?"

"Longer ago than... wait..." Max says. "Longer ago... longer ago... is that a phrase?"

"No!" I yell. "No no no!"

"The shooting." He nods, his motion exaggerated.

"Does your brother know?"

"Which one?"

"Either!"

"Not exactly," Max says, kicking a pair of boxers to the other side of the room. "Jon doesn't know anything."

"Callen, you don't even drink! That was a huge point of contention between you two."

"I don't really, um..." Callen stutters. "This is not—this is different, Liv," Callen says. "Have you ever tried it?"

"No, I haven't," I tell them, not wanting to freak out like this, but also realizing the addiction issues that run deep in Max's family. "It's never appealed to me. Smoking, nothing," I explain. "I almost brought the girls with me, guys, but I was afraid you might be messing around or something. But this? Oh my god. Do you have this shit here when they stay with you?"

"No," they both say it together, and by the looks on their faces, I believe them.

"Where do you put it? Your place?" I ask Callen, who has his own guest house on his Mom's estate in lower Manhattan, which he uses as a storage facility now that he's moved out.

"Used to store it there, but... no, not so much anymore."

"Then where?"

They look between one another. "Matty's."

"*Matty* knows?" I slant my eyes at them both, not sure who to be angrier at. The stupid 25-year-olds who have everything going for them and everyone watching them, smoking pot in the apartment I rented to them, or the 65-year-old uncle who should know better.

I storm out of their apartment and go back to my uncle's place across the hall. "Outside!" I yell at him.

"Mama?" Willow asks.

"Just stay here with Nolan, sweetie. Mama will be right back."

"Okay, I know women get hormonal and all," Matty says after he shuts the door, leaving us alone in the hallway, "but what could I have possibly done in the three minutes *we weren't even together*?"

"Max and Callen are smoking pot in there," I say, pointing to my old loft, "and you are fully supportive of this?!"

"I am no such thing."

"You're supposed to be *on my side* all the time," I tell him.

"I am, Little Liv. Calm down."

"I am calm," I say, gritting my teeth. "Max's dad was a drug addict. His mother was an alcoholic, and I know she dabbled in that stuff, too. Will has struggled with addictions of his own. Max is not allowed to smoke pot!"

"I am not his parent!" Matty shouts back at me. "He's a grown man!"

"He's a dumb kid!" I counter. "Have you seen what they've done to the place? It's a pigsty!"

"It's a bachelor pad... they have no woman to make it clean."

"That is so sexist of you! I can't believe you just said that!"

"I'm trying to make a point! You put two 20-something guys in a crazy-town Manhattan loft with a shit-ton of money, and there are two things that are likely to happen: it's probably going to get trashed, and there's a good chance there are going to be some drugs. Welcome to reality."

"How can you be so nonchalant?!"

"Because I did pot when I was their age and I lived to tell about it. You grow out of it. They will, too," he says, only this time quieter.

"You don't have addiction in your blood, Matty Holland!"

"I wasn't thinking about that," he admits, pacing in front of me. "Your parents will be very upset if you don't calm down, Liv."

"And my husband will murder you. So, please. Help me deal with this."

"I don't know what I can do."

"Stop being complicit in their drug use. Stop hiding things when my girls come over. The deal is, if they don't stop, they don't get to see my girls," I say, feeling so angry I could cry.

"Livvy, come on," he says. "I was a pothead when you came into my life... but I never used when I knew I'd see you. If your dad ever made those ultimatums, you and I'd never be close like we are now."

"I doubt my dad knew."

"Your dad knew. I lived in California. Everyone smoked pot. He wasn't crazy about it, but he knew." He puts his arm around me. "Let's go talk to them and get you a glass of water. You need to sit down and cool off."

"Don't tell me to cool off."

"I mean literally, sweetheart. Your face is beet red and I'm sure this isn't good for your blood pressure." Suddenly guilty, I follow him into my old loft after Max and Callen open the door for us again. Matty throws clothes on the floor so I have a clean place to sit on the couch. Callen brings me a huge glass of ice water, which even has a few pieces of cucumber floating in it.

"Guys, you cannot allow her to get this upset," my uncle starts. "And I don't know what bomb went off in here, but hire a maid, and get it cleaned. This is ridiculous. Callen, you're the CFO of one of the biggest companies in the country. How can you live like this?"

"I've just..." he starts, "I've never had to clean up after myself."

Matty and I both look at Max.

"I've never had things to clean up," he says with a shrug and a laugh. "And I guess, when I did, I lived at home with Mom or my brothers, and they did everything for me."

"So, in other words, we now have two spoiled brats living together," I say.

Callen's not ashamed to admit it. "Yeah."

"I've never been called that in my life, but sure," Max says. "This is a whole new thing for me."

I take a deep breath, and then drink about half of the water they gave me.

"Are you okay?" Callen asks. "Can I get you anything else?"

I shake my head, looking at the wall across from us at three paintings that I left here for them.

"Max, buddy, why?" I ask him. "Why'd you start? Or was it you?" I shift my attention to Callen.

"It wasn't him," Max says. "I, uh... started after the shooting. I do it for anxiety, sometimes for pain..."

"So, this is medicinal? Like... what your mom did?"

"Wellll," he says, his voice incredibly high-pitched, so I know that's a no.

"What's your excuse?" I ask Callen.

"He barely ever does it," my brother-in-law answers for him. "This is maybe the fourth time? And before you start blowing this out of por... por..."

"Proportion," Callen and Matty say together. Callen bursts into a fit of laughter at the end, which I'm sure is an after-effect of the pot.

"Yeah, that," Max continues, "I never did it when I lived with Trey. I never had shit at his place—it was a rule of ours—"

"*Trey* knows?"

"He doesn't know I still do it. Shhh... He thinks I stopped because I still take meds sometimes, and he got really squeamish about me mixing the two, even though I've got it all managed, so I told him what he wanted to hear. But it's good for me, Liv. It takes the edge off and kills the pain, all at the same time. A lot of people get hooked on opioids, but I found something non-addictive that works."

"Non-addictive," I scoff.

"Look it up and stop judging, princess," he says with a scowl. "And to clear his good image, Callen really doesn't do anything often at all. You caught him in a rare moment. I twisted his arm."

"Why aren't you at work today?" I ask his partner.

"I'm working from home."

"You're working *stoned* from home," I clarify. "Yeah, your dad would kill you. The CFO of his company getting high while he's making big business deals."

"I don't have anything on my schedule today," he says. "I'm just answering a couple emails. My assistant at the office is handling most of my stuff."

"Must be nice," I mutter.

"Yeah, it is," he says, a little defensive.

"So, I just need to know, Max," I start, directing my attention back to him, "when are you going to tell your brother?"

"Wasn't planning on it."

"It's time you start."

"Will knew about it a while back," he says. "I can bring him up to speed. He thinks I quit... you know... sometime."

"I'm not talking about Will."

"I can't tell Jon," he argues.

"Well, I can't keep this from him," I state. "You know the rules we live by in our marriage—no secrets from one another."

"No way, Livvy. You can't do this to me. He won't understand."

"Exactly. So, you better start thinking of ways to make him... or else quit this nonsense. What if you get caught? Do you want to go down the path of your father?"

"This is nothing like what my dad was in to, Liv." He rolls his eyes at me. "Jon doesn't need to know."

"Max," Matty intervenes. "Don't put her in this situation. Do you see that this is stressful to her?" My brother-in-law doesn't answer. "Stress isn't good for the baby—for your first nephew."

"I thought you didn't have that... *clampsy*—thing," he says.

"I don't, but my blood pressure is still too high most days, and this?" I say, looking around me. "This is not helping matters. I certainly don't mean to make you guys feel bad, because you're right, I invited myself over unannounced, but never in a million years did I expect this. You're smart guys. There are people constantly watching every move you both make! Wise up! You don't want to bring some sort of scandal upon yourselves. You don't want to make shit worse, do you? For you? For all of us?"

"I'm being careful," Max says.

"Right. And who's your dealer? Who could sell that story for a cool grand? Bring down a national hero and a business darling? And why haven't they yet? Huh? Or are they waiting to blackmail you for something? You guys could lose so much. You're not looking at the bigger picture here."

"He's cool," he answers, blowing me off. Max is still is that spoiled kid, and we're all guilty of fostering this behavior in him. I really just thought he was smarter than this. He's had moments of great maturity in his life, but Max has always done what Max wants to do. It's a blessing and a curse in him.

"Callen, what would your father say?"

He swallows hard and looks at the floor, possibly his first sobering moment of the day. "I'd lose this position. At least be suspended for a few years. It's actually in a contract," he tells me. "He was nervous about giving me the title at my age. Worried about me not having enough time to sow my wild oats yet or something."

I raise my eyebrows.

"I mean," he begins again, "you're not going to say anything to him, are you?"

"It's not my business—your dealings with your father. Your influence on Max is what I'm worried about."

"And he's not influencing me. It's the other way around—I told you that," Max insists. I don't feel like I'm going to get anywhere with him today.

"Callen, can you come into the hall with me? Just for a few minutes?" He nods, following me out the door. I walk as far away from the loft as I can and lean against the wall. "When you knew your relationship with Max was in jeopardy when you cheated on him all those years ago, you went to rehab to make sure alcohol would never be a problem for you. Remember that?"

"Sure."

"We were all so pissed at you for cheating but impressed at the steps you were willing to take to make things right. And as far as I know, you've never slipped up."

"Yeah, and?"

"Now, I don't know if alcoholism is a thing in your family; if addiction is something the McNares need to worry about. But I know it is in the Scott family. And I know when Will was about Max's age, he came to terms with his own demons. Faced his own battles with addiction. He doesn't drink a drop of alcohol. He won't take a step near a casino. Did you know anytime he gets a prescription pain killer, he has Shea give him his doses? To this day, he doesn't trust himself to make the right choices with things that have the potential to give him a rush—a high."

"I didn't know that."

"He's very aware. And I've always wondered if Max can handle his alcohol. Trey lived with him long enough to tell me he rarely got drunk and knew how to cut himself off after two drinks, but I don't know if that was because he always had someone watching him who would report back to Jon, or if that was just how aware he was. I tend to think it was because of the former and not the latter."

Callen nods his head. "He's had a few too many a couple times since we moved in here," he admits to me. "I've always been around, though. He's never been alone. But he's a happy drunk. He's cool."

I didn't expect his revelation. I feel the tears form in my eyes.

"Does Matty know?" He shakes his head. "Does anyone else? Trey?"

"No."

"Callen, you need to stop this. *All* of this. I don't think it's good for him, and I don't know if he has the skills to do it himself. He may be the influencer, but are you funding him? Don't tell me he's using his donation money for this..."

"He's never asked *me* for money for it."

"Then... if this is coming from the money people gave him for what he did—or even worse, the money his mom left him—I can't... Cal, I can't bear to hear that, and Jon will die before he lets that continue."

He thinks for a second. "I know," he says softly.

"I need *one* of you to be the responsible adult here. And if you can't handle it, Callen, then we'll have to take more drastic measures."

"But he's not an addict."

"He *is* an addict," I tell him. "It's in his genes. Maybe he's just not addicted to anything yet. Do you really want to wait until that happens? And deal with the aftermath? Your relationship is in jeopardy *now*. It may not happen for months or years, but it's in jeopardy *now*. Do what *you* do, Callen. Take the steps to make things right *now*. You did it when you were eighteen years old. And we were so impressed. Do it again now. For me. And more importantly for Max. Okay?"

"I'll think about it."

"I need you to do more than that."

"Just give me some time to deal with this, Livvy. Shit. I'm fucking high right now and this is coming at me really fast, okay?"

I sigh in frustration. "All right, Callen." I pull him into a hug before he walks away. "I love you. I just want what's best for you both. You know that, right?"

"I know. Love you, too."

"Please don't make me worry." He looks me in the eyes before turning to walk away from me. I feel like we're on the same page in the look we exchanged, but I won't be sure until I hear him say it out loud. "Tell Matty I'll be at his place!" I yell after him before he goes back into the loft.

. . .

*T*he girls and I have been trying to stump Nolan with songs to play on the piano, but he seems to know every damn tune ever written. We have to be careful about show tunes and Disney songs, too, because once he starts those, he doesn't stop. A few spontaneous singa-longs have happened while Matty has stayed across the hall.

When he returns, he's holding a cigar box and something else behind his back. After walking in an ultra-secretive fashion to his pantry, I can only imagine it's the weed and possibly the bong.

He glances at me, nodding once, answering my question. I have a million more, but I can't very well talk to him about them in front of the girls.

"I took all the asparagus they had," he says, joining us on the couch. "Max didn't say he wouldn't buy more. But he didn't say he would, either."

"Thank you," I tell him. "And you'll do what with it?"

"Asparagus doesn't agree with Nolan anymore, so I'll throw it out tonight. Along with the large, turquoise asparagus, uh... *fork*."

"Why don't we have asparagus forks, Mama?" Edie asks me.

"You can only get them in, like, South Korea." It's the best I can come up with off the top of my head. "Callen got it on a business trip."

"Can I have it?"

"No, honey," I tell her.

"They're not reusable," Matty adds.

"Okay," my daughter responds simply, leaning her head on Nolan's shoulder. "Shiny!" she yells to him.

"The Decemberists or Moana?"

"What?" Edie asks. "What's The Decemberists?"

"Moana it is," Matty's husband says, and yet another Disney singalong begins.

I'm ready for peace and quiet by the time our driver drops us off. Jon wrangles the girls together in the lobby and accompanies us up the elevator to our floor. "Did you little ladies have fun today?" he asks them.

"So much fun!" they both say at the same time, sending them into yet another burst of giggles.

"They've been like this since they went for smoothies with Matty," I tell him.

"So, no juice with dinner, huh?" he asks.

"Daddy, I want juice!"

"Me, too!"

"Please!? Apple juice!"

"We'll see. It won't be ready for another hour or so. Is that okay?" he asks me.

"Yeah, perfect."

"I'm making homemade tortilla soup. You said you were craving it, so I got your dad's recipe."

"Sounds perfect. Can I help?"

"Everything's done. It's just simmering on the stove."

While the girls go upstairs to their rooms, I pull Jon to the sitting area just off the kitchen. We cuddle close together on the plush couch and kiss a few times. "Listen," I say, interrupting his next move.

"Yeah?" he whispers right into my ear before taking my lobe into his mouth. "I missed you."

"Aww, well, I missed you, too, but your baby brother's smoking pot."

"What?" If I ever need to kill the mood quickly, I know exactly what to say. "What? How do you know?"

"I caught him and Callen in the act today. I went over unannounced and... there they were, bong and all."

"I don't believe it," he says, standing up and beginning to pace back and forth. "Max? My little brother, Max?"

"That one, yes," I say.

"He barely drinks."

"Yeah, about that... he's apparently been drinking more, too, according to Callen."

"What?" Now it's like I've kicked the air out of him and forced him back into the seat next to me. "What do you mean, he's drinking more?"

"That's what Callen says." I tell him how the entire day went down, start to finish. He's got his head in his hands—or more accurately, his hair—by the time I get to the end. "I'm sorry."

"What are you sorry for? You his dealer?" he says, pinching my knee. We smile sympathetically at one another. "You think Trey knows?"

"Max said he thinks he's stopped. That he knew he was using before."

"Trey would knock his lights out."

"Well," I say, "in a non-violent way." My brother doesn't fight.

"I mean, with his aspirations to hold political office? He's got to manage everyone around him, and that's not the kind of environment he can be in, you know?"

"Hence why they don't do it around him, I'm sure, Jon."

"I'm telling him. He's the best one to handle it."

I stare at him, mouth agape. "My brother?" He doesn't waver. "*My* baby brother? Their younger friend? I don't follow you."

"He's diplomatic. He's always been their moral compass. They'll do what he asks."

"Max will do what *you* ask!"

"No, no, because see—I don't know what to ask him."

"How about not to smoke weed, dude?" I say to him in my best stoner voice.

"Baby, I already have two kids and another on the way. Max is grown. I'm not his father."

"Jon! Will was this age when you had a talk with him about the way he was living his life!"

"And you see where that got me?"

"I see he ended up with his beautiful wife."

"I can't take credit for that. Do you not remember that Will and I didn't speak for months? That he decked me for intervening? Surely your pregnant brain hasn't wiped out those memories."

"No, I remember, Jon, but Will's a lot more hard-headed than Max is. Max will listen."

He shakes his head at me. "I'm not risking it, Liv. Maybe Will can handle this one, but I honestly think Trey's the best man for the job."

"They're best friends," I plead. "What if it ruins their friendship?"

"It won't."

"You don't know that."

"Max wouldn't choose pot over Trey. He knows the value of a good friend."

When he says it like that, I start to think he may be right. I've never seen a friendship as impermeable as Trey and Max's. They've been there for one another in the best and worst of times, and they're good friends to the people around them, too. When Callen cheated on Max, Trey stood by Max and helped him through the lowest point in his life, but he also kept in touch with Callen, who was still in love with Max every day they were apart. Trey could easily segregate the friendships and make sure both were nurtured. And Max did the same when Trey and his high school sweetheart broke up after four and a half years of dating. Max stayed friends with Zaina for quite some time, making sure she was okay after a significant heartbreak, but he was always loyal to my brother.

They were meant to be brothers as much as Jon and I were destined to be married.

"You know who *isn't* going to deal with this?" he asks me.

"You. You already said it."

"You," he corrects me. "I'll talk to Trey. He and I will map out a game plan. If he doesn't want to do it, then Will and I will tackle it. Okay? I just want you to know it will be okay and that you don't need to think about it another second."

"You know I'm not trying to be some meddling prude, right? I just know how your family works and I don't want to see Max in trouble."

"Liv, I get what you're doing. I appreciate it fully. And even if the little shit didn't show it today, I'm sure he does, too." He leans in to kiss me again. "Want me to go see Trey tonight?"

"No," I tell him. "I want you to help me with the girls. Or... rather... I want you to watch them while I take a really long bath and read a book for a little bit after dinner."

He nods. "I'll call him after you're all asleep. He and Coley stay up late."

"Okay."

CHAPTER 6

The next morning, the musical chime of the doorbell wakes me way too early on a Saturday. I look over, but Jon's already out of bed—not that I'm surprised. Either Edie got him up, or he set an alarm to go for a run with Will.

"Jon?" I call out, unsure if I need to answer the callbox.

"I've got it! Go back to sleep," he says from just down the hall. He runs down the stairs, and I strain to hear who's come over at this time of day.

"Send him up" is all I can make out. I decide to get up, put on a robe and run my fingers through my hair, waiting at the top of the staircase to see who it is. When the door opens, my brother appears with a bouquet of pink tulips. I start to descend the stairs.

"Nope, stay there," Trey says. "I'm coming up."

"Oh, okay." I smile and go back to my bedroom, taking a seat on the recliner by the window where I do most of my reading. Trey sits in the chair opposite me. It's Jon's, where he often reads his own nerdy books. My brother hands me the beautiful flowers, and I get up to hug him and kiss him on the cheek. "What are these for?"

"When's the last time you got flowers?" he asks.

I laugh lightly. "Not that long ago. Mother's Day, I guess."

"That's too long."

"Damn it, Trey," Jon says, walking in the room. "Why do you have to make me look like an ass?"

"You're the one who doesn't buy my sister flowers as often as she deserves them. How did I make you look like an ass?"

"Jon does plenty of other things, but these are gorgeous, Trey. Jon can go get a vase for them, and all will be right with the world."

"I'll do that," he says, taking the bouquet with him.

"So... I know you didn't come here just to bring me flowers," I tell him. "What's up?"

"I'm actually here to pick up your husband. We're going to go play ball. Three-on-three."

"With?" I ask.

"Max, Callen, Will and Joel."

"I forgot Joel was in town this weekend." Coley's twin brother is a personal chef who splits his time between Boston and Manhattan. Very often, he's helping Shea with catering events, too. "Is he with you?"

"He ran across the street to get bagels for everyone," he tells me. "He went to culinary school with the guy who runs the place."

"Has he had any leads on jobs here?" I ask him. His dream is to work full-time in a Manhattan restaurant, but he hasn't been able to find steady work with his disability. He went deaf at the age of eleven in a diving accident, and all the chefs that have hired him have found it too difficult to work with him in the chaos of a busy kitchen. He makes good money working with a few different families, but it's not what he wants to do for the rest of his life.

"Nobody's willing to take a chance on him. Chefs talk, apparently, and have heard about the experiences he's had in the past—which sucks, because no one has ever really tried to adapt, you know? It's, like, if a person with a wheelchair needed a special desk in an office, by law, they'd have to accommodate them. But, apparently, the rules don't apply in kitchens."

"The rules don't apply *yet*," I say, putting my hand on his knee. My brother has a lot of great plans for society; for this world.

"I'm definitely looking into it while I have some time this summer. I've got a task list of various things I want to research on my own time," he says with a laugh. "When we're in session, I barely have time to read the assignments. It's mayhem. I love it."

"You're crazy," I tell him.

"It's a rush. I can't wait to graduate and start doing some real work for people. Not that I'm not helping now," he adds. "I'm grateful the Legal Assistance Assembly is letting me volunteer. I can't do much without a degree, or you know, like, passing the bar."

"Minor detail."

"Minor detail," he agrees.

"But I bet they love having you around."

"Uhhh... yeah," he says, turning his trademark red skin tone when he blushes. "I get my fair amount of attention."

"I'm sure you do." I chuckle. "Anyone would hire you. The LAA would probably pay you, if you'd ask."

"That's not ethical, though," he says, looking earnest. *That's my brother*.

"You're gonna do great things, Trey," I say to him softly, admiring how truly good my brother is.

"Thanks."

"What are we talking about in here?" Jon says, going to the closet and putting on some sneakers.

"Bagels... and how good they sound," I tell him.

"I've got fresh waffles downstairs for you in the warmer," he tells me. "With whipped cream and bananas and pineapples."

"Even better. Thank you."

"You're welcome." He rubs my shoulder and kisses the top of my head.

I sigh, looking back at my brother. "So, I guess this means you talked to Max last night?" I ask Trey.

"Just to invite him to shoot some hoops with us. I talked to Will more... he talked to Callen. He's on board with not participating in any of it anymore. We just need to talk some sense into Max now." He nods his head and rubs his hands together. "I think we've got it under control."

"We're going to go visit Mom's gravesite first," Jon says. "Will's idea, but neither Max nor I have been since the funeral. Trey got some flowers for her, too."

"Ohhh, that makes more sense as to why I got mine," I tell him.

"Killing two birds," my brother tells me. "They're a thank you token for dealing with stuff yesterday. Shouldn't have been you, Liv, but I appreciate you caring enough to take the first steps."

"You guys don't think I overreacted?"

"I think nipping it in the bud is a good idea."

"You laid that pun out there on purpose, didn't you?" Jon asks him.

"I'm a wordsmith, genius, what do you think?" Trey sasses back with a smirk.

"Well played, buddy. Well played."

"I need to say hello to the little ones before we head out. Where are they, because they sure are being quiet?"

"Last I checked, Edie was giving Willow a makeover."

I push myself up from the chair immediately, remembering the last time Edie did this to her little sister. There were scissors involved, and six inches of hair on the floor.

"That was two years ago, Livvy, and you scarred her with your break-down. Chill out," Jon says. "They were using your makeup and those spongey things."

I squint at him. "Spongey things?" I head down the hall and knock on Edie's door to let them know I'm coming in. "Whoa."

"Hey, there, Edie. Where's Willow?" Trey asks as both girls rush to give him a hug. He kneels on the floor to see them at their level.

"I'm right here!" she says, the sponge curlers now removed from her head and her fine hair falling in dozens of airy tendrils.

"Not *you*." He shakes his head, inspecting her at arm's length. "You must be thirteen. Fourteen, at least."

She looks shocked. "Do I look pretty?"

"Always," her uncle tells her. "I think you look prettier without all that gunk on your face. Now you look more mature. Ready to hit the clubs. Got a hot date tonight?"

"No!"

"It's that Tanner boy you told me about, isn't it?"

"Shut up!" She covers his mouth. "That was a secret!"

"Oh, I didn't know," he whispers. "I'm sorry."

"Tanner?" I ask. "Tanner Dyer?"

"No, Mama! I never said that." Edie stands behind her little sister and nods her head.

I grin but respond to Willow. "Oh, okay."

I'm incredibly impressed with the makeup job Edie's done on Willow, especially since the girls have never been allowed to wear anything other than lip gloss outside the walls of this house. Maybe I've let them play with my makeup too often. "Edie, how'd you learn to do this?" I look up close at my youngest, seeing exquisite contouring that I don't even spend time doing. And Shea and Coley rarely wear makeup.

"Watching you?" Her response isn't the truth. I know this by the way she asks, as well as by the fact that I haven't applied my makeup with such precision since the girls were born.

"Nope," I argue with her. "Where?"

"YouTube," she says meekly. "They have makeup tutorials."

"Is this what you've been watching on your iPad?" I ask her. She nods. "When you're supposed to be doing your summer reading?"

"I think it's time for us to go," Jon says.

"No, Daddy!" Edie says.

"Stay, Uncle Trey!" Willow whines.

"How about... Coley and I bring dinner for everyone tonight?" he asks.

"Please, Mama?" the girls sing in chorus.

"I'd love to catch up with you and hear how your spring semester went," I tell him. "Jon?"

"Sounds great. We'll take care of drinks, desserts and entertainment. Right, girls?"

"Can we pick the movie?" Willow asks.

"Anything you want," Trey says.

"Great." I give him a hug before he heads downstairs. Jon tells the girls to be good, then wraps his arms around me and gives me a kiss. "Are you up for having company tonight?" he asks softly.

"Of course. Why not?"

"You were really restless last night in bed."

"Huh. I think I slept okay. If I feel run down, I'll just take a nap this afternoon. I'm sure I can get someone to come watch the girls if you guys are having fun and want to hang out for a while."

"I'll check in with you a little later. Wish us luck with Max."

"I know you guys will handle your brother perfectly. I'm not worried anymore." He kisses me sweetly. "But good luck playing against Trey and Callen. You guys don't have a chance in hell."

"We don't," Jon agrees, laughing. "But it's always fun playing against our resident NCAA champion."

"Go kick some McNare ass. Gah!" I exclaim, wishing I hadn't said it in front of both of my daughters. Jon gallops quickly down the stairs and out the door with Trey, leaving me with the girls. "Mama's going to get your money," I grumble, making my way back into my bedroom to find my stash of ones that I keep solely for this purpose. Just as I make it to the dresser, I feel a sharp pain in my back when I inhale. It stops my breath entirely.

"Ow. Ow ow ow ow ow." I grasp my side in pain, holding on to the dresser and my chair until I find my bed. It hurts to climb up on it, but I do, and find it most comfortable to lie in a fetal position, curled into myself.

Panic forces tears from my eyes. I concentrate hard on my breathing. At first, only shallow gasps make their way in, but after a few minutes, I'm able to fill my lungs better.

With my eyes squeezed closed in pain, I—cautiously, carefully—reach toward my nightstand where my phone usually sits on the charging pad, but it's not there. I open my eyes to make sure. *I must have left it in the kitchen last night or something.*

"Mama, where's my money?" Willow says, storming in with her hands on her hips.

"Mama?" Edie asks, following her younger sister in. "What's the matter?"

"I'm not sure, sweetie. I need you to find my phone, okay? It's probably downstairs." She takes off in haste.

"Mama, are you having the baby early?" I reach for Willow's hand, wanting to offer her comfort as much as I want to glean it from her.

"No," I exhale, and hope I'm right. I hope this has nothing to do with the baby. "I just moved funny or something."

"Should I call Daddy?" my oldest daughter asks, having returned quickly with the phone.

"Press the number for Memi, sweetie. Then put it on speaker."

With the phone on the bed in front of me, she crawls up behind me and rubs my back. Willow continues to hold my hand.

"Good morning, Liv," my mother answers.

"Memi!" Willow yells. "Mama's in trouble!"

"No, Mom. Gosh, Willow, it's okay."

"What is it?" Mom asks, serious.

"I just got this horrible pain in my side. I was having trouble breathing and I could barely move."

"Did you call 9-1-1?"

"I don't–" I pause. "No. What if it's just a cramp? It kind of just felt like a really bad cramp, like you get after a hard workout or something."

"How do you feel now?"

"I'm breathing. And moving a little better," I say, attempting to stretch. The sharp pain returns when my leg straightens out. "Or not. It still hurts."

"How's the baby? How do you feel there?"

"It feels separate from that, I think. I don't know."

"I'm calling your doctor and we're coming over," she says.

"Okay."

When she hangs up, I call Shea. "Hey, sweetie, are you still at home?"

"I am. I wasn't planning on going to the Kitchen until noon."

"Can you come over here? Like, now? I know it's early. I'm having some pain... and I'm scared." I didn't want to say it in front of the girls, but it's the truth. Both of them start crying loud enough for my best friend to hear. Willow's makeup is now making a mess all down her face and onto the sleeves she's wiping her tears on.

"I'll be there in five minutes," she says, the exact time it takes to walk from her apartment to ours, assuming she doesn't have to wait too long on the traffic lights.

"Girls," I tell them, holding them both next to me now. "Mama needs you both to be strong for her, okay? No tears. I'm sure everything's fine."

"What about Froggie?" Willow asks.

"The doctor will be here soon. We'll know soon."

"Can I put my hands there and tell him I love him?" Edie asks.

I smile at her. "Let's all do that."

Of course, I can't do that without worried tears streaming down my face, either. Seeing how sweet my girls are and knowing how badly they want their baby brother–I don't want anything to happen that would disappoint them, or Jon. God, if I lost the baby, Jon would be devastated. He's fallen hard for his son. I can't lose him. I can't lose Auggie.

*A*fter Dr. Northam leaves, Mom and Shea help the girls bathe and get dressed while my dad sits next to me on my bed, still holding my hand. "Feeling any better?" he asks me.

"Pain-wise? No. Relief-wise? Yes. I'm so glad it wasn't anything to do with Auggie." I try to prop myself on the pillows, but he stops me.

"You need to find a comfortable position and stay there," he says. "Relaxation is the best treatment for back spasms."

"And muscle relaxers," I add, only a little bitter that I can't take them.

"Your doctor said the anti-inflammatories would kick in soon. You need to get your mind off of it."

"Great advice from the man whose back isn't literally stabbing itself."

He chuckles. "Do I need to readjust the placement of the heating pad?"

"No, it's okay right now."

"Is it too hot?"

"No, Daddy," I tell him. "Thank you."

"Are you sure you don't want me to call Jon?"

"Only if you guys can't stick around. He had some family stuff to take care of, and I'd like to give him some time to do that."

"We're happy to help out all weekend, if you need us."

"Trey and Coley are coming tonight. I'm sure Jon can handle things but thank you. There is one thing you can do right now, though."

"Name it," he says.

"My hair is driving me crazy. Can you go into my bathroom and grab my brush and a rubber band? And do you think you can either put it in a low pony or braid it? I know you know how. I've seen you double team Edie when she wants two braids," I challenge him before he can get out of it. "Plus, you did used to help with my hair," I call after him as he goes to find the hair accessories.

"That was thirty-odd years ago, with you," he starts, "and with Edie, Emi's braids are always better; she always has perfectly divided strands."

"Yours have a certain spirit, Dad. A *je ne sais quoi* about them."

He huffs. "Edie's always critical of them." He looks a little hurt.

"She cares too much about her looks sometimes," I respond as he gently takes a brush to my tangled hair. "Your braid proves she's not perfect. Your braid builds character. In my mind, your braid is just what my daughter needs."

"You are too kind, Contessa," he says, smiling. "Look toward the wall and I'll give you an imperfect braid, too."

"Thank you."

Once the girls found out the baby was okay, they were bored hanging out with me and became restless in the house. Mom and Shea took them to the movies while Dad and I watched one of our favorite old movies—the Godfather—on the TV in the bedroom.

"We haven't had a day like this in a long time," he says to me before he starts Part II.

"I know. I was just thinking about that. It sucks that I had to become an invalid that you have to wait on hand and foot to make it happen, but it's one good thing about the spasms."

"We should make more time for one another, Tessa," he says. "I miss days like this. You're the only person who will recite movie lines with me while we're watching. Your mom shushes me. And Trey's always in his analytic mind, dissecting the film."

"Yeah, and you're the only one who doesn't make me share my candy," I respond. "My family is greedy." I decide to offer him the last Junior Mint, but he declines, like I knew he would. My dad has never had much of a sweet tooth. "Let's do quarterly father/daughter days," I suggest. "I have outings with Mom all the time."

"You do," he says wistfully. My heart hurts for a second.

"Daddy, I didn't know you felt that way."

"You're so busy. And I'm so proud of who you've become. I don't ever want to be in your way," he says. "And I certainly don't want to make you feel bad about anything right now. This is a two-way street. I could have made plans for us, too."

I nod my head and wipe the tears that had begun to form.

"We'll remedy it now. We can do another movie day just before your due date. Or maybe go out to dinner—just us, whatever you're craving."

"Or both?"

"Definitely both, Contessa. It's a date, for late-August."

"I'll put it on my calendar when I can successfully turn 30 degrees again."

"Sounds good," he says. "More chamomile? Or chocolate?"

"Tea, if you don't mind."

"Not at all. Don't start Part II without me."

"You're DeNiro, Dad. I can't start without you!"

. . .

*A*fter Jon gets home and my parents and Shea leave, we decide to talk to Edie about her YouTube habit. He makes sure I'm comfortable in bed first, then sits in the chair across the room and summons her to us with her iPad using the speaker system he'd had installed throughout the house.

Willow follows her in.

"Wils, honey," I say. "This is something we need to talk to Eeds about, okay? Why don't you go to your room and read for a bit?"

"Are you gonna play a game on her iPad with her?" she asks, looking a bit worried that we're about to leave her out of something fun.

"No, sweetie, that's not what we're doing," Jon assures her. "I'll come in to check on you in a few minutes. Maybe we can work on building that model from your science book when we're done."

"Okay," she says as she skips down the hall, obviously pleased to be getting her father's attention.

"Edie, shut the door," Jon tells her. She does so slowly, then walks to the center of the room with the device hugged into her chest and her head hanging low.

"Please don't take my iPad away," she pleads.

"How much time are you spending on YouTube?" I ask her.

"Not much time, Mama, I swear."

"And what are you watching?" Jon asks. "I thought we locked that down," he says to me.

"There were so many restrictions, she couldn't get to some sites she needed to do her homework." I shrug my shoulders, admitting that I did take off the restrictions a few months ago. I monitor her browsing history, and she doesn't have any social media apps. YouTube is one that slipped through the cracks for me.

"Let me see it." Jon holds out his hand and waits patiently for her to pass it over. When she doesn't, he finally gets up and takes it from her. "Let's see what you're watching..."

My daughter has mastered the look of guilt and innocence mixed together. I study her wide eyes as she stares at her father.

"What is this?" he asks. I hear the voices of both Edie and Willow coming from the iPad, directing my attention there. "Edie, what is this?" He stands up, facing her, but he continues to watch the video.

"*Then, you take the brush like so and gently drag it up the cheekbone,*" I hear her say.

"Jon, what is that?" I struggle to move, but it hurts too much. "Let me see it." He's ignoring me. "Jon!" When he looks up at me, his face is ghost white, but he's *angry*. I try to piece the story together. "That's not on YouTube, is it?"

He nods his head.

"Give it to me." Considering my current state, he walks over and sets the device in my lap. I survey the screen quickly, seeing a username of 'LadyEdieScott' above the video that continues to play, showing my daughters in Edie's bedroom as the oldest demonstrates how to put makeup on the younger one. "Edie, what did you do?"

"I made a video," she says softly, shrugging her shoulders and looking away.

"*How* did you make a video?" Jon asks her loudly.

"I borrowed Mama's phone. I set it on a pile of books and propped it against the wall."

"Did you know about this?" He turns to look at me. I simply glare at him, and he turns back around to confront Edie. "You didn't borrow Mama's phone. You stole it from her without her knowing, didn't you?"

"She was asleep," she explains.

"Eighty-six-hundred-and-twenty-three likes," I mumble, feeling sick to my stomach when I see the statistics for her makeup tutorial. "My god, Edie. How did you know how to do this?"

"I just know how to do makeup, Mama."

"Not the makeup!" I say tersely. Jon takes the iPad from me and looks at the page again. "Who set up an account for you?"

"I did it."

"Did you lie about your age? Isn't there a minimum age requirement?" I ask her.

"It's 18," Jon tells me, "or 13, with a parent's permission. I looked it up a few weeks ago when she asked me if she could have an account. And what did I tell you, Edie?"

"I don't know," she says, looking down at the floor.

"You *do* know," he argues with her. "I told you no. I told you we would revisit the question when you're 13."

"Edie!" I say, taken aback by what she's done and horrified to know that my precious, young daughters are being watched right now by God knows who. By God knows who, *times 8,623*. And those are just the people who *liked* it. My skin crawls and my eyes water. "Jon, you have to take it down."

"What do you think I'm doing?" he responds, sitting next to my feet on the bed, tapping away on the iPad.

"Daddy, no! I have followers already!"

"No, you do not have *followers*. Nine-year-old girls do not have *followers*. Do you understand me?" I tell her.

"I can't believe you put your little sister on the internet looking like that, bunny. You're supposed to protect her," Jon says.

"What do you mean?"

"Men look at things like that. *Bad* men."

Edie quirks her brows, not understanding. "I did it for girls my age, Daddy. It's a makeup tutorial. Why would boys care about watching that?"

"Jon," I say, shaking my head to stop him. He meets my eyes and immediately knows he's not sure he wants to venture into this conversation, either. She's innocent and has no idea about the seedy world her father is alluding to.

"Go get your sister," he says. She walks out of the room quickly.

"You're not going to talk to them about this, are you?" I plead with him.

"I have to say something... I'll talk on their level. I promise. We'll do this together. We have to make them understand the severity of this, Liv."

"Do not scar our babies," I say as they come back into the room together, holding hands.

"Sit down on the bed with Mama," he tells them. "Be careful. You know she's in pain."

They both climb up on the pillow to my right where Jon normally sleeps. Willow strokes my head with her hand a few times as if I were a pet of hers. It's sweet.

Jon pulls his chair over to the side of the bed to be close to all of us.

"Listen, girls," he says calmly. "What you did today is not okay. I know it seemed like a fun makeup video. I know it looked just like all the other ones you see posted out there on YouTube, but your mom and I aren't okay with it.

"You know how we try to keep people from photographing you two when we're out in public, right?"

"Yeah," they answer together.

"We want you to have a normal childhood, even though we are fully aware you don't come from a normal family. We have to take special precautions sometimes, okay?" From my peripheral vision, I can see both of the girls nod their heads. "We would prefer the world know as little about you as possible. It keeps you safer. You just have to trust us on this, okay?"

"Yeah, Daddy," Willow says.

"Do you think bad guys watched my video, Daddy?" Edie asks him.

"I don't want you to worry about that, girls, but I want you to know that there are some men in this world who will look to date girls no matter how old they are, and that's not okay. It's sick."

"But we're not old enough to date."

"No, you're not, but they don't care, and when they look at you, they don't see that. And that's why they're sick, bad men. So, we don't want to give them things to see, right?"

"Right."

"If there are no pictures and videos out there, then they won't look at you in that way. This is one way we have to protect you girls. It's why social media sites have those age restrictions, Edie. To protect you. Do you understand that?"

"Yeah," she says softly. "I didn't mean to do anything wrong. I just wanted to help other people."

"Eeds," I say, "there are so many other ways—better ways—to help people. We do volunteer work to help people and we donate clothes and toys to help people, right?"

"But you paint your murals for poor cities. And Daddy makes them look prettier somehow, too," she says. She's never understood Jon's job as an architect and his important work on the city planning board. "You donate what you're good at to help people. I'm just doing the same thing."

"A few things about that, bunny," Jon says, talking to her sweetly. "At nine years old, you are far better than any makeup... *designer*... I've ever seen. But you're only going to get better as you get older, so just imagine how amazing your videos will be when you're 18, right?"

"I guess," she pouts.

"And finally, I don't ever want to see Willow look like that—ever again."

"I looked pretty, Daddy," our youngest says. I put my head against hers.

"You looked like a 40-year-old street walker," he says. I purse my lips together and chuckle, feeling the pain in my back when I do.

"What's that?"

Neither of us answer.

"A hooker!" Edie yells. I cover my mouth to hide the laughter, not expecting her to know. I'll let Jon handle that. I have to manage the back pain and the giggles right now. "She did not!"

"What's a hooker?" Willow continues to ask.

"Edie," Jon talks over her before she can define it for her sister, "you're too wise for this world," he says, nodding his head. "I didn't know you'd understand that term and your little sister doesn't need to know it quite yet."

"Don't try to talk over me, Daddy," she instructs him sternly. "I have a big vocabulary."

"I'm sorry. But she had on too much makeup. Everything in moderation. It's a lesson you need to learn."

"He's right, Edie. But you gave your sister some very pretty hair," I add, trying to soften the blow. I crane my neck to see their responses. Both girls smile and touch Willow's hair.

"Go get your iPad, kid," he tells our youngest.

"I didn't do anything bad!" she protests, bouncing on the bed a bit too much for my back's liking. I hold my breath and pray she calms down.

"I'm not taking it away. I'm just going to adjust the settings and then I'll give it back." Willow scoots to the end of the bed to get off, then stomps off into her room. While she's gone, Jon doles out the punishment to Edie. "Two weeks, no screen time except for your math tutoring sessions... and when you have homework, Mama and I will be here to help you. We'll hold onto the iPad."

"This stinks."

"I know, right?" he says.

"And the next time you *borrow* Mama's phone," I tell her, "I'm going to *borrow* one item of my choosing from your closet and give it to charity."

"Same goes for Daddy's."

She climbs off the bed and stands in front of us with her eyes wide and her jaw hanging open.

"I've got my eyes on your denim jacket. The one with glitter," I tell her.

"That's a nice one," Jon agrees.

"I promise, I won't do it again."

"Okay. Go to your room and clean up that mess you made this morning, and then go downstairs and get your watercolors out of the spare room. Coley and Trey are coming tonight, and I want this house clean."

"Yes, Daddy."

"Thanks, bunny."

He immediately looks at me. "Now, if you don't want your brother coming over tonight, we can cancel the invite."

"I don't know that I can get out of bed," I tell him, "but I guess I'd like some company. He's seen me look worse."

"We can move that table and chairs over here," he says, pointing, "and bring in a few trays for the two of us. We'll just watch a movie in here and catch up with them. The girls can have a picnic on the floor. They'd love that."

"Is that okay?"

"Yeah, that'd be great. My muscles are already sore from the basketball game anyway," he laughs. "I may as well be bedridden, too."

"No, you have to take care of me," I say with a playful whine.

"Don't you see? We're inviting them over to take care of us *and* the girls? I've got plans," he jokes.

"You're cute."

"Okay, I'll take care of you. Do you need anything now?"

"No, I'm good right now. Maybe just some rest."

Willow brings in her iPad and hands it to Jon. He sends her back to her room to pick it up. "Mind if I join you for a power nap while they're cleaning?" He climbs onto the bed, carefully lying next to me and putting his arm around my torso.

"I don't want the company," I tell him, holding his hand.

"Oh," he says, trying to pull away.

"No, you're fine. But can you maybe ask Trey and Coley if they can come next Saturday instead? Maybe we can just do this all day," I suggest, having changed my mind.

"I doubt the girls will go for us lying here all day, but let's shoot for as long as we can get away with it."

"Perfect," I tell him, accepting the kiss he plants on my cheek.

CHAPTER 7

 y mind wanders to a million other things as I try to listen to an audio book on Saturday. I find myself in bed again, this time with a migraine. The back spasms didn't last long; they were gone by last Sunday, thankfully, but I've been overly tired ever since. A few days this week, I've had headaches, but this migraine that struck last night is the worst I've had in a while.

Meanwhile, the baby finally started being rambunctious, kicking up a storm. I should be enjoying these moments, but with my energy drained, I feel annoyed, blaming this pregnancy and its effect on my hormones for all the changes to my health this time around. And then I feel very guilty.

Touching the cushioned pack on my eyes, I remove it from my face when I realize it's warmed up to room temperature again. Frustrated with my current state, I do the only thing my body has the energy to do.

I cry. For the fiftieth time this week, I cry, feeling sorry for myself.

Jon must have been in the library down the hall, because he's in our room in seconds.

"What's the matter?" He stops the book that had been playing on my phone. Already, I'd tuned it out to the point that I didn't realize it was still going and wonder how much of the story I've missed.

"You're raising this one on your own, Jon," I tell him, at my wit's end.

I'm mainly teasing, but right now, I just want him to be born and out of my body. "I've gotten him this far."

"Stop saying things like that, Liv," he says, laughing. "I know this pregnancy hasn't been ideal–for either of us."

"Oh, *poor you!*" I come back bitterly. "I know you liked the first two better, when my hormones were all out of whack, working in your favor. This time, your boy-child's cockblocking you. Rest assured this has nothing to do with me. I'm innocent in all of this. The completely absent sex drive. The high blood pressure. The low energy. The headaches. I blame him."

"You'll never make me not like him, baby." Sweet like always, he sits down next to me and takes one of my hands in his. With his other one, he wipes tears from my cheeks. "Or even regret not making another beautiful little girl with you. I'm happy we're having a son. I'm so, so sorry it's been rough, but I promise it will all be worth it when he's here. You'll see. Boys are great. We'll have so much fun with him. Edie and Willow are so excited."

"You realize Edie's going to put him in dresses, right? He'll be the next star in her banned YouTube videos."

He nods and smiles. "As long as they're careful with him, and inclusive of him, that's fine with me. I will love our children the same as long as they're all nice to one another."

"They're almost the same age difference I was with Trey. So that's how it will be."

"You were... as expected with Trey. I think our girls are a little less spoiled than you were."

"Hey!"

"Liv, come on. You were the only child of Jack and Emi Holland. You wore a tiara and diamonds to my slum-high school prom."

"And you loved me in them."

"I did," he says, kissing the back of the hand he's holding. "Nevertheless, we've done very well raising our girls to get along with one another. They're... they're nearly angelic."

Against my better judgment, I can't contain my laughter. My pounding head gets tighter; pounds harder. I close my eyes tightly to try to counteract the pain. "You're wrapped around their little fingers," I argue with him.

"This headache's put you in some kind of mood, Olivia. What can I do for you?"

"Swap out my ice pack and get me another dose of pills," I request. He checks his watch to make sure it's okay for me to take them again. "Then rub my ankles," I say, softer.

When he leaves, I find a relaxation soundtrack on my phone to play in the background.

He comes back upstairs with sparkling water, my mild pain killers, a new ice pack and some magnesium spray. "That's a good idea," I tell him, closing my eyes as I let him apply it to my forehead. He rubs it in gently to my temples and massages it through my scalp. "That's nice."

"I know," he says, confident. "It's why you keep me around."

"You anticipate my needs."

"I love you," he corrects me. "That's why."

"And that. Listen, I want you to go ahead and tell Trey and Coley to come. I don't want to let the girls down again this week. If I'm not up to it, I'll just shut the door."

"Well," he hesitates, "Max wanted to tag along. Callen's on a business trip. Does that change your mind?"

"They get rowdy, but no. It makes me want you to make sure they come. You haven't seen him since you guys had the talk with him, right?"

"No. I was looking forward to catching up. Trey reports he's doing fine. He says he hasn't bought or smoked any more. I just know when my brother's lying, so I wanted to casually ask him... see if he was being honest about it."

"Then please... definitely get them here. And I'm going to lie here while you rub my ankles and then sleep some more and hope to God something makes this migraine go away," I tell him. "But before you start, your son's been listening to you and kicking up a storm. Come say hi."

The smile on his face is one I'll cherish until the day I die. He kneels on the floor next to me, lifting my shirt and putting his palms against my skin.

"Hey, son," he starts. "You having a good time in there?" When he feels a strong kick, Jon looks over at me in awe. "It never gets old, baby," he says to me.

"It kind of does," I tell him. "But sometimes, it's nice."

"Jonny," he continues talking to the baby, "can you do a big favor for me? Your mama's not feeling well today, and she needs some rest. Do you think you could take a good nap so she can get some sleep? And whatever you're doing to cause her headache," he adds, glaring at me, obviously not believing it's the baby's fault, but playing along with me nonetheless, "can you chill with that for a bit? If it's, you know, growing hair or fingernails or lungs or whatnot? I mean, keep growing, but maybe not at the migraine-inducing pace."

"No, Auggie," I say, placing my hand next to Jon's. "You keep doing whatever you need to do to become a strong and healthy little boy. Mama's fine." When Jon puts it that way, it makes me feel selfish.

"I don't think he knows you're talking to him when you call him that," Jon taunts me.

"Auggie knows his name."

"That is not his name," he argues, kissing my belly before he gets up. "Mark my words. When you see your son, you're going to realize that is no name for our child."

I smile widely to appease him. I'm sure he's probably right. It's cute to call him that now, but I can't imagine how an *Auggie* would manage in school nowadays. It's too different. Too old-fashioned.

And it *does* rhyme with Froggie, which is cute for his sisters to call him, but not bullies on a playground, and I worry that would happen.

"I'm going to get to work on your ankles while you try to get some sleep–both of you."

"Thank you, Jon."

*W*hen I wake up, I feel completely refreshed and have no headache to speak of. The door to our bedroom is closed, and when I turn off the soft music that had been playing, I can hear more voices than normal talking loudly downstairs.

7:45. I slept for *six hours* and missed most of the day. After drinking an entire bottle of water Jon had left for me on the night stand, I get up and take a shower since I hadn't been well enough this morning to do so. It feels amazing and I feel much more like myself when I get out.

Pulling my hair into what's becoming my normal hairstyle–a braid–I choose to dress in some stretchy, cotton pants and a flowing, yellow blouse. It's comfortable, but still cute. I opt for blush, mascara and tinted lip balm, but that's it. I'd rather be downstairs with our guests than up here fussing with makeup.

"How are you feeling?" Coley asks me as I round the corner from the grand stairway. She gently embraces me.

"A million times better. It must be something Jon said to the baby." I go directly to him and give him a kiss, showing him my gratitude. I put my hands on my belly. "He's moving, but calm, and he let me sleep for a very long time."

"You look rested," she says. "Do you mind if I feel him kick?"

"Not at all, but he's not doing anything at the moment. Let me eat something. I bet that will get him going." She nods, going with Jon into the kitchen. "Boys, how are you two doing?" I hold out my arms for Trey and Max.

"Awesome," Max says, getting to me first and holding me pretty tightly, kissing my cheek. "Thanks for telling my brother."

"Max, you know I had to."

"Or... you could have trusted me to handle things on my own." He shrugs. "I can, you know. I will."

"Okay," I say softly, squeezing his hands. "I hope you mean it." Without a job, I wonder what he's doing to fill his time, but I know he doesn't need the stress of my questioning any more than I do.

"I mean, you were right. Too much is at stake," he says, turning away from me when he speaks. I wish Jon was here – if he can tell when his little brother's lying, I'd like him to tell me if he's being honest right now. I don't get the sense that he is. "For Callen, for sure."

"For *both* of you," I state.

He steps out of the way for my brother.

"I'm sorry you've been under the weather, sis," Trey tells me. His stature and countenance have the natural ability of making a person feel safe when he hugs them. I love my brother's hugs. "You feel okay to be down here? Because there's no need to entertain us. Max does enough foolish things on his own."

That earns him a few fresh grapes to the back of his head.

"Willow loves those grapes," I tell him in an effort to make him stop.

"Willow!" Max yells.

"Pick those up, you dickweed," Jon mumbles. "My daughter doesn't eat floor food."

"Yes, Uncle Max?" He lifts her up quickly, the results of his physical therapy and extra workouts obvious, because my girls are too big for me to lift anymore – and *I* don't have metal parts in my arm and shoulder. Of course, maybe that's working in his favor now. She's laughing as he swings his niece around. "What did you want?" she asks.

My husband is left to clean up the mess. "I heard dessert would be ready soon," he says to her. "Strawberry shortcake, right?" he asks Jon, who simply glares at him.

"That's right," I answer for him. "And Kelly made the shortcake, so it'll be out of this world. Did everyone already eat?"

"Yeah," Trey says, "but we saved you a plate in the warmer."

"Smells like Indian food," I comment.

"Butter chicken with rice."

"You are my favorite brother in the world," I gush, hugging him again. "Did the girls like it?"

"They devoured it. It may not have worked out with Zai, but she left behind some great recipes."

"She definitely did," Coley says. "This is one of my favorites, too."

Coley hands me a full plate from the warmer, and I consider yet again how much I love her for my brother. Other women would be petty in situations like this, making a dish that was created by an ex-girlfriend, but not Coley. She's always been able to focus on the bigger concepts of life– friendship and family and love. She doesn't let small things weigh her down, which is good. Trey has a tough road ahead of him with the career path he's chosen, and I know she'll need to be strong for him and for their future family.

While working on the presidential campaign for a local senator right out of college, my brother decided he was going to run for president someday. His candidate won against a morally bankrupt narcissist. Senator Parker, a good man who had always done great things for his New York constituents, is the first gay president. The first *single* president. It was something we had all wanted to see, and although we were worried that racism and bigotry would win out over experience, acceptance, reason and love, Senator Parker was victorious—and Trey had a lot to do with it, being a speechwriter and organizer for the campaign.

We almost didn't see his presidency come to fruition, though with the assassination attempt at the inauguration parade. I still feel genuine fear when I remember watching the footage of Max getting shot, of him ramming into the gunman, and then of Trey rushing to Max's aid as police officers drew their guns on him. It was a horrific day for our family.

Trey was personally vested in the entire election process, though. He was happy his candidate won but surprised at how close a morally corrupt man came to running our country. It's now become his life's mission to ensure that people unfit for office have a lower chance of being elected, are held accountable if they *are* elected into office and are legally deemed unfit for office when laws are broken. It's why he's gone to law school. It's why he'll be running for public office one day. He wants to change the laws that have allowed current politicians to stay in positions we all revere, despite the fact that many seem to undo everything that is good for our country on a weekly basis.

Before the presidential election more than a year and a half ago, it was Parker's opponent's promise to repeal the Equal Marriage Act. He even talked about finding a way to nullify any unions that had happened since it had been passed years ago, although most lawyers didn't think there was any legal way he could follow through with that. Even still, the threat of reversing the act caused a lot of turmoil and needless worry. Callen even gave Max a ring, suggesting they get married if Parker lost.

After asking for many months, we finally found out from Callen that it wasn't how Max wanted to get engaged, so we don't consider them engaged, even though Max wears the ring.

There's still a lot of work to be done in our government. The House and Senate currently can't agree on anything, so it feels like everything is at a stalemate most of the time. It's not the way Parker had envisioned his presidency, but he does try, and he sets a good example, which is more than I can say for most other politicians.

I have big dreams for my brother. If he can't do it, I don't believe anyone will, but I think he's the one who will return normalcy and common sense to our government. No one is better suited for the job than Trey, and with his name recognition, he knows he has a huge chance of being elected once he meets all the qualifications.

When the dessert is ready, I grab my dinner plate and the adults sit down in the formal dining room to eat together. They do it for my benefit. Dessert is normally enjoyed in the family room, but we let the girls watch one of their movies in there while we talk.

"So, Trey, how was last semester?" I ask him. "You've been so busy volunteering; we haven't had a chance to catch up."

"I know. I have to get a certain number of hours in every week. I'm competing against a lot of talented men and women at Harvard and I want to make sure I stand out."

"I doubt you have any chance of blending in," Jon teases him.

"On my own merits," he says with a blush. "Not just by my stature and name."

"You were editor of the Columbia Daily Witness. You've written for the Times. You ran Parker's campaign. The three of you infiltrated Gluck's rallies to promote equality across race, gender and sexuality," my husband says with admiration, staring across the table at our guests. That is something we are all proud of, despite the way their activism ended. "While politicians are out there taking money from the gun lobby, you've done high-profile interviews against gun violence after the assassination attempt. You stand out, buddy. You're making a name for yourself."

"I'm just trying to do my part in the city now, though. Helping the people who can't help themselves."

"That's all you've ever done, Trey. If it's not directly, you do it by bringing attention to their causes."

"I guess," he says, modest. "When it comes down to it—to election day, whenever that is—it has to be enough. Everything I can do, every day, matters."

Coley holds his hand on the table to show her support.

"The video's always going to come up," he says softly, referring to a leaked sex tape of him and his fiancée that was recorded without their consent in college. "I always have to have bigger news to combat it."

"And we will," Coley says confidently.

"You're marrying that girl in a few months," I remind him.

"And even if you weren't," Max says, "the asshat that did that is behind bars for that crime until he's an old, repulsive, impotent dude."

"He's already repulsive," Jon, Coley and I say at the same time. We all laugh lightly, too.

"Anyone who brings that up will look petty. They'll look like they're trying to distract people from something relevant—likely something they're trying to hide. The fact is, that video is old news. It was a crime when it happened, and it's still a crime to show it, so..."

"You're not a worrier, Trey," I tell him, looking at him questioningly. "Why would you even be thinking about this?"

"One of my classmates brought it up in a mock debate with me."

"Well, that was a low blow," Jon tells him. "And if that's the worst dirt he can dig up on you, then you're golden. How awful that you were intimate with the woman you love, right?" he asks sarcastically.

"Yeah, I guess." Trey chuckles.

"You've got to stop feeling guilty about it," Coley says. "You didn't then. I don't know why you do now."

"Because then, I had pipe dreams. Now, I see a real future, and I don't want that to be a wall that keeps me from doing what I know I'm destined to do," he says, matter-of-fact.

"It won't be," I assure him. "That's not even *dirt*. That was just you living life. Everyone's done it." I shrug my shoulders.

"That is an absolutely untrue statement," Max says. "I have not done *that*."

"Let's not talk specifics at the dinner table, please, Mascot," Jon says to his brother. "I'm eating."

"Technically, so was Trey," he says with a smirk.

"This night is destined to end with a monumental food fight. I want to apologize in advance and offer to pay you for cleanup," my brother says just before he takes a handful of cake and whipped cream and chunks it at his best friend.

"No!" Jon yells.

Max reciprocates with two strawberries to Trey's head.

"Stop it!" I shout, but my laughter belies any attempt at being serious. "You guys are 25 years old! Coley? Stop him!"

"Do you see how much bigger he is?" she says, shaking her head. Having a better idea, she runs over to Max and attempts to hold his hands behind his back.

"Oh, no you don't, *Coney*." He breaks free easily, and smears whipped cream in her hair. She squeals loudly, and runs behind Trey, who's now standing up.

I continue trying to eat my dinner as the fight continues, and Edie and Willow come in to see what's happening. They immediately pick sides: Edie on Trey's and Willow on Max's.

"Girls? If either of you throw anything, you're both going up to your rooms and straight to bed," Jon says, laying down the law.

"We won't, Daddy," Edie says. Willow bounces on the balls of her feet, though, so tempted to help her uncle.

"Wils?" I say, my tone warning her.

"I'm not, Mama."

Suddenly, a large strawberry lands in my butter chicken, splashing sauce onto my blouse and face.

"Who threw it?" I ask, still staring at my food.

"Coley?" Max suggests, apprehensive.

"I did not!" she says.

"Mascot?"

"Yeah..."

"When's the last time you did dishes?" I ask him.

"Did what to them?" he asks, just like smart-ass Max would. "I eat off 'em all the time."

"*Washed* them. By hand. And *dried* them."

"They make machines for that now, Liv. I'm pretty sure you've got one," he informs me.

"Yes, but because tonight was a special occasion—having our sweet, youngest brothers over—we brought out the good china, and I don't like putting these dishes in that machine of which you speak," I tell him, finally looking him in the eyes. "Plus, that doesn't seem like much punishment for likely ruining one of my favorite shirts... so why don't you go ahead and get started on washing, hmm?"

Trey starts laughing at him.

"And you can dry, since you started it, buddy."

"Shit," he says.

"And pay your nieces a buck each on your way to the kitchen," Jon says.

"Coley, would you like to come upstairs with me while I change, and get that out of your hair?" I nod to the whipped cream.

"I think that'd be best."

"Can we come?" Willow asks.

"No. Since you were cheering them on, why don't you stay down here and help your father clean up the dining room."

"But we didn't do anything!" she protests.

"Wils, come help Daddy," Jon says, throwing her a wet rag.

Upstairs, I offer Coley the shower to wash her hair, but she decides to wipe it out as best as she can with a washcloth and water. To simplify things, she pulls her hair back in a ponytail, and somehow, she looks just as fashionable as she did when she came in with her hair in waves. Edie could learn from her natural beauty. Makeup and rollers and all the fuss are not needed to be beautiful.

"Did you get enough to eat?" she asks me as I change shirts in my closet.

"I may get a few strawberries once we go downstairs."

"That doesn't seem like enough food. You know, for two," she says.

Once I'm dressed, I come out and sit down on the edge of my tub. She sits on the vanity stool, facing me. "Nothing at all is normal with this pregnancy, Coles. I'm not hungry like I should be. I'm not healthy like I should be." I sigh, suddenly feeling burdened. "I'm not happy like I should be." Two tears slide down my cheeks, with more on the way. Coley moves next to me.

"Oh, Liv, it's okay," she says, putting her arms around me. "You're eating enough, though, right?"

I nod my head. "He's gaining weight. Not like the girls did, but he is. The doctor just says all babies are different. That all pregnancies are different."

"I don't know that from experience," my friend says, "but I'm sure that's true. I know he's taking a lot out of you, but it's going to be fine."

"Is it?" I ask her. "Coley, I have this feeling about it."

"What do you mean?"

"This... dark cloud looms over me daily. I don't have a good feeling about it."

"About what, exactly?"

"The baby. The pregnancy. Me. All of it. Nothing feels right. Don't tell Trey. I don't want him to tell Jon. I don't want him to worry about anything."

"I won't, Liv, but have you told your doctor?"

"She knows I'm frustrated with things. But I can't really tell her I have a weird feeling about it. What's she going to do? Some magic voodoo shit to make it better?"

"I don't know, maybe tell you to go talk to someone. Someone who can alleviate your fears and tell you you're not alone. That probably half the women who go through pregnancy have feelings like this. It sounds like you're depressed. The dark cloud? Come on. If anyone knows depression, it's me. It's nothing to be ashamed of or to hide from people."

"But I shouldn't be depressed. I'm having a baby! I should be happy!"

"He's changing your hormones!" she says with a laugh. "You can't control that. Don't feel guilty about it, for sure. And we're all happy enough for you and your son to make sure he knows he's going to be welcomed in this world." She touches my belly. "You'll catch up to the rest of us, I promise. It may take sorting through some other feelings, or it may take a little medication.

"But know this, Liv. There are people who can make you better. And it's okay to not be happy all the time. As long as you're working on it," she says, rubbing my arm. "If the doctor says the baby's okay and that you're okay, you have to trust her that nothing weird is happening. Just push that thought to the side. Let's work on figuring out what's getting you down, okay? I can recommend my therapist. She's very good—and discreet. She even does house visits."

"I'll think about it," I tell her, not sure if depression is my problem. I've never had issues with that outside of my breakups with Jon in my younger years. "And I know where to go when I need it. Thank you."

"Well," she says with a sigh. "You're not weird. Nothing about what's going on is weird, okay?"

I smile—it's not natural. It's all for show. "Okay."

She gives me a hug, playfully tugging on my braid twice.

"Listen," I say to her. "Can you maybe start, like, mentoring Edie? I know this sounds weird, but she's so obsessed with beauty and makeup and... I know she thinks you're so pretty, and I know your routine is, like, effortless."

She laughs a little. "It looks that way. I hate makeup but I have to take good care of my skin to not wear any."

"I think that's an important thing to learn. Did you know she asked me to go to a tanning booth a few weeks ago?"

"No!"

"Yes!"

"How does she even know about those things?"

"Apparently, she's discovered the power of YouTube. And we're working on that."

"Oh, no!" She giggles. "I would love to take her under my wing."

"That would be so awesome, Coles. I just don't want her to turn 12 and all of a sudden look 30, you know? And she knows how to apply makeup to do that. It's frightening."

"So... I've got three years to train her that natural is the way?"

"Is it possible, Dr. Fitzsimmons?" I tease her.

"I'll get my strongest team on it. But yes, Mrs. Scott. It is possible. And Willow?" she asks.

"I don't think we need to worry about her. Once Edie's got it figured out, Willow will follow suit. Plus, by the time Willow's 12, she'll probably be studying for the ACT so she can do early admission to NYU or something... she'll have other things on her mind than looking pretty. She only gets wrapped up in these things now because of her sister. If she could sit in her room all day and read, she would. But Edie likes attention, and Willow loves her sister."

"No doubt about Willow's aspirations. Both your girls are so exceptional, though, and so talented."

"I know. They're so different, too. But... they astound me daily. I love them to death, makeup obsessions and desires to go to the moon and all."

"You're a wonderful mother, Liv. I only hope I can be half the mom as you when it's my turn."

"Are you kidding? You and Trey are going to be great parents. I can't wait to meet your twins."

"Twins!?"

"You know you're going to have twins. They run in both your families. Get ready, Coles. It's your destiny," I tell her, nodding. "Double the feedings. Double the diapers. Half the sleep you'd get with just one baby. You'll have the time of your life."

She grins widely. "I hope it's a boy and a girl." Coley's obviously giddy at the thought.

I wash away all evidence of makeup–and tears–before returning downstairs. Because Trey and Coley only had to reheat the meal they'd brought, the dishes are finished and put away by the time I make it to the kitchen. I thank all of the guys and my daughters for cleaning up, choosing not to look in the dining room at the moment. I assume the rug will still need to be steam-cleaned, and that's not going to happen until tomorrow.

"Sorry about the mess, sis," Trey says.

"Hope we didn't stress you out," Max adds.

"It's fine, guys. I expect stuff like this when you two come over. I didn't expect you to change just because we moved to a bigger, fancier place."

"I did," Jon deadpans.

"Just because we grew up doesn't mean they had to," I remind him.

"And you're still set on having these two be our son's godparents?"

"Wait, who?" Max asks.

"Me and... *him?*" Trey adds, pointing to his best friend.

I withhold my response for a few seconds, just for dramatic affect. "As long as Max has his 'asparagus' thing under control," I say, glaring at him, "I definitely do. Look how much fun they have together. Auggie will learn a lot from them. How to be serious," I say, looking at Trey, "and how to cut loose every now and then." I smile at Max. "Appropriately and legally," I add, raising an eyebrow.

"Oh, man... wow!" Max says, giving me a hug.

"I'd be honored," Trey says, nodding his head. He shakes Jon's hand before embracing me—and then high-fiving Max.

"But we're not calling him Auggie," Jon mumbles.

Ignoring him, I continue. "I can only hope he and Charlie will be just as close as these two."

"What if they don't get along?" Max asks.

"I don't think that's a thing," I say, shaking my head. "I think if we bring them up together, they'll just naturally be, like, close. Right? That's how it works."

"What if they just *totally* clash?" he pushes.

I'd never even considered that our son and Will and Shea's son wouldn't get along. I think about it for the first time and look at Jon, worried.

"They won't," Jon says. "Will and I have similar sensibilities. You and Shea do, too. If we have the same parenting styles, they'll learn to be friends through what we teach them. I think that's how it works. I mean, look at the girls and Hampton," he says, referring to one of their friends. He's the son of one of Will's bandmates, and right around Willow's age, who lives next door to Will. "We brought them up together, and they get along great."

"He's in love with Willow," Edie says.

"He is not!"

"Is, too! He sent you flowers for your birthday!"

I look at her. "He did do that."

"They were yellow roses, and that means friendship." Willow's statement is punctuated by her crossing her arms and furrowing her brows.

"Well," Jon says, surprised. "That is true. How'd you know that?"

She covers her face with her hands. "Because I called his house and told him I didn't like him like that," she explains quickly, her voice muffled, "and he said that they were yellow 'cause we're friends and that maybe he didn't like me like that, either, and I felt really stupid."

Max goes over to her and pulls her hands away to reveal her watery eyes. "You know who's stupid?" he asks her. She shakes her head. "Hampton, for not liking you like that."

"He said *maybe*," Edie says. "But I know he looooves her. He told me so."

"No," Jon says, cutting in. "They're eight. Nobody should like anybody 'like that,'" he says with air quotes. "And nobody's stupid. Especially you, Wils."

"No, but someday he might," Coley says, "and if that happens, I want you to come talk to me or your mama so we can tell you how to handle it. When most boys send you flowers, they're trying to do something nice for you. Maybe there's deeper meaning behind it, but maybe it's just a kind gesture, like a gift for your birthday. You should assume he has positive intentions unless he's done something to make you think otherwise."

"I don't understand," my youngest says.

"Assume he's doing something nice just to do something nice. Don't assume he's expecting more from you."

"So, don't read between the lines?" she asks.

"What the...?" Jon looks at me, then back at our little girl. "That's such a big concept for your mind, sweetie. How do you know anything about that?"

"Uncle Will teaches me. It was part of a reading comprehension lesson he was showing me."

"I swear," I say to her. "The things your little noodle soaks up. Come here." I hold my arms out for her. She climbs into my lap carefully, sitting sideways to be able to put her hand flat on my belly. "You're going to have so many things to teach your baby brother."

I kiss her forehead and give her a hug.

"He'll have to keep up!" she says brightly.

"He'll probably be bored," Edie adds.

"We'll just have to let him decide, bunny, right?" Jon asks her. "Maybe he'll love fashion like you do, and you can show him the ropes."

"That'd be super cool."

"Whatever he likes, he's going to be so lucky to have such amazing big sisters," Trey says.

CHAPTER 8

*a*t Tiffany's, Shea and I look at trays of jewelry spread in front of us, both of us sold on the idea. Will's off in a corner of the store, trying to hide from some women who've recognized him and are trying to get up the nerve to approach him. With his headphones in and his nose in a textbook, he doesn't look very welcoming.

The book is a new one he picked up for Willow, though, and only his wife and I know that the headphones are silent—he left his phone at home today.

Periodically, Shea looks up to check on him to see if she needs to run interference, but so far, he's fine.

"I think we're onto something," she says to me. "I mean. He's the boy who has everything, really. He buys what he wants, but what's he going to need, going forward? Cuff links."

"He'll probably need tie clips, too, but I'm afraid they'll just get misplaced since he tends to rip off ties the second no one's watching," I tell her, knowing well my brother's adverse reaction to neckwear.

"Right, so cuff links are the answer! Didn't Coley get him some nice ones for Christmas?"

"She did. These," I say, pointing to a set with an X and an O with diamonds on each. "And now he can start a collection of them. I think it's a great idea. It's got to get boring wearing a suit and tie every damn day, and that's the life he's going into." I nod my head, looking at the salesperson. "I think we'll get one pair each."

"Yes," Shea agrees. "Which ones are you getting him?"

"I'm going to have to get him the comma ones, I think. The ones in black jade."

"Good, because I want to get him the sterling silver airplanes. They're just so cute."

"He's going to get so many compliments on those," I tell her, picking one up.

"But the commas will be very personal to him. He's going to love them. Oh, man," she says, looking at Will. "I need to rescue him."

Apparently, the women brought backup. He's swarmed by seven ladies now, all asking him for a picture. I focus on them while I take out my debit card and slide it across the counter to pay.

"Mrs. Scott, will you be paying for both?" the salesclerk asks me.

"No, just the comma ones. If Will can get away, he'll be buying the airplane ones. And can you giftwrap them for us? Separately?"

"Of course. Shall I get security?" He nods toward my friends and the crowd around them. Shea smiles politely, puts her hand on her belly, and pulls her husband out of the circle with her, apologizing.

"No, she's got it handled. She always knows what to say."

"Very well. Mr. Scott, how will you be paying today?"

"Credit," he says, securing himself between me and Shea.

"You're the envy of all men, walking around with these beautiful ladies flanking you today," the salesman says.

Will laughs assuredly. "Don't I know it? I keep telling Liv to leave my brother... I'm sure I can convince Shea to make room in our marriage for one more."

My best friend busts out laughing, one brow raised in disbelief at his arrogance, while I elbow him in the side. "You bigamist freak."

"You always gotta ruin the moment with your damn labels, Liv." He looks at me sideways with a charming smile, and in that one glance, I can see why Shea fell in love with him. He just has that *Will way* that could win over any girl—not me, because I have my own Scott brother—but any *other* girl.

. . .

*W*ill tucks the gifts in the messenger bag he carries over his shoulder as we leave the store, careful not to make neither Shea nor I handle anything today. It also makes us less of a target while we're out running errands in preparation for Trey's birthday. He puts his arm across Shea's shoulder and directs us east.

"Where are we going next?" I ask him.

"This... odds and ends shop. An antique shop? I don't know what you call it," he says.

"Why?" I ask him, thinking that doesn't sound like a place any of us would particularly like.

"Because that's where my gift for your brother is. I bought it online. I have to pick it up."

"You bought him an antique?" I look at him, judgmental. He puts his other arm around my shoulder and starts walking with a strut, obviously showing off the fact that he's got two highly successful, well-known women of Manhattan at his side—me for my art, Shea for her food. "Get that off me, you pimp-ass, polyamorous-wanna-be perverted prick." I shove him away, laughing.

"You let those alliterations fly, Liv," he says, laughing back as Shea giggles. "And yes, I bought him an antique of sorts."

"What is it?" I offer him my elbow, and he links his with mine.

"I just remember how much he loved Moby Dick when he read it in high school."

"Oh, god. I'm afraid to ask," I say, squinting now.

"Who's perverted now?" he scoffs. "There's this amazing, hand-carved, rosewood sperm whale—"

"See?" I say to Shea. "It always has to be something dirty with him."

"He can't help it," she says, shaking her head. "It's just how he is. Don't act like you didn't know."

"Will you two shut up? It's, like, a couple-hundred years old and in pristine condition."

"So... it's a statue?"

"No, it's a set of bookends. Gorgeous. I just thought he'd really like it."

"And the sperm and dick had no sway in your decision-making process?" I keep poking.

Shea high-fives me.

"I don't know why I agreed to go with you two today."

"Because you love us," his wife says, pulling him to a stop and leaning up for a kiss.

He lets go of me. "I love *you*," he says to her, putting his hands on her face and touching his lips to hers gently. I wait patiently for his playful insult. "I tolerate *this one* because you have no other friends." I know, in truth, he adores me.

"I have other friends," she laughs. "Just none I like as much as her."

"Thank you," I tell her, switching sides and locking arms with her now. We keep walking toward the shop.

"So, sperm and dick aside, do you think Trey will like it?" This makes me chuckle, and I know every time I see this set of bookends at Trey's house, I'll now think dirty things—which was probably Will's intent anyway, subconsciously.

"I have to see it," I say flippantly, "but he did love that dumb book. He read it twice."

"The second time he read it was to refresh his memory to help Max with his homework."

"I didn't know that."

"Yeah. As much as Max loves whales, he didn't like the sperm and dick so much."

"Stop it!" I laugh again. "Because he likes it now!"

"Yes, he does," Will says, grinning. When I realize which direction we're walking, I try to turn down a different street. "Liv, I'm trying to go this way on purpose."

"But Will," I say, reluctant, "I don't really want to see it."

"Please? I haven't gone by here yet. I've only seen the pictures Shea sent. I'm dying to go."

Seeing the corner of the building I'd been hoping to avoid peeking out at us already, I nod my head and agree to continue on his current path. Shea drops my arm and holds my hand instead, squeezing it to give me support.

A crowd has gathered on the sidewalks surrounding the twenty-six-story mural. It was the last one I painted before I got pregnant, for the Lexington Park Art Society. I didn't know it would be the last one I'd do for a while, and seeing it brings back feelings of joy, but also an immense longing to do the thing I love to do most in life. Painting was more than a hobby to me. More than my livelihood. It was my *life*. I'd been doing it since I was four years old, and I needed it like I needed air to breathe. Not being able to do it has left an emptiness in my soul and seeing what everyone in the art community had touted as one of my best masterpieces staring right back at me, it makes the pit inside me open wider. Those dark clouds I'd mentioned to Coley hang even lower. Perhaps I *am* depressed. I look away from the large painting and realize all the people are actually admiring my work.

"Oh my god," Will says. In fact, I think he's been repeating it since we stopped walking. He'd been in Houston when I had the unveiling, working with NASA on some top-secret project. He couldn't tell us anything about it. I'm convinced they'd located aliens in space, and since he's not allowed to confirm or deny it, I'm certain I'm right. I guess they're nice, since we're all still here.

"Better than the aliens?" I ask him, my attempt at levity to lighten my mood.

He chuckles. "Just... the pictures didn't do it justice, Liv." He's running his hands through his hair, unable to take his eyes off of it. I've always loved the way he appreciates my work, and Jon's, too. His intelligence gives him a very critical eye, so I hold his opinion in the highest regard. "It's incredible. 'Masterpiece' isn't a suitable word for this one. They need a new word."

"Oh, hush." I let go of Shea and push his shoulder.

"Everybody!" he yells.

"Will!"

People look at him and get excited—because it's Will Scott, guitarist for Damon Littlefield. "The artist of that wall is in your midst! Olivia Choisie is right here!" He points at me after shouting out my artist pseudonym.

People start to encircle us quickly, and I feel my pulse begin to race.

"This trip to New York was specifically to see your work," one woman tells me as I get separated from my friends.

"I'm going to art school because of you," and young man shouts out.

I smile politely but keep Shea and Will in my sight. The two body guards we'd hired for today, who'd been able to keep a safe distance, push in and grab me from the throes of the crowd, then pull me out.

"We have to get out of here," I say, only after they've removed me from the situation when I finally have my wits about me. Will was able to escape with Shea, and we're actually following them. I realize I'm only taking shallow breaths as I try to remove my arms from their tight grasps. I feel like everything is closing in around me.

"Fuck, Jon's gonna kill me," I can hear Will say. "Look, the shop's right here. We can just duck in." *Duck* is one way to put it. I get *pushed,* or at least nudged in an aggressive manner by the guards, who are now standing outside of the store and keeping other people from entering.

"Good afternoon," Shea says politely to the man behind the counter.

"You okay?" Will asks, his hands on my shoulders as he guides me to a chair.

"Sitting would be good," I tell him. "I just didn't expect any of that. I'm fine." I force a smile, but he knows it's less than sincere.

"I'm sorry. I just got caught up in a moment. You know me." He squats down in front of me.

"I know. It's good, Will. Really." I nod my head, appreciating his concern. "Just do your shopping."

"Liv, they have some tea, if you'd like it," Shea says.

"Chamomile, dear," the older woman with a British accent says.

"Oh, please, if it's not too much trouble. That'd be great."

"Happily. It's steeping in the back, just a moment."

Will stands up, keeping his hand on my shoulder as he turns around to face the man, who's now glaring at the front door.

"So, are those big guys gonna block my entrance indefinitely, or...?"

"Listen, sorry," Will starts, approaching him. "We'll make it worth your while, I promise. We just need some time to regroup. I've been emailing you about some bookends. I bought them last weekend."

"Oh, Auggie," the woman says as she comes out with the tea, "leave the kids alone. They need to escape for a minute. Don't you realize you have stars in your midst? You have a famous painter, a top chef and... what are you today?" she asks Will.

We're all smiling, and my brother-in-law laughs at her question. "Just an astrophysicist."

"An astrophysicist! He's very important!" After she hands me the tea in a dainty cup on what appears to be a very old saucer, she looks back at the man who, by the familiarity of her tone, I now assume is her husband. With her hands on her hips, she whispers loudly, as if it's a secret, "Some

CHAPTER 8 | 101

days he's a rock star! These are famous people! The Hollands? And Scotts? Don't you ever read Page Six?"

"If it's not on page one, no, dear, I don't," he says, grumpy.

"Wait," I interrupt, "did you say his name is Auggie?" I ask the woman, but he answers.

"It's August, but most people call me Auggie."

I relax, and it has nothing to do with the tea. I feel like this is a sign. "That's so strange. My son's middle name will be Augustus." With my free hand, I touch my belly. "I've been telling my husband that we should call him Auggie, but Jon's afraid he'll be teased."

"Oh, he'll be teased, but it builds character. That's what it did for me."

"That's what I keep telling him," I say, then my voice gets softer, "but he just wants to call him Jonny."

"That's so sweet!" the woman's voice erupts, startling us all. "He's going to be a second?"

"Yes," I say, smiling, watching Will as he finds the carved bookends he'd told us about. "But August... I mean, what a great name!" I begin walking over to Will but look at Shea. "If he's just born a couple days early—in August—maybe we can call him that!"

Will turns around to look at me curiously. "He doesn't have to be born early. His middle name will be Augustus. That gives you the right to shorten it however you like, right?"

I set down the tea next to one of the bookends and stroke the wood that's obviously been softened by age. "Yeah!" I say, nodding my head. "I think August is great! And I think Jon will one-hundred percent agree!"

"Whale's nice, huh?" Will asks, getting in a question.

"It's perfect. I don't know how you found it, but Trey's going to love it."

CHAPTER 9

*A*fter taking the last curler out of my hair, I put on a fresh coat of bright red lipstick and smile in the mirror. One on each side of me, my girls look up and grin back at me.

"Mama, you look so pretty," Edie says.

"Thank you, sweetie. Can you go get my shoes? They're the blue ones I set by the door."

Willow beats her to the closet and brings them to me. I sit down on the vanity stool, handing both of them a shoe. "Now. Can each of you put one on? Because there's no way I can bend over and tie the bows in the back."

"Oh, they're so beautiful, Mama! Can I borrow these when they fit?" my oldest asks, sliding her toes into my shoe. "They're Louboutin's, aren't they?"

"Yes, and yes," I say, shaking my head at her knowledge of shoes.

"They're too girly for me," Willow says, confused about the scarf accessory and fussing with the bow. "Can I just knot it?" Her frustration is quick and evident.

"No," I say. "Let Edie do it."

"I'll make them perfect," my oldest says, sitting with her legs crossed on the floor.

"Can I go downstairs with everyone?"

"Go ahead, Wils. Thanks for hanging out with me while I get ready." She takes off in a sprint.

"So, it looks like it crosses in the back, and then in the front, and then ties in the back. Is that right?"

"Exactly, and you want to make sure the scarf doesn't twist when you wrap it around. Does that make sense?" I ask.

"I'm not stupid, Mama. Like this?"

I lean to my side to get a good look at my left foot. "Perfect." I stand up to make sure it's not too tight. "Do the same on the other side, and these shoes are yours as soon as they fit... but you won't want them, because they'll be five years out of fashion by then."

"I'll bring them back into fashion. They're too pretty... you have such good taste."

I laugh at her compliment. "Thank you." I don't bother telling her that many designers contact me and ask me to wear their clothes and accessories, and more often than not, the clothes find me, and not the other way around. They'll do the same for her when she's older, I'm sure... and she'll love it.

"You look like a pregnant princess going to a cocktail party," she tells me when she stands up to review my overall look.

"The headband's too much, huh?"

"I like it! Leave it. It's a special occasion and you told everyone to be fancy, right?"

"I did. Daddy's in a nice suit, too. And I know what Shea and Coley are wearing. They're both wearing their really nice jewelry, so... I don't feel so weird."

"So, where are you *really* going?" she asks, nudging me and obviously implying that I've been lying.

"I told you!" I put my hand on her back and guide her out of our bathroom, and then our bedroom. "We just rented the party room downstairs. A catered affair. A very nice party for your uncle. He didn't want anything public, so... we're complying with that."

The doorbell plays its music, and I check the watch Jon gave me for our last anniversary. It's so bejeweled and dainty I can hardly make out the time.

"You know what? I bet that's Granddaddy and Memi. Go grab your pillow and overnight bag. I'll get Willow's." We split off into the rooms as

I hear my mom and dad downstairs saying hello to Coley's brothers and one of their girlfriends who are going to stay in our guest rooms tonight.

Edie beats me downstairs and is sitting next to my dad on the couch. Jon catcalls me from the kitchen when he sees me.

"You look gorgeous, sweetheart," Mom says, giving me a hug.

"I feel so... impregnated," I respond.

"Well, you are. You can't do anything about that, but the dress looks amazing on you."

"Listen to Emi!" Jon yells.

"You look great," Joanna, Nyall's girlfriend, says. Having only met her once before, there's an awkwardness about her greeting as she sort-of half-waves at me. I hold out my arms, inviting her in for an embrace.

"Thank you! So do you!" I tell her.

"Is this nice enough?" she asks, looking down at her black ankle-length gown.

"Oh, it's perfect."

"It needs a necklace," Edie says, and just as a look of insecurity crosses Joanna's face, she continues, "but we have one! Mama! She can borrow those pearls I got for you!"

"Oh, I wouldn't dream of it," our guest stutters.

"No, Edie's right. You look wonderful, but I do have a nice strand of pearls that would look great with that."

"I'd be afraid something would happen to them."

I lean back into her and whisper. "Edie got them for me. They're costume. It's okay."

"Oh. Well, if you're sure, then, yeah!"

"I'll get them!"

"Walk, bunny!" Jon calls after her as she races up the stairs.

"Nyall, how are you?" I ask Coley's oldest brother, giving him big hug.

"I'm well."

"That's good to hear." And it is. Nyall had been institutionalized for years for a violent mental condition that he had a hard time controlling. With the right therapy and medications, he was finally able to move out of the hospital—first into his mother's home in DC with in-home help, and finally into his own apartment nearby, after having a successful year with no incidents. He's been dating Joanna for over a year now. She actually has a degree in psychology but works in marketing. I think her education has really helped in their relationship, though; in turn, it's rekindled her interest in psychology. She's considering going back to get her PhD.

"And Joel," I say and sign at the same time. He's great at reading lips and can speak well on his own, but the entire family has learned to sign to support him. The girls particularly love seeing him so they can show him new vocabulary they've learned in weekly classes we send them to. "How is work?"

"Well, the only time I get to dress like this is if I'm serving food," he says with a sour expression. "I've got to find a way to stay in Manhattan. I've got to weasel my way into some restaurant. Who do I have to kill at Shea's place to make this happen?"

We all laugh. It'd been a running joke among the family. Shea's chefs had become close friends of hers; they were incredibly competent and trusted and would do just about anything for their boss. Shea had offered him a job as a prep cook, but they'd both acknowledged that he was too talented for that. It was just the only job she had available.

"Talk to her tonight and let her know you're serious about coming back to New York," Jon tells him. "I'm sure she'll start putting out some feelers."

"I just need someone to give me a chance. I just need a little time to prove myself," he says. "They just find out I'm deaf and close the damn door. In any other industry, it's discrimination. In the food industry, it's..."

"*Accepted* discrimination," Dad says with a tone of disgust in his voice. "It makes me want to start a restaurant to make a point."

"Jacks, you know nothing about that industry," my mother says. "You don't open restaurants on principle. Don't get those crazy ideas." She walks over to Coley's brother. "Joel, we'll help you in any other way... but I have to stop him from opening a restaurant."

Joel laughs. "Understood."

Once Joanna gets her necklace, Dad rounds up the girls and puts their things on the cart he'd been mindful enough to bring with him from the concierge. My dad's always three steps ahead of everyone, though, so I'm not surprised.

"Tell Jackson we said hello," he tells me. "Family dinner's still on for tomorrow night, right?"

"Of course. We have to take the mini-monsters back at some time," I say, tugging Willow's pigtails. "Jon and I will be there at five to give you and Mom a break from the girls—and cook—and we'll tell Trey and Coles to be there at seven. Right?"

"Right." He kisses me on the cheek.

I hug both of the girls as they pat my belly and say goodbye to me and Froggie. Mom and I embrace once more before Jon walks them out.

"Everyone okay?" I ask. "Did Jon get you all drinks?"

"Worst host ever," Nyall says, setting down his full beverage. "I asked for crushed ice and he gives me this?" he jokes.

"He's still learning... with the ice dispenser. I'll dock his pay," I assure him.

"Thank you. No, I think we're all good."

Joel and Joanna nod, both settling into the living room furniture.

"I invited a buddy of mine," Joel tells me. "He's just going to meet us downstairs. Is that okay? Trey's hung out with him a few times."

"Yeah, we should have plenty of food and drinks. Wait," I say, "any..." I stall, trying to think of the right ASL signs. "Dietary restrictions?"

"No."

"Okay. You have that vegetarian friend, don't you?"

"Not him."

"Cool."

"Hey! Did you see the lights in the bedroom and hallway?" I ask him.

"Yeah!" he grins. "Jon showed me when he brought me to the guest room, and I saw it in action when Jack and Emi showed up. You guys didn't have to do that."

"It was no trouble. We wanted you to be alerted if anyone came to the door, or if there was an emergency. They'll flash if an alarm goes off, too."

"You guys are the best."

"Well, I know," I tease him, leading him back into the living area, where Jon has returned.

"Did you pad Nyall's room?" Joel asks.

Because we don't see Nyall as often, I don't know if this is something they joke about as brothers. I look at Jon, walking toward him on the other side, and pretend I didn't hear the question.

"I brought the portable cushions," Joanna says, not missing a beat. "And the straight jacket."

"Jo, they don't need to hear about what we do in bed," Nyall whispers.

She picks up a pillow and whacks him with it, and all of the guys start laughing. I breathe a sigh of relief.

Jon finds the pulse points at the base of my neck with his thumbs and digs in, hard. "Relax," he says softly in my ear, pushing the curls out of the way. I lean my head back into his hands and let him rub away the tension that had been building up all day as we prepared for my brother's birthday party. "Ready to go downstairs? My brothers are there. Shea's apparently rearranging things with the caterer."

"She's not supposed to lift a finger," I say through gritted teeth.

"Then let's go stop her." He presses his lips against my temple for a second and puts his arms around my swollen torso. "I love you, baby." His thumbs now rub up and down my belly, exciting his son. "And you, baby."

*D*ownstairs, Will, Max and Callen are already playing pool while Shea rearranges place settings at the table. Jon and I both approach her. He takes the plate she was holding while I drag her away.

"Shea. Friend. *Best* friend. *Soulfriend.*" She laughs. "What are you doing?"

"It's like they let Max set the table here. Just look at it! Everything's out of place!"

"Okay, okay," I say. "If that's the case, then we tell the people I hired to fix it. I'm not paying your salary tonight. And oh my god, where did you get those earrings?!"

Large, pink, dangling diamonds catch the light from the chandeliers.

"Will's royalty check came in. You know he always does something crazy like this when he has hits."

"Good lord! Are those heavy?"

"A little! But worth it! I think I'll be too afraid to wear them out and about, though. I'd like to keep my ears in one piece," she admits. "But Liv. Stop distracting me. The place settings?"

"Look, Jon's already talking to them." I angle her in his direction. "And this doesn't have to be perfect anyway, Shea. It's for Trey, and he's forgiving of those types of things. He's forgiving of everything, in fact," I say with a laugh.

"I know. But when we throw a party, it should be perfect. It's how my mother raised me. It has nothing to do with Hollands or Scotts or anything like that."

"Okay. Well, I don't want you to worry about it anymore. They're fixing it now. You should go meet Joanna and say hi to Nyall. Plus, I know Joel wants a minute or two with you."

"All right. I'm stepping away and letting go," she says, releasing a sigh.

Just after Joel's friend, Booker, shows up, Coley leads Trey into the parlor, and we all break out in a very lively version of "Happy Birthday." The red on my brother's face must match my lipstick, the poor thing. He looks around, delighting in the custom-order sushi setup and the full-service bar before Jon and Max take him to the outdoor area and show him the three grills available to cook steaks, too.

"*Heaven,*" my little brother sings Sinatra poorly, "*I'm in Heaven.*"

"And we have pool and darts and trivia... and I was going to mention karaoke, but I don't want you to sing," I tease him.

"Coley is amazing at karaoke," he says. "Prettiest voice ever."

"We'll let her have a shot then."

"How are you feeling?" he asks, giving me a hug. "I hope you didn't have to go to any trouble putting all of this together."

"It was no trouble at all. Just had to make some calls and decisions. And I'd do anything for my baby brother's 25th birthday. You know that... it's not quite like the party for your 21st, but you didn't want all that fuss."

"No, I didn't. That was insane... but awesome. I got to surprise the hell out of Coley with a proposal, and that was worth every bit of all the extra attention I didn't really want."

"And now, you get to marry her in just a few months!" His smile is out of control. "You are too cute."

"I just can't wait for it to be official." He looks beyond me. "I want her to rest assured that she'll always be taken care of." The smile is gone, replaced with a contemplative look. I turn around to see her behind me; he's looking at her. "Since her father was killed, there are moments when she gets insecure about... *life*. The uncertainty of it all. Most of the time, she's great, but then she'll have moments of doubt when she worries about me going into politics; worries about some crazy person coming after me someday..."

"We don't help matters," I tell him, "taking all the extra security precautions because we fear that happening, too. And not even for our politics. Not even because we're divisive people. Just because we're *notable* people."

"Yeah." He takes my hand in his and squeezes it, looking almost morose now.

"You don't think she's having second thoughts, do you? About joining this family?"

His eyes water, and he nods subtly. "She does. Sometimes." He swallows hard. "But she loves me too much to walk away. I think she wishes I was just a regular guy somedays. A regular guy with similar ambitions. The same ideals and standards. Without the Holland name and money."

I keep listening, worried for him. I've been wrapped up in the idea of them for years. There is no cuter couple, and I know our family has a lot of dreams for what they'll do not only for our legacy, but for our country in later years.

"She still goes to her shrink weekly. They talk about these things. I go with her to some appointments, too. We discuss ways I can bring normalcy to her life. And she works on ways she can accept things that will never change.

"We're going to be fine, Liv. We are. We're happy and we're in love. We're just not perfect. But no one is."

"No, you *are*!" I tell him, wiping my eyes and shoving his chest.

He laughs at me. "This party was a good way to bring normalcy into our lives," he says softly. "So, thanks for agreeing to the low-key night. This is perfect. Just friends and family. This is all we need."

"And food," I add.

"Amazing looking food." He hugs me again, and his arm lingers around my neck. "Should we go tell them how we like our sushi?"

"You're going to tell them to put extra wasabi on mine, aren't you?"

"Damn straight."

"Ha! You think you can try to murder me tonight and get my part of the inheritance, but the joke's on you, buddy. There's no horseradish in this wasabi!" I inform him. Every time the two of us go out for sushi, he jokingly reminds me how easy it would be to get all the Holland inheritance by feeding me the one food I'm allergic to: horseradish. He'll then inspect every dish presented to me meticulously to make sure there is no wasabi on anything.

"What do they make it with, then?"

"See that weird green root?" I point it out. "That is *actual* wasabi. Shea told me about it. You grate it right before serving it, so it holds its flavor. It's why it's not served at restaurants here. We went all out for your birthday, buddy. And saved my life in the process."

"Foiled again," he says, mocking disappointment. "You ready to order?"

"No sushi for me tonight, I'm afraid. Unborn babies and sushi don't mix. Plus, I'm going to say hi to the others and wait for Jon. I'll send Coley over here. You two can start the process since you're the guest of honor. Have a wonderful birthday, baby brother."

"Love you, Liv. Thank you."

Walking over to the pool table, I tap Callen on the shoulder just after he takes his shot. He's not as good as the rest of the guys and doesn't pocket any balls on his turn.

"Hey, Livvy." He smiles, giving me a hug.

"Glad you could make it!"

"Didn't think I would. I had just enough time to throw my shit inside the loft, grab Max, and head over... so I apologize for the business attire."

"Oh, you look handsome as ever. And Max looks... it's gross if I say he looks hot, isn't it?"

"Not to me. He does. I'm loving the new haircut."

"That's what it is... he looks really good tonight. For once, Cal, I think he may elevate your look," I joke with him.

"I deserve a break from being Adonis sometimes." He rubs his palm over his blonde, day-old whiskers. "I don't look homeless, do I?"

I roll my eyes. "You need to take a walk beyond 5th Avenue sometime, honey, and see what homeless people look like. Trust me, they look nothing like you."

I finally meet Max's eyes after Will loudly informs him that he hit the wrong ball type into the pocket. He looks away from me and starts to walk toward the windows overlooking the outdoor area. We haven't even said hello tonight, so I begin to wonder if he's upset at me for something.

"Max!" I call to him. Even though the music playing over the stereo is loud, I know he can hear me. He doesn't turn around, though. I walk toward him, shouting his name again.

It's not until I put my hand on his shoulder that he finally acknowledges me. "Hey, Liv." His smile looks anything but genuine.

"What's the matter?"

"Nothing. Why?"

"Well, then give me a hug. You haven't even said hello to me tonight."

"Didn't I?" he steps back.

I huff, a little offended. "No, you didn't."

"Oh, well, hello, Liv. Nice party."

"Thanks, Max." I look at him strangely. "I was just telling Callen how nice you look tonight. You got a haircut?"

"Yesterday, yeah." He's struggling to even converse with me.

"Did I do something wrong? You seem very... short tonight."

"Same height I've always been. Maybe an inch taller with the shoes." He clicks his heels together.

I look him directly in the eyes, trying to ascertain what's going on—his *bloodshot* eyes. He's got a soda in his hand. I don't think he's drunk.

"Give me a hug, Max." Before he can escape this time, I put my arms around him and take a deep breath, inhaling the odor I'd smelled a few weeks ago in their apartment. He knows exactly what I'm doing, too. When I realize I don't even know what to say to him, I just push him away, sloshing the Coke out of his glass and onto his stupid shoes, and walk back toward the center of the room.

Jon is at my side quickly. "You feeling okay?"

I'm biting my bottom lip as I smile and nod quickly.

"That doesn't look good."

"We'll talk after the party. I want Trey to have a good time," I tell him. He takes my hands in his, placing his thumbs on my pulse points and rubbing deeply. He looks into my eyes with an assuring smile.

"Okay. You're okay. You are stunning tonight, and whatever it is, it will all be okay. Do you believe that? Because if you don't, we're going upstairs to talk right now. Just me and you. No one even has to know." He kisses my cheek, then adds with a whisper, "Seriously. Nothing matters more than you and the baby."

I pull my hands away and place them on his cheeks, putting my lips on his. "I'm good for now. Thank you."

But I know that he has to do something about his brother before this baby is born—before I decide to give Max the title of godfather. Honorary or not, I expect more out of him, and right now, he's making stupid decisions and lying to us about them, and I don't want that sort of person influencing my little boy.

We'd thought long and hard about Max. All his life, he'd been so strong. In his teens, he displayed such maturity. He was resilient. He'd known himself so well and was never afraid to be who he was. These were qualities we loved about him. These are the qualities we wanted him to pass on to our child.

But here he is, at 25, acting like the teenager he never was.

*J*on and I sneak upstairs with two extra slices of cake when the party starts getting a little louder than I like my social gatherings these days. He's very giddy, likely the effects of one too many beers, but it's helped to lighten my mood from earlier. Still, I think it's necessary to mention to him what I noticed.

After we've both changed into pajamas, we meet back in the downstairs living room with our second desserts and forks. I settle myself on the floor, leaning into him, wanting to be close to him. We take turns feeding each other the delicious marble cake, laughing at the deliberate mistakes each of us makes with the frosting.

"So... I think your brother is still..."

"Still what?"

"Smokin' the weed."

"What? No."

I look at him, shocked. "Yeah."

"Why do you think that?"

"Because he was high tonight."

"*My* brother? Max?"

I scoff at his response. "Yeah. That one."

"He was not."

"Yes, he was."

"Liv. I talked to him for half an hour. We played pool together. He even beat me. He wasn't high."

"Did you see his eyes? They were totally bloodshot."

"He looked tired, and I told him that. He said he'd been having some nightmares... something about the shooting."

"He said that?"

"Yeah."

"He reeked of pot! You didn't smell it?"

He shakes his head. "I wasn't all up on him or anything, though."

"I gave him a hug, and he was... skunky."

"Skunky," he repeats as if he doesn't believe me.

"Yes, like that nasty skunk pot smell! He was definitely high! And he knew that I knew he was and didn't try to defend himself, either. He let me believe it!"

"Liv, I just... I don't think that's true..."

"It totally is!"

"Hey, hey..." he says, rubbing my arm slowly. "Don't be upset. I mean, I get that you're upset. Let me handle it, okay?"

"Are you going to confront him? Or just let me believe you are, and then you're not going to do anything because you don't think he was high?"

"Liv," he says seriously, his smile now gone, "I'm going to ask him point-blank. If he says yes, he was high, I'll address it. If he says no, he wasn't, I'm going to let it go this time and give him the benefit of the doubt. I have to build trust with him. But in the future, I will be more aware, okay? I'll look harder for signs. I'll be more suspicious. Can we agree on that plan?"

I frown but nod, wishing now I'd said something to him in the moment instead of waiting. "That's fine," I tell him. "I agree to it, but only in exchange for a calming massage tonight."

He grins. "Full body?"

"Yes."

"Are you gonna... get naked?"

"There are people staying in our apartment tonight, Jon."

"They're all going to be downstairs, and we have a lock on our door..." He raises his brows.

"We're not going to do anything, baby, but... okay. I want the full massage. I'm stressed out."

"Understood... and I will take whatever I can get. Let's hurry and get upstairs before the party's over."

"Okay." Before we go, he sits up and presses his lips to mine, delivering a sweet, yet sultry, kiss.

CHAPTER 10

*S*hopping at the farmers market was a much different experience than either of the two other outings Matty and I had been on today. We'd started with a few different baby boutiques, looking for clothes. It was, well... hell, with lullabies. Paparazzi pushing borrowed carriages made their way into every shop we went into, capturing otherwise precious moments spent with my uncle with their invasive lenses and shouting out questions to which they were never going to get answers—no matter how loudly they asked them, nor how many times.

There were multiple hand-made outfits that I would have loved to have purchased for August, but due to the fact that none of the boutique owners had bothered to try to protect us, as customers, and instead reveled in their temporary fame, Matty and I left most places empty-handed.

Not that I didn't take a picture of one crocheted, winter cap that looked like a frog that my newborn son would have to have come winter time, and that I would beg someone to come and buy for me on my behalf some other day. Matty took note, though, and assured me he'd be back.

At the grocery store, my uncle and I had planned to divide and conquer to get everything on our lists, but we knew as soon as we entered the small, two-story market, we may never find one another again with the rush of people who'd followed us in.

And these weren't people with grocery lists of their own. They were more vultures, cameras poised to record every mundane moment, to discover every brand I preferred over others. I'm sure companies would pay them money to know these things. They'd probably pay *me* money to endorse their brands. That was not a life we chose to live.

The truth was, it was a rarity to spot me in a grocery store. Normally, I'd have someone do this task for me, but Matty had a few things to pick up and I thought of an item or two, as well.

After we dropped off those groceries at home, we took a short walk to the local farmer's market for some fresh vegetables. It was a risk, knowing we'd be spotted, but somehow, the hoodies concealed us enough to get off my main street and the people shopping among the produce couldn't care less that the Hollands had invaded their space. The people working there were excited to tell us about their fresh limes and handmade soaps, and my uncle and I took our time browsing every booth in every aisle, buying far more than we'd intended, requiring us to take a taxi back home.

To be honest, the two of us together can be pretty dangerous as shopping companions when left to browse unfettered. We don't do it often, but we have the best time when we do. We have similar taste and encourage one another endlessly.

When we get home, Matty and I work quickly in the kitchen, putting away fresh fruits, vegetables and spices we'd picked up at the market. Once we're finished, we wipe down the countertops, returning the room to the pristine condition it was in when we entered.

"Now, where's this recipe?" he asks.

"On my iPad. It should be open to the page."

"You have the strangest cravings," he says. "That's not going to stop me from trying one."

I hand-wash the plastic molds we'd bought earlier while he finds the ingredients necessary for our experiment. "One," I tell him. "Just one."

"I've learned to never argue with a pregnant woman. What does Shea crave?"

"The boring shit. Pickles and ice cream. Can you believe it? She's such a stereotypical preggo."

"Gah. Can't she be more original?"

"Right?"

"I'm assuming that's why you bought the pickles and ice cream, huh?"

"I have to have them on hand for my bestie," I respond, shrugging my shoulders. "I'm here for her."

"Doubt she'd make these for you," he counters.

"Oh, come on. She's a chef. If I was craving mashed jalapeños on banana bread, she'd perfect the recipe and package it with a pretty bow on top. She's the best."

"Hey, Little Liv. Who's making this nut-job dessert with you now?" my uncle asks, offended.

"You're the original best, Matty. You know that." I give him a big hug.

The click of the front door opening interrupts us.

"The house looks amazing," Jon says, walking in. "I guess the maids came today."

"They did. Matty and I are making sure to leave no trace of the goings on in the kitchen." I give him a kiss and my uncle follows that up by shaking my husband's hand. "How was work?"

"It was great. Things are moving at a perfect pace," he says, smiling. "I can't wait to finish up this project... because that means Jonny will be here and our family will have some time to get acclimated to its new member." His hand is on my belly as I start drying the plastic parts.

"Hey," I say, "did you know you could make popsicles with avocados?"

His expression is what I expected. "Why would you want to?"

"They're supposed to have the consistency of Fudgsicles. I can't wait to try them."

"That's what you're making?" Jon asks, removing his tie and setting it on the back of the couch. "Not dinner?"

"They have to have time to set in the freezer," I tell him. "And I figured we'd have that casserole Shea brought over last night for dinner. We just need to pop it in the oven. Matty's staying, if that's okay."

Matty claps his hands together, as if he's begging my husband, which he needn't do.

"Fine with me. Should I do that?"

"What?"

"Put dinner in the oven?"

"I can get it," I assure him.

"Those popsicles. Are the girls going to eat them?"

"I'm not making them for the girls," I tell him bluntly. "I guess I'm making them for me and your boy."

"Oh," he says, nodding. "Speaking of the girls... why no welcome?"

"Mom and Dad took them to see that new movie. I told you last night."

"Oh, yeah, you did. And they're going out to dinner after."

"Exactly. Hence the casserole."

"I'm with you now," he says. "What other trouble did you two get into today?"

"I resent that," Matty says.

I nod to the formal dining room. Jon turns on his heels and walks in to see the life-sized sock monkey sitting in his seat at the head of the table. "Is this what I look like to you?" he jokes.

When Matty and I saw it today, we knew we had to buy it for August's room. Jon and I had rediscovered our affinity for the iconic character last Christmas when my Aunt Anna bought the girls personalized sock monkey ornaments for the tree. When I found out I was pregnant, Jon and I deliberated over how to decorate the room. We wanted something that would suit a boy or a girl, and the sock monkey was the perfect solution.

"It resembles you," I tell him. "I think it's the ears... just as cute."

"Good god, it's just as big as me." He picks it up and puts his arms around it, doing a little waltz with it. "Where are we putting this?"

"In the far corner of the baby's room. Don't you think it'll look perfect there?"

"It'll look great." He sets it down on the couch, facing the TV, and puts a remote on its leg. I get a giggle out of that. "This child's going to be even more spoiled than the last two."

He begins looking through the neatly-piled mail on the counter. "Yes, August *is* going to be so spoiled." I hold my breath, waiting to hear what he thinks about this newly proposed name. Matty and I hurriedly glance at one another before he returns to spooning avocados into a bowl.

Jon doesn't even look up as he begins opening an envelope. "No. I don't like it."

"What do you mean? You haven't even given it a thought."

"Will told me about it a few weeks ago when you had that *fated moment* in the antiques shop." He scoffs a little, taking me aback. "It wasn't *fate*, Liv. It was just a coincidence, and I don't like the name."

"Why?" I press him for a reason.

"Listen to the name. *August*. Is it not the saddest name you've ever heard?" he asks, looking at me as if I'm stupid for thinking it had any value whatsoever.

"No, it's not," I argue with him.

"Come on! It's the saddest month of the entire year!"

"No! There aren't sad and happy months, Jon. They're... divisions of time. There's no emotion tied to them."

"Sorry, but there is. It's the month when things start to die; when leaves start to fall off trees; when the kids have to go back to school–"

"But we like that part!" I interrupt his list.

"That's not the point. There's a depressing overtone to the entire month and I don't want my kid to have that name."

"When did this all become about what *you* want? What *you* get to name our child?" I ask him angrily.

Matty takes the clean dishtowel I'd been clinging to for confidence and dries his hands. "I'm going to take the monkey upstairs," he says softly.

Jon waits until he hears the bedroom door close before he continues. "Well, it should be our decision. You've been pushing names on me all this time!"

"Pushing?" I say, rolling my eyes. "So, then, what name would you choose?"

"Jon? Or maybe Jonny?"

"I don't like that," I say in a pleading manner, in no way intending to be mean.

"What don't you like about it?"

"It's so... pedestrian," I say, looking down. "Normal."

"It's *my name!*"

"I know it's your name! I like it for you, but I don't want it for our son. Doesn't that make sense?"

"No!"

"We have a chance to call him something special, and that's what I want to do," I tell him. "That's what I like about Augustus."

"I just don't like it! It's been assumed from day one that we're going to name him after me, and, like maybe we don't have to," he suggests reluctantly.

My jaw drops. "I thought you would want that! That you would want your son to carry your name!"

"I don't really give a shit about that, Liv. I just want to raise our son well, and god! If you hate my name so much, I'd hate for you to have to call him that. I mean... what about variations on Jonathan? What about Nathan?"

I stare at him, waiting for him to catch up, but he appears to need a full explanation. "Nate was my mother's ex-boyfriend! We can't call him that. It would hurt my dad and bring up bad memories for my mom."

"Oh, shit," he says as he turns away, almost blowing me off. "Then we call him something else, Liv. You know, I don't want you to be repulsed by our son's name because I wasn't born in a glass castle like you were, with a stately name like *Olivia Sophia*..."

I stomp up to him in the living room angrily and turn him around to face to me. "Need I remind you that I wasn't born into that, either, Jon? As far as I know, my mother was poor and had nothing when she had me. She had no friends and a meager, trashy apartment. She was no better off than your mom, so don't go writing me off as privileged. I was adopted into that and my name came way before the Hollands ever met me.

"And I didn't say your name was bad. I just don't want to go around calling him the same thing everyone has called you all your life. I want it to be something different. You know, August is different. I knew I'd never win you over with Auggie, but it was fun to joke about it," I tell him, trying to deescalate the situation.

"It drove me nuts." He's not being kind or forgiving.

"Get a sense of humor," I say, shaking my head in disgust. "And August Scott sounds really nice."

"Not to me."

"Okay," I say, "let me get this straight and see if I remember everything correctly. Augustus is too pompous. Auggie is too silly. Gus is too... what did you compare it to? Oh, right. Too 'gas station attendant-y.' And now August is too depressing. Was that right?"

"No, don't make this all about me!" he shoots back. "Let me go over all of your objections to my suggestions. Ready?"

"Sure!" I say, ready take him on.

"Jonny is too pedestrian. Jon reminds you of me, God forbid."

"Stop it," I jump in.

"Nope," he says, continuing. "Nathan reminds you of your mom's dead ex. Jonathan, what was that one? You know too many of them. Oh, and let's not forget Junior, which *reminds you of your favorite candy*."

"How can you *not* think of Mints after saying that!?"

"I don't know, because my mind isn't always on food!" he shouts at me.

"I'm pregnant, idiot," I say, hurt, crossing my arms, spent and out of energy. I feel my lip beginning to quiver. He stares at me, obviously not pleased that I've started calling him names. I sigh and sit down on the club chair, still facing him. "Fine. We have time to think of something entirely new, I guess." I'm biting my lip so I don't start crying. "It's not good for me to fight about stupid things like this. I just... I just thought all men liked namesakes."

"Maybe the men in your family do." He still stands over me.

"Well, you're my family, aren't you?" The tears fall now. "Excuse me for fucking this up. Whatever." I begin to make my way to the stairs, hitting him with my shoulder when I walk past him. "You can put the casserole in. The directions are written on the lid."

"You trust an idiot with your dinner?" he calls after me. I ignore him, going straight to our room and slamming the door.

I grab the blood pressure cuff from my nightstand and put it on, angry with myself for letting the fight get so out of hand and equally mad at Jon for not taking things down a notch when he saw it escalating, either.

157/100.

Lying back on the bed, I find the first acupressure point in my hand that I'd read was supposed to help lower blood pressure. At the very least, following the instructions I'd found had a calming effect on me, so I put them to practice anytime I have measurements this high. I switch back and forth between hands a few times before moving to the next point in my wrists, all while lying still with my eyes closed and my mind focused on my current task and not on the fight.

Jon knocks and waits for me to invite him into our room. He sits next to me, looking contrite.

"Can I do your neck for you?" he asks.

"Sure." He helps me into a seated position in front of him and digs his thumbs into the base of my head, putting just enough pressure on the points to feel good. We don't speak while he repeats the exercise four times in thirty-second intervals.

When he's finished, he puts the cuff back on my wrist to do another measurement.

136/92.

"Want me to do it some more?" he asks me.

"No. I'm fine," I tell him.

"You're an ass," he tells me, putting his arms around me and pulling my back into his chest.

"What, for assuming?"

"Mm-hmm." I can hear his smile.

"I'm sorry I called you an idiot."

"No, it was a stupid thing for me to say. And I love Junior Mints, too, so, like... who could blame you? Not me."

"Right?" I say softly with a chuckle.

"We just start at square one, Liv, with his name, okay? At the end of the day, we need to give him a name we can both live with, wouldn't you agree with that?"

"I would. Yes."

"Then I think the original plan goes. We come up with something all new. It'll be fun. Let's ask the girls for some help."

"No," I whine. "I want it to be our decision. Can we... I don't know. Can we keep this between us? We'll figure it out together."

"If that's what you want. Maybe we should call him Matthew for putting your uncle through this fight today," he jokes.

"Are you kidding? He got a front row seat to family drama. He loved it."

"He came downstairs and started to work on popsicles. He just said, 'you know I'm always on her side, right?' I'd have punched him if he wasn't family. And if I was my brother."

"Sure, you would have." I say with doubt. "But he is always on my side. Right or wrong."

"You saying you were wrong?" he challenges me.

"I'm saying we're not calling the baby anything remotely related to your name. I'm even going to give him my maiden name just to play it safe. I know you'll love that."

He laughs. "You break my heart."

"Never," I say, craning my neck to give him a kiss.

"I saw you got some Pom today. Want to split a bottle?"

"That sounds awesome. Maybe with a little ginger ale in mine?"

He nods and helps me off the bed. At the staircase, he puts my hand on the handrail before we take the steps down. I would have done it myself, but he's overly cautious. Sometimes, I think he'd rather me take the elevator. I'm sure in my later months of pregnancy, I'll opt to.

"Do I have to awkwardly excuse myself?" Matty asks when we get to the kitchen.

"What for?" Jon goes to the cabinet and gets a couple tumblers.

"Either because you're still fighting, or you *really* want to make up with one another."

"We took care of that upstairs, Matty," I tease him.

"Super quick," Jon plays along. "Probably put another baby in there."

"That's how it works," I agree, patting my stomach.

"Gross. Both of you. Gross," he says. "And to think my encouragement is probably what led to all of this." His arms flail dramatically, and avocado flies off the spoon landing across the room on the floor. Jon snatches the utensil from his hand and grabs a paper towel to clean up his mess.

"Whatever!" I laugh. "We were destined for each other from child-hood. You believed in our love so much that you encouraged it. Not the other way around."

"You believe what you want, Little Liv. Your love is the egg. I'm the chicken. The conundrum will always be: *which came first?*"

"Tonight, I did," Jon says, patting my uncle on the back when he cringes at the bad joke.

"Can we end this now? I was thinking maybe a salad would be good with this—what is this casserole, anyway?"

We're both laughing, knowing how uncomfortable Matty is. "It's cauliflower, bacon and... Brussels sprouts, I think she said?"

"What?" they both ask.

"It's a test kitchen side," I tell them.

"Where's the protein?" Jon asks.

"Bacon," I say with a shrug.

"No," he laughs. "You even just said a 'test kitchen *side*.' Is there no protein?"

"I think she's planning to serve it with rotisserie chicken."

"That's..." Jon looks down at me, smiling. "That's awesome for Shea and Mrs. Livingston's Kitchen, but what about us, tonight?"

"I didn't really think about that. I bought some chicken breasts. I'm sure they're not totally frozen yet."

"The popsicles are in the freezer," Matty says. "I'm on chicken detail now. Are we thinking fried? Roasted? Grilled?"

"Grilled's good," Jon says. "I've got some seasoning we can throw on it."

Matty looks at me. "Bacon was a good enough protein for me," I say again. "You make it however you like. I'll eat whatever."

"What am I going to do with you?" Jon asks.

"Just feed me. Give me juice. Put me to bed at night. Rub my neck when it gets stressful. Take me to the hospital when the baby's done. I'm *very* low maintenance."

"Like hell you are, Ms. Avocado Popsicles. Why can't you just eat fruit pops like everyone else?"

"First of all, avocados are fruit, and secondly, you did not marry a woman *like everyone else*, Mr. Scott. If you wanted that, you'd have married that girl you met in Utah that was so nice to you."

"Just-a-friend-Audrey."

"That's right. *Ut-Audrey*," I continue with the nickname *I'd* given her long ago. "Remind me, was she tawdry?" I tease him.

"For the millionth time, Liv, no." He grins and rolls his eyes.

"If she was, would you still have picked me?"

"There was no *choice* in the matter, baby," he says just before his lips press against my forehead. "I knew it from the day I met you. Hell, even Just-a-friend-Audrey knew it. She was a smart one."

"*Ut-Audrey*. You've mentioned that," I tell him, standing on my tiptoes, requesting a full kiss on the lips.

CHAPTER 11

*S*ince they left the door open on this beautiful, summer day, I hear Dad and the girls talking about me in the courtyard at Nate's Art Room. He's telling them how their dad and I used to lie down in the grass and draw the limbs of the tree when we were just a little older than they were. I remember those days, when what I felt for Jon was something I didn't even have a name for yet. I was too young to recognize romantic love. But I respected my friend as an artist, and I thought he was the cutest boy I had ever met. When I was 12, the combination of those two things proved too much of a threat for my father. He feared Jon's influence on me for years—until the day he finally buckled and accepted that he'd probably be in my life forever.

Many, many times since then, both of my parents have told him how grateful they are at his persistence in pursuing me. Any misgivings they'd ever had were lapses in judgment about him. They'd admitted it. "There's no better man for my Contessa," I'd overheard Dad tell him on our wedding day. The truth is, Dad started seeing the similarities between him and Jon somewhere along the way—things he'd been ignoring when we were teenagers to protect himself from the fact that I had to grow up someday. Jon had big shoes to fill, but he filled them perfectly.

Mom brings twenty brand new, plastic pans of watercolor paints out from the back room, setting them on the side table.

"Let me help, Mom."

"No, Liv. I'll just make a few trips," she says. "It's not a problem. I'll get Jacks to divvy up the water at each station."

"Okay." I pick up the small pans and start setting them on the workbenches, two per table. As she makes her deliveries to the side tables, I follow behind her and pass out the supplies to the desks: paper, brushes and bowls for water.

When I'm finished, I go to the familiar closet and pull out enough smocks for the room: ten adult sizes and ten children sizes.

"Daddy?" I shout. He comes into the room. "Can you get water for the bowls? There's a pitcher in the closet. They only need to be about half-full."

"Of course." I take his place in the courtyard, watching the girls perched on a thick branch of the same tree Jon and I used to draw. My phone in hand, I snap a picture of them and send it to their father, sure that he'll appreciate the photo in the midst of his workday.

He texts me back immediately.

Jon: *I'd love to be lying in the cool grass with you today. Can you believe we have daughters climbing that tree that you struggled to draw?*

Me: *I never struggled to draw that.*

Jon: *I still have the proof somewhere in my old boxes of things.*

Me: *I will find it and destroy it. I'm a famous artist now!*

Jon: *Love you. You guys have fun today.*

Me: *:**

"Girls, we're getting ready to start."

"Don't you think I'm too advanced for this?" Edie asks, climbing down the trunk first. She waits for her sister and spots her as she makes her way out of the tree.

"I think you will inspire the other students and help Granddaddy paint a very nice picture," I tell her. "And you don't have to sit there and be silent. When we start, if you think you can help someone else, you're free to offer assistance."

"Can she help me?" Willow asks.

"Of course, but you're going to have Memi with you, and she's a pretty bad-ass watercolorist. She did that picture in your room with your name and the tree, remember?"

"Oh, yeah," she says. "I won't need you, Edie."

"I won't have time to help you, anyway," my oldest says, her nose stuck high in the air. "And you owe us both a dollar, Mama."

"For what?"

"Bad Ay-Ess-Ess," she says, matter-of-fact.

I make a face. "Go get it from Granddaddy. I don't have any cash on me. But be careful–he's holding a full pitcher of water."

*A*fter giving my last demonstration, I look over at the small classroom of students and smile. It's been a couple of years since my last stint at Nate's, but it was easy to jump right back in, and my mother was right. It filled that creative void that I'd been feeling ever since I gave up my own painting when I got pregnant. I wish I had been helping her with drawing classes or something all along. I'd probably be in a better frame of mind.

This week is my first teaching adults, too. The free course invited underprivileged kids to bring a guardian with them, be it their parent, sibling or grandparent. The diverse group is busy concentrating, creating two works of art to be displayed in their home. A few decide to make diptychs to be placed side-by-side, so extra coordination is needed between those pairs. I start to make my rounds, answering questions along the way.

"How far along are you?" one mother asks.

"Oh," I say, smiling. "I just passed thirty-one weeks."

"Are you so excited?"

"I'm... ready to meet him, yes. It hasn't been the easiest one. Those two girls at the back are mine," I tell her. Another thing I love about Nate's Art Room is that, while people who attend or send their kids here do know who my parents are and who I am, they don't really pay much attention to our lives. They appreciate that we're normal people, too, who like to share with our New York Community–on our terms. This is one of the ways we've done it all my life.

"You don't look old enough to have girls that age!"

"Oh, I am. Trust me. Thirty-five here."

"What is your secret?"

"Sunscreen and fresh air. Lots of both... and just living life."

"Are you concerned at all, being a high-risk pregnancy? I'm a nurse, so... I was just wondering."

Having been on the low-end of the high-risk scale, I liked to pretend I wasn't on it. Sadly, feeling unwell so often has put it top of mind at times, but no one has ever come out and asked me the question before. I start to move to the next table, a natural move as the instructor of the class. "No, not at all," I lie, maintaining the kind smile. "Let me know if you have any painting questions." I nod and look to the next table, zoning out as I stare at the blurry blobs in front of me.

"What do you think?" the young boy, Peter, asks me after I realize I've been silent for a good minute and a half.

I blink to focus on his obvious portrait of his older brother, Zion. It's incredible. "Oh, my gosh, Peter! That is... Zion, look at that! What do you think?"

"I think Petey's a pro! And I don't know what the hell I'm doin'."

I grin, turning his paper toward me. It's a bunch of abstract shapes that don't appear to be related to one another.

"Well, you definitely have a different style than your brother, but all's not lost. I don't think you're finished with it. Also, it could be that you're working on a mixed media piece, and you don't even know it."

I talk to him about how to connect the shapes with a stroke from a larger brush; a darker paint, and possibly oil. Since we're using very heavy paper, I go to the back room and get a few extra supplies for his table. "Watch this."

After squeezing out the black paint on the palette, I immediately feel sick to my stomach. "I'm sorry. I'll be right back."

In the bathroom, I stand over the sink, eventually talking myself out of throwing up. My face flushed, I decide to splash some cold water on it, wiping away the makeup I've messed up afterwards. Edie meets me outside with some iced water.

"Oh, thank you, Eeds."

"Are you okay?"

"I'm good. I shouldn't have opened the oil paint. I was just excited about Zion's artwork."

"Memi's working out in the courtyard with him, showing him what you meant. She told everyone what happened."

"Great," I say, mildly embarrassed.

"You're doing really good in there, Mama."

"Really *well*," I correct her. "And thank you. How's Granddaddy's painting?"

"It's bad. Really bad. He's good at a lot of things, but he's not good at this," she says with a frown. I laugh at her honest response.

"Is that what you told him?"

"I told him he was doing really good," she says with a shrug.

"What? How do I know you're not lying to me, then, if you lied to him like that?"

"I didn't want to hurt his feelings. But I don't lie to you."

"You do," I argue, challenging her with a smile.

"Well. I didn't right now, for sure. And I usually don't."

"That's good enough for me. Right now, for sure." I set down my water and give her a hug, returning to the room to face the class again.

A few of the students have questions before our time is up. We offer to let them keep the paintings in the studio overnight so they can dry out properly. For a few of them, we even make arrangements to deliver them to their homes in instances when they don't have a way to come back tomorrow.

"Let's look at your painting, Dad." He turns it upside down so I can see it from the other side of the table. "Is this us?" I ask, trying to stave off the laughter at his stick figure family.

"Isn't it obvious?"

"I guessed it, right?" I look up at him adoringly, wanting to put my fingers over the images of my daughters. Over Jon. Over the mop of straw-berry blonde hair of the figure that towers over all of us—my little brother. "This was pretty ambitious, Daddy. But... you did it perfectly." Its childlike quality nearly brings me to tears. It's one of the most beautiful things he's ever created—my dad's not the most creative person. "Oh, look. You even painted the baby. I'm holding the baby. Ohhh..."

"Yes. It's a portrait of all of us. There's Trey and Coley. I envision this being early next year. After their wedding, you know. I thought they might get a dog." I hadn't noticed the addition, but it's adorable. "The Holland/Scott family. If we'd had more time, I would have painted *all* the brothers and their families, too."

"Maybe another class, Daddy. I'd love to see it." I go to his side of the table and give him a hug. "I know you did this for you, but... can I have it?"

"Really?" he laughs. "You'd want that?"

"It's... my favorite thing." I start crying.

"Well, Contessa, don't cry." He holds me tightly. "Of course, you can have it. I'd be honored if my daughter, the artist, wanted to hold on to it."

"I'm going to frame it and hang it prominently in the living room."

"Oh, don't do that," he says, blushing. "Maybe a guest room," he suggests.

"Then I won't see it every day. My room, then."

He nods. "I should probably autograph it." He takes one of his nice pens out of his shirt pocket, as if he's always prepared to sign a contract, and meticulously signs his name in the corner.

"Thank you, Daddy." I hug him again.

After Mom has hung the other paintings to dry, she finally comes to take Dad's. "Adorable, isn't it?" she asks.

"Incomparable." I wipe my eyes. "What did you paint?"

"The girls," she says, nodding across the room. Sure enough, in her illustrative style, there's a divine work of art from her, too. "I'm holding onto it."

I laugh. "Darn it."

"Feel free to visit it regularly."

I walk around the room, looking at the work hanging up, admiring all the different styles done by today's students. I can pick out Edie's without even seeing her well-practiced signature at the bottom. Her innate talent is evident. I have a harder time finding Willow's, but I should have guessed by the subject matter—a bunch of stars on a dark background.

I finally get to Zion's and breathe a little shallower instinctively. My mother did a perfect job showing him what I had intended to do, and the technique brought out his watercolor strokes beautifully. I hope he was happy with the end result—even if it still wasn't quite as good as his brother's.

After everything is cleaned up, the five of us go outside into the court-yard for a picnic my dad had prepared. The old table isn't the most comfortable in my current state, but I find it easy to forget about it when I'm surrounded by the people I love on this beautiful day.

"Livvy, you did so well in there."

"I'm glad you suggested it, Mom. I wish I'd been doing this weekly. I really think I'd be in a better frame of mind if I'd had a creative outlet all this time. I mean, I know this about myself. I don't know why I couldn't think of an alternative."

"Maybe because you've been busy feeling under the weather," Dad says. "Sometimes you need help seeing the light, that's all. We have our weekly drawing classes. We have an instructor, but I know they'd love the assistance. There's always room for more people to mentor the class. You know this."

"I'd love that—for as long as I'm able to keep up." My palm soothes the kicking baby, who's obviously been awakened by the meal. "I love this place," I tell them, suddenly contemplative and grateful. "It's as much home to me as my apartment and your house."

Mom and Dad clasp hands across the table. "It's pretty great," Mom agrees.

"It's where Jon and I met. I mean... it's where we fell in love. It's where I spent so many amazing days with Granna." Nate's mother had become a surrogate grandmother to me, as she had become very close to both of my parents once they opened Nate's Art Room. "It's where I honed my art skills. I hope this place never closes. It does so many good things in this city. For kids like Peter, who are so naturally gifted."

Dad smiles. "I see you and Jon running it someday... in the far, far future of course. And then maybe Edie will want to. Who knows?"

I'd thought the same things many times. It was a part of the *non*-retirement plan Jon and I had. This could be just a part of the work we do. He shared my affinity of the place.

"I know Jon and I would be honored to. And we wouldn't change a thing."

"I would call it *Edie's* Art Room," my daughter says.

"Well, then," I scoff, "we haven't done a good enough job teaching you its history. I will tell you tonight about the grand gesture of love that created this place to begin with. And then the only alternate name you may *ever* consider would be to change it from Nate to Jack. Period."

My mother smiles, looking at Daddy.

"Granddaddy's not an artist!" my oldest daughter argues. "Did you see his watercolor?"

Immediately, I tear up and choke out tears. "You have no future as an art critic, Eeds. The sentiment behind that painting, it... he... you'll never understand what that means to me. And you apologize to him right now."

"Mama, don't cry," she says, shocked. Willow's eyes start to water, and she comes from behind to give me a hug.

"I'm sorry," I say, wiping my eyes with a napkin. I look at my father, who appears to be swiping at tears, too, but he's looking away from us, trying not to let us see. Mom clings to his bicep and rests her head on his shoulder. "I'm sorry," I repeat, turning around and embracing my youngest, who hates to see me cry. "Mama's okay."

"Sorry, Granddaddy," I hear Edie say softly. "I didn't mean to hurt your feelings."

"Oh," he laughs. "My feelings aren't hurt, bunny. You can always be honest with me. It's okay. Go give your mama a hug."

She quickly comes around the table and throws her arms around me. "Sorry, Mama."

"I'm sorry, too, Eeds. You know Mama gets emotional because of the baby." I take a few deep breaths, calming myself. "But I *do* need to teach you more about empathy... and just... being polite."

"Empathy?"

"Yeah. Understanding and anticipating how other people feel."

"But Granddaddy said I didn't hurt his feelings."

"And *that's* what it means to be polite. We'll discuss this at home tonight with *your* father, okay?"

Her face is drawn as she sits back down. "Fine."

Once I confessed to my parents that I wasn't feeling great after we ate lunch, they insist on coming back up to the apartment with me and the girls until Jon gets home. Dad does a puzzle with them in the library upstairs while Mom does a load of laundry and watches the news with me.

"How are the girls doing with their reading goals this summer?" she asks.

"Willow already met hers. She's trying to be the top reader at the library in her age group now. I keep telling her she'd have a better chance if she read books that were actually written for her age group instead of the books Will keeps choosing for her, but I'm not her *literary mentor*, as she keeps reminding me," I tell her with a chuckle. "And Edie doesn't understand why fashion magazines don't count toward the goal. So... she's protesting and trying to change the rules. She believes it's discrimination."

This makes my mom laugh. "I don't know why this surprises me at all."

"Yeah, it shouldn't. Matty even made a nice, glittery poster with her, and they picketed in front of the library for an hour a few weeks ago. I can't believe you didn't see it on the tabloid sites. We nearly killed him for it."

"You know we don't like to look at those. It's always invasive nonsense that's no one's business but ours."

"I know. I always worry that you will see, though, and think we're doing a horrible job at parenting," I admit with a shrug.

"Well, that would never happen." She puts her hand on my knee. "You just told me one of my granddaughters is out-reading everyone in her age group and beyond, and the other one is standing up for what she believes. I see nothing wrong with either of those things."

"Thanks, Mom."

"I'm immensely proud every day of what you and Jon have done, and what you continue to do. I can't wait to see what will become of little Auggie, either."

I confide in her quietly. "That probably won't be his name."

"What?"

I shake my head. "Huge fight about it. Jon hates it. We're starting from scratch. The kid'll probably be named Bobby George Scott, for all I know," I tease sarcastically. "Hopefully he can keep the last name. I may need to clarify that."

"God, no. So not even Jonathan Augustus?"

"No. Literally from scratch. No Augustus at all." I frown.

"But he's Auggie to me!"

"I know. He's Auggie to a lot of people." I smile, and it's bittersweet, because I did kind of fall in love with the name. I fell in love with a baby named Auggie. I still love the baby, but it's hard to separate the two. "He's Froggie to the girls. Still. We haven't told them yet."

She puts her hand over her heart. "Well. I think Memi might just call him what she wants. Memi doesn't care what's on the birth certificate."

"Yeah, we'll see how long that lasts ya," I say as a challenge. "Don't tell him I told you. We want to keep it between us. We don't want any outside interference."

"Okay."

Jon comes home a few minutes later, surprised to find my parents here. He listens to them brag on my instructor skills—ones he'd seen many times in the past—before they finally head home.

*A*fter dinner, we corral the girls into the library upstairs and talk to them about empathy. I could tell that Willow was born with it—or that she had been around Uncle Will enough to glean it off of him, because he could read people like no one I'd ever met—but our 9-year-old needed a good lesson in it. We decided to have an open discussion with them both, defining what it means and talking about the consequences when one doesn't use it.

And then, I told them the history of Nate's Art Room, start to finish. They learned about Nate and where he fit into my mother's life. They learned about the night Nate died; the same night my dad's feelings for Mom were rekindled at a New Year's Eve party. And they learned about how, as a wedding gift to my mother, Dad had opened up Nate's Art Room and the Nathaniel J. Wilson Gallery on the second floor, to always keep Nate's memory alive, knowing that the man would always have a place in Mom's heart.

I think both girls had a newfound respect for their Granddaddy that night, and more empathy for their Memi. After the conversation, Edie vowed that she would keep the gallery, but change the name of the charity to Jack and Emi's Art Room when it became hers someday in the "far, far future."

There aren't many nights that I go to bed wanting to high-five my husband for the great parenting we did that day, but this night, I wanted to, and I did.

CHAPTER 12

I can't calm down.

My eyes wide open, I stare at the darkness around me, trying to identify a recognizable shape. I see spots in my vision. I'm sure of that. I can see the moonlight peeking through curtains, but there are *definitely* spots in my vision. I try to sit up, but I can't.

My pulse beats loudly in my ear, uneven and annoying and I want it to stop. But I don't. I want it to slow down. *Calm down.*

Pulse points.

Breathe.

Where are my pulse points?

I'm sweating.

I grab the webbing in my left hand between the thumb and forefinger of my right, but I barely feel anything. No numbness. No pain. Just panic. And the drumming gets louder and louder and faster.

I kick Jon. Nothing. I kick him again. Twice.

"What?" he asks.

"I can't calm down," I tell him, out of breath.

"Do you need the monitor?" he asks, his speech slurred, as if he's not quite awake.

"No!" I shout. "Wake up!"

He sits up, grabbing his phone to turn on the lights through the app.

Spots in my vision, but I can see the room now. I can see him. He looks over at me as I lie flat on my back. "Do you want me to rub your neck?" He stretches lazily.

"No! Call 9-1-1."

"What?" His body turns to face me, and he takes my hand in his, rubbing my wrist. No, he's feeling my wrist. "You've got to calm down," he tells me, worried.

"I can't!" I tell him for the millionth time. *I think.* "Call 9-1-1." He's out of bed quickly, pacing the room in his boxers with the phone to his ear.

He speaks urgently to an operator, telling them who I am. *How* I am. *Where* I am. And how fucking fast they better get here. *Good. I need him to be stern.*

He pulls on some jeans and a t-shirt, then makes another call to the concierge downstairs, warning them. After that, it's a call to his brother.

"Will, I need you over here in five minutes. No, four minutes." That's all he says to him. I know Will will be here in three.

It feels like an eternity, but the EMTs and Will all show up at the same time.

There are three strangers next to me, but it's quiet as I lie in bed, as I feel them poking and prodding; all I hear is the pulse in my ear that doesn't quiet, doesn't slow. They finally move me to a stretcher and take me down the elevator to the first level of our apartment.

"If the girls wake up, don't tell them what happened. Just tell them we went out for a while. I'm sure we'll be back in a few hours," Jon says to his brother.

"It's okay, Liv," Will says right next to my ear, kissing my forehead before we leave the apartment.

But is it? When I can't calm down?

In the ambulance, Jon sits next to my head and constantly strokes the hair away from my face. His eyes never leave mine. He looks strong. He looks assuring. He looks confident. He shows no fear.

I want to feel all of those things.

Panic. All I feel is panic.

"Baby, did you have a nightmare? Are you worrying about something?"

I nod my head rapidly.

"Don't worry about anything. You're in good hands, right?" he asks the two attendants with us.

"Great hands, Mrs. Scott. You're doing fine. Just hang in there."

I see a flash of what I'm feeling cross Jon's face as he looks at the EMT who said that. *Hang in there.* That gave him reason to worry, too. But just as soon as that flash came, it's gone, and his façade of strength is back. "I've got you, baby. I'm right here." He starts rubbing my wrist. I feel it this time. That must mean I'm calming down. It must mean that.

I sigh, but it still feels shallow. I'd expected more relief. A deeper breath. It wasn't.

In the hospital, they separate me from Jon, and I start to cry. I want him here. The panic's worse.

"Where is he?"

"He's in the waiting room, Mrs. Scott. I'm Dr. Irving. Can you tell me how you feel?"

"I can't calm down. I have high blood pressure. I'm scared for the baby. Am I hurting him?"

"Well, that's why we need you to calm down."

"I can't calm down!"

"We're going to give you an injection to help, Livvy. Can I call you Livvy?"

"Will it hurt my baby?"

"There are very low risks for him. The risks are much greater for both of you if we don't do it."

"Then just do it. Do it now!" I cry. "And bring Jon back!"

"Go get her husband," the doctor says. "And we're implementing the dose right now."

"Okay." As I wait, I get to listen to not only the thumping in my ears, but the stereo effect of the monitors I'm hooked up to. It's driving me crazy. "Can you turn down that noise, please? I can't stand it."

"Just a tad," the doctor tells a nurse. "Livvy, we need to be able to hear subtle changes."

"Baby, I'm right here." I look over and see Jon, standing two feet behind the doctor.

"Is it getting better?" I ask. "Shouldn't it be slowing down?" I've memorized the rhythm in my head, and nothing has changed.

"Livvy, can you close your eyes?" The doctor turns to Jon. "Help her out."

"Baby, try to close your eyes and take some deep breaths. Let's pretend this is Lamaze, okay? You remember how to breathe, right?"

"I can't do that," I tell him, choking on my tears.

"Okay, okay," he says, caressing my face. "No need to get frustrated. Just breathe with me." He matches my quick breaths, but then tries to slow them down. I can't stay in concert with him.

"I can't do it. What is that other beeping sound?" I ask, finally tuning in to another noise.

"Livvy, that's your baby's heartbeat, and he's in distress. We're going to need to deliver him now to help him out."

"No!" I yell. "It's too early for him. No!"

"Baby, calm down," Jon says, his eyes watering.

"It's best for both of you," the doctor says. "I think the hydralazine will work better on you once he's on his own, and I think he'll be much less stressed, too. Please." Dr. Irving looks at both of us.

"Olivia, what did you just tell me just the other day? He's 32 weeks. Or, now, he's 33. He's viable. He'll be small, but he's very viable. Look at Trey, right? He was born early and look at him now!"

"We need a decision," the doctor interrupts.

I shake my head, feeling weak.

"Trey is six-foot-four now and healthy and strong and in fucking law school. Why? Because he's a fighter! Right, baby?"

I nod. "Okay." I squeeze his hand and look at the doctor. "Okay."

"Hollands are fighters!" Jon says with a smile, nodding, as if he's trying to make sure I heard him.

I shake my head at him as they begin to wheel me toward the exit.

He stops the gurney to kiss me, and I exhale deeply as he embraces me, whispering my response into his ear. "I'm not."

CHAPTER 13

PART II | JON

*D*umbfounded, I stand still as I watch them wheel her away from me. "You are," I mumble. Someone nudges me in the back, pushing me forward hurriedly. *I get to go with her.* "You are!" I call after her, even though she's twenty feet ahead of me by now.

They take her in a freight elevator, but another nurse accompanies me to a standard one next to it.

"Are we going to the same place?"

"Labor and Delivery, yes."

I hear her in my head again as we ride silently up to the seventh floor. *I'm not.* I don't even know what she meant. Not a *fighter*? Not a *Holland*? Why would she say either?

When we get to the floor, they're already pushing her through two secure doors. The woman I was with rushes to follow them. "You'll take good care of them, right?" I call after her. "Um," I say, desperate to make sure she gets the attention I need her to have, "her father's given so much to this hospital they named the pediatric unit after him."

"We know who she is, Mr. Scott," she says, friendly and assuring. "We take care of all of our patients. Just let the doctors do what they're best at. Your wife and baby will be fine."

"Okay," I say, nodding, looking around the room, finally seeing other people there. "I just... wait here?"

"Have a seat and we'll be out to report on their condition as soon as possible."

"Thank you. Just... so much, thank you." I watch her disappear behind the doors.

Did I tell Livvy I love her? Did I reassure her enough?

I walk quickly to the doors and try to pull the handle to deliver the message, but they're locked. The windows are covered, and I can't hear a thing happening behind them, either.

I turn to my side and lean my head against the wall, letting out a heavy sigh.

I'm not. She sounded scared when she said it, but she'd sounded scared since she woke me up. Of course, she's scared. She couldn't calm herself. She worked herself up somehow, and that's how we ended up here in the hospital tonight.

And they're going to deliver the baby.

"Holy shit," I say aloud, just now coming to grips with this reality. "My baby's coming." I face the room and announce it to the ten people waiting with me. "My baby's coming!"

"Congratulations," a few say, while a couple others laugh.

"He's early." I smile but feel a lump in my throat. "But he's gonna be okay." I put it out into the world to make it happen.

"Of course, he is," an older woman says, standing up and walking over to me. She takes my hand. "Why don't you come have a seat?"

"Yeah." I nod my head. "Yeah," I respond again, sitting down next to her and staring at some vast nothingness across the room. We haven't even finished the nursery. I don't even think we have diapers at home. She hasn't had her shower yet. He has a place to sleep. I'm comforted by the image of the bassinet. He'll have a place to sleep. I'll move it to our bedroom as soon as we get back home. I'll see if Emi can go get diapers and wipes– "Shit! I need to call her parents!"

"I was just going to ask if you had someone to call," the lady says.

I must look like hell in my Columbia hat and glasses, because no one in the waiting room has openly acknowledged who I am, and that rarely happens. I didn't take the time to put in my contacts, and I don't often go out in public with my glasses.

I go to the far corner of the room and dial Jack's home number. It's the one I know to call for emergencies. He always answers that line.

He clears his throat first. "This is Jack."

"Hey, Granddaddy, the baby's coming."

"What?"

"The baby's coming early. We're at the hospital. Livvy said she couldn't calm down and she had a spike in her blood pressure—"

"Is she okay?"

"They're getting it under control. They said the medicine would work better once the baby wasn't in distress."

"He's in distress?"

"I'm screwing up this call. They said everything was okay. They just had to deliver him tonight. That it was what was best for both of them."

"We're on our way," he says, and promptly hangs up.

"Shiiiiit. Shit shit shit." I take a deep breath, not meaning to worry him like I did. *Or maybe I should be more worried?* But the nurse assured me they'd be fine. Jack was definitely worried, though. *I have to calm down.* This is what got us here in the first place. We can't both be nervous wrecks. They said she'd be okay, and *I* have to calm down.

While I'm waiting, I fill out the requisite paperwork and get tagged with a bracelet that identifies me as Baby Scott's father. It's really happening, and I can't imagine how anyone would expect me to calm down. It was different with the girls. They came when they were supposed to—not out of the blue in the dark of the night, six weeks early.

I haven't heard anything by the time Jack and Emi show up, but we only have about two minutes together before a team of nurses comes out of the secured area pushing a baby in an incubator. I see SCOTT labeled on the front of it.

"That's my baby," I say, walking up to them. "Is he okay? Where are you taking him?" I see a glimpse of him, tubes coming out of his tiny, red body. "Is he okay?" Jack and Emi are right beside me. The three of us stop their progress.

"Yes, Mr. Scott. It's a boy. He's small, but he's doing well. Four pounds, 2 ounces, and he's 18 inches long."

"He's so little. That's really small, right?" Jack asks.

"Shouldn't you cover him up?" Emi asks.

"He's small, but average size for a preterm baby. And we're going to find a nice, warm place for him right now, Mrs. Holland."

"And how's Livvy?" I ask.

"They're suturing her now."

They start to walk again, but I just met my son, and I don't want them to take him yet. "Where are you going?"

"To the private NICU, down the hall."

I look back at Jack and Emi, who wave me off to go with the nurses. "Let me know the second I can go to see Liv!" I call to them, running to catch up to my son.

"Did she do okay?" I ask them. "Was she awake for it? We've never done a cesarean before."

"She was. She was sort of in and out of consciousness, though. Maybe a side effect of the medicine they injected beforehand."

"That's normal?"

"Well, emergency C-sections are never the norm, Mr. Scott."

"Did she get to see him?"

They stop me at the door. "You can wait out here and watch through the window for now."

"I can't... hold him... or anything?"

"Not at this time, no, but soon. You'll be needed very soon."

I smile and watch them through the glass as they carefully transfer him to a large, somewhat enclosed bed. It has holes on each side for arms. I can't wait to feel his little hands and feet. To count his fingers and toes. They don't cover him up, though. I wonder if it's a safety issue or what. I just keep thinking how cold I feel right now; he must be freezing.

And just as I think that, another chill comes over me that makes me shiver. It lasts for a good ten seconds. The strangest feeling. It's unnerving. So much so I look harder at the monitor to make sure everything appears normal. When I realize I don't know, I knock on the window to get the attention of a nurse.

"Is he okay?"

"He's good. He's in a warmer; his body temperature is already rising."

"I don't mean to be impatient, but... how long do I have to wait? I just want to touch him. I want him to know his daddy's here."

A different nurse comes up behind the first and signals for me to walk to the other end of the hallway to a separate door, leading to a side room. She meets me there.

"I need you to disinfect. Leave the bracelet on, but wash your hands, your arms, your face and neck."

"Anything," I tell her, turning on the water.

"Hotter," she says.

"Got it."

"When you're finished, knock on this door, and I'll let you in."

"Thank you so much," I say, tears in my eyes. I wonder if I should wait for Livvy, but I know she would want one of us to be here with him. I know how important it was for her to have constant contact with the girls when they were born. She said it helped with bonding. While she had much more contact with them than I did, I was able to get my fair share of time, too.

I scrub hard, not wanting to be the reason our boy is exposed to anything harmful. I'm grateful that they're giving me this time with him. I feel raw when I'm finished, but I'm excited, and knock at the door, ready to meet...

We don't have a name for him. We still haven't come up with anything. We fought about it and abandoned the conversation. I guess it needs to be the next conversation we have.

"Right this way." She checks my bracelet before offering me the seat in front of the large, enclosed bed. "Now, you can put your hands through there. Don't pick him up or disrupt the tubes, but feel free to introduce yourself. Just be gentle."

"He can hear, right?"

"We haven't done the test yet, but this late in the pregnancy, babies' hearing has already developed. We'll do the tests soon, but feel free to talk to him."

I rub my hands together to warm them before placing them inside the enclosure. Even still, he seems to jerk away from my finger when I touch his foot. I think that's a good sign, though. I keep rubbing the bottom of his foot, back and forth, the size of it not too much bigger than the top section of my thumb.

"Hey, little guy. Did you have a bit of a scare tonight?" His eyes open lazily, a little crinkle between them as if he's not sure he meant to do it. "Who's that talking to you, huh? Do you recognize Daddy's voice?" I move my hand up to his torso and put four fingers against his belly. I can feel him breathe. I'd forgotten how wonderful it is to feel little babies breathe. "Happy birthday, baby. You know what? I think you're going to look like your mama. Maybe you'll have brown eyes like her, but I can tell they're going to be big, man. And your lashes? You are going to be one handsome little thing. I bet your mama already fell in love with you at first sight, huh? Did she? I'm sure she did.

"You have the best mama, little guy. I'm not just saying that. She'll spend so much time with you, feeding you and cuddling with you. You'll never want for anything. Unless you're a loner... and you want privacy. Then we got a problem," I say, laughing at my own statement. "She won't be able to keep her hands off you. No way."

I find one of his tiny hands and gently hold it in mine. "And you have two sisters who are gonna be loads of fun. They'll show you the ropes and blame you for all sorts of things, I'm sure. Edie's the troublemaker, so watch out for her. But she'll make sure you always look your best. And Willow will read you all the good bedtime stories. They're best friends. It's pretty great, but I know they're going to make room for you. They're so excited to meet you. And—fair warning—they're going to call you Froggie. Just go with it. We did your room in monkeys, but there are a bunch of frog items at the house. I mean... they were too cute for me to get rid of.

"You've got Granddaddy and Memi. They already love you so much. You'll meet them tonight. They're just outside. They're your mama's parents. And you have a ton of uncles who you'll probably confuse for a few years, and then you'll learn what each one is good for. Your aunts are going to spoil you rotten.

"Oh! That's the best part!" I tell him. "You're going to have a cousin that's just a couple weeks—no, months now—younger than you. Can you believe that? You two will go to school together and share toys with each other. He'll live down the street from you. Oh, yeah. He's a little boy, too. So, you won't have to face this world alone. It'll be like having a brother of your own. I have two of them. Brothers are pretty cool."

I smile and look up at the nurses, who had been listening to me while they tended to other chores in the otherwise empty nursery, but I noticed their movements ceased a minute or two ago. They all look shocked. One is crying and looking beyond me, outside the large glass window. The other two are staring right at me.

CHAPTER 14

JACK

"*He's* bigger than Trey was," Emi says. "I don't remember Trey having that many tubes in him, though, do you?" She walks into my awaiting arms, embracing me.

"He did," I tell her, remembering the day our son was born with perfect clarity, even if it was 25 years ago. "You were a little out of it, but he did." She sighs and looks up at me. I give her a kiss. "Congratulations, Em. We have a grandson."

"Our lives get more surreal every day. How are our kids this old?"

"I don't know. How are *we* this old?" My thumb brushes against laugh lines next to her pale green eyes as I admire her smile.

"You think he'll be okay?" She takes my hand and leads me to two seats in the waiting area.

"He's been healthy in every checkup, Poppet. And the nurses just said he's doing well. The next few days will tell us more. We just have to be strong for Liv and Jon. If they need to be at the hospital, we'll keep the girls with us. Baby Jonny can get everything he needs here."

"You know, I don't think they're going to name him that," she tells me.

"What?"

"Just a hunch."

"What do you know?"

She looks away, a blatant show that she's hiding something. "We'll just have to wait and see."

I stare at her, but she keeps her secret. I check my watch, noting the time. "They did an emergency C-section on you, too, and it was... quick, right? It didn't take this long."

"It didn't seem like it, but... like you said, I was a little out of it."

"I'm going to go ask the woman at the counter." I squeeze her hand and start walking toward the front of the room when a doctor and two nurses come out of the secured doors. He's clearly looking for someone else, but when he sees me, he recognizes me.

"Mr. Holland," he says, extending his hand. "I'm Dr. Irving. I was the attending doctor when Livvy was brought into the emergency room tonight." I glance behind me at Emi, who quickly comes to join us. "I assisted with the delivery of your grandson." His smile is faint, and I can hear him swallow before he speaks his next word, a very somber "Congratulations."

The look on his face stops me from thanking him. "How is my daughter?"

He doesn't hesitate. "Please step through these doors with me."

"Oh, god," Emi says, faltering where she stands. One of the nurses rushes to her right side while I hold the weight of her as she tries to recover.

"Em, come on." We follow the staff into the secured area to a small office where the five of us barely fit. "Where—" I have to clear my throat, as fear has taken residence there. "Where is she?"

"Mr. Holland, where is your son-in-law?"

"He's with his son in the NICU. Where is my daughter? She's my number one priority, and if you don't answer me, I *will* start looking for her."

"Sir, as you may know, Mrs. Scott was brought in with severe hypertension. After the dose of hydralazine didn't have the desired effect on her, and appeared to put her baby in distress, we knew the only option to save either of them was to deliver the baby."

"Is she okay?" Emi chokes out.

It feels like hours go by before anyone speaks again.

"I'm sorry."

"Oh, god." I fall into the seat behind me.

"No," Emi cries. "No no no no no no..."

"After the baby was delivered, we were suturing the wound, and she went into cardiac arrest. We tried everything—we had seven doctors down here, and our full staff of nurses, Mr. and Mrs. Holland."

Sobs erupt from my chest. "Not Contessa. Not my Contessa!" Emi's arms are around me quickly, her tears hot on my neck. "No. It can't be happening. This cannot be happening."

"We couldn't revive her."

"No. Oh, god, no. Where is she now?"

"She's still in the delivery room."

"Take me to her." The doctor nods and I stand up, but Emi holds on to my arm, keeping me from moving.

"Jacks, I can't," my wife says. "No, she can't be gone! No. This is a dream, right? We're in a horrible, horrible dream, but this isn't happening."

"I don't believe it. Let me see her."

"Jacks, I don't want to see her. She's not gone. Nooooo," she sobs. I embrace her, and we hold on to one another so tightly, it's difficult to breathe. But I don't care. Breathing seems a luxury if my daughter can't be here anymore.

"Em, I have to know," I whisper. "Please come."

Two doors down, a dim room is in disarray. An eerie silence fills the space, and a thin sheet covers a body on the table. Let this be a cruel joke. Let her be hiding under there, waiting to surprise us. I don't care if it's sick and twisted. I'll hug her first and reprimand her for nearly destroying us later. But please, let it be a joke.

"I'll wait here," Emi says, standing just outside the door. "I can't go in." She continues to cry as I slowly enter, following the doctor to the head of the table where she lies. He puts his hand on the edge of the sheet and looks me in the eyes. *Ready?* he asks me without words.

In twelve lifetimes, I will never be ready for this. Tears thud onto the sheet beneath me. Carefully, he folds it down, revealing thick, dark hair. Pale skin. She never had pale skin in her life. No matter how sick she was, or scared—never was she pallid. And there are her beautiful, long, brown lashes.

I break down.

"Can I have a moment?" I ask him.

"Of course." His footsteps mark the way to the door, and then I hear it close. It's only me and my Contessa. I find her hand and hold it in mine, surprised at the difference in our body temperatures. It's not a cruel joke.

"Oh, god, Tessa, what happened?" I cry over her. I find the handkerchief I'd expected to use when I got to see my grandson up close and personal for the first time. "This isn't how it works, Livvy. I can't take this. Your mother—she can't take this, either. You can't do this to us. What about your girls, and Jon? Huh, Contessa? And your little boy? Oh, god. How are we going to live without you? I don't—I don't know how to do that. You made me a father. Don't you know that?"

I choke out more tears. Some fall on her skin. I dab at them gently. I think about what she went through and realize I don't want to go there. I will destroy myself if I do that. To die without anyone she loved by her side? She must have been so scared. Did she feel our love? Did she know we were right outside?

And suddenly I'm angry. The fact that they could have gotten us. The fact that we were right outside while they made futile attempts to save her. Maybe we could have said goodbye. Maybe seeing our faces could have revived her.

And maybe they truly did everything they could. Seven doctors, he'd said. They know who she is.

Who she *was*.

"God, Livvy, no." I lean down and wrap my arm around her, lifting her torso from the bed, holding her head in my hand, hugging her into my chest. "Come back, Contessa. Please, come back to Daddy. Please, I'm begging you. I can't do this. I just can't. I can't bear not seeing your beautiful smile again. Seeing you with your girls. How they look up to you. Seeing you raise your son. He'll never know you. How can that be? Come back... please, come back."

Her body is limp in my arms. Cold and lifeless and limp. Supporting her head like a baby, I settle her back down onto the bed. Her arms are tucked back under the sheet. I make her comfortable. *Appear* comfortable. I know it's just for my benefit. She's not here anymore.

"I don't know myself without you, Contessa." I kiss her forehead and wipe the lingering tears from her skin. "I love you more than life itself. Thank you for the life you gave me. But I don't know how to go on."

I walk away, but turn back to see her, her face still exposed, before I open the door. *How do I let go? How do I go on?*

Emi looks up at me from a bench in the hallway, and I catch a glimpse of hope on her face before her expression crumbles into devastation. I guess she was wishing for a miracle, and although I feel we've experienced many in our time together, I have failed her this time.

The little girl we met in this exact hospital 31 and a half years ago will not be leaving with us today, and there's nothing I can do to change that. I join Emi, and she cries into my chest as I stroke her hair and let my own tears fall where they may. I have never felt such loss in my life. I don't know how Emi has lived through so much of it and maintained her sanity. It makes me respect her even more in this moment as I realize the strength she really has. It's a quality I doubt I will ever match; nor will I want to.

"I love you so much, Emi. I am so sorry. I am so, so sorry."

My wife gasps, looking up. "The girls," she says, covering her mouth and shaking her head.

"And Jackson. We have to tell our son."

"Jon first," she says, unable to stop the flow of tears.

I look away from her, unable to imagine the pain he will feel. The shock. "Emi, he'll be devastated. Absolutely destroyed." I start sobbing again, but in truth, I haven't stopped. "If I ever lost you..." I'm not sure she can even understand what I'm saying to her.

She squeezes my wrists. "I'll talk to Jon."

I look at her, displaying all of my weaknesses to her. I've never felt more inadequate. "Do I call Jackson?"

"No, love," she says, soothing me by running her fingers through my hair. "I don't want him to hear this in a phone call. Call your brother. Matty can go over to Trey's to tell him in person. And see if he and Nolan can also call the rest of our brothers and sisters."

"And our parents?" *How do people deliver such news?*

"We'll handle them in a few hours. It's too late at night... or early? I don't even know what time it is. We'll wait until the morning." She says, hugging me again. "It's okay."

"What about her friends? Shea? Jon's brothers?"

"Shhh, Jacks." She angles my head to face her. "Let Matty work all of that out. Maybe Coley can help; she can go to Shea's. We don't want her to be alone in her condition, and Will's at Jon's apartment right now with the girls."

"Oh, god... Will. How do you think he'll handle it?" I ask her.

"I think it's going to be horrible for all of us. In my experience, some people become pillars of strength for the others who need it." Her voice is calm and assuring when she says it. "Do you think you can make the call to Matty?"

It's about the only call I think I could make, even though I know she was his favorite niece. Matty has always been able to handle anything. His work has prepared him better than any of my life experience has. "I can. How... with Jon?" I look into her eyes, greener because of the tears she's been crying.

"Gently. With all the love I have." We embrace again and I walk her to the beginning of the hallway, watching as she makes the dreadful trek to deliver the worst and most unexpected news, what will destroy one of the happiest moments of my son-in-law's life.

Going back to the front desk, I ask if I can have a private room. Immediately, I'm led back through the secured doors, back into the office just two doors away from where my daughter now lies, lifeless and alone. I dial the phone quickly, hoping to get that thought out of my mind. I can't stand to think of her like that, but I also don't think I can see her again. Not without completely falling apart.

"Everything okay?" my brother answers, having never received a call from me at this time of night.

I exhale slowly, unable to speak and trying to tame the sobs that want to choke out of my tightened throat.

"Jacks, are you okay?"

CHAPTER 15

MATTY

"It's Livvy," my brother says. His voice sounds foreign to me—weak and strained. "My Contessa."

"Nolan, wake up." My heart pounds in my chest as I shake my husband in the bed next to me, startling him to alertness. "Is she sick? Did something happen?" I ask quickly, needing more information. My brother stalls for more seconds than is comfortable. "Jack, say something."

"She passed away tonight, Matty." I feel like someone just cold-cocked me in the stomach. "They did a C-section, and... uh... she went into cardiac arrest?" His breaths are shaky; emotions he'd been trying to hide from me begin to gush out. "They couldn't save her, Matty. They couldn't save my little girl. Oh, god." I pull my knees into my chest, hugging them into me and wishing they were my oldest brother. Wishing I could be comforting him in his obvious pain.

"Jacks. No. Not Little Liv. Nolan," I turn to see him staring at me with worry, "Livvy's gone. Cardiac arrest?" I whisper. He covers his mouth in shock. "Jacks, just, out of the blue?" I ask my brother, putting him on speakerphone.

"She went in complaining that she couldn't calm down," he explains. "Her blood pressure was high and endangering them both, so they had to deliver the baby."

The baby. "Is he okay? Please say he's okay."

"He's tiny, but they're optimistic." Nolan and I look at one another and smile, although it's bittersweet. Definitely more bitter than sweet. "After the surgery, the doctors say she went into cardiac arrest and..."

"Oh my god." And suddenly it hits me. I imagine her in distress, my beautiful niece that I feel like I helped raise for the past 30 years. I begin to cry; to wail. I let it out for a good minute or two but remember that what I feel is likely only a fraction of the pain my brother must be experiencing. Nolan hands me a couple of tissues, and I wipe my nose and eyes, taking some deep breaths.

"I know," Jacks says softly.

"I don't even know what to say. I don't believe it."

"I know," he repeats. "I have to ask some favors of you, and Nolan... I wouldn't ask if I didn't think you couldn't handle it."

I clear my throat and sit up a little straighter. "I'll do anything for you. Nolan and I both. Do we need to make some calls?"

"Yes, I need you to call Kelly, Steven, Chris and Jen for us. But before that, I need you to go to Jackson's apartment... and be there when you tell him. We don't want him to find out over the phone," I explain.

"Trey doesn't know?"

"No, Matty. We just found out. Emi's telling Jon right now. We need to be very thoughtful about how everyone gets the news, okay? Shea's seven months pregnant and home alone right now because Will is watching the girls. Will's going to take it very hard, and it can't be in front of Edie and Willow. I think Jon will want to be there when they find out, either from him or... Emi..." I notice my brother doesn't offer to deliver the news to his granddaughters. "We need to bring them here somehow without giving too much away."

"Nolan and I can handle it. Just do me a favor and let me know if there's any news on the baby. If his condition... you know..." I don't want to say *worsens*. I don't want to put that out into the universe.

"I understand."

"Hang in there, Jacks. We'll all be there soon. I want you to do *me* a favor and go find your wife now. Don't let her tell Jon alone, and please. I don't want you to be alone, either."

"You're right," he says. "I know."

"I love you," I tell him. "And we all love her so much."

I hear him gasp into the phone, like he was trying to say something, or maybe just to breathe. "I have to go," he finally manages to say, his voice not one I've heard before. The line disconnects.

When I hang up, Nolan is there to comfort me. He holds my hands in his as he lets me deal with the news in my own way and my own time, but I know we have to act quickly.

"What do you need me to do?" He's calm and steady, although I know this news hurts him as much as it hurts me.

"I'll go to Trey's."

"Alone?"

I nod my head. "I can do it."

"I know you can."

"They need us to call my brother and sister, and Em's brother and sister. Can you do that for me while I'm gone?"

"Of course, I can." I get up and put on some clothes, giving him all the details I know. "Have them get down to the hospital. Jon and Jacks and Emi are going to need all the support they can get... and if word gets out—and it will, people at the hospital will talk—we're going to need to protect them as best as we can."

"Understood. I'll just start heading down there and make the calls on my way. Should we... wake up Max and Cal? They're right across the hall."

"Not before telling Trey... or Will. We'll... figure it out after."

"You're right."

"I'm going to go to Trey's," I say, thinking this out, "and then Shea's, and to Jon's place, where Will is. I have to bring the girls with me so they can somehow... tell them."

"Those poor babies," he says, the tears finally falling from his eyes. "Jon's going to need so much help from us. As Edie's godparents. As their great-uncles. You need to be strong, Matthew."

I nod my head. "I know. I just loved her so much. She had my heart the moment I met her."

He hugs me again. "You can cry alone with me anytime," he whispers. "Anytime."

"Thank you. And thank you for doing this... making the calls."

"It's part of my job as your husband. I'll take great care."

"I know you will." We kiss before I head out of the apartment, barely saying hello to the doorman when I leave.

. . .

*T*he New York City streets seem unusually quiet, but it's been awhile since Nolan and I were out past midnight. I take a cab around the perimeter of Central Park to Trey's penthouse, just above Morningside Park. The doorman of his building senses the urgency of my visit and rings the apartment immediately.

It takes about a minute for anyone to answer.

"Yes?" Trey's voice is tired.

"Trey, your uncle is downstairs. Matty Holland?"

"It's two-thirty in the morning." My nephew doesn't sound awake.

I'm silent as I watch the man do his job. "Shall I bring him up?"

"Of course."

CHAPTER 16

TREY

I pass through the patio doors, the quickest way to my bedroom, to find a t-shirt. I'd hoped the buzzer hadn't awoken Coley, but she's sitting up in bed, the moonlight shining on her.

"What was it?"

"Matty's here." I scratch my head, feeling the mess of hair up there.

"Why?" She picks up her phone, and then mine. "We didn't miss any calls."

"Not sure. I'll handle it."

"He wouldn't just come over in the middle of the night," she reasons with me.

"Maybe Nolan kicked him out."

She scoffs. "No." She climbs out of bed, wearing nothing but her satin underwear, and ambles to the dresser. I walk over to her and kiss her deeply, feeling down the sides of her body.

"Didn't we just do that?" She laughs, moving her mouth to my bare chest.

"Couldn't we just do that forever?"

"Not with your uncle coming up!" We hear the ding of the elevator, which means he's in our apartment. "Get out! I'm naked!"

I laugh and grab my t-shirt from the floor, sliding it on as I navigate the dark hallway.

"Trey?" my uncle calls out to me.

"All lights on," I say aloud, watching the whole apartment become bathed in a bright yellow, mimicking the sunrise. "Hey, Matty." When my eyes focus on his face, I can tell something's not right.

"Hi, Matty!" Coley follows me into the room, now in leggings and a short robe.

"Hey, kids." He signals to the couch. "Can we sit down?"

I reach for my fiancée's hand. "Sure." We take the couch while my uncle chooses the recliner on the other side of Coley. "What's going on?"

"Are you okay, Matty?"

He opens his mouth, as if to speak, but nothing comes out. Tears immediately fall from his eyes. I squeeze Coley's hand, nervous. "I took a cab over here and tried to think of what I was going to say to you, but there is no way to tell you this, Trey. It's... the worst."

"Just say it, Matty. Who is it?"

I already know it's dire news about someone we care about. I can tell that by the way he's acting. Anxiety is eating away at me as I consider everyone I love.

"It's your sister."

"Is she okay?"

"Oh my god," Coley says. "The baby?"

I put my arm around her. "What happened?"

He shakes his head. "She had the baby... but she didn't make it."

"What?" I feel like I didn't hear him correctly.

"No..." Coley puts her hands over her mouth in shock. I hear her gasping for air.

"What do you mean? She didn't make it..."

"It was a heart thing, Trey. After the operation to deliver the baby."

I stand up, staring at him in disbelief. "Who–" My voice falters. "Who told you?"

"Your father."

"No," I fall back onto the couch where my girlfriend is already crying; where she's already accepted the news. "No." She wraps her arms around me, but mine are limp and unable to move. I continue to look in the direction of my uncle, but the vision of him blurs. When I feel one, lone tear fall on my right cheek, I hold Coley to me with all of my strength and let her cry. The empathy in my uncle's eyes is of comfort to me. It gives me courage. "It's okay, laureate. Shhh... it's okay." I sniffle back the remaining tears.

"It's awful," he says to me.

"How's the baby?" I ask.

"He was doing well. Small, but the doctors are hopeful."

"And how's Jon?"

"When I talked to Jacks... they hadn't told him about her yet. He was with the baby."

"Oh, shit..." I take a deep breath, considering the unimaginable pain he must be going through. "And my parents?"

"Devastated," he whispers, getting choked up. I nod.

"Who else knows?" I ask him.

"Nolan's calling your aunts and uncles. I need to go see Shea, because she's alone... and Will–he's with the girls. I've got to take them to the hospital to be with Jon."

"Edie and Willow," Coley sobs. "How are they going to handle this, Trey? They're so young."

"With our help," I tell her. "All of our help."

"Matty, can I go with you to Shea's?" Coley asks.

"We'll both go," I suggest. "And then to talk to Will. I'll bring the girls to the hospital with you."

"Thank you," he says. "I don't know if I can see them and not fall to pieces."

"I think I can. We can take my car, too. Coley, let's go get changed."

"We'll just be... five minutes," she tells him. We go back to our master bathroom with the same idea. I know I still feel like sex, and I don't want to go to the hospital like this. We strip off all of our clothes and start both shower heads, each taking our own. We share the soap and shampoo, but don't say anything to one another. I stand under the hot water until she shuts hers off, at which point I turn around and reach for her hand. She steps under my stream and, eyes still flooded with tears, gives me a desperate kiss.

With our hair towel-dried, we find fresh clothes and dress quickly. I throw on a college tee and a button-down and Coley chooses a hoodie, even though the warm air outside doesn't necessitate it. It's a smart choice–it's probably only a matter of time before word gets out, and this will be the biggest news story to hit Manhattan in quite some time.

"We're ready," I say, grabbing my keys. "Do we need to pick up Nolan?"

"He'll meet us there. He was heading over already."

"Good."

Coley hands me a cap and dons one herself as we secure the alarm and exit the apartment.

The car ride to the Flatiron District is quiet, save for the lingering sniffles in the backseat. Coley and Matty sit side-by-side and are holding hands when I look back there.

"Do you think Shea suspects something's wrong?" I ask Matty.

"I have no idea what she knows... about where Will is, if she knows he's gone... nothing."

"They were best friends," Coley says with a sigh. I try to put myself into her shoes. I remember how it felt when I saw Max get shot, when I thought he was dead. The pain was unbearable. "Should we call her doctor first? Is there a risk of her going into labor?"

And then I consider Shea, and what I know of her. She's a woman who's suffered many losses in her life. Tremendous ones, like the loss of both of her parents. Life-altering ones, like the business her mother handed down to her. The home that was essentially repossessed from her. And she said goodbye to all that she knew when she made the move to Manhattan. Shea knows how to survive. Shea knows strength.

"I think she's the only one who can tell Will," I say, feeling certain of that–knowing how he cared for my sister. "And I think she'll be equipped to handle the news, as horrible as it is."

"She and Livvy had the same obstetrician, right?" Matty asks. I nod my head. "I'll see if I can get the number from Emi, just in case."

"I'm sure she's already at the hospital tonight," Coley adds. "Surely they called her."

I pull up to the curb in front of their building, leaving my keys in the ignition.

"We'll be leaving in a couple of minutes. This is an emergency," I tell the valet. "If you can just watch it with the hazards on." He nods.

Inside the building, we tell the concierge we're there to see Shea Scott. She takes no time to answer the buzzer, allowing us all to come right up.

CHAPTER 17

SHEA

I take a deep breath and wait by the door, patting Gunner's head. "Release," I tell him. "Relax," I say to myself, knowing that two Hollands and Coley coming to my apartment in the middle of the night is not a good sign—not on the same night my husband's been called away to watch Livvy's kids because she's been rushed to the hospital in an ambulance.

If she was okay, Will would be home. If the baby was here, I would have received a phone call. When I hear the ding of the elevator, I open the door, letting the dog out into the hallway to greet everyone. I'm still in my pajamas and a long robe but realize I could have better used that time to change when I see Trey, Coley and Matty.

"What happened?" I ask, letting them all in. Trey and Coley sit on the couch; Matty leans against the end of it. I take the love seat across from them, where Gunner—too large for the small sofa, normally, but welcome right now when I see their faces—stretches across the whole thing, with his upper body draped up the back pillows and his head just behind my neck. I rub his belly, which soothes us both. He's a perceptive animal, sensing the mood of the room as well as I can.

Coley's already crying. I shake my head. "She lost the baby," I say, breaking down and putting my other hand on my belly. "Oh, no..."

"No," Matty says quickly.

I gasp, looking at them all. Trey gets up and walks toward me, taking a knee in front of me. The dog smells him and gets off the couch to lick his face; Trey's red nose gives away the fact that he's been crying, too, although I see he's trying to be strong.

"The baby made it, Shea." He takes a deep breath, then swallows. "Livvy didn't." His eyebrows shift in disbelief, showing that he's still in shock.

"Gunner, down." Trained, he's lying on the floor with his head on his paws immediately. I reach for Trey and embrace him tightly. "Oh, Trey," I whisper quietly as my tears fall on his shoulder. "Oh, don't say that."

"I'm sorry, Shea."

"No, I'm sorry, sweetie. Oh, no..." I wave Coley over, wanting to hold on to her, too.

"Are you okay?" she asks. "Are you feeling... I mean?"

"Charlie's fine," I assure her. "I've been worrying about Liv for the past couple hours, ever since Will left. I just had a bad feeling. I just... didn't think it would be her. Oh my god. How is Jon?"

"We don't know."

"And your mom and dad?"

"Heartbroken," Matty says.

"I can't imagine." I let out a few more tears. "We were gonna raise them together," I say, feeling sad. "She was going to teach me how to be a good mom. What am I gonna do?" Suddenly, I feel panic, realizing how much I'd been relying on my friend through this pregnancy, and had planned to rely on her in the coming months.

"You're gonna be a great mom, Shea," Coley says. "You've been watching her for years."

"Surely you know all the tricks by now," Matty says, taking the seat Gunner had.

"She was my best friend, though. It was always going to be Jon and Livvy and Will and Shea. That's just how we are. How we were always going to be. They moved down the street to be closer to us, and now... I'll never be able to walk down there and see her again. I can't... this was the life we'd dreamed of."

"I know, Shea," Trey says.

"Both of us. I sound so selfish, but we couldn't wait to push our babies around in strollers, going to Sunday brunch together. Taking them to the private school two blocks away. We had it all figured out."

"I know, honey." Matty's arm is around me.

"Now what happens?"

"We all help," Coley says, stifling away tears and wiping them with her hoodie sleeve. "I'll help. I'll go to brunch with you. I'll push the stroller. Jon will need help. I know it's not the same, but we're friends, too."

"Of course, we are. Sisters," I assure her, giving her another hug. "Poor Jon. How's he going to manage?"

"Just what Coley said," Trey responds. "We'll all pitch in. He'll never be alone in this."

"The girls," I say, looking in the faces of all of them. "Do they know? Does Will know?" I reach for my phone in between Trey and Coley. "I don't know how he'll take the news."

"We want your help... telling him. We want to take the kids to the hospital. But do you think you can tell Will?"

"Of course. Oh, he'll be sick. He'll be so upset. He figured they were taking Liv as a precautionary measure, but he's been waiting for news. He's been texting Jon for the past hour with no response. Now I understand why..."

"Yeah," Trey says. "Matty, did you tell Max and Callen?"

"No, we wanted to tell you guys first.

"Okay. Coley, someone needs to tell them. If I call the car service to take you, do you think you can handle that while we get Edie and Willow to the hospital?"

She nods her head. "Yeah. And they can bring me to the hospital."

"Right."

"We should go now..." Matty says.

I nod, then go to the bedroom and change. I grab some clothes for Will, remembering that he only pulled on some lounge pants and a t-shirt before he ran out the door.

*S*ince Will and I each have a spare key to Jon and Livvy's apartment, we bypass the doorman and head straight up to the 55th floor.

CHAPTER 18

WILL

*A*s I sit in the upstairs library just outside the girls' rooms, I hear the main door open. Relieved, I set down the book I'd been reading and start downstairs to greet Jon and Livvy, but from the top of the steps, I see my wife, Trey and Matty, instead.

I stop dead in my tracks. "What?"

Shea signals for me to join them on the first floor of the apartment. I shake my head, reluctant, but take the stairs, one-by-one, anyway. I don't even need to look in their eyes to see something bad has happened. I can feel the tension surround me. I can sense the words that no one is speaking. My throat gets tight in the silence, and I'm drawing my own damned conclusions—none of which are good.

"Somebody tell me what happened."

"I'm going to take you up to the third floor," Shea says with an empathetic smile.

"We don't go up there," I remind her of the strict rule that was issued months ago by both my brother and sister-in-law about their studio, which took up the entire top floor of their penthouse home. "Livvy will smell the paints on us from a mile away."

She tugs on my arm, leading me toward the elevator. "Let's go."

"We'll see you there," Trey says softly, heading up the staircase with Matty.

"What are they doing?" I ask Shea once the elevator doors close. She shakes her head, not wanting to say. "Going to wake the girls?" She looks up to stop tears from falling down, just as the doors open to the third floor of their apartment—the 57th and top floor of the building. We had only been up here once—when it was still under construction, and Jon was showing us the small corner where his workspace would be in contrast to the vast openness where Livvy would be allowed to paint with a nearly unobstructed, 360-degree view of Manhattan through floor-to-ceiling windows.

It's a cloudless night, and the moon casts an eerie glow on all of the unfinished paintings that sit on easels and drop cloths all around us. And the paint smell is strong, as the room's been closed-up for months. I remember how to open the venting windows that Jon had installed and do so immediately—not only to keep the smell from soaking into our clothes, but to stall from whatever bad news is on the tip of Shea's tongue. I can tell she doesn't want to deliver it, anyway.

I start to look around the room at different pieces of art, standing in front of each incomplete painting and trying to figure out where Livvy was headed with it. Shea remains standing in the middle of the entire floor, still next to the elevator, leaving me be.

I know in my heart something has happened to Liv. If it doesn't matter that we come out of this room smelling like paint, something has happened to her. I start crying while looking at the fourth oil painting, this one nearly finished. I touch a deep, red swirling object that appears to fall deeper into the canvas. It's kind of how I feel right now.

When I audibly gasp for air, I hear Shea's footsteps quickly approaching. "Will," she says softly.

"It's her, right?" I ask. Her response is simply a hand on my shoulder. I fall to my knees as guttural sobs erupt from my chest and echo within the cavernous room. Shea kneels behind me with her arms around my neck. "Is she..." They're the only words I can choke out.

"She's gone, Will."

I turn around quickly and she welcomes me into her arms. *She* steadies *me*, and it should be the other way around, I know, but Livvy was too special to me. Her artistic soul was so much like mine that I often felt we were connected in that way.

I hear words coming from Shea, but I'm not really listening. I'm thinking about the pretty girl I met for the first time one Christmas Eve. She'd made me an ornament. She was *famous* and she had dinner at *my apartment,* and I told the boys at school who'd bullied me that she'd come over, and they called me a liar. They didn't believe that Livvy Holland came to my shitty apartment. They'd even made me doubt that she had–except I had the ornament to prove it.

"Cardiac arrest..."

I'm thinking about the girl who I swear would flutter her long eyelashes at me when she'd say, "Hey, Will," to greet me. My stomach would erupt in butterflies. I had *such* a crush on her.

"Tried everything..."

I'm thinking about the time I got caught by my brother ogling her breasts at dinner with her whole family, *at* the Holland house.

"Nothing they could do..."

I'm thinking about the woman who forced me to dance with her at her wedding, even though I was nervous as fuck and had two left feet and knew everyone would be watching. Even though I had slept with a multi-tude of women by then, but still lost my breath at the sight of her in a wedding dress that day. And at the end of that day, I went back to my hotel room alone, still thinking about her, but no longer with the unrealistic dream that someday she'd realize I was the better brother.

"Saved the baby..."

For one thing, I'd always known Jon was *it* for her. For another, he'd convinced her to marry him. And lastly, she was carrying his baby.

"Livvy wasn't like a sister to me," I interrupt Shea, feeling the need to confess; to spill my emotions to my wife in this moment.

"I know," she says.

"She wasn't an object of desire."

"It's okay, Will." She releases me and holds my hands in hers, then leans in to kiss me.

"She was an unobtainable, indescribable, beautiful girl that I was fortu-nate enough to know and my brother was lucky enough to marry. And I can't imagine how he feels, because I know how I feel, and it hurts so fucking bad."

"Oh, Will," she says, enveloping me into her arms again. "Baby, I know... I know you loved her."

"I did," I tell her, pulling away and nodding, tears falling quickly down my face. "I did."

"It's okay," she says, crying, but with a smile. "I did, too. It was impossible not to fall in love with her, Will. That's what she did to people. And it's okay."

"Okay," I breathe.

"It hurts," she says. "I know it hurts."

"But I love you, Shea. So, so much."

"Will?"

"Yeah?"

"Baby, nothing that's happened today has me doubting your feelings for me. Understand that now."

"It shouldn't."

"It doesn't. You have proven your love to me in so many ways. We are good."

"I couldn't live without you, Shea," I crumble into her as more tears find their way out.

"I wouldn't want to live without you, either. Not a single day. I love you, Will."

"I love you," I say again, nuzzling into her hair. "You said the baby made it?" I ask her.

"That's what they said. He's a preemie, of course. I'm sure he'll be in the NICU for weeks, but... there's a blessing in that... in him, right?"

"It's hard to look at it that way right now, but... yeah."

"We should get to the hospital. Your brother's going to be needing us... and the girls."

"Wait... how are you feeling?" I ask her.

"I'm fine, baby. Really. Everything feels just like it should. Please don't worry about me."

I stand up, then offer her both of my hands to help her.

"Thank you."

Hand-in-hand we walk back over to the switch that closes the windows. I can't imagine how long this room will stay closed up now... we may be the last to see it for quite some time. I take a deep breath of the smell of paints that remind me so much of my sister-in-law. I start to cry again as I exhale and realize that smell will always be associated with her, and also that I may never smell these paints again.

CHAPTER 19

COLEY

*I*n the back of the town car, I slowly thumb through the pictures I'd taken of Livvy just a few weeks ago when we'd met for our spa day. She looked beautiful. Healthy. So happy to be among friends. When she and Shea were together, they were constantly laughing, comparing husbands in jest. "Sister Scott!" They'd always yell that to one another. Now there would only be one Sister Scott, and I'd never heard the phrase shouted without an echo. They were as good as sisters, not only to each other, but to me, too.

I feel like I've lost a big sister today. I reach for another tissue—the last one in the box. I wipe my eyes and blot my nose, happy that we're turning onto 5th.

Two blocks later, we arrive at the loft. For so many years, I used to visit her here. Now, I have to deliver the news of her passing to Callen and Max. I weep quietly to myself, even as the driver holds the door open for me.

"Take your time," he says.

"Thanks." After a few deep breaths, I take his hand and get out of the car.

"Miss Coley, I don't know what's wrong," Edgar, one of our regular drivers, says, "but can I offer you a hug?"

"That would be nice, thank you." He whispers assurances that it will all be okay while he embraces me.

"Shall I wait?"

"No, no." I wipe my nose once more. "Callen can take me to... yeah... I'm good."

"If you change your mind, you know how to reach us."

"Yes, Edgar." I hand him a generous tip. "I used your last tissue."

He nods and says goodbye. I sigh, turning into the familiar building.

"Good... morning, Miss Fitzsimmons," Luis, the concierge, greets me, looking at his watch. "It's awfully early. Is everything okay?"

I try to wave him off but burst into tears when I look into his kind eyes. He knew Livvy well–would be devastated to know what was happening. I'm surprised Matty didn't tell him already. He puts his arms around me and takes me into their small office, handing me a box of Kleenex.

"I know something's going on. Matty left a while ago; then Nolan ran out with his phone to his ear... and now, you show up crying. What happened?"

"It's awful, Luis, but... you can't tell anyone. It can't get out until we tell the family."

"Oh, Coley, no... what is it?" He knows it's serious.

"Livvy." I barely get her name out before the sobs erupt. I fall into him, my arms around his neck. "And I have to tell Max and Callen."

"Livvy what? Don't tell me she's gone, Coley..." He pulls away slightly and I nod my head. His face crumples in sadness. "But I just saw her the other day. She can't be."

"I know." My words are caught in my throat.

He gasps in recognition of her condition. "The baby?"

"I think he's okay. I don't know for sure. We all have to get to the hospital."

"Oh, no. Coley, I am so sorry for your family."

"I know. Thank you."

"Let's get you upstairs. Shall I call the boys and let them know?"

"No, I have the elevator key. I'll just go up and knock."

"I won't tell a soul, but I will start saying prayers for all of you–and especially for Jon and the baby and their little girls."

"Thanks, Luis." He summons the elevator for me and stands by the doors until they close me inside. I probably shouldn't have told him, but I couldn't pretend everything was fine. And Luis is like family. I remember Livvy cried when she said goodbye to him on the day they moved out.

Once on the 12th floor, I take a seat on the bench in the hallway, trying to find an ounce or two of courage.

Finally, I clutch the box of tissues in one hand and knock with the other—softly, at first, but loudly the second time, when I don't get a response.

Callen opens the door, dressed in jeans and a tank top, looking as confused as one might expect when they have an uninvited visitor at four-thirty in the morning. "What are you doing here, Coley?"

"Livvy died," I blurt out, surprised at the way I've delivered the news. I gasp and cover my mouth, my eyes wide.

He ushers me inside the loft, taking the box from me and pulling a tissue out to give to me. Tears are streaming, but I feel composed.

"What?" he asks me, shocked.

"She died, Callen. She had a C-section and died before they finished operating on her." Noticing that Max isn't in the unmade bed, I look around the otherwise surprisingly clean apartment, walking around the corner to the second living area. "Where's Max?"

"He's out."

"*Out?* In the middle of the night?"

"Yeah... he needed some fresh air. Come here," he says, his arms open wide. "I don't understand, Coles. Why'd she have a C-section? The baby isn't due until September." His voice sounds funny.

Callen isn't the most emotional person, and it hurts to hear him upset; to feel him struggle to breathe normally.

"She woke up Jon telling him she couldn't calm down. It was her blood pressure again. Just out of control, apparently. And they tried to treat her, but they couldn't."

"Holy shit." He squeezes me tighter. "Holy shit," he repeats. "She lost the baby?"

"No."

"Well, that's something, right?"

"Yeah," I say, trying to smile through tears.

"How is Jon?"

"I don't know. We need to go to the hospital. We're supposed to meet him there. Can you call Max and get him home?"

"He, uh... he'll be home soon. Why don't I get you a car so you can get down there? When Max gets home, we'll meet you. Okay?"

"Just call him, Callen," I urge him.

"He doesn't have his phone on him, Coley."

"Why not? I'm not allowed to take a cab by myself, and Max is out walking the streets at four-thirty in the morning with no way for anyone to get in touch with him? That's crazy."

"It's not that, okay? I'm just trying to shield you from the truth... let's just leave it at that."

"Are you guys okay?"

"We're perfectly fine. He's close by... as soon as you leave, I'll get him here. Trust me. But he'd want to be alone to hear this, okay? Just trust me."

"You're acting weird," I tell him.

"I know." He frowns and shakes his head. "I'm sorry. Let's get you a car so you can get to the hospital."

"I've got the card for the service here. I'll call and wait with Luis downstairs. Promise me you're right behind me?" I plead with him.

"I promise you." He hugs me again and kisses my cheek. "I'll be there soon."

"Okay."

I'm halfway down the elevator as I replay what he said in my mind. *I'll be there soon.* Not *we*. But *I*.

What the hell is going on with Max?

CHAPTER 20

CALLEN

*A*fter showing Coley out, I go to the windows on the other side of the loft, grabbing the keys that sit on the leather stool that I use as a nightstand. I touch the glass to estimate the temperature outside. Deciding I don't need a jacket, I head out of the loft, down the hall, past the elevator and out the locked door that leads to the rooftop terrace.

Having gotten used to the heavy metal door at the top of the stairway, I open it quietly and shut it behind me. Max lies on one of the loungers with his headphones on. I'm sure the volume's up so loud, he wouldn't have heard me had I banged the door on the brick wall behind it, as most people do who aren't used to its weight or the lofty winds that often blow at this elevation.

He exhales a puff of smoke as I approach and greets me with a moderately startled, "Hey." I know he didn't expect to see me up here. The agreement was that I didn't want to be an accomplice to him smoking weed, and this was the compromise we'd come up with.

I take one of the teak chairs from the outdoor dining set and pull it next to him, sitting down with my elbows on my knees and leaning into him. He pauses the music on his phone. "Put that out, okay?" I nod to his joint.

He starts to dab it out in the ashtray between us, with the obvious intent of saving it for later. Frustrated, I grab it and toss it in the waterfall to my right.

Max and I had both agreed that this form of self-medicating wasn't hurting anyone. That it wasn't something he could get addicted to. I could even appreciate his reasons for doing it—sometimes for pain relief, but tonight, it was another nightmare. Right now, though, I hate that I let him continue doing it when we'd told everyone he quit. Tonight, I have a sinking feeling it's going to cause a shitload of problems for both of us, and—while he's the one guilty of smoking the weed—I feel responsible.

My boyfriend takes his headphones off and looks over at me out of the corners of his eyes. I know he's annoyed, but he also knows how many concessions I've made for him to continue doing this. How many lies I've told on his behalf.

Shrugging his shoulders, he smiles that charming smile that makes me forget any feelings of frustration or anger. "C'mon, why'd you do that?"

I huff, wanting to be light-hearted with him. To carry on easy banter. To let Max be Max so I can laugh all night and not have to face what's ahead of me later. I look up at the sky—beyond the sky... *is there a heaven?* I haven't been religious since high school, but right now, I wonder if there's any truth to what we learned in our religion classes, or to what was lectured to me in church on Sundays. Because if there is a heaven, there's a good chance Livvy's up there right now watching this. She's disappointed in Max for smoking this shit. She's mad at me for not stopping him.

I look down to face him, noticing the blur in my eyes brought on by heavy tears that aren't brave enough to drop yet.

"Cal, it's not that big a deal," Max says.

"You're about to hate yourself in ways you never have," I mutter to him. I know him. I know his conscience. It's worse than my own.

"What do you mean?"

"This... this... this weed shit, Max. I wish we'd kept up with therapy or found another solution. I just wish I'd kept my promise to your brothers... to Liv... especially to Liv." I look up again, and this time, the tears fall.

"What they don't know..." He's not looking at me now. He's trying to be cocky, but already, I can tell he feels guilty.

"But they're going to know, babe. Jon? Will? They're gonna know."

He turns abruptly. "Why?"

I hold his hand in mine and caress it sweetly, rubbing his palm with my thumb. "We need to go to the hospital." I nod my head, looking directly into his glassy eyes.

"What? Are they randomly drug testing me now? I don't think so—"

"This isn't about you, okay?" I interrupt louder; stern.

"Okay." He sits up slowly and swivels his feet toward me, setting them flat on the rooftop. "What's up, Cal? Are you okay?"

Instinctively, we reach for each other's remaining hand at the same time. This small gesture makes us both smile.

I start to speak but swallow my words. Then sigh. Then shake my head as he waits in anticipation. I have no idea how to deliver this news to him. I've never had to tell anyone such a thing.

"Your nephew came early," I start, deciding to ease my way into it, feeling immediately like a coward when I see his smile grow—when I realize he thinks this is good news.

"Which one?"

"Jon and Livvy's."

"Is he okay? He's way early..."

"I think so... I guess. He was when I got the news from Coley."

"Okay, good. Then we can go see him later in the morning. I can sleep this off," he says, shrugging everything away like it's not a big deal. "Don't worry about it."

"Livvy isn't," I continue softly.

He doesn't breathe for a few seconds as he tries to process what I said. "Livvy isn't *what*? Okay?"

"No."

"What's wrong with her?"

I look away from him and try my damnedest not to allow any more tears to break free. I have to be strong for him.

"Oh, fuck, Cal. What?" I nod my head subtly, hoping that's enough of a response. He stands up and shoves me in the chest—not hard, but enough to snap me out of my bleary haze of avoidance. "Yes, what?"

"She's gone, Max. She died in surgery."

"Fuck," he says, his voice wavering as he paces in front of the chairs. "No fucking way." He looks at the rooftop, watching his bare feet as he walks back and forth. His rubs his injured shoulder, his trademark move of frustration. It replaced the pulling of his hair, which I'd hated–the one I'd seen all of the Scott brothers do so many times we'd make jokes about it. "No way, Callen."

"Coley was just here–"

"No fucking way, Callen!" he yells at the top of his lungs, ceasing his pacing and putting his hands on his knees as he shouts at me. He turns around and walks to the edge of the building, placing his palms flat against the wall. My heartrate quickens. I hate this. He knows this. He swore he'd quit doing this.

"Stop, Max," I tell him, walking to him quickly and wrapping my arms around him to pull him back. "I'm sorry. It's the worst news, I know."

"What next?" He turns into me and cries on my shoulder briefly, then pushes me away. "Who the fuck are you gonna take next?! Huh?" he shouts to the sky above us.

"Don't ask those questions." I'm not a superstitious person, but it does feel like a lot of shit has happened recently.

"He takes Mom, just over a year ago," he starts recounting, as if I need a reminder. "Coley's dad is fucking *murdered* protecting the president. Fuck, Isaiah just died earlier this year! And now... why her?" The expression on his face and the pause that follows his question leads me to believe he expects a response.

"I–I don't know. I just don't know."

"She's the best thing that happened to our family. Do you know how fucking different my life would be today if she and Jon had never met? If they hadn't fallen in love?" I don't respond, but rather listen to hear more. "I would never have met Trey, and I would never have known you.

"And holy fuck, Callen, what is my brother gonna do without her? She's been his whole life for 20 years! And the girls... and the baby? Fuck this world!" he shouts again.

"Max..."

"I mean it. Fuck any world that takes someone like her... in the prime of her life. I can't... I can't make sense of this shit anymore."

Even though he's pushed me away multiple times, I approach him again and embrace him tightly, hating his words and wanting so badly to fix everything that's been off with him lately. "Max, I love you more than anything *in this world*. Nothing is ever going to change that. You know I'd do anything for you. Please don't say things like this, okay? It hurts me. It worries me. It fucking scares me."

"I'm fine," he mutters.

"You're not. I know you're not, but I will do whatever I have to do to get you there. Do you understand me?" I back away just enough to look into his eyes. The sadness I never used to see when we were younger swells deep within them.

He puts his hands behind my neck and pulls my head to his, kissing me slowly. I relax into him, happy that he's taken the initiative this time. With his mood lately, I feel like I've been constantly making the first move to be romantic, sexual, flirtatious, whatever. I understand, though, and take whatever I can get from him. "Thank you," he whispers when we part, still holding me close.

I kiss him once more. "I'm so grateful for Livvy, because I can't imagine not knowing you, Max... or... what my life would be like had you not been in it." I get choked up. "She played such an important role in all of our lives."

"We need to go," he says, making his way to the door.

"Yeah. You need to change clothes, though," I tell him. "Your shirt smells. And maybe put in some eye drops or something."

"That's not gonna do much." I know this but want to try anything and everything we can. I follow him down the stairs, watching his leisurely footfalls.

"How high are you?"

He nods his head. "I don't know, the news of someone dying sure puts the smack down on ya, but I still feel kind of distant. Foggy. Like this might all be a dream or nightmare or something."

I open the door to the apartment for him. "I wish I could tell you it was. Will a shower make you feel any better? I think maybe you should–"

"No," he says, stripping out of the jogging pants he'd been wearing. "Not at this point. It'd probably enhance it. I'll be fine."

"We'll just lay low," I add, going to the closet and finding a pair of jeans and a black V-neck tee for him. "Hoodie?"

"Just grab my Long Beach cap." I find it, as well as my UCLA one. "You think Jon needs anything?"

"Uhhh..." I shake my head. "No idea, man. I think just our support right now. He'll need lots of stuff in the coming days and weeks. We'll do whatever we can to help. Don't worry about it."

"Your trips?" he asks.

"I'll reschedule. My dad will understand. Ready?"

"Yeah." He grabs a box of tissues on the way out and weaves his fingers through mine as we walk down the hall.

CHAPTER 21

MAX

A crowd of journalists and paparazzi has gathered around the hospital entrance and are shouting questions at Callen and me as we make our way inside. Even high, this stresses me the fuck out.

"Is it true that Livvy Holland passed away last night?" I hear one of them ask.

"Livvy *Scott!*" is my response.

"Are you confirming the rumor?" she follows up.

"We have no comment," Callen says, but he stops walking. I take a few more steps away from the crowd before I round the corner and wait for him, but I can still hear him talking. "We're just walking in, but I'll tell you one thing: if two little girls come walking up and you yell out that question, your career will be over. Do you understand?"

"We heard Edie and Willow are already inside," someone else pipes up.

I go back to confront the assholes myself. "So, they could be within earshot? Then shut your fucking mouths, you dicks."

"All right," Callen says, putting his hands on my waist and directing me back around the corner. "That'll do."

"The nerve of those fuckfaces. What if they did ask that question when the girls came? Holy shit, Callen." I try to turn back, but he stops me.

"Stop trying to be a hero." *Hero.* That's what they all think of me, and what did I just call them? "Remember, we're trying to lay low."

"Right." I nod my head in agreement, rubbing my shoulder. "You don't think they'll, like, quote me in the papers or anything, do you?"

"Not sure they can print 'shut your fucking mouths, you dicks' in their papers, but it's a question we can ask Trey, as our resident journalist and lawyer-in-training." I snicker, but my mood is quickly sobered when I see Nolan standing by the elevator we're walking toward. He's with a uniformed officer, and they're both waving us forward.

"Hey, guys," he says, reaching out to give us both hugs. "You okay?"

"As well as we can be, right?" Callen answers. "You?"

"Hanging in there. You're going to go up to the seventh floor. Check in with the woman at the front desk. She'll take you to another room where everyone is."

"You're not coming?" I ask him.

"I'm waiting for other people to show up. Jen and Stevie went to tell the grandparents, so they'll start filing in soon."

"Do you need anything?" Callen asks.

"No, I'm good. And I've got backup," he says, motioning to the officer next to him.

"Is the baby still okay?" I'm grateful Callen's here and mindful, because he's asking all the questions I should be asking.

He nods. "Last I heard, nothing had changed. Jon's been with him most of the night."

"Good," I say as the elevator doors open. "We'll see you later, I'm sure."

"Yeah. Give Jon a big hug from me."

"We will," Callen assures him.

I exhale heavily in the elevator, still feeling cloudy, but now wired, too—like, suddenly highly attuned to everything around me. Once we exit onto the seventh floor, a woman sees us and immediately escapes from behind the desk to greet us by name.

"Max, Callen, I am so sorry for your loss," she says softly, whisking us away from the main waiting room and down a hallway.

"Thank you," my boyfriend says. I wasn't sure of the appropriate response. In truth, I never have known what the appropriate response is to that. "*Yeah, it sucks,*" is always how I want to respond.

"The family is in here," she says, standing outside of a door simply marked PRIVATE WAITING AREA.

"My brother?" I ask.

"He's been in and out. The NICU has needed him."

"Is something wrong?"

"No," she says, holding my forearm tightly and smiling. If she knew that her attempt to be empathetic actually caused me pain, she wouldn't do it; I look down at her hand, though, realizing just how high I am because I don't feel any physical pain at all. "I believe the baby is doing well."

"Cool." I nod my head, staring at the door in front of me. "I mean, do we knock?"

"You're family. They're expecting you."

"Okay, yeah. Thanks." I turn the knob, pulling a door that's much heavier than I expected it to be. It was also more soundproof than I was aware, because once we enter the room, it's an assault on my senses. I feel tension and sadness and there's a cacophony of cries coming from all four corners of the room. I take a step back, only to be impeded by Callen's more muscular stature. I'm sure the pot is fucking with my hearing right now, or at least the way I'm processing sound. In any other instance, I'd turn around and leave.

"Go on," he encourages me, his hand on my hip.

Livvy's aunt, Anna, is the first to notice us.

"Max," she says, her face tear-streaked as she approaches me.

"Hi, Anna." I want to curl up into a ball right now, but her arms are welcoming me into a hug. I embrace her and try to calm my frayed nerves. "You okay?" *What a fucked-up question...*

"It's hard," she barely manages to respond. I nod and step aside so she can hug Callen, and I pray that he can manage the small talk. I want none of it.

My ears tune in to both of my nieces crying: steady, quiet wails. I know each of their sad, distinct voices. Edie's is a little higher-pitched than Willow's. Finally feeling brave enough to look around the room, I see my middle brother holding his goddaughter, and Shea, rubbing her back and talking to her soothingly. Jack is on the couch against the wall in front of a window, with Edie curled up in his lap. They're both inconsolable. It's about the saddest thing I've ever seen. Coley's sitting next to Jack on the edge of the couch, her arm across his shoulders, trying to be of comfort. Trey is squatting in front of them, trying to talk to our niece.

Emi's standing by herself in the corner, looking out the window. I can see the pain in her reflection. Feeling compelled to say something to her, or to join her in her solitude, I start to walk over to her, but Anna stops me.

"Not right now, Max." I turn around and look at her, confused. "She's praying."

"Oh." Callen pulls my back into his chest as he leans against a wall and wraps his arms around me. In this moment, I feel grounded and safe, but still overrun with the emotions of everyone in this room. It's odd that no one else has even acknowledged us, but it seems as if the girls just found out about their mother, and I don't want to ruin this moment.

"You okay?" he whispers in my ear.

I shrug my shoulder. I glance over at Jack again and feel immense loss. I've never seen a man so sad—not in movies or on TV, and especially not in real life. It's rare that I imagine a life where I have kids, but I allow my mind to wander there now. Then I take it 90 steps further, and consider a life where I've raised a child, watched *her* grow up, have a successful career, fall in love, get married, have children... and die. I feel my chest cave in on itself, and I cry, feeling more empathy than I knew I was capable of feeling. Maybe it's the pot. Maybe I'm maturing. Maybe I'm some freaky empath. Whatever it is, it's an unbearable loss, and I understand why Jack is the saddest man I've ever seen.

The door makes a tiniest click as it opens, and I seem to be the only person who hears it. I glance over to see Jon enter the room; he looks like he's fifteen years older than he was the last time I saw him just a few days ago.

My jaw drops as I read the shock and devastation on his face when he sees me. "I'm so glad you're here, Mascot," he tells me, walking toward me. I fall into him every bit as much as he falls into me.

Both of the girls cry for their daddy, and they run over to hug him, waist-high. He doesn't let go of me, but instead tries to compose himself with a few deep breaths. I imagine him trying to be strong for them, like he was strong for me and Will when our mother died last year.

When we separate, the look on his face has changed completely. I struggle to make sense of it. *Confusion? Betrayal? Anger?*

"Go home, Max," he says tersely, and loud enough for everyone in the room to hear–and to make them go silent.

I shake my head. "No, Jon. I want to be here for you... for the girls."

"One thing!" he yells at me. Instinctively, I jump back as he points in my face. "She asked one thing of you–in all of her life." It dawns on me what he's talking about. What he's angry about. I guess he smelled the pot on me somewhere. Maybe in my hair, I don't know.

"I won't go," I tell him, defiant.

"Not around my girls, Max! Go!" he shouts again.

"Jon–" Emi pleads from behind me. Callen takes my hand in his.

"Don't," Jon warns his mother-in-law, less forcefully than he spoke to me. He stares hard at me for a few seconds, then shifts his attention to Callen. "Are you, too?" He pulls my partner in front of him by his shirt.

"No," he tells my brother. Jon looks him over, accepting his response as the truth, and nods. Putting my hand on Jon's shoulder, I try to diffuse the situation; to be supportive.

"Get the hell out of here, Max!" He's not even focusing on me anymore. His eyes are steady on Callen's. "I can't even stand to look at you right now."

Callen steps in between us, a defensive posture to protect me from my brother's obvious aggression. I feel like absolute shit. "I'm sorry," I cry softly, looking first at Jon, and then around the room to see if everyone else is watching me. Disappointment from Will and Trey. Confusion from Jack, Emi, Shea and Coley. And the girls? Their father has now scared them by yelling at me, and they're huddled with Jack. I'm not sure if they're scared of him or of me.

"I'll take him," Callen speaks clearly. "I messed up. I'm sorry."

"Yeah," Jon says, his response clipped.

My boyfriend puts his arm around me and starts to lead me out of the room, but I don't want to leave him and everyone else in the room that I love. "Jon! Don't do this!" I sob, poised to get down on my knees to beg if I have to. "I need to be here."

I hear Jack say something behind me. "I'm not sure what's going on."

"Don't worry about it, Dad," Trey answers.

"Daddy, don't!" Willow chokes out, running up to me and holding onto my leg. Will swoops in and picks her up, taking her across the room.

Jon looks at me severely, but my other brother appears to have a little more sympathy. "Go home," Will tells me. "Callen, please?"

And with that, there's no more arguing. No question what we'll do.

"Come on," Callen says, his grasp around my back tight as he walks me to the door. "Will, I'll call you."

"That's fine," he says. "Thanks."

As soon as we're out of the room, I struggle free of him. "*My* side!" I holler. "You're always supposed to be on *my* side!"

"I am, babe. Come on. Let's not make a scene here. We can fight at home."

"My brother needs me," I plead with him, crying. "I can't go home."

"You can't stay here. Not like this. I should have never let you leave home the second I got a whiff of your hair. I should have known he'd react like this."

"No! You shouldn't have! These are extenuating circumstances, wouldn't you say?"

"You know what, Max?" he says, pulling me into a family bathroom and squaring off. "I think Jon calls the shots this morning. Period." He locks the door to make sure we're alone.

"Even if it's not what's best for him?"

"He thinks it is what's best for him—and probably, more importantly, for his daughters. That was Liv's big hang up, too... being high around the girls. This shouldn't surprise you."

"Well, it does, because his wife is dead. My sister-in-law is dead, and how am I supposed to grieve... huh? I need family, too. Fuck him!"

"You're talking shit again. You need to sleep this off, babe. Just... get it all out. Get your... I don't know... balance back. You're all over the map tonight, and I don't know if it's a bad batch of weed, or Livvy dying, or your general malaise, or a combination of all of it, but we need to get control over what we can. Sober up and we come back later today. That's all he's asking."

I sigh and kick the wall, hurting my toes in the process.

"This is temporary, Max." He puts his hands on either side of my jaw. "And I'm your family, too. Let's go home and go to bed. We'll get up after we've slept and start fresh, okay?"

"And you'll tell me this is all a fucking nightmare, right?"

"I'll tell you that I'm going to help you through everything. The pain.

The grief. The nightmares. The boredom. The need to escape. The feeling that you have no real purpose in life. I'm going to step up, babe. I don't want you to feel lost anymore."

For the second time tonight, he's said exactly what I needed to hear, and I feel the need to thank him appropriately. I pull his head to mine and kiss him firmly; quickly. "I need you, Callen." I wrap my arms around him and hold him close.

"I know," he whispers.

"Like I have never needed anyone in my life. I need your help."

CHAPTER 22

JON

My head resting against the hard plastic that covers my newborn baby's body, I watch him rest peacefully. I like to think the hand I have gently pressed against him is providing some warmth–doing some bit of good–but he's been doing well on his own. I know how much he's going to need me, and already I feel unable to provide for him in ways that his mother would.

More tears drip onto the surface that divides me from my son, and I wipe them away quickly with my sleeve. It's hard not to reflect on the last three hours, because it seems like a lifetime of events have occurred within that time. And in a way, I guess they have.

It was just three hours ago that I was sitting in this very room, in this very chair, when I looked up at the nurses, hoping to get nods of approval or some other emotional support for the first few minutes I'd spent with the baby. I'd never been in a NICU before. It was scary, seeing him hooked up to so many monitors and watching so many displays of readings that I didn't understand. Medicine is one field that I never studied. I just wanted a bit of encouragement from the other women in the room with me.

They were all in shock, though, and experiencing obvious sadness. At first, I thought they must be watching something on a TV–*another terrorist attack? Mass shooting?* But when I turned around, I saw Emi peering through the glass at me, her posture deflated and a look of despair such that I've never seen on another person's face before. My stomach fell as I slowly rose from the stool, and she couldn't contain her tears. I shook my head at her, not understanding what she was saying—and yet knowing *exactly* what she'd come to tell me.

After making sure someone was watching after my son, I hurried into the hallway and took the hand that my mother-in-law offered me. She squeezed me so tightly it caused actual pain. I didn't need the words that came from the doctor who had joined her, but he was the one who ultimately delivered the news. Jack showed up a few moments later, unable to look me in the eye; unable to look up at all.

Livvy died just after surgery, Dr. Irving had said. My precious, beautiful, young, healthy, love-of-my-life Olivia had died.

When I brought her here tonight, I hadn't considered it a possibility. Even from the time she woke me up, I never sensed the urgency. I offered to rub her neck. To get the blood pressure monitor. She needed the *hospital*. I was just wasting precious seconds with every fucking question I asked her.

Did she know?

Her final words haunt me now. I'd told her Hollands were fighters. She'd responded, "*I'm not.*" In all the years I'd known her, she was always a fighter, though. If she felt weak, why did she let the surgery happen? Why didn't she speak up? What if there were other options? We could have talked about them.

I choke out more audible tears in the NICU. One of the nurses brings a tissue and dabs at my eyes, since me doing so would require another disinfection. I'm not sure how long we can keep this up.

"Thank you," I tell her.

"You're doing really well," she says. "His vitals are stable. He's doing great."

"That's good." But when I try to smile, I cry again, knowing that I can't go to Livvy and bring her this good news. I can't tell her how well her baby boy is doing.

I think of her lying on a hard, cold table. I needed to see her, so the doctor took me to the room where they'd delivered my son. Jack was standing by the door, holding a handkerchief. His eyes were bloodshot. He wouldn't go in with me, but I found out after that he'd already gone in to say goodbye to his daughter. Emi accompanied me, still squeezing my hand. It was just the two of us with the doctor.

I pulled back a thin, white sheet that covered her face. "How could they cover her beautiful face?" I asked no one in particular; her mother, crying. She buried her head into my shoulder, unable to look. Livvy was pale. Her skin almost matched her mother's and brother's, a genetic improbability with her biological Italian heritage. Her natural tone was olive-colored. She passed it along to Edie, and I think to our son.

I ran my fingers through her dark, thick locks, and a million memories came flooding in of the times I had done it before. When I dropped the tresses, they still bounced against her cheek, as if they still contained life. As if she was still alive. But that cheek had no color. I'd never seen it pallid like it was in that room. I'd brushed my thumb across it to make sure it was real.

"Did she even see the baby?" I asked the doctor without taking my eyes off of my wife.

"No."

I let go of Emi to find her daughter's hand, gripping it tightly in both of mine. I leaned down close to her and cried, the tears dripping on her angelic face. "He's beautiful," I whispered to her, kissing her temple. "Perfect. He's a fighter. A Holland. A Scott." I felt Emi's hand on my shoulder. "He's part of you, baby. So much of you. Every bit of you. I can see it already. And he's going to be okay. I'll make sure of it. I promise you that.

"You did good, Olivia. You did so *much* good. And *I love you* so much."

I struggled to get air to my lungs. "How could you leave me?" I tucked my head into the pillow, next to hers. "How could you leave me, baby?" I sobbed until the pillow was soaked with my tears; her hair, too. I sobbed until I felt I had no tears left—which was a temporary feeling, I'd learn a few seconds later. I pulled back and caressed her face. I found her lips with mine and kissed her for the last time, so heart-broken that the kiss wasn't returned. I was devastated. I fell into my mother-in-law, who could barely hold me. The doctor helped to support me.

A few minutes later, when I was able to stand on my own, I turned back to Livvy, took her hand one more time, and promised I'd take good care of our son and our two daughters. I kissed her hand... and I walked out.

I walked past the doctor, past Emi, past Jack, and directly into the small room to de-sanitize, where a nurse was waiting to help me prepare to see my son again. I'd needed to be alone to take in the news.

I got fifteen minutes of relative privacy before a different nurse came over to do some tests on the baby. She also told me that Emi was out in the hall, wanting to talk to me once more. I'd already been thinking about Edie and Willow. I knew telling them was going to be her first concern, and it was.

"Matty's on his way to your place to get the girls," she told me. "I think we should tell them together."

"Right. Right." It was all I had to say. I didn't know what I was going to tell my daughters. Those perfect words hadn't come to me yet, and the truth was too terrible to utter to an eight- and nine-year-old. "But... how?"

"I don't know," she cried.

"How is he getting them here?"

"He's just telling them that she went into early labor. We've been letting him know how the baby is... to make sure he's..."

"Still alive?" I asked, shaking my head. "This is awful."

"I know, Jon. We'll get through it together, sweetie. I promise you that."

"I think she knew she was dying, Em," I told her. "Before she went in, I was trying to encourage her. I reminded her about Trey being a preemie... I told her Hollands are fighters, right?" Emi nodded, following along. "And Liv responded, 'I'm not.'" I looked at her, confused, and scratched my head. "Did I push her? Pressure her?"

"No," Emi said as she pulled me into a hug. "The doctor told me he wouldn't have done the surgery so readily if he thought she couldn't handle it. He said she was okay during the surgery. It all happened after."

"But I think she had some premonition. Some feeling about it."

"You can't think like that, Jon. Not now. It will eat you up. She could have said no."

"She wouldn't have—not if it was a choice between her and the baby," I told her mother. Wracked with guilt, I'd made an admission. "I don't know if I would have made the same choice. I love her so much. I don't want to go on without her. I've loved her for more than half of my life. I've never imagined a world without her in it. I need her to raise our children. I need her to grow old with me."

"I don't think it was your decision to make. Or Liv's. There was a greater plan–"

"I don't believe that shit, Em!" I shook my head vehemently. "No decent god steals a mother from her two daughters. From a baby boy who needs his mother's milk, for Christ's sake! I can't compensate for that! How does a father fill those shoes? Huh?"

Crying, she'd turned to walk away from me. I'd offended her. I'd offended the one person I needed most.

"Mom?" I called out to her. I hadn't called her that since my own mother passed away last year, but it was time I'd accepted her in the role she rightly played in my life and had for twenty years. She turned around, wiping her eyes. "I'm sorry. I'm really sorry."

"It's okay," she'd said, coming back for a tight embrace. "Your son is going to be just fine, Jon. Trust me. And the girls, too. We're all going to help you. That's what families are for, and we are your family. Okay?"

"I know," I'd said, clinging to her.

"Let's go get ready for the girls."

The girls. *My girls.*

*T*he tears stream from my eyes steadily as I remember their reactions. I'm sure, in my lifetime, it's a moment I will never forget, though I will want to every single second.

I'd made a stop to splash cold water on my face, a failed attempt to even out my blotchy skin tone from the crying. I'd hoped to start off neutral, and not in the valley of despair where I'd found myself after hearing the news. There was no way I could look neutral; nor could Emi or Jack.

As soon as the girls stepped into the room with Matty and Trey, they knew something wasn't right. Both carried stuffed animals, though. New ones, from the gift shop.

As Trey went to comfort his parents, Matty cleared his throat. "They insisted on getting something downstairs for their baby brother." He nodded, and his eyes started to water they moment they met mine. I started crying as he hugged me, and Jack, Emi and Trey were enveloped in their own circle of tears.

"Daddy, what's wrong?" Willow asked softly. I fell to my knees and held my arms out for my young daughters, unable to tell them. They rushed me. Hugged me. Cried with me without knowing what or who they were mourning.

"What's wrong?" Edie repeated. "Memi? Granddaddy?"

None of us were prepared. Or maybe we just weren't brave enough. I took a few deep breaths before I released them from my arms. I threaded their messy, silky strands of hair through my fingers, admiring how much they took after their mom—Edie especially.

"You got these for the baby?" I asked them, taking a teddy bear and a puppy from them, both of them blue. They nodded. "He'll love these... but why don't you two hold onto them for now?"

"Why are you crying, Daddy?" my youngest asked again.

"Girls," I started. "Mama wasn't feeling well when we came in tonight. She, uh..."

"No!" Edie shouted. A high-pitched squeal erupted from the back of Willow's throat, evolving into full-scale crying. I pulled them both back into me and held them tight, but they both fought against me.

"Girls, please," I begged them. "She did fine during the delivery," I tried to tell them, hoping they were listening, "but as they were finishing the operation she had to have, she had a... heart problem."

Willow finally squirmed away. "Like Pop did?"

I nodded. "Kind of."

"Mama's not okay, is she?" Edie asked.

She already knew. She slipped away from me and ran to Jack, who was crying behind me. I looked into Willow's little green eyes and shook my head, delivering the answer to her. "No. She's not okay. Your mama didn't... survive. She's gone, baby." I reached out to hold my youngest, but she turned and ran toward the door. Matty tried to grab her, but she eluded him. It was lucky timing that Will and Shea showed up right then. She ran right into my brother's arms and sobbed into his shoulder.

He looked like hell; they cried together, and I was glad they had one another. Happy that they'd forged such a strong bond, because there was no way I was going to be able to do this on my own. I stood up and looked around, completely broken. I felt completely alone as I watched my daughters being comforted by other men in my family—other men who hadn't just delivered to them the worst news of their young lives. Other men who hadn't allowed their mother to go into that delivery room in the first place when she'd obviously had misgivings about it.

I'm not. My mind will always remember her scared voice uttering those last words to me. *Were they her last words?* Did she say anything more after they took her from me?

Shea wiped her face, which had grabbed my attention. We approached one another, searching the other's eyes for answers. But I didn't know how to get through the next hour without Livvy, much less the next day, or the next sixty years. I didn't know how I was going to raise my son on my own. That wasn't the deal. I could see Shea thinking the same thing as she put her hand on her pregnant belly. We hugged each other. I suspected, in the end, I would be helping her as much as she would be helping me.

"How are you?" she asked me.

"I just want to rewind a few hours. Maybe a half a day. Analyze every second of what she did last night to figure out why she couldn't calm down. Was she reading a scary book? Did she get a threatening email? Was it just a bad dream? And why couldn't I help her? I'd helped her all the other times."

"I know, Jon."

"I should have been in that room with her. They wouldn't let me in there with her. But if I had been, I could have helped. Right?"

She shook her head. "It was worse than normal, Jon. This wasn't hypertension. She went into cardiac arrest."

"But why?"

"I don't know." She hugged me again. "I wish I knew."

I turned around and walked over to Edie, taking a seat next to Jack on the couch. I'd put my hand on her knee to get her attention, as her head was nuzzled in my father-in-law's neck. "Bunny?"

Instinctively, she reached out to me and climbed into my lap. I rubbed her back, trying to soothe her. "Daddy?" she asked, her voice muffled in my shirt.

"Yeah?"

"Did the baby die, too?"

I sighed into her hair, glad that not all the news I had to deliver was terrible. Willow must have heard her sister's question, because she'd quieted at that moment. I looked up to see her staring back at me, waiting for my response.

"No, Edie. He's okay."

"That's stupid!" Willow shouted angrily, kicking to be let down. Matty backed against the door, ready to keep her from escaping. My brother couldn't hold onto her. I stared at her, confused by her outburst. She walked right up to me. "*He* should have died. *Not Mama!*"

"Wils, no," I'd pled with her, reaching for her, but she moved as far away from me as she could. Edie squirmed off of my lap and joined her. "Girls."

"He killed her," Edie cried. "She'd still be here if it wasn't for him, right, Daddy?" Willow grabbed her hand, and they stood by themselves against the far wall, trying desperately to understand what was going on.

I opened my mouth to speak, but I didn't want to lie. I just didn't know.

"Girls," Emi said, kneeling down with her arms open. "Come here."

"No! I want Mama back!" Edie called out.

"I hate that baby! I don't want him here!" Willow added, and my heart broke. *I* broke.

As the girls both began crying in fits of hysteria, fueled by one another, I felt helpless and overwhelmed and it was so fucking loud and I wanted Livvy back as much as they did, but I'd already fallen in love with my son, and I was crushed that this is how he was welcomed into the world. I faltered as I stood back up, but when I did, I only had the energy to stare at the devastating scene in front of me. My brother eventually broke them up and took Willow back into his arms. Matty hugged Edie, and the two of them joined Jack.

I met Emi's eyes. She looked just as shattered as I did when she backed into the other corner of the room. Trey joined her, putting his arm around her when she turned away from me to face the window. Unable to stand the noise anymore, I walked out of the room and back down the hall to find solace in the NICU. They were running some tests on the baby, and I suddenly felt lost and out of place.

I turned around and went into the first door available to me, a family bathroom. I locked the door and cried some more, trying to figure out how to handle my girls. *Were their feelings temporary? Would they always resent their brother?* Feeling like I had to go back and say something to them, I returned to the room.

Any words of wisdom failed me when I smelled pot on Max. My emotions raw, I ripped into him, scared my daughters in the process, and left the room once more, knowing I'd need a plan next time I returned. I'd hoped the plan would come to me after spending a little more time with the baby, who seemed ready for another visit when I slipped back down the hall.

*M*y son begins to move against my hand. I sit up and watch his arms move, a stretch of sorts. I want to hold him so badly. I look up to ask a question of one of the nurses, and they're all watching me.

"Is it okay if I put my other hand in? Put it on the other side of his body?"

"Of course," one of them says. As she approaches me, I purposefully make note of her name: Katie. "Just be gentle. Did he wake up?"

"Yeah." I smile as he squints his eyes open again. "How is he?" I nod to the machine displaying his vitals.

"Really good." She puts her hand on my shoulder. "How are you?"

"I keep thinking it's the worst day of my life," I admit to her, "but then I see him, and I know that can't be true. He's going to save me." I choke on my tears again. "She lives on in him, and I have to be grateful for that gift. I'll have to remember that every time I'm sad. He has no idea how important he is to me right now. All my kids, for that matter. She's not really gone when I see her talent in Edie. Her strength in Willow. It just kills me that he'll never know her. How wonderful she was."

"But we all know. Everyone... in the city, in the country... in the world," she says with a wistful laugh. "He'll know all about her, Mr. Scott. She was so special to so many people. People like Livvy Holland aren't forgotten."

"*Scott*," I say with a huff. "It's Livvy *Scott*." I smile at her, letting her know her slip-up was okay.

She shrugs. "I grew up wanting to be Livvy *Holland*," she admits. "I don't know any little girl who didn't."

"And I grew up wanting to be *with* her." I exhale deeply. "I don't know how a person moves on from that. She was my soulmate. If there's something beyond that, she was it for me. I did everything to get her, and to keep her. I just can't believe I've lost her."

"I'm so sorry," Katie says, grabbing another tissue to wipe my eyes.

"When can I hold him? Like, really hold him?"

She looks at the machines again, then at the other nurses. One of them nods to her.

"Let's roll the incubator over here," she says, putting her hand on my back to signal for me to go with her. We move behind a makeshift curtain in a corner of the room where a reclining chair is set up. "You sit there."

"Yeah?"

"Yes. He needs to stay warm, so you need to take off your shirt. I'm going to place him on your chest."

"Okay. You're sure he's okay for this?"

"His vitals are great, Mr. Scott. He'll stay connected to his breathing and feeding tubes, see?" she says, holding him up as I settle into the chair.

I nod, anxious to feel the weight of his tiny body on mine. He's so small that his weight is hardly noticeable when she sets him on my chest.

"Just hold him upright. Here's a blanket to cover you both."

"Oh, wow," I say, keeping one palm firmly on his back while the other hand feels his legs and feet and toes and arms and hands and fingers and the little patch of dark hair on his head. His eyes stay open for about 30 seconds; after that, he's asleep. His breathing is quick, but steady, undoubtedly helped with the machine. But he is calm.

And I am calm.

"You're doing so well already," I whisper to him. "I have to think of a name for you, kid. Your mom and I were supposed to do that together. But... I honestly don't think we'd ever agree on one, so I had one in mind for you before we got here tonight. I'd never told her. I was ready to discuss it. Debate it. Fight for it. But now that I know you, I don't think it suits you.

"And more than that, I want you to have a part of your mom with you all the time. I want to name you after her."

As I hold him against my skin in the privacy of that small corner of the room, I go over the night again, and her last words echo in my head. *Hollands are fighters*, I'd said. *I'm not*, she'd told me.

I will forever wonder what she meant by that, but she gave me the perfect name for our son in that one puzzling response.

"You know who you are, little guy?" I ask, lightly running my thumb on his scalp. "Luca Paxton." I smile at the sound of that, but then think I can do one better. "Luca Paxton *Augustus* Scott. Because Mama loved that damn name. Welcome to the world, son."

For thirty minutes, they let me hold him. For a half hour, I feel at peace. I know he's going to be the one thing that gets me through this.

"Katie?" I ask the nurse as I pull my shirt back on and watch her check his diaper. "Do you think I can bring Jack and Emi in?"

"Sure," she says.

"Thanks."

CHAPTER 4

CHAPTER 23

EMI

She's not alone. It's the only thought that brings me any comfort this morning. I watch the street below as traffic starts to pick up with the sunrise. A crowd of reporters and photographers lines the sidewalk at the main entrance. I can see people approaching with flowers, too, but I've yet to figure out where they're leaving them. *Are they for Livvy?*

Has the news gotten out already?

Ignoring the countless text alerts, missed calls and voicemails on my phone, I opt instead to bravely check one of the tabloid sites that has notoriously followed my daughter around for years. Her picture is the only one featured on their home page under a large headline: *UNVERIFIED: Livvy Holland Scott DEAD.*

My phone slips out of my hand and crashes to the floor. I cover my face as I weep with shaking hands, trying to hide the sorrow from my granddaughters. Trey's presence next to me is obvious before he even speaks or puts an arm around my shoulders. "It cracked," he says.

"I don't care."

"I know. I just don't want you to cut yourself."

I shake my head. "Throw it away." I wipe my eyes and catch a glimpse of the page again as he examines the phone.

"Oh, Mom." His strong arms bring me into his chest and hold me tightly. "Why'd you do that?"

"Look out there." He leans toward the glass and glances down.

"That pile of flowers?"

"Is there one?"

"You can't see it?" I shake my head again. His height gives him better visibility of the street directly below us. "Hundreds of bouquets."

"Do you think they're for her?"

"Yeah, Mom. After seeing this? Yeah. I do." My son has been so strong all night, but I can tell he's fighting off tears right now. "I'll hold onto your phone, okay?" he says, changing the subject.

"Thanks." The room gets silent all of a sudden, only to be broken by Willow crying out for her daddy. I look up and see that Jon has finally returned. He picks up his youngest daughter and kisses her cheek.

"Where were you?" she asks him.

"I was with your brother."

"I don't like hi–"

"Wils," he says seriously, "that talk stops right now. Edie?"

She looks up at him, her head laying on a pillow in Jack's lap as he strokes her hair. "Yes, Daddy?"

"That goes for you, too. We'll have many more conversations about this, but right now, I want you both to come with me."

"Okay," she says, climbing off the couch and taking the hand Jon offers her.

"Jack? Emi? I, um..." He pauses and sniffles. "I want you to meet Luca." He nods his head, and my heart falters when I hear the name. "The NICU said you can both go in."

"Luca?" I ask.

"Yep," he responds with a smile. "Luca Paxton Augustus Scott."

I start crying again, and Jack collects me in the corner. He puts his arms around me and smiles, his eyes still wet. They haven't been dry since we got the news tonight, but I haven't seen him smile in hours.

"I love it," he tells Jon. "It's a beautiful name."

"She named him... in a way..." he responds.

"I want to see him," I state, filled with a sudden burst of hope.

"Daddy, I don't want to," Willow whines.

"You're just going to look through the glass. Anyone else want to come?"

"I have to see him," Shea says, and Will nods.

"I can't wait to meet him," Coley agrees.

Matty, Anna and Trey all gather around, and Jon leads us out of the room together.

It's easy to spot Luca–he's all by himself in the big room, with the full attention of three nurses. "That's him," I point to the only baby there, showing Jack his grandson. He laughs at my obvious observation and takes my hand.

"I think he's grown since we last saw him," he teases.

"Maybe he has," I say, shrugging. Coley and Shea are both cooing at the sight of him. I realize in that moment they're... they're the only 'daughters' I have anymore. It doesn't matter that Will isn't our son. We've considered him that for many years, just as we have Jon and Max. And we don't need vows exchanged for Coley to be a part of this family. She has been for some time now.

Every single second, a new revelation hits me about how our lives have changed. Every single second, the night moves on into daylight, but gets sadder and sadder as time goes on. Right now, the sadness is mixed with sweetness, as our daughter's tiny baby sleeps just on the other side of the glass.

A nurse taps on it, getting my attention. She points at the door to our left, and Jon steps aside, telling us to go in and wash up.

"We get to actually go in with him?" I ask.

"Yeah," he says. "I think he'll... I don't know. I think he'll bring you some peace."

"*Paxton,*" Jack comments to Jon as he walks by.

"Coincidence?" my son-in-law asks. "Destiny? We may never know."

Jack and I have to scrub with hot water before we're allowed into the larger room with the baby. *Luca.* From DeLuca. Livvy's birth surname. I appreciate Jon's desire to name him after Liv, but I don't like it. I don't like it because of what he told me earlier.

My daughter was a Holland up until the moment she took her last breath. She'll always be a Holland. Or *he* would argue that she's a Scott. But a DeLuca? We removed that name from her, legally, when she turned four. It wasn't until she was an adult, after she met Isaiah, that she started identifying with it again. And that was fine... but to name our grandson that?

Isaiah. I look up to the heavens and pause.

"Poppet?" Jack says, snapping me out of my thoughts. "Go ahead."

They've moved his bed closer to the glass so everyone else can have a better look at our new family member. He's even tinier up close, especially when they tell us we can slip our hands through the side holes and we compare the size of our fingers with his.

"He's so delicate," I say. "Was Trey like this?"

"Yes, Em," Jack says, laughing again. "Have you lost all the memories from that time?"

"I just... it was so difficult," I remember. "I think I wanted to forget a lot of that time spent in the NICU. I remember when we brought him home. I remember knowing he was okay."

"Those were the better memories," he admits, but his voice sounds even farther away as he feels the soft skin of Luca's legs with his thumb. "Just look at him. What a wonder..."

"I hope he does amazing things with his life, Jacks." I start crying again and wipe my face on my shoulder. "For everything she sacrificed."

"I hope he's healthy. I hope she's watching over him now." His voice cracks. "Tessa, we've got him from here."

"Oh, Jacks," I sob. We both let go of Luca and hold onto one another. "She should be here."

"I know, Poppet. I know."

"Mr. and Mrs. Holland?" one of the nurses says. "We want to keep the environment calm and stable in here for him. Maybe it's best if you both come back a little later?"

"I think that *would* be best," I say, looking back into the incubator. "We'll be back, sweetie."

Jon and Matty are the only ones left in the hallway when we come out. "I'm sorry," our son-in-law apologizes quickly.

"Oh, no, no..."

"He's beautiful," Jack adds. "It's just so hard."

"I know." He hugs us both.

"Nolan's downstairs," Matty says. "I... I think I should make a statement or something. The rumors are out there."

"This isn't their business," Jack says, frustrated and so much more emotional than I've ever seen my husband.

"No, it's a private, family matter," his brother agrees, "but Jacks, you have to know, she was loved by this entire city, state. She was loved around the world. And people in this hospital have obviously talked to people on the outside. My phone's blowing up with friends asking me questions. I... I don't want to repeat the words a million times; I'll be honest with you. It hurts too much."

"He's right," I say. "She meant so much to this city. Trey says there are hundreds of bouquets outside... probably for her. Let's make a statement. Just short and sweet and get it out there and over with. And we'll ask for privacy. I had too many texts and calls to go through, and I don't want to deal with them, either."

"All of your parents know," Matty follows up. "Your siblings, nieces, nephews... Finn and Katrina are trying to get a flight up."

"I need someone to call Ariana and Kora in Brazil," Jon says. "I don't want them to find out from a press conference." He hands Matty his phone after unlocking it.

"Anna can handle that," he assures him. "Should I write something for us to say?"

"No," I tell him. "You don't need to do it. Jack and I will go out there."

"I don't know, Em," my husband says. "I don't feel like I have anything to say."

"Jacks, you've always been the one to speak to the press and ask for privacy. They listen to you."

"I'm a wreck."

"Of course, you are. You think people won't *expect* that? *Forgive* that? They need to *see* that to respect our time and our ability to grieve in peace." He nods. "Is this okay, Jon?"

"Yeah," he says. "Thank you."

"Of course." I hug him. "Can we... announce the baby?"

"As long as it's clear we need people to give us all space. And I want security at the NICU 24/7, although I don't plan to leave here."

"Well, you can't stay here forever," Matty reasons with him.

"Someone needs to be with him. It would be Livvy if she were here... well, she's not. So... I need you guys to watch the girls while I do what needs to be done here."

"We'll do anything," Jack assures him, "but you'll need breaks. And we'll gladly cover for you then. Matty, I want you to call the private security company and get a guard scheduled, full-time."

"I can do that."

"Let's go back to the room and try to freshen up," I suggest. "Maybe Trey can let you borrow his shirt." I remember my son wore a pressed, blue button-down, which looks nicer than the clothes we threw on in the dark of night when we were summoned here for the joyous birth of our first grandson. That seems like *days* ago.

*T*rey accompanies his father, uncle and me outside, standing to my left on the top step just outside the side entrance of New York Central Hospital. He looks even more youthful in the Columbia University t-shirt he'd had on under the button-down. I'm used to seeing him in dressier clothes, now that he's busy volunteering at the law center on his break from Harvard.

The crowd silences as we stand in front of them, something that never happens. *Where are the shouted questions? Why aren't they yelling about the latest rumors?* Our family hasn't been respected by the press in years. But today is different.

Matty clears his throat. "My brother, Jack Holland, and his wife, Emi, would like to make a statement. There won't be any follow-up questions this morning, but you can expect more news from the family in the coming days. I'll let Jack take it from here."

I watch Jack as Matty nods in his direction. His shoulders slump, and the corners of his lips are heavy as they begin to quiver. Composure has always been one of Jack's best qualities, but I'm watching him fall apart beside me.

"Tonight, at around 12:30 this morning, our daughter, Olivia Sophia Holland Scott, was brought to New York Central in a state of distress. Doctors decided..." His voice is shaking. "To deliver... the baby." He chokes out a sob, and the reporters, paparazzi and citizens of New York who have gathered react in one of many ways. Some gasp, undoubtedly at Jack's emotions. Some stare in stunned silence, mouths agape. And others cry with Jack, not even knowing for certain the news we're about to confirm.

My husband looks at me for only two seconds, shaking his head before turning and going into the double doors behind us.

"I'll handle it," Matty says, following him quickly.

"Mom, I can take over," Trey says.

"No," I say to him, grabbing his hand in mine and holding on. I take a deep breath and look into the faces of the crowd. Another slow breath is required, but I continue for Jack. "Luca Paxton Augustus Scott was born at 1:05 a.m. and weighs four pounds two ounces. He is currently being doted on by multiple nurses in the NICU, but Jon, Jacks and I have all been able to go in and see him. He's very handsome, and they say he's doing well, even though he was born early."

In the silence that follows as I wait to build up the courage to continue, someone asks the obvious question. "What about Livvy?"

"Yeah, could she go in and see him?" another person adds.

Two tears drip down my cheeks and I squeeze my son's hand tightly. "No," I say softly as I exhale, shaking my head. I swallow, then speak. "Livvy never recovered from the surgery."

There are audible reactions of shock from the people who stand in front of me. Wails of sadness. Exclamations of 'oh my god!' Things I've heard over and over all morning from the people who loved her and knew her best. But she touched so many lives.

"After the delivery, something happened to her heart, and the doctors couldn't save her," I say, surprised that I was able to get it out in one breath. I remember her lifeless body lying on the table, and then break down. "She's gone. I'm sorry."

As Trey and I embrace, the rest of the crowd reacts. Echoes of collective sorrow. It's a haunting—yet comforting—sound, and at the same time, I know I never, *ever* want to hear it again.

"We'd like to ask for privacy while we deal with the loss of our sister, daughter, mother, and friend, and the birth of this beautiful new family member," Trey says, looking back into the crowd. I'd forgotten that part. "Thank you."

"How is Jon?!" Someone shouts.

"Do Edie and Willow know?"

"Are the girls here?"

The questions continue as we escape into the building. A guard stands at the doors to make sure we aren't followed by anyone not needing assistance from the hospital.

"I love you, Mom," Trey says, hugging me close. When we separate, we both look to his father; my husband. "Did Dad drive here?" my son asks.

"Yeah," I answer him.

"Let me and Coley take you two home."

"What about the girls?" Jack asks.

I pull him to the side, away from everyone else so I can speak to him in private. "You know, Jacks, I know they just lost their mom, but we just lost our daughter. We can try to start being grandparents of the year tomorrow, but right now, about the only thing I think I can do is lie in your arms and recount every precious memory we ever had with her, so there's no threat of losing a single one of them."

"What if it hurts too bad?" he asks.

"It will hurt more if we forget her. Your parents are at our place. Let them take care of us today. Tomorrow, we figure out how we move on from this." Reluctantly, he agrees to let Trey take us home.

"Matty?" our son says. "Can you drive the Rover to your place? I'll pick it up when I swing by to check on Max later."

"You're gonna handle that?"

"I'll take care of it." Trey nods and hands his uncle the key to his car. We all get back into the elevator, and I wrap my arms around Jack, who's inconsolable at this point. I wish I had the words to help, but I never thought I'd have to mend his broken heart. I'm not prepared for this.

He stays in the hallway, careful to hide his emotions from his grand-daughters, as Trey and I let Jon know we're going home for a little bit.

"I'll be back soon. Whenever you need me," I tell him.

"We'll be here with them, Emi. Don't worry," Shea says.

"Don't hesitate to call, though," I continue. "We just need a little time to let this sink in. Alone."

"I understand," Jon says. "We've lost so much tonight." I hug him tightly and kiss his cheek. "I love you. Tell Jack... tell him I did everything I knew to do." Tears drip down his cheeks.

"He knows, honey. We love you, Jon," I tell him. I kiss the girls and tell everyone else goodbye before following Trey and Coley out of the room.

"Let's go," I say to Jack.

"I don't want to leave her," he says, shaking his head and glancing down the hallway toward the operating rooms. "I don't want her to be alone."

"Dad," Trey says, then hesitates. He exchanges a look with his fiancée. Coley links her elbow with his and leans into him. "She's... Dad, she's not there... anymore... you know?" I'm sure he's speaking *spiritually*, but I'm also certain that her body has been moved to another part of the building by now. The thought of her being in a cold, sterile morgue makes me want to find her and take her to a more comfortable place, but I know we can't now... and I also know there will soon come a time when we, as a family, will be charged with making those arrangements. This is why we need to go home. We will need to help Jon, and someone has to be better prepared, mentally, to make decisions. He will be in no shape for it.

"Jacks, she's up there watching over Luca right now," I say, trying to assure him that she is in a better place—and, more importantly, if he's also having visions of her in that morgue, to get his mind off of that. "She's making sure her girls are okay. She's giving Jon the strength to get through this night, and morning... she's not alone."

The focused look down the hall becomes a vacant stare in my husband's eyes. Coley releases Trey to take Jack's other hand, and we guide him to the elevator that will take us to the parking garage.

*J*ack's parents are at our brownstone when we get there. The aroma of French vanilla coffee greets us when we come in through the back door, but there's little comfort in our own home when we're met with the sorrowful grief in their eyes and their tearful hugs. It stirs up the loss and pain again, feelings that had just begun to settle like the bubbles in a freshly poured soda. I feel shaken up again as they begin to ask questions, especially as I watch Jack completely shut down.

"Sharon, Jack, let me take Jacks upstairs," I tell them.

"I'll explain things," Trey says as he takes a seat on the couch next to Jack's mother. "Coley and I can hang around for a bit."

"Stay," I say, urging my son to not leave. "Please." I look at Coley. "It's early. You probably haven't had much sleep at all. You two can take the other guest room. Just stay here. Just today, please? Don't go," I plead, my eyes welling up with tears. "I want my family together."

"It's okay, Mom," Trey says. "We won't go anywhere for a while. I need to see Max later, but... I'd rather be here with you two right now."

I kiss the top of his head, then do the same to Coley. "Thank you."

Jack walks like a zombie up the steps to our third-floor suite. I think he would have just stood in the doorway had I not walked him over to the bed and urged him to sit.

"Can I get you something?" I ask him.

The faraway look hasn't left his eyes, and he doesn't bother to look my way when he finally speaks, even though I'm standing right next to him. "I wish I were Isaiah," he says softly. I gasp at his admission, putting my hand over my mouth. He reaches out, his palm up, and I place that hand in his, listening to him. "It's selfish, but I'm jealous. He doesn't have to know this pain." He pulls both of our hands to his heart, bringing me closer to him. I sit with my body touching his on the bed. "It's unbearable. No father should have to deal with this sort of pain."

I know this pain. No parent should have to deal with it, but we have to. It's our reality... and we have other children and grandchildren who will keep us going. I find relief in that.

"Honey, listen." When I'm not sure he is listening, I angle myself toward him and tap his leg to prompt him to face me. He finally does, and I get a brief second of eye contact, too. His blue eyes have never looked so sad. "Think of it this way." I speak softly, now holding both of his hands in mine. "How lucky is our daughter to be able to grow up with us... to spend her life with us... and then be welcomed into the next one with another set of parents who love her unconditionally, so she's not alone and she'll never be alone? And we don't ever have to worry about that. We never have to worry about her." Jack sighs as tears fall. "And she'll never have to worry about her children not being taken care of because Jon's still here and we're here. We get to see her children grow up. We still get that. We know she's safe and loved where she is now.

"Maybe this is how it was always supposed to be. As painful as it is for us, maybe this is all the time we were ever supposed to get with her. What a wonderful life we had with her!"

"No, Em," Jack says, crying.

I nod, though, trying to be convincing with my theory even though I'm weeping, too. "Maybe it's Isaiah and Simone's turn now." I release his hand briefly to wipe my eyes and nose. "Jacks, we did such a good job. We raised such a beautiful and talented woman. And she raised amazing daughters. She gave us a grandson. What a life we have, Jack! But don't wish yours away.

"It hurts. It hurts so bad. We have so much to live for: Trey and Coley. They're going to have kids someday, too. Edie and Willow, and now Luca. Jon's going to need us. He has nobody. He's our son. All of the boys.

They're our family. We brought them into our lives, and they're always going to be a part of it. We love them."

He nods his head, and as much as I know he agrees, nothing and no one can take the place of our precious Livvy. We both recognize this.

"We always knew our life was too perfect. We always knew a day like this would come; we just didn't know what it would be. And this is one of the worst things that could happen to us.

"But Livvy has another family up there. And that brings me peace."

He searches my eyes with such sadness and despair but releases my hands quickly to pull me into him. He cries hard on my shoulder. "I know," he says.

"I hope it brings you peace, too... eventually."

"Me, too."

"You know," I begin, running out of optimism, consoling words *and* energy. "If I can just make it until midnight tonight, I'll know I can make it through the worst day of my life. And if I can do that, I think I can get through just about anything."

He pulls away from me and kisses me softly on the lips. "We'll do it together."

"Thank you."

CHAPTER 24

PART III - JON

While I'm struggling to keep my eyes open, I see two familiar faces peering through the glass of the NICU. Knowing my hands are bringing warmth to Luca's small body as he sleeps against my chest, I'm reluctant to wave at my daughters, but the looks of pure joy on their faces change my mind quickly. I open my eyes wide, smile, and attempt to match their enthusiasm without waking my son.

I haven't seen my girls in 36 hours and my heart aches to be with them now, when I know how badly they need me. Jack and Emi finally appear behind them, looking worn out and ready to hand over Edie and Willow to anyone who will take them. It's not fair for me to ask my in-laws to watch my daughters now, when they're still coming to terms with grief that's so insurmountable, fresh and raw.

I'm grateful Matty and Nolan have agreed to take them home after I visit with them for a bit.

"Jon?" Katie speaks softly. "Time's up. Looks like he's sound asleep. I bet he'll get in another few hours of good rest in the crib." She points to the incubator. I hate that he has to stay in there. Nothing about it says comfort or home. I want nothing more than to get him out of the hospital and into... well, into some place that's welcoming. I haven't been to the apartment in four and a half days; not since that night. Neither have the girls.

Will has been kind enough to supply me with the things I need, not that I've asked for much. What's to need when you feel as if you've lost everything?

I kiss Luca on the head and hand him over to the nurse, who walks him to the bed by the window where my family waits. Jack and Emi admire him adoringly. The girls move to the door, waiting for me to meet them in the hallway. After buttoning up my shirt, I hurry out to give them both big hugs and kisses.

"Daddy, when are we going home?" my youngest asks as I kneel down so I'm not towering over her.

"Soon, Wils," I say to her, not knowing if there's any truth to my answer. "Look how pretty you both look."

"You stink, Daddy," Edie informs me.

I imagine I do. In two days, the only real washing I've done is in the sink at the NICU, before I get to see Luca. In the times they take him to do testing and diagnostics, I've been jogging up and down the stairs of the hospital to keep my mind occupied. Not a great mix for stellar hygiene.

"Sorry, bunny," I tell her, feeling a blush come across my face. "I haven't found a shower here."

"There's one at home."

"Very astute of you," I mumble sarcastically, exhausted. "How are my girls doing?"

"We miss you," Willow says, enveloping me in a hug. "I don't care if you stink."

"I miss you, too."

"Then why do you spend all your time with him?"

"Honey, I've told you... he has nobody here but me."

"Jon," Emi says, "we've told you we'll relieve you. We'd love some time with Luca."

"I just feel like he needs to know me. Like, these first few days or weeks are precious for bonding or something. The nurses say his vitals are better when I'm with him. I want to get him out of here, so the more time−"

Jack puts his arm around my shoulder and walks me down the hall, away from the girls. "A few hours," he says. "A good night's sleep. Even taking a break to have dinner with your daughters. That would mean the world to them, and Luca will be fine. You'll pick up where you left off. Emi had a tough time leaving Jackson when she was released from the hospital and he had to stay, but she had much more energy for him after she'd gotten rest at home."

"It's different," I say argumentatively. *Everything's* different now.

He frowns, but nods. "What about tomorrow?"

I look beyond him, not wanting to think about tomorrow. "I'll be ready. Of course, I want to be there for Edie and Willow. As much as I never wanted to go to Liv's funeral, I'll be there to... to say goodbye. Somehow." I wipe away the tears that fall. "I just hate that Luca won't be there. I just want us to all be together. In the same room." I scratch my head, knowing what I'm saying makes little sense. "Just once. And after tomorrow..."

"She's in Heaven," Jack says to me. I stare at him hard, hoping he's right.

"Is that what the girls think?"

"Yes," he responds. "I know your faith is different than ours, but–"

"No, Jack, I want them to think that. It's... a comforting thought. I want there to be a Heaven, I do. And if there is, I know she's there."

"She's there."

His assurance brings more tears to my eyes, and he embraces me. He's holding up much better than he was the last time I saw him, and I begin to hope that I, too, may begin to feel strength soon, or at least the will to get on with my normal life. The only things keeping me here so far are my kids. Without them, I wouldn't want to be here.

"Son, you need a shower." He says this just before he pats me on the back twice and releases me.

"Luca doesn't seem to mind."

"Luca can't speak yet," he says with a smile in his eyes.

"I'll bathe before the funeral. Don't worry."

"Maybe a shave, too," he suggests.

"Now you're pushing it." I feel the stubble on my chin and cheeks. This is about the length that began to drive Livvy nuts–and *not* in a good way. It was rare that I ever went four days without shaving, but the few times I did, she'd let me know by not returning my kisses, or by approaching me with the razor and threatening to do the job herself.

I let out a huge breath, realizing those moments are gone.

"She hated it like this," I admit tearfully. He looks at me with sorrow.

"Every fucking hour, Jack, it's something different." I look back at my daughters, still far enough away to not demand payment for my curse word. "Every hour, I realize the divergent path my life just unwittingly fell upon... and I hate it."

"I know. Emi and I are going through the same thing."

"I'm sure you are." I swallow and try to compose myself. "It wasn't like this with my mom. I thought that was loss, but... *this?*"

"Your relationship with Margie was always complicated. You can't compare the two. You love people in your life in different ways, and I know you gave Liv everything, Jon. That's why it feels like you've lost so much."

"Jacks? Em?" Matty says from behind me. Willow and Edie run down the hall to greet their uncles. "You're officially off-duty. Go home and rest, please."

Jack looks at me, uncertain. "Go," I urge him. "Or ogle your grandson for a bit, and then go home. I'll go have a snack with the girls in the cafeteria before the guys take them."

Emi puts her hand on my back. "I think we *will* go ogle Luca. I've missed him." I thank them both for watching my daughters and tell them goodbye, taking from them a pink duffle that they'd brought along.

"You girls want to go get some ice cream in the café?" I ask, looking at my daughters, and then at Nolan and Matty.

All four of them answer in the affirmative, and I drag my leaden body toward the elevator to take us to the first floor. Apparently sensing my exhaustion, Nolan takes the bag from me.

The girls both seem happy to be having dessert before their dinner, even if it is at a dingy hospital table. They seem less affected than I expected them to be, but I know it's good for them to have some distractions. Tomorrow will be difficult for them; tomorrow will be the day when they have to deal with the loss of their mother head on. The permanence of the situation will begin to set in at that point, I'm sure.

Tonight, it's nice to see them smiling, to hear them chatting about the time they spent with Livvy's parents. They watched a marathon of Harry Potter movies, and their imaginations are still soaring from the fictional world they'd lived in all afternoon.

"Do we need to do anything tonight for them?" Nolan asks me as Matty tells the girls a story about the first time he saw the films.

"They love getting their nails done. I know Liv was planning on taking them next weekend," I tell him, then swallow the lump of sadness that tries to settle in my throat. "Would you guys mind taking them? I want them to... I don't know..." I say, tugging on my hair. "I know Livvy would appreciate it."

He puts his hand on mine, bringing it down to the table to stop my nervous habit. "We'd love to. Maybe you should go to a barber?" he suggests.

"I don't have time for that." I shrug him off.

He looks at his watch. "I've got a stylist who could do it at his place right now. He's about fifteen blocks south. You'd be back within the hour."

"Nah, thanks, Nolan."

"What can we do for you?"

"You've already got the girls," I say, looking at him with confusion. "That's plenty."

"For *you*."

I think for about three seconds, then answer reflexively. "I want her back. The mother of my children. My wife. My best friend. Wake me up from this nightmare, Nolan. That's all I want."

"I wish I could, Jon," he says. "Edie and Wils are in good hands. We'll bring them in the morning, so you don't need to worry about a thing. Just meet us there... and if you think of anything we can do, let us know."

"Thanks." I push away the cup of ice cream I haven't even touched. "If they need anything, text me and I'll call right back. Doesn't matter what time."

"Daddy?" Edie interrupts.

"Yeah, bunny?"

"I need to get something from our house."

"What do you need?"

"Some shoes."

"Memi got your dresses and shoes, right?" I ask. "I thought you went shopping."

"They're Mama's shoes."

I frown at her and shake my head. "That's been handled." I force a cough, an attempt to disguise the urge to cry at the thought of Shea and Coley picking out clothes for her. I didn't want them to touch a thing, and yet I knew someone needed to take care of tasks that I was completely unable to do. I knew my sisters-in-law would be respectful of Livvy's things and pick out something that she loved to wear.

They'd asked me if I had any preference. I didn't, because I wasn't certain I'd even be able to look upon her at the viewing. It wouldn't matter to me anyway because she looked beautiful—always. She was gorgeous the last time I saw her alive: her hair messy, her face clean of makeup, dressed in a comfortable t-shirt and cotton pants with an elastic waistband that adjusted to her growing belly.

"They're not for her. She said I could have a pair of her shoes."

"Sweetie, you can't fit into her shoes yet."

"Daddy..." She rolls her eyes and throws her hands up in frustration. I await her rebuttal patiently. "Remember the shoes she has with the ribbons that tied around her ankles?"

"The blue ones." I remember them well. She'd worn them to Trey's birthday party. I took them off her that night, her back too sore to bend over all the way to untie them. "I do."

"*Those* shoes. I want to take the ribbons from them and put them in our hair tomorrow." She looks at her little sister. "They'll look pretty with our dresses... and we'll have a little piece of Mama with us all day. Please?"

I smile at her eager expression. "Of course." I look at Matty with instructions. "The doorman will let you up... just you, though, okay? Not the girls."

"I can draw you a picture of the shoes, Uncle Matty," Edie adds.

"I can handle that."

"Thanks. Girls, your uncles are going to take you to that nail place tonight... pick something simple, but colorful, okay? Nothing too out there. Wils, I'm talking to you." I remember the time she came home with cat faces drawn on each of her fingernails.

"I'll pick a color for her," Edie assures me, and Willow surprisingly doesn't argue with the offer.

"Okay. Daddy needs to get back upstairs. Be good for your uncles. Go to bed when they tell you to, okay? And I don't want you going to Max and Callen's. Not tonight. Understood?"

"Got it," they say together.

"Jon, the guys feel awful," Nolan says.

"I've seen them," is all I say about it, still coming to terms with the situation. "I love you both." I hug my daughters for a long time, not wanting to let them go. "We'll go home soon. I promise," I whisper in their ears.

I get a kiss on each cheek before I release them. My soul's been lifted, if only for a few minutes.

That time with my girls was exactly what I needed.

*W*hen I get back to the NICU, one of the pediatricians meets me at the glass window. I've talked to her numerous times about Luca; every time she examines him, she has good news for me. I smile at the sight of her.

"Dr. Mayer, did I miss a checkup?"

"You did, but he's doing just fine. Thriving, even. We're about to remove the CPAP and go to the smaller nasal cannula that we talked about."

"Really?" Less machinery is *great* news.

"His breathing has improved so much. And tomorrow, we're going to try some formula... just a little. We'll keep the feeding tube in, but we need to start teaching him to eat on his own."

I nod, apprehensive. "Formula. Yeah."

"Jon, ignore any negative things you've heard about breast milk versus formula, okay? Don't consider Luca at a disadvantage because of this. He's off to a great start, and so much nourishment and development comes from the love you give him. He's got an abundance of that already. Like I said, he's thriving. Your involvement helps him along. Okay?"

"Okay." I smile, feeling a little better.

"I have more good news."

"Hit me."

"We got you a private room down the hall. A maternity suite. Well–paternity, for you."

"I don't want to take a room from a new mother."

"Jon, we have extras, and I insist. You need rest. Maybe your experience isn't like that of a new mom, but you've been through a lot the last few days, and you've been going non-stop. A warm shower and a comfortable bed will do wonders for you. They've even put some brand-new New York Central scrubs on the bed for you... clean clothes."

"That'll be nice. After my cuddle time with Luca–"

"Nope," she says, stopping my forward progress toward the door. "Now. We'll bring Luca to your room in half an hour. Can I show you the way?"

"I smell that bad, huh?"

"Ripe," she says kindly.

"I couldn't find my brother's deodorant at his place," I explain. "That was two days ago."

"I'll have someone pop down to the sundry and get you some. It will be on the dresser when you get out of the shower."

My cheeks burn hot as I follow her. "Thanks."

"We know you've had a million other things going on. And we're doctors. Please think nothing of it."

"Well, I would, but you *literally* won't let me see my son again unless I shower," I say with a chuckle.

"We all think you'll feel more refreshed. We deal with new mothers all the time. We know what works. Can't be so different with the dads, right?"

"You're the expert."

She walks into a room and holds the door for me. "Once Luca's in here, a nurse will check in hourly."

"Will he still be in the incubator?"

"Yes, but you'll have your skin time with him, just like in the NICU. The nurse will get everything set up with you. And there's a button on the bed that will call someone if you need assistance. There are cold drinks in the mini-fridge, too. If you want a coffee maker, I can make that happen."

"This is pretty nice. It's like a hotel."

"That's the idea."

I glance around. "When do I wear out my welcome?"

Her expression is warm. "Your daughters need you, too." She puts her hand on my forearm. "A few days. I think you'll know when it's time to go home."

"Yeah. You're probably right. Thanks for this."

*A*ll the bath products were selected with women in mind. While I'm showering, I can't help but think how much Livvy would have appreciated the lavender and tea scented soap I use to clean myself. It was her favorite aroma to use when she needed to relax. Being in the enclosed space with the scent of her concentrated around me summons tears to fall alongside the cleansing hot water from the faucet.

How can she not be right here, fresh from a bath? The fragrance is so familiar, I practically feel her presence as I look upon myself in the mirror, the bright lights bringing focus to the dark circles under my eyes. Is it exhaustion or sadness?

Both, I'm sure.

I hardly recognize my reflection, though. The facial hair. The puffy eyes. The red nose. The corners of my lips that are weighted to the ground. I can't even force a smile, my heart shattered, my body tired and my mind wondering how time can still tick on as if nothing has happened; as if she isn't gone, or that she never even existed at all.

"Where are you?" I ask quietly, but aloud, hoping in vain for some supernatural response from the only woman I ever loved. After a minute or two of silence, and no signs, I decide to put on the scrubs that were left for me and go back into the main room, making sure I apply the deodorant that's sitting on the counter.

Settling onto the bed, I turn on the TV as I wait for Luca, hoping for a suitable distraction from reality.

*W*hen I wake up, someone is in the room talking softly to my son, and it's dark, except for the light coming from the TV. I sit up quickly, trying to get my bearings and startling Katie with my sudden movements.

"What time is it?" I ask, wiping sleep away from my eyes.

"Fifteen until midnight," she answers. "You've been out for hours. I left the television on in case it was helping you sleep."

"I didn't..." I say, looking around, "I didn't mean to fall asleep. I was just waiting for him to come to the room."

"He's been in here since five. Right by your side. I've been checking on him hourly. He's doing great with the cannula."

"Can I hold him?"

"If you're up for it."

"Definitely," I assure her.

She comes over to the bed and presses a button, moving it to a seated position. "Want some more pillows? We can make it like an armchair."

"Uh, sure." I start to get up to help her, but she puts her hand up to stop me.

"Daddy can stay put. They told me to go easy on you."

I chuckle lightly. "Well, thank you. I'm a little thirsty, though."

"Water? Soda? Coffee?"

"Water's good."

She builds a fort around me with pillows, then brings me two bottles of water before carefully lifting my son out of his incubator. She holds him in her arms, facing me.

"Shirt off," she directs me.

"Right." I strip out of the scrub top and reach for Luca, feeling the chill of the room on my own bare skin and knowing he must be cold, too. Katie untucks a blanket from beneath my feet and pulls it up to my torso. "Thank you."

"I just changed him. I'll stop by in an hour, but he'll probably be fine like this for a couple, if you're good."

"I'm great," I tell her. "Don't you worry about us." I look at Luca's blue eyes, already blinking closed, and kiss the top of his head, cradling him into my chest.

Once the nurse leaves, I speak to him quietly, wanting him to know my voice and feel comforted by the sound of it. I talk to him about having ice cream with his sisters and I tell him his mother's favorite dessert. "She loved lemon cupcakes. Aunt Kelly makes the best ones. Any special occasion, man... she had to have her lemon cupcakes. And sometimes, the special occasion was simply having the cupcake." I smile when I remember *her* smile. "She was so funny, Luca. And *fun*." I feel heartsick at the realization that so many of our family's happiest moments were due to something she said or did; when I think that Luca won't get to experience these things. *Will there even be any happy moments anymore?*

What do I even bring to the table?

I have to search the depths of my memory, past all the thoughts of her, and go back to times with my brothers. We had a rough childhood, but I still managed to be the source of fun with Will and Max when we were younger. I'm sure I still do plenty of things that make people happy, but every time I try to remember anything more recent, I stumble upon another thought of Liv... one that makes me stop... one that gives me pause... one that brings me immense sadness in the middle of the night.

CHAPTER 25

*I*n the morning, after I've had my cuddle time with Luca, I continue to watch him with wonder as he sleeps in his incubator. I'm still tired, but the feel of the occasional wiggle of his tiny toes and fingers keeps me alert. I watch the clock, dreading the approaching hours and putting off leaving for as long as I can.

"Knock knock."

I turn around to see Will in the doorway with a backpack and a half-a-dozen helium balloons, announcing *It's a boy!*

"What are you doing here?" I ask him, not at all upset to see a friendly face.

"I," he says, tying the balloons to the end of the bed, "am relieving you."

"What?"

He sits down next to me on the bed and puts his arm around me. "I'm taking over for a bit. It's time, Jon."

"It's still early."

"No," he argues. "You only have two hours. Your suit's at my place. Shea's there with a hot meal and a new razor." He pats my cheek with his hand. "Go get cleaned up."

"I still have time. I'm not shaving."

"You are," he says. "Why? Because you love Livvy and she hates wooly Jon. Do this for her."

I swallow. "Hat*ed*."

My brother sighs and sets down his backpack. "Yeah," he says softly.

"I don't want to leave him. Just look at him."

"Is he gaining weight?"

I shake my head. "But it's normal. Or so they say. Tonight, I get to try and feed him. Formula."

"That's great, Jon."

"It'd be better if she were here."

"Hey," he says, serious, "he's going to get everything he needs—from you."

"I know. I know he'll be dependent on me in ways the girls never were, too." I sigh and start tugging at my hair. "I don't want him to wake up and... I don't know, like... miss me, you know?"

"He won't," Will assures me. "It's why I'm here." He pulls on my arm, bringing my hand out of the incubator. Palm to palm, he compares the nuances of our fingers. Our hands are the same size—his fingertips are just more calloused from his guitar playing. "At this point, he'll never know the difference."

"But he'll have skin-to-skin time in a few hours."

"So, I have a little more hair on my chest. It's soft—wanna feel?" He grabs my wrist, holding my hand in front of his left peck.

"No," I say, laughing. "I don't."

"I'll take care of him."

"So, wait. You're not going to the funeral?"

"I'll be there in spirit." I see his eyes tear up before he looks away from me. "I just can't fucking see her like that. I want to remember her like I knew her—full of life and love."

"Don't we all?"

"Yeah. But I have a good excuse to not go, anyway. You need someone to stay with Luca."

"Are you... sure? I mean, Willow would want you there."

He stands up and paces beside the bed. "I know. I've thought about it... but I can't. I wrote something, though. Damon, Peron and Bradley will be performing—just acoustic. It'll be..." He scratches his head and clears his throat. "I hope it honors her well." His voice is still affected by his tears.

"Come here," I say, standing up and giving him a hug. He cries on my shoulder. I know how much he admired Livvy. "I'm sure it will. And I know she'd love it and understand your absence. I'll tell Willow I asked you to stay with Luca. Maybe we can all meet up tonight."

"That sounds good," he says.

"Shea's going to stick with me today?"

"Absolutely, and I need *you* to stay close to *her*. She'll help with the girls, if needed, but right now, she's there to help you get ready. She also expects me to know how to change a diaper by the time I leave here."

"The nurses normally do it, but I'm sure they'll make an exception. Let me get one in here so they know what's going on." I push the button, and Katie appears a few seconds later. "Do you know my brother, Will?"

"Not personally," she says, blushing, "but I love your work."

"My research?" he asks, knowing that's not what she's referring to. She looks confused. "My music. Got it," he says with a flirtatious smile. Being married to Shea didn't remove his ability to charm women; fortunately, he was more devoted to his wife than nearly any man I knew, and she had full trust in him and their relationship. She was the match I'd always wanted for my brother. "Thanks."

"Katie," she says, her hand reaching out.

"Will. Nice to meet you."

"Katie, Will's going to be staying with Luca while I'm at the... service." She gives me an empathetic frown but nods her head in understanding.

"Oh! I need to get him an ID bracelet. I'll do that. Are you leaving now, Jon?"

"I guess so... yeah." I look back down at my son, who's still sound asleep. "Katie, do you have any scissors?"

"I could get some."

"I want a lock of his hair... for her."

"Ohhh," she exhales, putting her hand over her heart. "I'll be right back."

After she exits, Will gives me another hug. "I love you," he tells me.

"You, too."

"I'm gonna do everything I can to help you out, man. You were always there for me, teaching me shit growing up... it's time for me to step up."

"Shut up," I tell him. "You've made me so proud and paid me back tenfold in seeing this remarkable man who's standing in front of me today. You owe me nothing."

"But... I want to be there for you and your kids. Shea does, too. I mean it, whatever you need. She's already been making you a bunch of food. Stuff you can freeze and unfreeze or whatever. You should be set for a month—and then she'll have the restaurant make more."

"That's helpful, for when I go back... there." I look him in the eyes. "How the fuck can I go back there?" I whisper. "I built our dream home. *Her* dream home."

"And your girls love it," he reminds me. "It's still your home. We just start making new memories to add to the old ones."

"But her studio... on the third floor."

"And yours," he adds. "You have a corner. Shea and I went up there the other day. Everything is just as you both left it."

"You went up there?"

He nods his head. "Shea took me up there to, uh... tell me the news away from Edie and Wils. Safe to say I won't be going back up anytime soon. But... I don't know, someday, you can make it into something for the kids. It's not something you need to worry about now, though."

I bite the inside of my cheek in thought but am interrupted when Katie comes back into the room. "I should probably do it," she says, showing me the blunt-tipped scissors.

"Maybe from around the nape of his neck, where it's longer," I suggest, watching over her.

"This much?" she says, pulling together a small tuft.

I see Livvy in the curve of Luca's lashes. A subtle detail that confuses my heart.

"Jon?" the nurse asks.

"Oh, yes. That's fine." She hands me the soft, ultra-fine, dark strands of his hair and a plastic bag. "Thank you."

"One more thing," Will says, grabbing his backpack. "Can you hold him?" He looks at Katie for her permission. "Can he hold him? Just for a second?" He pulls out an instant camera—one that Matty got Willow for her birthday, in fact.

I can't contain my emotions as the nurse readies my son for our first official picture together, and it's not one we'll keep, either.

"Try to smile for her," my brother says. "Remember how much you love her. Think about how much you love Luca."

"Yeah," I say, smiling through the tears as he takes two photos of us.

He hands me the undeveloped film. "One for Liv—this can go with the picture Shea's set aside of you and the girls from Father's Day. And one for the baby book."

"We don't even have one yet," I say, carefully handing Luca back to the nurse.

"Yes, you do. Shea bought it for her—it was one of her shower gifts. Liv had told her exactly which one she wanted. She's been filling shit in already. So, give one picture to Shea. Okay?"

"Will do." I hug him once more. "Katie, show him how to wash up and stuff, will ya?"

"Of course."

"And he wants to change all the diapers."

"I don't—"

"He'll be a new dad in a few weeks. So please," I insist, interrupting Will's trepidation.

"Happily," she says to him. "And I think he needs one now."

"Great," my brother says. "Jon?" He stops me as I walk toward the door. "I'll treat him like he's my own. Please don't worry about a thing."

"I won't," I tell him. "I truly appreciate you doing this."

CHAPTER 26

*A*fter the service, family and friends share memories of Livvy in the pews behind me while I stand next to her casket, holding one of many roses placed on top of it in my hand. After I leave here... I don't want to think about that. We'll have ashes of her, and although that's what we had both agreed upon, it seems so final and morbid in reality, rather than theory.

I look at the picture of her, beautifully displayed on a simple easel three feet away. *I just want to hold you again. Just one more time.* One tear turns into many. *Fuck that. Not one more time, Liv. I want our lifetime back.*

Always. Everywhere. Like our vows, and like the song Will wrote for her. I open up the program and read the lyrics of *Affection*. I'd only listened to the song as Damon sung it and am happy to have all the words here to reflect upon now.

> *We met her as a gust of wind*
> *taking us by surprise,*
> *taking our breath away,*
> *taking some by the hand to lead them out of darkness.*

Guarded, safe, in her sole possession,
Our affection was hers—to handle with care.
I cannot deny, in this final confession,
That I am affected; always, everywhere.

We knew her as a force of nature
wanting to know the world,
wanting to express herself,
wanting to share her love with only the lucky among us.

Guarded, safe, in her sole possession,
Our affection was hers—to handle with care.
I cannot deny, in this final confession,
That I am affected; always, everywhere.

We saw her as a shooting star
leaving many in wonderment,
leaving questions unanswered,
leaving this planet long before we were ready to let her go.

She was meant for this world in ways we will never understand.

Guarded, safe, in her sole possession,
Our affection was hers—to handle with care.
I cannot deny, in this final confession,
That I am affected; always, everywhere.

"*And* somehow, Will makes a better showing than I do and he's not even here," someone next to me mutters. I glance to the side to see my youngest brother standing there, flapping the end of his tie against the casket. "Fuck that guy," he continues in jest. The sight of him today brings calm and comfort, and oddly enough, a little humor. I laugh at his opening lines to me.

"We're in a church, Max," I remind him, still chuckling, but wiping away tears with a handkerchief.

He had come up to the hospital once since I kicked him out on the day she died, but a pane of glass separated us, and I made no effort to talk to him. I was still too angry at him then.

"What does Coley say?" he asks.

"All words are created equal in God's eyes," I respond with the beginning of a quote Trey's fiancée often rattled off, still smiling.

"Except around children and the Hollands," we both say together. Falling into an embrace, we laugh together, but before we let go, I can tell my little brother has started crying.

"It's okay, Mascot," I whisper softly, holding him tighter.

"I'm so fucking sorry, Jon. I should have been there for you. I should have been better for her. I know I fucked up."

"Max?" I push him away to look into his eyes. "We're all going to have to live with regrets of what we should have done differently, okay?" He nods, tears streaming down his face. "Some of them will have us wondering for the rest of our lives if we could have saved her. And others?" I point into his chest. "Others are just changes you can make going forward. Be better *now*. Be the person she wanted you to be. Be the man she thought you were when we decided you'd be one of Luca's godparents."

"I will. I am," he says. "I'll stop lying." He stares hard at me and nods his head. "I shouldn't have been lying to you. It's not who I am. I want to live up to every idea she had of me. I am where I am and who I am because she came into our lives, Jon. I recognize this. I owe it to her."

"No. You owe it to yourself. You never owed her anything. I mean, me, maybe, but her?"

Max smiles. "That's probably true."

"You don't owe me anything, either. But I want you to be well, Max. I don't want you to follow in the footsteps of your dad or of Mom—her bad habits. I want what's best for you. That's all I've ever wanted, and I'll be on your ass to make sure you're working toward that. Got it?"

He nods.

"I love you, Mascot. I'm sorry I treated you the way I did."

"No, I deserved it. I've gone over that night in my head many times. Callen shouldn't have let me go in the first place—no, I should have known better than to go. I can't blame him. You were right to kick me out."

"Still. I don't like how it all went down. Life is too short. We should never part ways like that, you know?"

"Yeah." We hug one another again. "The service was perfect... but where's Will?"

"At the hospital with Luca."

"Doing things a godfather should be doing?" he asks.

"Nah, it's not like that. Let's just call it training to be a new dad. He needs it anyway... and he said he couldn't see her like this. You know how they were."

"Yeah. I don't think he ever really got over his crush."

I shake my head and smile. "Probably not. Who didn't love her, though?"

He turns around and encourages me to do the same. For the first time since I came in, I see the church, packed to capacity. People are lining the walls on the sides and in the back—and this was a private ceremony for friends and family, by invitation only. "Everyone did."

A woman approaches us and asks us to return to our seats in the front row. Apparently, all of these people want to give their condolences to us.

Over the next hour and a half, some sort of defense mechanism kicks in, making me numb to all the consoling looks and kind words so I don't spend the entire afternoon crying. It helps that the girls are restless and require my occasional attention. More than once, I consider leaving with them. It must be hard for them—confusing, even—dealing with the loss of their mother and the unfamiliarity of hundreds of strangers, wanting to share random stories with them.

After everyone else has left the chapel, we all discuss meeting back at our apartment for a meal. It's already been arranged by Shea and her restaurant staff. Apprehensive as I am, I realize it's the best way to ease back into the home I'd been afraid to go back to because she wouldn't be there anymore—with the family that loves us unconditionally and knows what's best for us.

I call Will before we leave and ask him to join us, knowing it's the time of day when Luca puts in a good four hours of sleep.

*a*s the limo turns onto our street, a hush comes over the car. Not only is our entire side of the block lined with flowers, but a crowd is gathered on the sidewalk. There must be hundreds of people, many with signs with Livvy's name and pictures.

"Daddy, look," Willow says. "More flowers."

Jack and Emi had told me their home had been inundated with visitors and gifts in the days following her death; still, I didn't expect this today.

At the entrance of our building, two security officers stand alert, keeping the path clear for residents. It's an obstacle course to get around the thousands of bouquets, though. The night doorman greets us at the curb, since Leon was in attendance at the funeral today. Jack and Emi get out first, followed by Edie, Willow and Shea. I'm the last to emerge, taking my time, not knowing if I'm ready to be in the public eye already. I can hear people gasp and sigh the second I step out. I can *feel* their pity.

I wave anyway, appreciating those that came to pay their respects, although I know many just came to gawk at me and my family. We take a few minutes to look at the flowers and cards left in the clearing of the entrance. Emi and Shea encourage my daughters to pick a few of their favorites to take inside. The question occurs to me: *What do I do with the rest of them? Is that my responsibility?*

Overwhelmed, I'm the first inside the building. Another attendant approaches me with a ridiculous display of flowers—it's completely over the top and inappropriate for the occasion.

"Mr. Scott, these came for you. I was directed to hand-deliver them to you."

"Thank you." I set them on the concierge counter and look at the card, wondering who would send such a gift. Someone who doesn't know our tastes, obviously.

Dear Jon—My most sincere condolences. The country has lost one of its most beautiful assets. It was such a great pleasure to have met her. Harris Gluck.

No mention of her cultural significance, or of the contributions she made to so many communities in her young life. He didn't bring up the fact that she was part of a movement that began the beautification of many older cities in our country. He had no idea of the great influence she had on millions of young artists across the globe.

He only mentioned her physical beauty. *It's so much like that misogynistic pig.* I'm grateful he didn't win the presidential election. I can remember the day he came to a grand opening of a new office space downtown for a building my company designed. We'd invited all the tenants and many of the top employers in the state—Gluck being one of them. I couldn't believe how he'd embraced Livvy as if they were familiar with one another, even though it was the first time they'd met. He even attempted to kiss her—on the lips—but being who she was, she put her shoulder between them and fought her way out of his grasp. *A fighter.* She proceeded to give me the evil eye for a good half hour. I probably should have done something to protect her better, but—honestly—I was in shock by the whole thing.

I crumple up the card and give it back to the man who handed me the outrageous display. "Please arrange to deliver these to the 181st Street Women's Shelter. No card, no signature. And for God's sake, don't let anyone know that Gluck had anything to do with it."

"Yes, sir."

"*Harris* Gluck?" Jack asks. I nod.

"He has some nerve," Emi adds.

"No shit," I say, then catch myself. "Sorry, girls. I owe you, okay? I don't have any cash on me."

"Daddy, who is Harris Gluck?" Willow asks as we get into the elevator.

"He was that clown that ran against Parker for president. The one that Coley and your uncles Max and Trey used to protest. Remember?"

She shrugs her shoulders. "Why didn't you like the flowers?"

"Because I don't like *him*. Nobody here does, baby. He has... no integrity... horrible character... zero respect for women."

"Why? What's not to respect about women?"

"Exactly," Shea says.

"What's protest?" Willow continues.

"It's one way to show you disagree with people. You have the right to publicly protest," Emi says.

"So, I could protest my bedtime? Because it's too early at Memi and Granddaddy's."

"I want to, too!" Edie chimes in.

I chuckle, guiding them off the elevator and into our apartment, where everyone else has already arrived and is getting comfortable. "Girls, you can't protest Memi and Granddaddy. You can only protest bad people until you turn... twenty-one," I say, making up a rule. "Emi and Jack certainly don't qualify. They just have slightly different rules—and for good reason, I'm sure."

My in-laws both smile at me. "Thank you," Jack says. "When they're twenty-one, bedtime will be at one A.M., at the earliest."

"That's awesome!" Willow celebrates.

"No, it's not," my oldest argues. "When we're twenty-one, we can do what we want, dum-dum."

"I'm not a dum-dum! I just didn't know! I'm smarter than you! Did you know that Mercury—"

"I don't care!" Edie yells over her sister. "*Nobody* cares!"

"Girls!" I shout to get their attention, startling nearly everyone in the apartment in the process. I lower my voice to a whisper. "Upstairs to change clothes."

"Daddy," Willow says sweetly, taking my hand at the bottom of the steps, "did the *president* send us flowers?"

"He did, sweetie. They were at the funeral today. They were the white lilies at the end."

"Those were really pretty."

I comb my fingers through her hair and nod.

The girls, Shea and I are the only ones to ascend to the second story of the apartment. Everyone seems to respect that as a sacred space, the more intimate space of our bedrooms. Shea assists Edie and Willow as they find other outfits to wear.

I venture through the closed door of the room I shared with Livvy, making sure I shut and lock it once I'm inside. It still smells like her in here—and nothing has changed in the room since that night.

Other family members have been here since then and have made the conscious decision to leave things as they were—and I'm grateful.

The bed is still unmade, the indentation of her head in the pillow, still there. A glass of water is half full on the night stand next to where she slept. I pick it up to see the mark her lips left there, moistened with peppermint balm that she often wore at night. *Like half a kiss, preserved.* Carrying it with me to the master bathroom, I empty out the liquid in the sink, but tuck the glass itself high on a shelf behind a pair of shoes I hardly wear.

On another day, when the home is empty, I'll wrap the glass up in paper and put it in a box to protect it from dust and general carelessness. Today, I just want to know it's safe.

When I turn around, I'm faced with a closet full of her clothes. I stare at them for a solid five minutes, remembering how beautiful she was wearing different items. Some moments, I smile; other times, I cry. This is the life I can expect to live in the coming weeks and months.

Out of the corner of my eye, I jump at the sight of her, turning quickly in shock and disbelief. A coatrack stands erect in the corner, just as it always has, with Livvy's brown robe hanging from one of the top hooks. It's the color of her hair. Reality is shrouded in disappointment and despair. It takes a few moments to catch my breath.

Eventually, I change out of my suit and into some jeans. Instead of putting on one of my standard Columbia t-shirts, I find a Yale one that Livvy had bought me a few years ago for a volunteer event we did at her alma mater. I didn't want to wear it that day, even though it was the required uniform. Today, I vow to get more Yale clothes to represent the school she loved, too.

Multiple hands knock on the door to my room, and someone tries to jiggle the knob. Once fully dressed, I open the door to find my daughters waiting on the other side.

"Are you coming out, Daddy?" Edie asks, her hair still in a ponytail with the ribbon from Livvy's shoe, even though they've both changed into summery outfits. Willow is wearing her ribbon as a headband now. She looks precious, and their eager looks bring a smile to my face.

"Yeah, I am."

"Can we go inside first?" Willow asks.

"There's nothing to see in here," I tell them, "but if you'd like." I open the door wide for them both.

Edie walks over to where Livvy slept and crawls onto the bed. A part of me wants to stop her, but I don't. She curls up into a fetal position and lies her head down on the pillow. "I miss her."

"Me, too."

"I know, girls. We're all going to feel that a lot... for a while. But we've got each other, and that's how we'll get through it."

"Can we sleep in here with you tonight?" my oldest asks.

"Well, bunny, I'm staying at the hospital tonight. Luca still needs me."

Sadness spreads across Willow's face as she moves her arms to cross her chest. "It's not fair."

"We need you, too," Edie tells me bluntly. I look back and forth between the two of them, seeing the truth in their eyes. I nod my head, realizing this for the first time.

"You know what? Tonight, you two are coming with me to the hospital. There's a great bed for you guys, and I'll sleep on the couch. It's just like a hotel. Then we'll all be together. And tomorrow night? Well, we'll figure that out tomorrow."

"Compromise!" Willow says, happily throwing her arms into the air. I laugh at her response.

"Can we stay up and watch movies?" Edie asks.

"We'll see how good Luca's sleeping... but maybe. If not tonight, we'll do that the first night we come back here. I promise."

"Okay." I reach for her hand to help her off the bed. "Daddy, can I have Mama's pillow?"

I start to tell her yes but change my mind. "No. You've got a pillow. Too many pillows, actually."

"But this one smells like her."

"I know." I raise my eyebrows and smile at her. *Daddy needs that.*

I can't say why, but I feel lighter once I get downstairs. Everyone is talking and snacking on catered appetizers. Soft music is playing in the background. All the people I love are here—except for Luca, who Will has assured me is sound asleep and being watched after by the nurses—and, of course, Liv.

When I look around, I notice everyone has changed into more comfortable attire except for Jack. He's still got on his slacks, a dress shirt and a tie, but it's not out of character for him to be dressed that way, so I don't know if he's comfortable or not.

"Jack, I've got some other shirts upstairs."

"I'm perfectly fine, Jon. Thank you." He glances down. "I like yours."

"Thanks. Can I refill your glass?"

"Sure." His smile is subtle as I take the tumbler from him. Emi follows me to our bar.

"Let me do that, Jon. Go relax."

"You go relax," I argue, pouring the scotch we have on hand for Livvy's father into his glass and adding a fresh ice cube. "This is just as bad a day for you both."

"Then let someone else do this."

"I'm okay. Really." She gives me a hug. "How are you holding up?"

"I feel strangely unburdened today."

"I know what you mean. I guess the funeral was one... dreadful... milestone that we've all survived." I swallow hard, regretting my word choice, but she squeezes my hand and nods.

"If you help me get some things together for the girls, we can take them tonight."

"I'm actually going to have them with me at the hospital. Hopefully they can start getting used to having their brother around—maybe begin to understand that he's a welcome part of our family."

"Jacks and I have been working on that."

"Thank you. I've noticed a shift in their attitudes. Or at least they haven't been verbal about it."

"We've just stressed how much Livvy wanted Auggie."

I flinch, and my stomach drops when I hear that name, but I force a smile anyway. "She loved him," I respond.

"She did."

I turn my attention to my kids. "Bunny, when's the last time you had something to eat?"

"I had a grapefruit for breakfast."

"She said she wasn't hungry this morning," Nolan tells me. "Same for Willow."

"It's fine, man." I pat him on the shoulder on my way to the kitchen, picking up two plates at the end of the island.

"Let me help," Coley says, taking one of them. "What do they like?"

"Just put a little of everything on the plate," I suggest, making my way down the buffet line. She follows me. "This looks really good."

"My brother and his friend, Booker, made it all."

"What? Joel did this?"

"Yeah. Shea hired him to cater and do a little cooking for you on the side."

"That's... awesome. Why isn't he here?"

"They went out with Nyall and Joanna... to give us all some time alone."

"Coley, they're family. They're welcome here, too."

"It was Joanna and Booker. They felt weird about it all."

"I wish you would have said something. I would have invited them at the church," I tell her. "How long are they in town?"

"Well, Nyall and Joanna are staying with us for a few more days. Joel is... well, he's staying with Booker at the moment, but–"

"Hold that thought. Edie? Willow?" I call out to my daughters, who are enjoying being the center of attention with all of the aunts and uncles in the house. Everyone's doting on them.

"Yeah, Daddy?" Willow says.

"Go sit down at the dinner table for me. You both need to eat."

"We're not hungry."

"You say that now, but I saw you eyeing the desserts Aunt Kelly sent, and you're not having any of them until you eat everything on that plate. Got it?"

"All of it?" she asks.

"All of it."

"But then I won't be hungry for her pie," she whines.

"Wils, we'll be here for hours, and I bet you anything there will be a constant supply of sweets coming into this house for a while. You'll get her pie, okay? Just take this into the dining room and eat."

"What about Edie?"

"I'm going to get her now," Coley says. After she has a similar discussion with my oldest, Edie drags herself into the dining room, too. We stand at the end of the island where I can keep an eye on them as they eat, and Coley and I continue our conversation.

"You were saying... about Joel?"

"Well, he wants to find a permanent job in the city, right?" she starts.

"Yeah, I remember him saying that last month."

"How do you feel... and you can say no, but... what do you think about him staying here with you in your guest room for a while? Maybe he could be your personal chef until you've got things under control with Luca, and then he'll be able to start looking for a job in a kitchen somewhere. He's very helpful to have around. The girls love him. And he'll give you privacy. He likes his, too. He's got plenty of friends here to hang out with. I swear he won't be in your way."

I think about it for a minute, then look back into the dining room to see that both girls are eating heartily with huge smiles on their faces. "How's your dinner?" I ask them.

"So good," Edie tells me.

"I want seconds of this one," Willow says, pointing to something green.

I turn back around at the serving trays behind me to see what I actually fed my daughters. In a haze, I didn't pay much attention to what I spooned on the plate. Spaghetti squash. Grilled chicken. Some sort of fresh vegetable medley in a light cream sauce. Parmesan crisps. They actually had a healthy meal... and they want more.

"Once we get settled in," I tell Trey's fiancée, "I'll give him a call. I'd love his help. I'll pay whatever."

After getting some extra veggies for my youngest, I grab a plate for myself and join them. Shea, Will, Trey, Coley, Max and Callen make their way into the dining room shortly after.

"Do you two have any questions about today?" I ask my girls.

They look at one another, trying to think of something.

Edie eventually speaks. "Who was that man at the funeral in the lime green jacket and black glasses?" When I don't answer immediately, she continues to describe him. "He had on black pants and a black and green striped tie. And his pants seemed too short. And you seemed to be gritting your teeth when you shook his hand. And also? Granddaddy put his hands in his pocket when he came up to him."

I didn't need the additional info. I'd wanted to deck the guy the second I saw him in his flashy hipster suit. "That was your mother's first agent. His name is Abram."

"Do you not like him?" she asks me.

"You're quick on the uptake, Eeds," Max says.

"What's that mean?"

"That you're astute... perceptive. You know what that means?" She nods her head.

"Why don't you like him, Daddy?" Willow asks.

"Do you know the word smarmy?" Will asks.

"No."

"Exploitative?" Coley adds.

"No."

"Bumptious?" Trey gets into the fun.

"Stop it!" Edie says, getting frustrated.

"He, uh... kissed your mother when she didn't want to be kissed," I say simply. "Do you know what we call that?"

Both my girls shake their heads.

"Assault."

"*Sexual* assault," Coley says. I shake my head subtly, trying to stop her from saying it, but it's too late. I'm not sure my daughters are quite ready for this conversation. It dawns on me that I don't know what conversations Livvy had with them. I know we decided to not have a full anatomical conversation with them when they asked how babies were born last winter, but rather a very vague discussion about how when couples fall in love, they decide to share that love by bringing a baby into the world... and sometimes, if they're lucky, sleeping in the same bed can make that happen.

I felt like we'd gotten away with it, but I had a feeling the girls had more questions that were likely *not* asked in my presence. Or it's possible Livvy just wanted to be more honest with them and told them.

Plus, Edie knows the term *hooker*. She must know things beyond what I think she knows.

Willow's cheeks blossom red. "Oh," she says, returning to her plate of food.

"Why?" Edie asks.

"Why what?" Trey responds.

"A kiss isn't sex." She looks at me, wide-eyed, after she makes the declaration. I'm pretty sure I'm looking at her with the same expression.

"Can I be excused?" Willow interrupts.

"It's okay, Wils," Coley says. "It's okay to talk about—"

"Sweetie, go ahead. Take your plate in with Memi and Granddaddy."

"Thank you."

After she's gone, I direct my attention to Coley. "Don't push her, if she's not ready... she'll let you know."

"I'm sorry."

"It's fine. Just... you'll figure it out. Don't worry about it." I look back at Edie. "Bunny, what were you saying?"

"Just that... I know that a kiss isn't sex so how can that be sex... assault?"

I let out a long sigh and tug at my hair. I can feel everyone looking at me. "Eeds, do you know what sex is?"

She shrugs her shoulders. "Where babies come from," she says, looking down, embarrassed, after she says it. "And you can't have babies from just kissing. Or else there'd be a lot more babies in the world!"

We all laugh at that comment, appreciating the boost of humor injected back into the room.

"Well, that's very true. Women can't get pregnant from just kissing," I confirm, choosing to breeze past defining sex; that's far too complex for her young mind. "But because some kinds of kissing can be an intimate act between two people, it can sometimes be categorized as sexual. Sexual doesn't only relate to sex. It can relate to physical attraction, intimacy, contact... those kinds of things. Does that make more sense?"

"The way you and Mama kiss is sexual, right?"

Whereas before, all eyes were on me, now everyone looks away. Forks are set down on plates; heads are bowed into laps.

My eyes water, thinking about kissing Livvy. *My Olivia.*

"The way we kissed..." I linger on the past tense of the verb. "It was everything, bunny. Just... everything," I tell her, wiping my eyes.

"I'm sorry, Daddy." She starts to cry, too. "I didn't mean to bring her up."

"Don't apologize." I shake my head and pull her into my chest. "And certainly, don't cry. *Always* bring her up. It's going to take time for me to not be sad, but I always want to think of her and remember her." *Always. Everywhere.* "Okay?"

"Okay."

"I mean it. The last thing I want is for you to think I'm too fragile for you to talk about her. I'm not."

"Okay," she repeats.

"I want to be strong like you. I'm just going to need your help... and I think there will be moments when you need mine, too. Right?"

"Right." We all go back to eating, following Edie's lead after she swallows her tears. "Daddy?"

"Yeah?"

"Did that man go to jail for sex assaulting Mama?"

"No, he didn't. We didn't press charges. I walked in right when it happened... he did lose his job, his most lucrative client and his credibility."

"What'd you do?" she asks me.

I consider lying but decide to tell her the truth. If she asks Jack, he'll tell her what really happened with no shame whatsoever, and he's not a fighting man. "I hit him. Nearly broke his nose. And I don't condone violence, bunny... but I lost my temper that day. Your mom and I were in a rocky place in our relationship, so... a lot of factors played into that moment. I was handcuffed by security... afraid I'd be arrested. But Granddaddy came just in time and cleared things up. Saved me from any jail time."

"Was that before or after I was born?"

"Way, way before. I was a freshman at Columbia. Your mom was a senior in high school."

"Can I date college boys when I'm in high school?"

"No," I say, giving no thought whatsoever to her question. When I look around at my family members, they're raising their brows, knowing that I will be powerless to stop the force of nature that will be high-school-Edie-Scott, just like Jack Holland couldn't control high-school-Livvy-Holland.

But I can think that I have that power for now—and make her think that, too.

She takes her plate to the kitchen, then joins her sister and the others in the living room. I notice everyone is still looking at me. "What?"

"Your nine-year-old seems to know a lot about sex."

"About that," I start. "Don't trust that girl alone with any computer, phone or tablet, you got it? Liv unlocked her iPad and she figured out how to create her own YouTube channel."

"Sure, blame the girl who can't be here to defend herself," Max says. My heart falters, but a smile breaks across my face, and we all start laughing out loud. It feels damn good to laugh together.

CHAPTER 27

*F*rustrated, I tap the bottle nipple against Luca's lips, which he refuses to open. It's the third day I've failed at bottle feeding, and he's losing weight, even though he's still being fed with a tube.

"Try your finger again," Katie encourages me.

"We've established he'll suck on my fingertip," I say, unable to mask my anxiety. "He likes the natural feel of it. I get it. What he doesn't like is the fucking rubber tip of this fucking bottle."

I bow my head and close my eyes as I murmur an apology to my little girls. "There's a five in my wallet on the dresser."

"It's okay, Daddy," Edie says, coming over to me and rubbing my arm sweetly.

"It's not, bunny. Your brother needs to eat, and I can't do it."

He starts crying in my arms, his hands flailing. *I feel the same exact way, kid, but somehow, I've got to hold it all together.* I set the bottle down and find a different position to try to calm him.

Willow comes up from behind her sister and takes the bottle from the countertop, then pops it in Luca's open mouth as he wails. He fusses for two seconds, then tests out the nipple a couple times. He opens his eyes, blinks once, and keeps suckling the formula. I take the bottle from my daughter, holding it at the proper angle.

"Well, why didn't I think of that, Wils?" I say, grateful for her quick actions.

"I don't know, Daddy. You've been fighting to get his mouth open *forever*," she exaggerates. "Seemed pretty obvious to me."

"I guess it did. I must be overthinking things."

"So, can we go soon?" she asks.

"Sweetheart," I start, my heart racing at what I consider a momentous occasion, "this is such an important thing that's happening here. We're watching your little brother eat for the first time. This is huge! And we're all witnessing it together."

"Big whoop. I'm hungry, too, but no one's feeding me anything."

"Shut up, Willow. Daddy said he'd take us wherever we wanted on our way home if we were good. So, shut up and be good."

"Stop telling me to shut up."

"Girls, stop arguing. Edie, don't say shut up, but... Wils? Let's be quiet while Luca has his dinner, okay? Don't rush him."

"He doesn't know what I'm saying anyway," she mumbles as she crosses the room to the couch where her book lays. She crashes onto the cushions and buries her nose into the pages.

"Daddy, can I try?" Edie asks. Her interest in Luca has been surprising—and a total relief.

"You can hold the bottle for me. Just make sure you keep it like this," I say, showing her. She's careful as she grips the bottle, and she strokes her brother's head softly as he drinks the formula.

"He's so cute."

"I know. You think he looks like your mom?"

"He has dark skin like her—and me. He's not pale like you and Willow."

"We aren't pale. Memi's pale," I argue. "Uncle Trey is pale."

She smiles. "They're ghostly."

"Yeah, they are," I agree. "And he has lashes like yours. I bet he'll have brown eyes like yours, too."

"He has *girl* lashes." She giggles. "And his hair's dark like mine and Mama's."

"Mmhmm."

"So, he's going to be a pretty little boy, I guess."

I laugh with her. "I guess he will." I think he'll look even more like Liv, though, than Edie does. He has his mother's nose, too.

I take over bottle-holding duties when she moves to give him a kiss on the forehead. She baby-talks to him, too, and I don't want to do anything to discourage their bonding.

"Looks like he was hungry," Katie says, coming over to us as he finishes off the bottle.

"Oh, my gosh. That's crazy. That's not normal, right? Should he have eaten all of it?"

The nurse nods her head. "You didn't overfeed him," she assures me. "I measured out an appropriate amount for his little tummy."

"Now we burp?" I ask.

"Do you remember how?"

"I'm a pro at this. Give me that rag." Edie hands me the cloth that the hospital had provided, and I drape it over my shoulder. Luca's much easier to handle without the feeding tube attached. I know we're not finished with it, but it's nice to have him a little less tethered. I hold him close to my heart and pat his back gently.

After a couple minutes, Katie approaches me. "Sometimes, it's difficult for preemies. We may need to—oh!" She stops talking when she hears the air escape his throat.

"I said I was a pro. This was my job with these two. Liv fed them; I burped them."

"Ladies don't burp, Daddy," Edie says.

"Mmhmm," I say, rolling my eyes. "You keep thinking that. And tell your sister, won't ya?" Give Willow a soda and put her in a room with her Uncle Max, and she will challenge herself to burp the alphabet. I'd admonished my little brother multiple times for encouraging my daughter's behavior, only to find out he really had nothing to do with it—except that she had no trouble being her true self with him.

And, really, I didn't want to discourage that, even if it wasn't ladylike. She knew better than to do it in public.

"Who wants to change a diaper?" I ask the room. No one volunteers. "Daddy gets to pick the movie tonight, then." I get up and take the baby to the changing table.

"What movie are we watching?" Willow asks.

"Something... I don't know. Black and white. A *classic*," I suggest. My girls hate black and white movies. Hell, I'm not a fan of them myself.

"Oh, I'll do it," my youngest says, dragging her feet as she walks toward me. "Show me what to do again, Daddy." I exchange a look with the nurse, who totally saw through my manipulative plan, and grin.

"Great job," Edie says sarcastically.

I'd forgotten about Willow's current fascination.

"Sharknado 4!" she exclaims, holding the clean diaper over her head in victory.

"Oh, man..."

Katie bursts out in genuine laughter. "Darn, and you're sure you have to go home tonight? I'll have to miss that one?" she asks Willow, her hands on her knees.

"Have you seen the first three?"

"No," she admits. "I couldn't finish the first *one*. My boyfriend loves those movies."

"You're missing out!" my youngest gushes, waiting for me to remove the soiled diaper and clean up her brother. All I really want the girls to do is help at this point and putting on a clean diaper is pitching in right now.

"None of this leaves this room," I tell the nurse. "I don't want anyone finding out my family watches this trash."

"It's not trash, Daddy. They're my favorite movies."

I lift up Luca and nod to her, letting her know it's time to put down the fresh diaper. She spreads it out carefully and looks up at me for approval. I lay the baby down and show her how to fasten it around his tiny waist.

"I cannot fathom why, Wils, but... since you did such a good job with the diaper, I can't argue." I smooth down her hair and kiss the top of her head, then pick Luca back up and cradle him in my arms.

Sadness and apprehension suddenly overwhelm me. It's the first night since his birth that I won't be with him, but it's time to vacate the room for a mother who needs it. More importantly, it's time for me and the girls to return to our home full time.

"Now you be good for your nurses, little guy," I say softly as he drifts to sleep. "Daddy will be here first thing in the morning for cuddle time, and we're going to do that bottle thing again, right? You liked that?" I ask him, realizing I've crossed over into baby-talk. "Memi and Granddaddy will be coming by, too. Lots of visitors tomorrow. We just want to get you eating and breathing on your own so you can come home with us. Right girls?"

"Right," Edie answers. Willow's gone back to her book.

"We can't wait for you to come home, Luca. Sleep well, my little one." I kiss his forehead. "Girls, you want to say goodnight to your brother?"

"Bye, Froggie," Edie says, pushing his dark hair back. "Be a good boy."

"Bye, Froggie," Willow repeats. *Froggie.* Livvy would love to hear them calling him that. It breaks my heart a little, honestly, because it reminds me of her. It reminds me of *Auggie.* It reminds me of the fight we had over his name. It was a moment of stress that I caused that didn't help her one bit. And it was senseless. Did that contribute to her health situation?

Was it situational?

Or was it possibly *genetic?*

Could our children have some sort of heart defect that I don't even know about?

I kiss Luca again before handing him back to Katie. Before I tell the girls to get their things, I gather them into my arms and tell them I love them.

That night, after both girls have fallen asleep on sleeping bags in the living room, I turn off the horrible movie that Willow had picked. Before shutting off the lights, I admire their peaceful expressions for a few moments. I'd told them I'd sleep on the couch downstairs to be close to them, but even after the week I've had–dealing with such immense loss and being awoken hourly every night with Luca–I'm not tired enough to go to sleep yet.

With my phone in hand, I find my way to Luca's room and close the door behind me for privacy, just in case one or both of the girls wake up.

I sigh heavily when I realize this is the last place Livvy and I made love, and stumble into the new rocking recliner we'd had delivered just a couple weeks ago.

I'm so grateful for that night–that it was so memorable, and that it happened at all, really. Otherwise, I fear that I may not be able to remember specifics of the last time we were together.

I'd planned to call the NICU to check on Luca, but I call Jack first.

"Is it too late to call?" I ask him once he answers. It took him five rings to pick up.

"Never," he assures me. "You know that."

"Have either of you ordered a copy of the autopsy report?" I ask him, not in the mood for small talk.

"Uh, yes, we did."

I nod my head, realizing no one can see me, but I feel better knowing this. "Can I see it when it comes in?"

"Of course. Worried about... her heart?"

"Yeah. Jack, what if she and Isaiah had some condition? Do we have a copy of his?"

"I think she ordered one," he answers. "I don't know where it is. Do you know where she kept important documents?"

"Yeah, yeah." They're all in file cabinets in the studio upstairs—somewhere I don't want to go yet. "Third floor."

"Oh," he says simply, not needing a further explanation. "It'll take a few weeks to get hers."

"What if?" I start, but can't finish. My throat tightens up to the point that the horrible thoughts I'm having won't vocalize.

"For one thing, you can't worry about it now. There's no point," he says. "And another thing, knowing will allow us to prepare. Possibly get preventative treatments."

"What if she knew her biological father had a congenital condition that she could have had? What if she found that out from his autopsy?"

"Well, she didn't have much time to take in that knowledge or prepare for it."

"But Jack, come on! Her blood pressure kept skyrocketing throughout the pregnancy! That had to set off some alarms for her, right? Why wouldn't she say something? Do something more?"

"Jon," he says, obviously trying to calm me down. "Perhaps his heart issues weren't genetic. Maybe she didn't have his reports. It could be that she didn't put two and two together." I wait for him to say more. "Do you think for a second that she would have purposefully put her own life and her baby's at risk? Or don't you think she would have done everything she could, if she knew?"

That does make more sense. "I guess."

"Doesn't that sound like Livvy?"

"Yeah," I say softly.

"I *do* know that Isaiah didn't take great care of himself. He didn't eat well at all. And he was a workaholic. You and I both know that. He never said no to a job, and if he had a creative idea, he'd pursue it relentlessly, even if that meant no sleep for days at a time.

"In my mind, that's what caused his heart attacks. But we can find out the truth, if need be. Let's get her results first. If we need his, you can either search for them or we can request them."

"Can we? I thought it was next of kin only."

"You have his only grandchildren. Three of them."

"Right," I say, temporarily forgetting that important fact. I exhale a long breath. "I don't want it to be something that my kids could have," I rattle off, just speaking whatever comes to mind, "but I don't want this to be something that could have been prevented, either, you know? I don't want to find out that getting her to the hospital five minutes earlier could have saved her life. Or not giving her the hydralazine would have been an option—that she could have survived without it and we wouldn't have had to do the C-section that night."

I stand up and walk over to the empty bassinet to run my hand across the smooth padding that lines the bottom of it. I imagine my son asleep in it, free of all the tubes—healthy and able to breathe and eat on his own.

"This report isn't going to come with a list of things you could have done differently," my father-in-law informs me. "It'll be congenital or... stress, Jon. And you did everything in your power to try to alleviate the latter. The doctors gave you their recommendations. What they did just wasn't enough to save her.

"Listen to me. You. Couldn't. Save. Her."

I push the basket back and forth, wishing Luca was asleep inside. I look forward to the day that I can rock him to sleep in his tiny bed.

"Did you hear me?"

"I did," I assure him. "I hope you're right."

"When am I ever wrong?" I huff into the phone. Jack is so rarely wrong these days. But this... he's no expert on these types of issues.

I politely respond to appease him. "Right. Never."

"Right." He laughs. "I promise we will call you the second we get the results. We'll wait to open them with you, and we can talk about them together. Okay?"

"That would be great. I'd like that."

"Good." It's his turn to sigh. "We'll see you tomorrow at the hospital?"

"I'll be the one with the baby."

He laughs. "Are the girls coming?"

"No, they're tired of the hospital after two days. Will and Shea are coming to stay with them, and I think Joel may stop by... check out his new digs."

"That's right. When is he moving in?"

"This weekend."

"Does he need help?"

"I think he and Trey and his friend, Booker, are taking care of it. He doesn't have any furniture to move. Just his personal effects, for now."

"Makes sense. All right. Well, it's late, and Emi's already gone upstairs."

"Yeah, the girls are asleep in the den. I need to grab a pillow and some blankets for the couch."

"Not going to try the bedroom?" he asks.

"No. It doesn't feel right tonight."

"Well, you're in the apartment. That's what's important. Try to get a good night's sleep and tell the girls I love them when you get the chance."

"Of course. We love you both, too. And I'll see you tomorrow."

I pick up one of the quilts, laundered and folded inside the crib that I'd originally made for Edie. She and Willow both used the bed while they were babies, and we'd stored it in a closet at Livvy's gallery for the past six years.

The blanket was handmade by Livvy's grandmother—truly the coolest quilt I've ever seen. She'd asked how we were decorating the room, and when we told her 'sock monkeys,' we expected patchwork in browns, tans and reds to match. But no. She actually created five little quilted sock monkeys and surrounded them in bright colors. "I heard bright colors were best for babies," she'd told us.

I'm glad she delivered this gift early, so Livvy got to enjoy it. She loved it, and I hope it's something we can pass down to Luca's children someday.

Feeling a draft in the rocking chair, I drape the blanket over my chest and decide I need to adjust the vent in the ceiling later. For now, I call to check on my son.

"Mr. Scott! We were just talking about you!" Katie says.

"Shouldn't you be at home by now?" I ask her. "You were there when we left earlier today."

"Double shift," she says. "The glamorous life of nurses."

"How do you stay awake?"

"I had a two hour break earlier. I napped," she tells me. "You didn't call to talk about me, though."

"No," I admit.

"Well, Luca is doing great!" she says. "He's taken every last drop of every last bottle today. He hasn't needed the feeding tube, although we'll put it in tonight so he can get a good night's sleep."

"Wow. That's incredible. He just... he just picked it up that fast?"

"It's natural to him. Sure."

"That's... amazing. I miss him. How's his breathing?"

"Oxygen flow is great. He's 34 weeks today," she says.

"Holy shit. He's one week old today. And I'm not there."

"It's okay, Jon."

I pull at my hair, sad that I didn't realize this milestone while I was with him earlier. Livvy took pictures of the girls when they were one week old. I'll have to take one tomorrow.

"He's making great progress. At the rate we're going, you may be able to take him home in a couple of weeks."

"That long, huh?" I know she was trying to be positive, but the thought of him sleeping apart from us for fourteen more days distresses me. I just want my little family together, under one roof, where I can watch them all and make sure they're all okay... all the time.

"Time will go quickly. You'll see. We'll keep working with him and he'll be so strong by the time you get him home. We may even have him walking," she teases.

"I'm not ready for that," I tell her with a laugh. "Chasing a toddler? Nope. This place isn't even baby-proofed yet. I guess I need a little time to finish getting everything ready."

"See then? Everything will work out... and you'll still visit him."

"Of course. I'll be there in the morning with Jack and Emi."

"I look forward to seeing you all."

"Will you tell him I love him? And that I miss him?"

"I will." And I'm confident she will, too.

"Thanks. Goodnight, Katie."

CHAPTER 28

*E*mi, Jack, Edie and Willow are all waiting in the lobby while I go into the NICU. When Luca sees me, I swear he smiles at me.

"Hey, Champ!" I greet him. "Did anyone see what he just did?" I ask the other nurses.

"What'd he do?"

"He grinned. The second I walked up, he cracked a smile."

"I believe it. He's a little flirt. He smiles at me all the time—when he's gassy," she tells me.

I look at her sideways and put my hand over my heart, offended. "He smiles often?"

She shrugs. "I've seen it a time or two. But seriously—when he has gas. Not out of the blue, like now... when he's seen his daddy."

I feel a little better. "You think he knows he's going home today?"

"We've all been telling him for the past twenty-four hours. If he has any grasp of the English language—or can sense the excitement from you or the Hollands—then yeah, he knows."

"We are over the moon about this. Just to have the family together..." My thoughts drift to Livvy for a second, and I swallow. "We need this to move forward."

"I'm sure." She puts her hand on my shoulder. "Katie went over everything with you yesterday?"

"Yes, I'm prepared. And I have our doctor's number ready if we have any questions. I can't thank you guys enough for what you've done for him." I give them all hugs before returning to my son's crib.

"Well, he's all yours. Freshly fed and changed. He'll probably be hungry again around three."

"Got it. Thank you." I pick him up and hold him against my chest with both hands, making sure to support his head. He's still tinier than the girls were when they were born, but he seems much bigger than he was on his birthday three weeks ago.

In the hallway, Emi hands me the sock monkey blanket and tucks it around Luca's body, giving him a little extra protection from the wind outside, as well as from the awaiting paparazzi. The world has yet to get a glimpse of him, and they're clamoring to, for sure. They've been at the hospital every day, not knowing when we'd be taking him home.

I decide not to expend too much energy trying to hide him, not willing to play their game. Once they get the picture they want, there's a better chance that they'll leave us all alone.

Even though Jack had brought in the stroller, there's no way in hell I'm putting him in there. He's been out of my grasp and out of my control for too long. I want him to feel the protection of his father's arms for now—for hours, if need be.

Like I'll be able to keep him from Emi for hours. I chuckle to myself. I can't say no to that woman when she asks to hold her grandson. Or to Jack, for that matter. The comforting thought is that I know they will love and protect him just as much as I will.

Edie takes Jack's hand; Willow takes Emi's, and we all ride down the elevator together and exit the hospital using the back entrance to the parking garage, where my SUV is. The flashbulbs are blinding, and for that reason, I do shield Luca from the onslaught of their cameras.

"Cut it out with the flashes," I say loudly enough for everyone to hear. "His eyes are still getting used to the world, all right? I don't mind pictures, but do the right thing, yeah?"

"Sorry," a few of them actually respond. While most of them are kind enough to heed my request, a few don't seem to give a shit. Because of that, I keep my son's head tucked close to me and drape the blanket over both of us until we reach the car.

"Should I drive?" Jack asks.

"Would you mind?" I hand him the keys, letting the girls into the very back before I work on getting Luca strapped into the car seat that seems to swallow him whole. "You've got some more growing to do, little man... Emi, can you see if this feels right to you?"

She went with me to a car seat safety class last week, so I feel like her second opinion would be helpful.

She adjusts the shoulder straps lower, something I forgot to do. "There you go."

"Perfect, thanks. Girls, are you buckled in?" I peek in the back to visually check their booster seats, since I get no response. They've both already put on their headphones. Even though they're both older than the age requirements for the child seats, they're too small for the regular seatbelts. Livvy and I decided to use them until each one met the height requirements. They'll both be there soon. Already, none of their friends do, and occasionally, they remind me how stupid it is that we make them sit in them.

That's normally when I turn up *my* music and wish I could escape under a set of noise-cancelling headphones.

"You can have the front, Jon," Emi offers.

"No, thanks," I tell her, grinning. "I see your angle here."

"I think he wants to sit by his Memi."

"You'll be the first to hold him when we get to the apartment. Deal?"

"Okay," she says, pleased with the compromise.

Luca's a little fussy once we get out of the garage and the sun assaults his eyes. Even through the tinted windows, it's too much for him. I pull the canopy over the seat, which calms him down. I notice one bare foot. "We lost a sock," I announce.

"I've got it," Emi says. "It fell off when you were getting him in the car." She passes it back to me.

"Thanks. His feet are too tiny for them. Everything's too small." I slip it on, but it's loose.

"He'll grow into things. Very soon," she assures me. "We were astounded at how fast Trey went through clothes those first few months. Once he started gaining weight, he wouldn't stop growing."

I sigh, knowing that Luca isn't genetically related to Trey in any way. "I hope it's the same with Luca."

"There's no reason to think it won't be. We're gonna fatten him up,"

Jack says. "We'll get him on a good feeding schedule. He's already proving to be a really good eater. And then you've got a gourmet chef for a sister-in-law and another one living with you."

"Well, Joel's just here temporarily. I don't imagine he'll be here by the time Luca's ready to eat solid foods," I tell them.

"You never know. Maybe he'll get into the custom baby food business. It was Shea's way into the New York culinary scene."

"True," I say, remembering the months when she lived with us to get her business off the ground while Will was still on tour. It gave us a chance to get to know her. It was when Livvy found her true best friend in life. I'm so glad my brother met her. "But Joel's made a name for himself with quite a few people in Boston. And he knows people here, too," I remind them as I look beneath the canopy and see Luca fighting to keep his eyes open. I lower my voice when I speak again. "He's got the chops; he just needs someone to go out on a limb for him. I really wish Shea had a slot for him."

"I do, too," Emi says. "But on the off chance it didn't work out, you know... I hope he finds something elsewhere. I wouldn't want things to be weird between Shea and Coley. They need each other right now."

"That's... true," I say, wanting to ask why it wouldn't work, but also not wanting anything to split up Shea and Coley. They've lost Livvy, an important link in their relationship. It's not that they need her to be there to be friends, but Liv *was* the one that brought them together.

From what I hear, though, they've been hanging out a lot, just trying to get through the loss of their sister together in whatever ways they can.

When we get to my building, Leon helps to corral us into the lobby, away from the photographers. I don't go immediately to the elevator, though, knowing he wants to see the baby.

"Well, would you get a look at that head of hair?" the doorman says. I cradle Luca, sleeping, between us. "He's a handsome one, Jon... and I think he's gonna look like his mother."

"I know," I respond. "I hope he does."

"Those lashes."

"Yeah. I have a feeling he's going to get her brown eyes. Mark my words."

"He's so little. Are you afraid to hold him?" he asks.

"Not now. I was a little a first... but I'm getting the hang of it."

"He's wonderful with him," Emi says.

"I'm sure he is," Leon answers, and I notice tears in his eyes. "I better get back to work. You bring him down every once in a while, to let him see Uncle Leon."

"Of course, I will."

As he turns around, he swipes at his eyes. I sigh, wondering if everyone who knew Livvy will respond this way when they meet our son. It hurts, but I realize it should. She's gone and she's left a hole in everyone's hearts.

"Jack's holding the elevator."

I follow Emi to meet him and the girls, and we go straight up to our floor. Joel is standing at our entrance, wiping his hands, waiting to greet us.

"How'd you know we were here?" Emi signs to him.

"I was tracking Jon. My watch buzzes when he's close. He's okay with it," he communicates back to us, both verbally and with his hands.

"I am," I say aloud when I know Joel's watching me, since I can't sign with Luca in my hands. "We've got a system."

Joel nods.

"Joel?" both of the girls are pleading with him.

"Girls, sign, okay?" Jack says. Emi makes herself comfortable on the couch, then motions for me to hand her Luca. I smile and place him gently in her arms.

"Can you make us that... that..." Edie and Willow look between each other, confused, then look at me. "Daddy, how do you sign strawberry salad?"

"Edie, he can read lips if you go slow. Ask Joel." He's already laughing and asking them to watch him as he shows them the signs for strawberry and salad. When he's done, I get his attention. "And by the way, Joel, if you had other meals on the menu, you do not have to cater to their every whim."

"I have the stuff to make it... plenty for everyone. It's not a problem. And it's healthy, so it's all good," he responds.

"Thank you," both Jack and I sign.

Joel finally has a moment to come and meet the baby. He doesn't try to communicate anything, but I can see everything he has to say in his expressions. On the couch next to Emi, he holds on to my son's tiny foot while he watches him sleep. His smile is bittersweet, his brows asking the question, *"why?"*

He sighs, then finally signs, "He's definitely your son."

"You think he looks like me?" I communicate back. "No."

He shakes his head. "But he looks tough. He looks like a fighter, who can make it through anything. He looks like your son."

A smile spreads across my face. "He is a fighter." In those words, though, I'm taken back to Livvy's final ones. *Why didn't she fight that night?*

"I think Auggie's going to grow up and be strong like his daddy," Emi says.

"Auggie?" Joel spells out. "Are you calling him that?"

"I'm not," I respond. I sign it first, but then say it aloud. "His name is Luca..." I only briefly glance at Emi when I say it.

"Auggie's just a nickname," she adds. "Something his Memi can call him."

I turn around and go into the kitchen to fix myself a drink. "Does anyone want anything?"

"Soda, please."

"Me, too."

"No," I tell the girls. "No more sodas. I have some sparkling water for you."

"What?" they both protest.

"It's... too much sugar. We're all cutting back on it." Joel and I had been talking about dietary changes, and this was one I'd wanted to implement. The girls were addicted to sugar already, but I didn't want Luca to be brought up that way.

"Why?"

"Because I said so."

"Forever?" Willow asked.

"All of it?" Edie followed up.

"No and no. We'll have it for special occasions, and there's sugar in fruit... Joel's making you the strawberry salad you wanted, right? So, there's that. Some types of sugar are okay. He's going to help us figure it all out. And you like his food, right?"

They both nod their heads as I hand them glasses of carbonated water. They cringe at the flavor. "What? It's good. Your mom loved it."

"Daddy, it sucks."

"It's that or regular water," I tell them. Edie opts for regular water, but Willow likes her "fizzy water," so she drinks both hers and her sister's.

Joel taps me on the shoulder. "Trey and Coley are on their way over. Is that okay?"

"Of course. I expected a lot of company today. Should I see if Leon should arrange for some more groceries? We use a service," I tell him.

"She said they had a big breakfast."

I nod and help him get out everything he needs for his salad, trying to remember the ingredients he used last week.

"I've got this. It's what I'm here for." He signals for me to join my in-laws and kids.

"Okay. Thanks."

Jack starts to stand up to offer me the seat next to Emi, but I tell him to stay put. "Girls, put your tablets away, okay? Let's have some family time. It's Luca's first day home."

Willow turns hers off immediately. After Edie rolls her eyes, it takes about twenty seconds for her to wrap up whatever she was doing and set hers to the side. I collect them both and put them on the top shelf, above the TV, where neither of them can reach.

"Did you two go with your dad to work yesterday?" Jack asks them.

My youngest responds. "We did!" She bounces on the edge of the couch. Both girls were showered with attention on my first trip back to the office since Livvy's death.

"What did you do?"

"We got to draw on the walls," she says.

"They did," I confirm. "We have dry-erase walls in my office. Edie, want to tell them what you drew?"

She shrugs her shoulders, but eventually speaks. "A lady."

I stare at her, wanting her to say more. "It wasn't just a lady. Who was it?"

She shakes her head.

"It was Mama," Willow says.

"Yeah, it was," I confirm. I pull out my phone and bring up a picture, handing it to Jack. The drawing has its limitations, mainly in the fact that the only media she could use were fluorescent dry erase markers, but anyone close to Liv would know it was her.

"It's beautiful, bunny," he says to her, showing Emi.

"Looks just like her."

"No, it doesn't," Edie argues. "It wasn't any good."

"I disagree," I tell her, just as I'd repeated to her multiple times yesterday. "And if you flip through them, you can see Willow's drawings, too."

"Hers are dumb. She can't draw."

"Eeds, come on. She has a different style," I argue, not wanting to discourage Willow from trying, even if she hasn't shown much interest in the arts yet. She'd been to quite a few one-day courses at Nate's Art Room but would always spend more time daydreaming through the classes than actually participating.

I say *daydreaming*, but a more accurate description of what she was doing would be... hypothesizing about the world around her. Something about being in the creative environment would inspire a whole other level of thinking for her. Will said he could relate; he'd get that way when he listened to music. The *superconscious*, he called it.

I understood it. I could get that way sometimes, and Livvy would get in that zone every time she painted, but I couldn't fathom my eight-year-old transcending her conscious mind at her young age. My brother told me not to doubt it; that he began when he was in elementary school, too.

"I don't care that I can't draw well," Willow says. "But they aren't dumb."

"No, they're not," I agree with her.

"She just can't possibly understand what I'm trying to say in my drawings. They're too complex." I look at Jack and Emi, and we all smile and nod our heads.

"I think she just called *me* dumb," Edie says.

"No, she didn't," Jack says. "You girls just have completely different talents. Someday you'll learn to appreciate your differences. Today, I don't think you understand them. Give it time."

"Jon, what did they say at work?" Emi asks, still speaking softly as Luca sleeps in her arms.

"Just, you know... take my time coming back. Work from home as much as I want. They've got everything under control there with all the projects. Salvatore had a few questions, and we went over those, but other than that, it did seem like everything was running very smoothly. We brought home some plants," I say, nodding to a few new additions in the window sills. "Plants were a popular gift. There are still a ton that Angel is caring for at the office."

"I'd love a few," Emi says, "if you would like to re-home some of them."

"Oh, sure, yeah. We can go up together next week and grab them."

"Thank you."

The doorbell rings, and even though it's not the traditional, abrupt bell sound, the chimes still wake up the baby. He starts to cry. Emi bounces him in her lap as I get up to answer the door.

"Hey, there." I hug both Coley and Trey, welcoming them into the apartment.

"Oh, did we wake him?" Coley asks.

"He's just not used to doorbells... or much of anything, yet. It's okay... want to see if he'll stop crying for you?" I ask her.

"Sure!" she says, happily taking on the challenge. I carefully pick up a fussing Luca and place him into my soon-to-be sister-in-law's awaiting arms. "Oh, Luca... I'm sorry, sweetie. Don't cry." He begins to wail. "No, no, Luca." She looks up at me, worried, and I can tell she already wants to hand him off.

"Wanna give it a shot, Godfather?"

"I mean... he doesn't really know me," Trey says.

"Copout." I give him a side-eye and take my son back, holding him against my chest. He immediately knows where he is; recognizes that he's safe. He stops crying and clenches his fists, catching my shirt in them. I know he's not purposely grabbing my clothing, but it's still nice to think he's clinging to me like he needs me. "He'll need to get to know you eventually."

"I'll hold him later. When he's sleeping. Or just, like, settled. I don't want him to associate me with negative things, like the mean doorbell or whatever."

"Or whatever," I repeat. "He'll get used to you quickly and love you both. I promise you that. Have a seat," I offer.

"You didn't have work today, Trey?" his mother asks him.

"I asked for the day off. Told them I wanted to be with my family today. Seemed like an important day, I don't know," he says modestly.

"That's so sweet," she responds.

"Thanks, Trey." It *is* very thoughtful of him. With my brothers coming over later, it'll be nice to have everyone here. I have no idea how

Luca will handle the crowd, but I guess it's good we have multiple floors; if he's overstimulated, we can simply go upstairs, or even to his room.

Looking down at him, already asleep again, he seems to be fine with the growing crowd. I guess he's probably used to people coming and going, with multiple doctors and nurses coming in and out of the NICU all of the time.

I hear a familiar noise coming from his diaper. Even though he's sleeping, I know he'll be uncomfortable in a messy diaper soon, so I decide to go upstairs to change him.

"I'll help," Coley offers.

"Really?"

"Yeah. I need a refresher course. I do intend to take on some babysitting duties, so... show me what to do," she says.

"You're on."

She follows me upstairs and into his nursery.

"It's so cute," she says. "Shea and I peeked in the other day to make sure everything was in order."

"Did I forget anything?" I ask.

"I mean, I don't know, but Shea thought everything was here. We love the sock monkeys."

"Yeah. It was Livvy's idea. It's perfect."

"Except then Froggie came along, so now we have a mishmash of animalia in here."

"Pretty sure that's not a word."

"I'm a creative writer, Jon. I can make up words." She is known for that, and I can't argue with her. It's never anything I don't completely understand, either.

I smile at her, letting her keep her word. "So first," I say, "we wake up the sleeping baby." I cringe when I say it sarcastically, because it's the last thing I want to do right now. I start by unsnapping the onesie. He sleeps through that, but once my cold hands touch his tummy, he awakens with a jolt and starts crying again. "Take off the old diaper."

"Figured that out," she responds. "I can just watch. You don't have to talk me through it."

"All right," I say with a laugh. She watches as I start to go through the motions.

"I do want to learn this, but I wanted to get you alone for a minute to talk to you about something."

"Sounds serious."

"Not really." She hands me a wipe, and I forget that we'd bought a warmer. I don't remember where it is. Luca's really unhappy when I clean him with the cold cloth. Coley waits for him to quiet down to continue. "Just, um... wedding stuff."

"Okay." I make eye contact with her, encouraging her to continue.

"You know Livvy was one of my bridesmaids," she starts.

"Yeah," I say softly. I'd looked forward to making another trip down the aisle with her this winter, since I was one of Trey's groomsmen.

"I've come up with two options, and I want you to make the final decision."

"Sweetie, it's your wedding, okay?" I shake my head. "I can't pick her replacement."

"There's no replacement for her, Jon. That's not really an option."

"Okay... I'm not following, then."

"My initial thought was that I just wouldn't ask anyone else to join the bridal party—for that reason. I'd never want Livvy to feel replaced, I mean... even though... you know?"

I smile at her. "I know."

"And I don't want people to see some, like, fringe friend standing up there with me. Everyone close to me will know she doesn't belong. But then, like..."

She hesitates for a few moments as I finish putting on the clean diaper. I take a seat on the recliner with the baby as she makes herself at home on the ottoman next to it.

"Like, what?"

"I don't want you walking down the aisle by yourself."

I huff audibly. "Coles, I'll be doing a lot of things by myself. It'll be the new norm. Something we all have to get used to. Don't worry about me."

"I think people will be... sad... melancholy... reminded of her absence in a, uh... very abandoned sort of way. And I don't like that."

"Well, what's the other option?" I ask her.

"I was thinking that I might have a junior bridesmaid and promote Edie to that role. I know they were both going to be flower girls and Liv already bought their dresses, but—"

"I love it."

A wide smile grows across her face; tears fill her eyes. "Yeah?"

"Yeah."

"So, Liv bought their dresses, but she was going to use them for their Christmas dresses, too. She had little sashes made to go around their waists for that purpose."

"I haven't even seen them. Do we have them?"

"No, my seamstress is holding onto them in case she needs to make any final alterations..."

"Okay. Do I need to get Edie a new dress?"

"Don't worry about it. Let me take her shopping."

"Oh, no, I can handle it–"

"I insist, Jon. And, you know, before she... um... Livvy asked me to take Edie under my wing."

"What? When?"

"It was one night. She wasn't feeling well. The night of the food fight," she says, pointing out a detail she knows I'll remember.

"She was better when she came downstairs," I recall.

"Her headache was gone," she confirms, "but she'd confided in me that she was worried about the pregnancy."

I stop rocking the baby and look at her; listen to her intently. "What?"

"She'd told me that nothing felt normal. I don't think it's anything you didn't already know. I suspected it was depression, but I don't think she thought so."

"What do you mean, nothing felt *normal?*"

"She said she didn't feel healthy... or happy... she said she had a bad feeling."

"She said that? That she wasn't happy?"

"Not in general, Jon. Just that she wasn't, I don't know... happy in the way an expectant mother is supposed to be. Of *course*, she was happy with you. But she sensed something was off with the pregnancy."

"Why wouldn't you tell me that?"

"She asked me not to."

I stare at her, but her gaze doesn't waver. She doesn't blink.

"Do you regret that now?" I ask her.

She shakes her head. "No," she whispers. "She was going to her checkups, Jon. She was taking her vitamins. She was doing everything right.

Everything by the book. If there was a way to stop her death from happening, the doctors would have done it. It had nothing to do with me keeping this from you or from Trey. Nothing.

"She needed a friend to confide in. Someone she could trust. I was that to her," she avers. "And I offered her help. I told her I'd hook her up with my therapist if she wanted to talk to someone else... but she didn't. She was content on handling things alone. With you."

"But something was off with the pregnancy and *she knew it*. You just said it."

"She *sensed* it. She couldn't *know*. All she knew is that it was very different from her previous two pregnancies, Jon. *No one* could have predicted what happened. If the doctors couldn't, there's no way you could have."

We sit in silence for about ten minutes as Luca falls asleep. Tension fills the room around us, but fortunately, the baby doesn't seem to feel it or care. I think about her request to take Edie shopping, to take my oldest daughter "under her wing." I can't help but feel the slightest bit of betrayal, but I know deep down she's right. What would I have done with the information anyway? Liv and I would have had a conversation about it. My wife would have downplayed it, and all would be forgotten.

"You wouldn't mind taking Edie shopping?"

"Not at all," she says. "Maybe we could make a day out of it. We could go out to lunch. Get mani-pedis. I could give her the news when it's just the two of us... would that be okay, or do you think Willow would be upset and feel left out?"

"They can't always do everything together," I respond. "I think it's a great idea. I'll make sure Willow has something to do, too, and I'll let her know she'll be the star flower girl on your wedding day. That way you don't have to see any sort of negative reaction, which I don't think the bride should see. I'll make sure to spin it into something awesome."

She smiles. "You don't mind?"

"Not at all."

"Thanks. You can tell her she gets Hampton all to herself."

"That might make things worse. Edie teases her relentlessly about him... says he has a crush on her."

"I forgot. Then don't mention that as a 'positive.'"

I nod and take a deep breath. "Coley, I want you to promise me something."

"Anything."

"If my girls ever confide something like that in you, like what Liv said—or anything serious, for that matter—you tell me. As adults, we have to stick together, and I need... help. I appreciate your loyalty to my wife, but I need there to be no secrets between my girls and me. Not while they're still kids, growing up," I tell her. "It's something I intend to tell them, but something I need everyone to be in agreement on.

"I don't care what it is. I'm the parent here. Mom *and* Dad. I need to know what's happening with them in all aspects of their lives."

"Of course, Jon. No secrets."

"I just want them to feel comfortable talking to me about anything. And it'll be weird because I know Liv has had some discussions with them about periods and... it sounds like she's talked to Edie about sex... they've never really come to me with questions about that. Somehow, I need for them to know it's okay."

"They may never feel comfortable talking to you about those things, though, Jon. I mean—it doesn't seem like it's a problem for Edie, but still. You can't force that level of comfort on a young girl.

"But that's why you have me and Shea and Emi and all the aunts and cousins. Sure, you're Mom and Dad, but you don't have to do this alone. Let us be present for some of these tough conversations. Maybe we can talk to them together... maybe they'll be okay with that."

I nod my head.

"But we really have to wait and see what they want to do. What you don't need to do is tackle all of this and make decisions about everything in the first month. Just let things happen naturally."

I roll my eyes at her but smile anyway. "Damn. You give good advice."

"I'm in touch with feelings. It's kind of my specialty."

"Hmmm..."

"Can I hold him, now that he's sound asleep?"

"Sure." I hand him over to her awaiting arm.

"Oh, my ovaries..."

"That's all it took, huh?"

She starts laughing. "He's the cutest thing! He already has a great summer tan," she jokes about his olive-colored skin.

"I know. Liv had pretty strong genes."

"I don't know... Willow looks a lot like you."

"Maybe a little," I concede. "So, about Edie... you're going to teach her how not to wear makeup, I hope?" I've always noticed that Coley rarely wears any, and I have to admit, I think she looks prettier without it because it allows her freckles to show through. Her freckles are one of her best features.

"That's one reason Livvy wanted my help. She didn't want her to be 12 going on 30, or something like that," she explains.

"Then I'm all for it. And maybe one day when you've got her, I can secretly throw away all the makeup she's somehow managed to collect, even though we've never bought any for her."

"That's a great way to build her trust," she says sarcastically.

"Yeah... I don't have anyone to blame it on anymore, either," I respond. "Maybe not such a great idea."

"I'll get her to a point that she doesn't want to wear it. You have my word."

"You've got some real confidence there..."

"Except for the wedding. We'll let her wear a little to the wedding, right?" she asks, blinking her lashes quickly to win my favor.

"As long as she doesn't look any older than... like... a tween," I bargain with her. "The second she looks 13, I'm washing it all off."

"That's fine. I can work within those parameters."

"Okay."

Someone knocks lightly on the door frame. "Can I come in?" Trey whispers.

"Sure," I say, standing to offer him my seat. "Why don't you two get acquainted with your nephew, and I'll go downstairs and help finish getting lunch ready for everyone else?"

"Sounds good. He's clean, right?" my brother-in-law asks.

"For the moment..."

*A*fter we have lunch, Jack decides to try his hand at feeding Luca. After I'm sure he's getting the hang of it, I head upstairs to look for the warmer for the wipes, which can only be in a couple of different closets.

In Luca's room, I notice things are even neater than they were when I left. Coley and Trey have folded the quilts, which I'd left pretty messy. The wipes and powder are back in their side pocket on the changing table, and the pillow that I'd tossed off the rocker and onto the floor earlier to get it out of my way is back where it belongs.

Not only that, but the head of the larger-than-life sock monkey has been propped up, so the animal doesn't look downtrodden like the natural plush stuffing makes its head lay. Somehow, it brightens up the room and lifts my spirits.

His closet hides a treasure trove of items that I know Livvy and I didn't buy. I find the warmer, but in addition to that, there are items of clothing I've never seen, toys, blankets, shoes, a Pack 'n Play folded up in the back and even a swing. They're things I'd still needed to buy, but not items that were terribly high on my list.

"Can I come in?" Emi asks, standing in the doorway.

"Sure." I scratch my head, surveying all the gifts. "You have something to do with this?"

"Not much. Shea had been planning the shower, you know... most of those are the shower gifts. We didn't think a party was appropriate, but people wanted to pass along the gifts."

"Wow. That's... unexpected, and so thoughtful. Like... who do I thank?"

"She kept a list. It's in his baby book... which is in this drawer." She opens the bottom one in his dresser. "When you're ready."

"Shea?" I ask, knowing she's the one behind it, but asking anyway.

"Yeah."

"How can I ever thank her for everything she's done? I mean, she's eight months pregnant. She doesn't need to be going to all this trouble. She just needs to be taking care of herself and Charlie," I say.

"I have an idea."

"Really?"

"We have to find Livvy's sketchbook," she tells me.

"It's in her nightstand, I'm sure. That's where it went every night when she went to bed. And her old ones are either on the bookshelf in our bedroom or up in the studio. What's in there?"

"She told me she did a drawing of a mural for Charlie's room. I'd love to find it... and I think you and I together we could figure it out. You could easily sketch it, I'm sure, and I can mix the colors. We can paint it together... it will never be as good as what Liv could do, but I know it would mean the world to Shea. Livvy wanted to do it for her after Auggie was born." I flinch a little when she says *Auggie*. Even though she and her mother sounded nothing alike, I still hear Livvy's voice every time Emi speaks the word.

"Let's go see what she had in mind."

After finding her book, we have to flip back a hundred pages to find what appears to be the perfect mural for Charlie, even though it's not labeled. I flipped quickly, because it pained me to see all of the art that would never see the light of day. Street art that would never be painted on buildings. Ideas never realized. It was crushing, and I didn't want my thoughts to linger on that. I wanted to be able to bring one more master-piece to life.

"The astronaut's alphabet," I say, reading a little note she wrote to the side. Emi and I both study the drawing. She's assigned an adorable illustration for every letter and spaced them across a neatly sketched wall. If an 'astronaut' is present, it's an animal–a monkey, a hedgehog, a sloth, a panda bear–there's even one that looks like Gunner, their Airedale terrier. "You've got to be kidding me. This is about the cutest thing I've ever seen."

"Did you notice all the animals are eating fruits or vegetables? A little nod to Shea, maybe?" Emi points out.

"Oh, how perfect." The mural will be simple to complete. I think either one of us could paint it, although I think I'm definitely the better candidate to draw it out, knowing my mother-in-law's weaknesses. She's never been great at drawing by hand, but she'll be the ideal collaborator on this. "This will be simple."

"Absolutely," she agrees. "I think she was taking into account a limited work schedule in the weeks between Auggie's birth and Charlie's."

There's that name again.

"Maybe."

"While we're in here, did you ever find the ring?" She'd asked me last week if I'd seen the green ring that Jack and Emi had given to Livvy on our wedding day.

"No... we can look. It's not in her jewelry boxes. Maybe in one of those other hat boxes?" I suggest, pointing to them in the closet. "I'll look in this other one by the table."

Before she'd gotten pregnant, Liv wore it often when we went out, but I hadn't seen it in months. It wasn't with her engagement and wedding bands, either, which she had been keeping on a small ring stand on the vanity.

The one thing I hated about cremation is that they wouldn't take jewelry. I still have her wedding band, and I feel like it should be with her. *"You'll have a ring to give each child,"* Jack and Emi kept telling me. But I still hadn't found Emi's green engagement ring.

"Daddy? What are you doing?" Edie asks me, sitting on the poorly made bed.

"We're looking for a piece of jewelry of your mother's."

"Which one?"

"The green ring that once belonged to Memi."

"Oh," she says, walking over to Livvy's chest of drawers and reaching toward the back. She pulls out a pair of pink fuzzy socks and hands them to me. They're heavier than socks. I separate them and reach inside one, pulling out a small box that contains the keepsake.

"Well," I say with a chuckle. "I didn't ask the right person."

"Thank you, Edie!" Emi hugs her granddaughter.

"Hey, I have a question," my daughter segues, barely accepting the embrace. I nod, encouraging her to continue. "Can I get my ears pierced?"

"No," I say, giving the request no thought whatsoever.

"Why not?"

"Because your mother said no." She had said no when Edie asked two months ago. "Nothing's changed."

"Yeah it has. She isn't here anymore." I look at Emi, who looks away, saddened.

I strain to smile at her challenging response. "That doesn't change what her wishes were, bunny," I explain, my voice measured. "We don't dismiss those, just like we don't dismiss her. Have some respect, okay?"

"Jon," Emi scolds.

I bite my lip, knowing I took it a bit too far, but my daughter still glares at me angrily. "Do you have something more to say about it?"

"Why didn't Mama have her ears pierced? Everyone else got theirs pierced when they were *babies*, practically."

"Because she wanted to be different. She never wanted to be like *everyone else*. She liked the idea of being a blank canvas. And in the end, in her mind, not having them pierced and being the person she was created an air of mystery around her. And she liked that." And there are *other* reasons that I'll never explain to her or her mother.

"Do you like earrings on girls?" she asks me.

"Frankly, Eeds, I don't like anything that draws attention from boys to my eight- and nine-year-old daughters. That goes for pretty jewelry and makeup and some of the clothes you ask us to buy you. You're a little girl. When you're 16, you can ask me again."

"Sixteen?!" she yells dramatically. "I bet Memi got her ears pierced before she was 16!"

I don't even wait for Emi's response. "I'm not Memi's father, now, am I? That was a decision she made with her parents... and times were different then. I bet her dad didn't have to worry about her starting a YouTube channel. Let's ask her that."

Edie's cheeks blossom in a deep crimson. "They didn't even have computers back then!" She storms out of my room and into her own, slamming the door. It's not allowed in our house, but I'll talk to her about it later when we don't have company and we're both calmer.

"She's almost right. We barely had computers," Emi says with a laugh.

"You just proved my point."

She smiles, now holding all of Livvy's most precious rings in her palm. "So, Jon," she starts.

"Yes?"

"I want you to put these somewhere secure. Locked away. You should do that with any of her jewelry you intend to keep. Do you have a fireproof safe here?"

I nod my head. "It's in the back of the bedroom closet."

"If you can ever part with them, I think you should consider passing one down to each of the kids."

"No, I know. I think it's a good idea."

"I'd like Edie to have my ring," she says. "As the firstborn." I don't disagree. "Willow should have Livvy's engagement ring, and I think Luca should have the wedding band. He could use it as the base for an engagement ring or something someday, right? You could use jewels from a necklace or bracelet of hers, if he wanted, like we did with Coley's ring for Trey."

"We've got a long time to plan for that." I rub my fingers against my beard. Fortunately, no one had said a word about the fact that I hadn't shaved since the day of the funeral. I was getting used to seeing myself in the mirror—and used to people's reactions who I hadn't seen in a while.

"Should we put them away?"

"Yeah." I take them from her and go to the closet. "Em?" I say loudly to make sure she hears. "Should anything happen to me, you know... everything you need is in here." I think about that for a second. "I guess I need to check in with Danny... change my will... although I think the wording will still get everything where it needs to go."

"You, Jack and I should probably make a trip together," she says, now behind me. "And we'll show you where the safety deposit box is. Trey knows, but... just in case."

I stand up and give her a hug. "Yeah."

"Can I wash up your sheets for you while I'm here?" she asks, her speech tentative.

I look down at the floor. "Why? Do you think I haven't washed them?" I ask, testing her out.

"There's makeup on her pillowcase, Jon. Unless you're sleeping with another woman already—"

"Fuck, no!" I exclaim at the mere suggestion of it, then realize what I just said to my mother-in-law. "Sorry."

"That language doesn't bother me," she says. "Or, one of your daughters is playing in the makeup again, I was going to add."

"It's Liv's."

"I understand if you're not ready. I remember when Nate died, they washed up all of my sheets while I was still in the hospital. I'd hoped to... smell him again, feel his presence or something in the linens or when I laid my head on my pillow. I was crushed to smell the fresh detergent."

"The girls have been sleeping in here..." I shrug my shoulders. "I can't smell her on the pillow anymore. But I still have her shampoo... and perfume. I take a whiff of those all the time."

"How about I wash up all the linens? Yours and the girls' sheets. Then you can all sleep in your own beds tonight. I mean, really... Luca's probably going to sleep in his bassinet in here anyway, don't you think? The girls don't want to wake up to him crying all night."

"I've washed Edie's and Willow's sheets, hoping they'd go back to their beds. I think it'll definitely take Luca to get them to do that. But... yeah, let's wash the sheets."

"Okay," she says, squeezing my arm in a mothering way. I strip the bed for her, shaking away thoughts of Livvy watching me as I made the bed a couple of days before she died. She hated wrinkles in the bottom sheet and wasn't shy about pointing them out to me. I realize it's one of the reasons the bed hasn't seemed so comforting lately. It's not only her absence, or the presence of two squirmy little girls. I'm not making the bed every day—not straightening out the wrinkles. *She was right. There is a difference.*

When I look up, Jack's standing in the doorway, holding a framed object that's facing away from me. I hand Emi the linens, and she pats his arm on the way out. I glance down, curious, as he nods to the mattress, suggesting we take a seat.

"Where's Luca?" I ask.

"Trey and Coley have him. He finished his bottle, he's been burped... he's good."

"Okay."

"He's perfect," he says with a plaintive smile. "Now, before I give this to you, I have to explain." He clears his throat. "It's a painting."

I stand up and begin to pace. "There's enough going on today to bring me to tears, Jack. Maybe seeing a new piece of her art could wait a few days."

"It's not hers." He waves me back. "It's nothing *like* hers, I can guarantee that." He's laughing to himself. "Remember that day when she taught at Nate's Art Room? Well, I painted with Edie... and it's horrible; truly, I am not artistically inclined in any way, but... my Contessa, she saw it, and she said she loved it." He closes his eyes to stave off tears.

"Well, shit, Jack. *You're* gonna make me cry."

"I'm trying not to. I just..." He places a painting in my lap; how he expected me to not become emotional is a mystery. Sure, it looks like a painting Willow may have done when she was five—a stick figure family—but it's my family. My *whole* family, if there ever was such a thing. "I added to it since that day. I'd only done the top row in class, but I painted your brothers and their families down here."

I haven't even made it to the bottom row. I'm stuck on the image of the dark-haired woman holding a baby, standing in between two little girls, one who's standing beside a man who's supposed to be me. "Damn it, Jack."

"How was I supposed to know?" His voice is only a whisper.

"How could anyone know?"

He picks up the Kleenex off my nightstand and hands me a couple before taking one for himself.

"Livvy wanted to hang it in here," he says. "If you don't, then... you can do with it what you will, but she wanted to have it."

"I want her to have it. *I* want to have it," I state. "And yeah, I'll hang it in here."

He produces the necessary tools. "Where would you like it? I'll hang it right now."

I smile and set it aside so I can give him a hug. "Thank you. How about... right over the headboard? She was going to paint something there someday, but... this will be all I'll ever need."

"Consider it done."

*M*ax, Callen, Will and Shea all show up together just before seven, and the whole apartment is swarming with chaotic conversation. Normally, I'd be in the thick of it, but it feels strange without Livvy jumping in with her sassy comebacks or arguing with Will about something or other. Ordinarily, she would whisk Coley and Shea upstairs for some girl time, but there's no one to do that anymore. I hope they feel comfortable enough in my home to go upstairs and get away from all the guy talk, but I don't want to make it weird by saying something about it. I don't want to point out the fact that Liv's not here, just in case other people aren't dwelling on it like I am.

While I'm overthinking that, Will comes over and takes a seat next to me at the kitchen island.

"You're hogging the baby. I'd like to hold him," he says.

"Really?" I ask, looking down at Luca, who's alert and swaddled in my arms at the moment. He'd just had another bottle and seemed to be drunken with contentedness ever since.

"Yeah. We bonded. Plus, Shea really hasn't had much time with him, and I know she wants to get to know him."

"Well? Here you go, Uncle Will. Be prepared for a diaper change," I warn him.

"I'm an expert," he brags. "Katie taught me well."

"We'll see about that. Oh, but when you do it, I want you to take Max and Trey and show them. The godfathers need to know this shit, right?"

"Watch your mouth, Daddy!" he scolds. "You owe this baby a dollar. Does he have a piggy bank up there?"

"It's a sock monkey, but yeah. I'll pay up. Promise."

"Don't think I won't check."

"Do I lie?" I argue. "Get ready." I place my son in his cradled arms. Luca starts to cry immediately.

"What do I do?"

"Go sit down with Shea." Everyone's watching him since the baby's now taken over the conversation. Will makes his way back to the couch and takes a seat next to his wife. She struggles to sit upright, obviously in discomfort from her own pregnancy, but finally gets situated and starts to stroke Luca's head, trying to calm him. After two minutes, my brother hands the baby to his wife, who's made a little place for him with one arm and a throw pillow next to her body. With his feet tucked under her armpit and his head near her belly, she continues to tickle his scalp and talk to him sweetly.

He seems to like this a lot.

I walk up behind her and put my hands on her shoulders. "You don't have a thing to worry about, Shea. You're gonna rock this motherhood thing."

She looks back at me, uncertain. "I just want him to be here already. I want to get the birth part behind me."

I nod, understanding. "You'll be fine. You'll do great."

"I keep telling her that."

"I don't think I'd be so afraid if Liv was still here. Not because..." She sighs and looks away from me, shaking her head. She doesn't need to finish that sentence. "I just know she'd make me feel more confident about the whole thing."

"We'll be there with you, Shea," Emi says. "I've been there, too."

. . .

*E*mi and Jack leave before we order a late dinner, with time having gotten away from us. We'd fed the girls sandwiches a little after five, but never figured out what the adults would eat. I decide to give Joel the night off since everyone's over and let him have a little fun with the rest of us.

After Trey and Coley take and place our orders online, I ask Max to help me put the kids to bed, wanting a little alone time with him. I can see a look exchanged between him and Callen before he agrees to come with me, but he follows me and the girls nonetheless after Edie and Willow tell everyone goodnight.

"Go brush your hair and teeth and put on your PJs, girls, while I change Luca. Uncle Max and I will be back to tuck you both in."

"Aren't we sleeping with you, Daddy?" Willow asks.

"Not tonight, Wils. I have to move Luca's bassinet into my bedroom. He wakes up every couple of hours to eat, remember? He cries a lot, so I want you both to get some uninterrupted sleep."

"What if I don't care if I do?" she argues in the hallway as Edie grabs her pajamas and heads into the bathroom.

"You lose. I care if you do, and my vote's a little more important."

"Come on, Willow. You can sleep with me, if you want," her big sister offers. She grins and nods, taking off in a skip to her bedroom to get her things. I signal for Max to come with me to the nursery.

"How are things with you?" I ask him.

When he doesn't answer immediately, I look over to see the expression on his face. He hasn't been his bubbly, funny self tonight. "You know. Fine."

"Come here," I say, handing him Luca. He looks afraid to hold him. "The worst he can do is throw up on you, Mascot, and I can fix that with some hot water and detergent. Babies vomit and pee and shit on you sometimes. You did it to me and I lived. He'll do it to you, and you'll survive it. I promise."

He closes his eyes and sighs, taking the baby into his arms.

"What's the matter with you?"

"I'm..." he starts. "I'm going through some shit."

"Smoking again?" I ask, my tone purposely measured and non-threatening. I want to be here for my brother, no matter what. "I'm not going to be angry. We'll get through it together. I can get you help."

"It's not something I can just quit. Honestly, Jon, it's not something I want to quit."

"If you're not ready, then..." I think back to the times I'd tried to help Mom before she was mentally prepared to give up alcohol, "there's not much I can do except try to monitor it, and I'll try not to be a nuisance, but I can't just turn a blind eye—"

"I don't need you to *monitor* it. I'm not a kid, and I'm not abusing it."

"Are you mixing it with anything?" I lay out a clean diaper to have everything ready.

"No," he says, turning away from me and bouncing Luca lightly.

"Not alcohol?"

"I drink. I only smoke at home, Jon, and Callen's with me most of the time."

"*Most* of the time?" I take my son and start to change him.

"Why is that a concern?"

"Because..." I hesitate. "Because you haven't been yourself in a long time and I worry about you. I hate that you spend so much time alone—to think you're spending your days alone, getting high... it just makes me worry that much more."

"It's not every day. I don't need it every day."

My ear is keenly attuned to that word: *need.* "Is this an addiction thing?"

"No. It's a recovery thing."

"Is that an excuse?"

"No!" he argues defensively. "I'm in pain, I smoke. I get flashbacks, I smoke."

"And when do you drink?" I add.

"When I just want to feel numb," he answers.

"Doesn't the weed do that?"

"Sometimes it's not enough. Sometimes it's not the right kind of numb. With alcohol, I get happy before I get mellow. If it's a social situation, that's the better way to go. I adapt."

"Why do you want to be numb so often?" I ask what seems to be the obvious question.

"I don't want to be here anymore—in New York," he clarifies quickly.

Even with the addendum, I'm stunned.

"God, Mascot, don't say shit like that." Luca begins to whimper as I finish putting on his diaper. "Can you grab a onesie out of that drawer?"

"Any particular one?"

"Your choice." Instead of picking one off the top, he holds up a few until he finds one he likes. It has a whale on it.

"I got this for him."

"Thank you," I tell him.

"And I have to say shit like that," he continues our conversation. "I've been holding this in for... years, Jon. Literally."

"What? Really?" He nods. "You're unhappy?"

"Is that news?" He looks hurt when he asks, as if I haven't been paying attention.

I swallow and concentrate on getting my son secured in his soft clothes, slipping past Max once to grab a pair of socks from the dresser. "I mean... no. I didn't know you were *that* unhappy. I didn't know you felt like moving was the solution."

"I've been bugging Cal forever."

"Where do you want to go?" I don't wait for him to answer, but instead say it with him. "California. Yeah." I exhale a long breath, eventually making eye contact with him again as I pick up Luca and sway him gently from side to side. "What's there that isn't here?"

"The rest of my life," he says as his face falls. "I know you guys are all here." I find a blanket and start swaddling Luca while he talks. "I know it would be hard to be so far away from you and Will and Trey, but fuck, Jon, I need to... reconnect with nature. With the ocean. I need to surf," he says, nodding, and making no apologies. "You have your career, Livvy had art, Will has his music and his... whole purpose in life, right? Trey and Callen are both fucking geniuses and have their lives planned out, but you know, I don't seem to have something useful to contribute," he tells me. "The thing is, when I'm on the ocean, I feel whole.

"And there aren't many other times when I do. I'd really like to have the opportunity to feel... *good* about myself again."

"Max..." I set Luca in his bassinet and pull my brother into my arms. "I wish you knew how much I think you contribute to our family, because I think it's really important. You were always the life of the party. The one to make us all laugh in any situation. The one to break the ice and ease the tension. The one to remind us all to stop being so damn serious all the time and have some fun. The one to convince us all to be ourselves, above everything else.

"*Were.*"

"Huh?"

"You said that in past tense. I *was* those things... so you admit that things have changed."

"I know you've suffered since the shooting. No one expects you to be the same person you once were after surviving such an ordeal, but you're no less important. Your contributions are no less impactful on me or the guys... or my kids. I'd love for you to be more involved."

"Don't ask me that."

"Why?"

"Because then I'm only gonna let you down, and that's just one more thing to add to the list."

"Nobody's keeping a list."

"I am... and for once, I want to put some things in the positive column. I've got to get back to the West Coast."

I look away from him and back into the cradle at Luca. My heart feels even heavier than normal. "I don't know what I'll do without you, buddy."

"Don't start that, Jon. Don't make me feel bad about my own needs. Please," he pleads. "I wouldn't go if it was something I didn't think I needed to do for my own sanity."

"Daddy?" Edie interrupts. "We're ready to be tucked in."

"We're coming," I say, wiping wetness from my eyes and following her to her bedroom. Willow's already in Edie's full bed, her nose stuck in a book. "Teeth are brushed?" I ask them both.

"Yes, Daddy," they say in unison as my oldest crawls into bed.

"Uncle Max, want to give the girls a hug?"

He leans over to embrace them, and I hear both of my daughters give him kisses on the cheek. When he pulls away, he's smiling. "Breakfast date on me before you go back to school," he promises them. "Anywhere you want, but make sure it's somewhere that serves something with tons of syrup and whipped cream. Somewhere your daddy hates."

"Yay!" they both cheer.

"And donuts!" Willow adds, closing her book.

"Only if you finish that chapter," Max says. "You weren't finished yet, were you?" She shakes her head. "Edie, do you have a book?"

"I have a magazine," she hedges.

"Nope. A book." My brother looks at me, and I point to the bookshelf. Max picks a random book and shows it to Edie. "Have you read this one?"

"No."

"Let's shoot for chapter one..."

"Will you take me somewhere after our breakfast date? Anywhere I want to go?"

"Within reason. Sure."

"You're asking for trouble now," I warn him. "This has lead-singer-of-a-boy-band-meet-and-greet written all over it," I add. "Trust me. I fell for something like this last year."

"That's well outside of reason," Max clarifies. "Wait—which boy band?" I roll my eyes at him.

"I just want to go to the store to get some more bows for my hair... for school," she says, exasperated.

"I can get you those, bunny."

"I want Uncle Max to take me," she says.

"Okay, then." No questions asked. After what Max told me, I'm not going to discourage the girls from spending time with him, and I won't be offended even if it is in my stead – provided he's sober, and now I know that's something I have to watch closely for. *Livvy was right. But at least he's being honest with me now.* "Finish chapter one. We'll discuss what it's about in the morning."

"Right," she laughs. "You've never read *Matilda*."

"Oh, but I have," I say, "and you're going to love Miss Honey. Mark my words."

"I bet there's no Miss Honey."

"Bet me all the money in your swear jar." I hold out my hand to show her I mean business. She bites her lip, considering my offer, but a smile breaks through.

"Nope. Now can you boys leave so we can read our books?"

"Can I get kisses, too?" I ask. Both Edie and Willow put their books aside. I sit on the edge of the bed, letting them hug me and offer a kiss on the cheek.

"Tell Froggie goodnight," Willow says softly. Edie repeats her, and they both go back to reading.

Before Max heads back downstairs, I ask for his assistance once more. "Help me carry the bassinet. I don't want to wake him." Together, we lift the heavy wooden bed and slowly carry it into my bedroom, settling it next to the place where Livvy once slept.

After turning on the baby monitors, I toss him the handset. "Thanks. Now go downstairs and let me know if you can hear me. You have to press to talk back."

While I give him time to make his way to the living area, I rock the crib back and forth, watching my son sleep soundly. Prying my eyes away from him, I stand up and walk across the room.

"Testing, one-two," I speak in my normal voice.

"I can't hear you," my brother returns. I smile at his joke, lame as it is, simply because it's a joke and I'll never again take for granted his play-fulness.

"How's the sound?"

"The voice... the voice! It's coming from inside the house!" he says excitedly. I start laughing.

"Is it clear? Will I be able to hear him crying, do you think? And breathing?"

"I dunno. Whimper like a little girl for a second. Let us hear that."

"Fuck you," I respond with a lighthearted chuckle, and I hear an uproar of laughter from everyone downstairs. Luca didn't seem to hear; his long day must have caught up with him. I barely put my hand in front of his nose just to make sure he's still breathing. "Can someone who gives a shit give me a straight answer? How about his godfather? The *real* one..."

"That's low," Max says.

"Well, the serious one, anyway..."

"We can hear you clearly," Trey answers me. "Why don't you have a camera for that thing? What decade are you living in?"

"It's in his room, and I don't want to rewire just because he's sleeping in my room. I figure I'll be with him most of the time. I just... want to hang out downstairs a little more tonight."

"Then get your ass down here."

"I'm on my way." I clip the handset on the bassinet, out of his reach but close enough so that I'll be able to hear him breathing. I turn up the sound sensitivity to ensure that I'll hear him. It's his first night in the house, and I don't want to miss anything important.

CHAPTER 29

*I*t's quiet upstairs on the morning of the first day of school. Too quiet, I think, but not wanting to jinx things, I let that notion go and continue feeding Luca, who's happily enjoying his bottle after a restless night's sleep for both of us. I'm actually looking forward to dropping off the girls, getting Luca settled back down at home and taking a long nap.

"So, no breakfast? Really?" Joel signs after taking a sip of his coffee.

"They get a full breakfast at school," I explain to him. It was part of the deal with their private school. Healthy breakfasts and lunches, so it was something we never had to worry about, and there were people on staff there that kept track of what the girls ate. A daily report was sent home to us every afternoon. Both Edie and Willow knew what kind of foods would earn them a lecture when they got home, so over the past year or so, they'd done really well at adjusting their diets accordingly.

"I feel useless," he says back to me.

"Hell. I'd go back to bed if I were you."

"Isn't Emi coming over? Wouldn't it be rude?"

"Not one bit. Get some sleep for me and little Luc here... will ya?"

"Yeah," he mumbles, pouring out the rest of his coffee. "I'll fix you something when you get back, if you want."

"Lunchtime," I respond. "Let's just shoot for lunch."

"Got it."

After all the formula's gone, I lean against the back of the chair at the kitchen table and close my eyes, putting the baby on my shoulder to burp him. We'd both become pros at this by now. I could do it in my sleep, and in a way, I want to.

And almost do. I jump at Willow tapping my arm, having not heard her approach me.

"Daddy?"

"Yeah, baby?"

"Edie's still in bed."

"What?" I get up, inadvertently kicking the chair abruptly as I stand. "What do you mean, she's still in bed? I saw her get up."

"She just got up to go potty, and then she crawled back in bed."

"Well..." I'm frustrated, but I can't be frustrated with Willow—that is, until I notice she's made very little progress at getting herself ready. I head upstairs, and she follows closely behind me. "What have you been doing since you got up?"

"Reading. Waiting for Edie. She always gets ready first."

"Seriously? That was the best use of your time? You're smarter than that Wils, right?"

"It's just how we always do it. Mama helps her first, and then she helps me."

I stop before I reach Edie's room and turn around. When I do, I catch a whiff of something a little acrid and mildew-like. I realize Luca's spit up on the burp cloth. After taking the rag off my shoulder, I wipe his face while Willow verbally expresses her disgust at her brother's indigestion. "Grow up, Wils. He's a baby. You're not." And then I remember what she just said to me. "Honey, things aren't going to be like they used to be. You understand that, right? Our routine is going to change a little."

"Why?"

"Because Mama isn't here to help."

"But you're here."

"I have Luca. And you know what? Your mother would have had Luca to take care of, too. This year would have been different than last, regardless. Now, I need you to go brush your hair and teeth and wash your face while I'm dealing with Edie. And you've got your clothes laid out?" She shrugs. "They're at least in your closet, right?" She nods. "You tried them on, though." Although I say it like a sentence, I do mean for her to respond. She rolls her eyes and flips her messy hair as she walks to the bathroom.

I turn on Edie's lights as bright as they can go when I enter. "Bunny! You're going to be late on the first day of school! You'll miss breakfast. You won't get to pick your seat... some boy you don't like will pick your seat for you. Is that what you want?"

"No!" she says, panicked.

"Up. Now."

"Why do boys get to pick my seat?" she asks, wiping her eyes as she climbs out of bed.

"Got you out of bed, didn't it? Your sister was waiting on you to get ready, so you've made her late, too. Edie, I'm counting on you to step it up and help out here, okay? I've got a baby to take care of, too. I can't be everywhere at once in the morning, and I trusted you'd be on schedule, like normal."

"Mama always kept us on schedule."

"That is... good information to know," I say. "I guess I'll get up earlier from now on." I realize I've never helped the girls get ready on my own. Livvy always took care of this. Even when she was sick, she'd bark orders from her bed. The girls knew what needed to be done. "What are you doing with your hair?"

"I need to take a shower."

"We don't have time for that. It's eight. We have to leave in twenty minutes. You're not going to school with wet hair."

"It's dirty, Dad!" she exclaims. "I can't go with it dirty!"

"You washed it yesterday morning. It looks clean. You just need to brush it... maybe pull it back in a ponytail or something. Put in one of those bows Uncle Max bought you. Right?"

"Not on the first day of school! That's so lame! You never get a second chance to make a first impression!" I stare at her for a few seconds after that, wanting to laugh, but holding it in.

"Don't you know most of these kids?" I ask her, tentative.

"It's a new year. You don't understand!" She starts crying.

"Bunny, come on." I shuffle Luca to my other arm and reach out for my oldest daughter, taking a seat on her bed. "Work with me here."

"I can't go to school like this," she whines, looking in the mirror.

"Go get your hairbrush and let's see what we can do, okay?"

She literally stomps to the bathroom, opening the door on Willow, who screams at her sister to get out.

"Girls!" I have to go in there to break up their shouting. "What is going on?"

"I was going to the bathroom," Willow tells me. "She's supposed to knock first!"

"Edie..."

"You told me to get the brush!" She storms past me and into my bedroom.

"Wils, I'm sorry. Continue." I shut the door behind us, leaving Willow to her privacy. "What are you doing in here, Edie?" I ask, following her into the master bath.

"Sitting at Mama's vanity." She starts to run the brush through her hair, but it's knotted. "Daddy, it's not working," she pouts.

Wanting to help her, I quickly retrieve the bassinet from the bedside and bring it into the bathroom with us, laying Luca down in it. He fusses at first, then throws a fit that rivals his oldest sister's both in frustration and volume as I attempt to brush her hair. I'm hurting her, and still can't get the bristles through the ends of her long tresses.

"Sweetie, why is it so tangled?"

"Because I need to wash it. I didn't put conditioner in it yesterday."

"Why not?"

She shrugs. "Mama told me not to."

"No, she said not to *wash* it every day. I remember this conversation. She didn't say not to condition your hair. If you wash it, you have to do all of it... or else... this happens. Your hair's too thick. You dry it out every time you wash it. Conditioner adds a little oil back in. If you skip a day of washing, your scalp produces natural oils. Isn't that what she told you?"

She nods her head. "Daddy, can I stay home today?" I barely hear the question over Luca, but even if I hadn't, I could have guessed the request from the puppy dog eyes that look up at me from the mirror.

"No, Edie, you can't." I pull a rubber band off of the brush handle and pull all of her hair back as best as I can. "We're just putting it in a ponytail today. We'll wash it tonight when you get home."

"Jon?" Emi's practically shouting over all the noise, and she taps on the doorjamb outside my room.

"Come on in," I call out to her, happy that she's a little early. She'd said she'd be here to see them off, so I wasn't expecting any help getting them ready.

"Should I take him?" She points to my wailing son; I simply nod my head.

"Memi, do I have to go to school like this?" Edie asks.

"Like what? You look adorable!" my mother-in-law answers—perfectly, I might add.

"Maybe if I could wear some of Mama's blush..."

"Go get dressed." I nudge her along with a pat on her back. Once she's in her room, I let out a sigh of relief. There's silence for a few seconds. Emi's calmed the baby. Edie's changing clothes. Willow's—

"Daddy?" I smile briefly at Emi as I walk past her into the hallway to see what my younger daughter needs. She's got the shorts of her school uniform up to her hips, but they're not going any further.

"What's the matter?"

"They don't fit," she says, her brows contorted in worry.

"Well? Go get your pants."

"I already tried them, too." She shakes her head. "I can't pull them all the way up."

I'd noticed the other day how much she'd grown over the summer. She was almost Edie's height, when she'd always lagged behind a few inches, but I didn't expect her to grow out of the clothes she'd worn to school just a few months ago—especially since I'd asked her to try them on last week, and she reported that they were fine.

"So, you have nothing to wear?"

"My shirt fits. Kind of." I notice the last button doesn't come together. My eight-year-old is growing hips. The thought of it makes me sad. Edie comes out of her room, dressed in her khaki jumper over a pressed, white blouse. Her hair *does* look like a bird's nest from behind. I'm only grateful of the fact that she can't see it, but I do start to worry that kids will tease her.

"Jon, why didn't you have her try them on?" Emi asks.

"Wils," I start, not looking back at my mother-in-law, "tell Memi that you told me you did. Okay?"

She shrugs again, just like she did earlier. I start to wonder if she ever told me she tried them on at all. Maybe she's been passively shrugging for weeks, and I've been too tired to notice.

"She did tell me that," I finally say, certain that we actually had a conversation about it. I distinctly remember it now. It was a discussion between me and both of the girls. "Willow, go borrow one of Edie's skirts and shirts."

She shakes her head violently. "I can't wear a skirt!"

"Yes. You can. And you will."

"I hate skirts, Daddy!"

"I don't care, Willow. You're going to school today, and you have to wear the uniform. Period. Yours don't fit. Hopefully Edie's will. Come on."

Begrudgingly, she follows me, but only after the tears have started falling down her cheeks. I know she hates dresses and anything girly. This is probably her worst nightmare, but I'm not sure what else to do. I take out the clothes and hand them to Willow, who proceeds to change in the middle of her sister's room.

"I'll go buy new uniforms today, okay? This is the only day you'll have to wear this. Tomorrow, it's back to shorts and pants. I promise."

"I hate it," she cries, wiping her nose on the back of her arm after she's dressed.

"I know, baby." I get down on my knees and give her a hug. "I should have made sure you'd tried them on, right? Daddy should have double-checked. But you look pretty."

"I don't either."

"Yes, you do," I whisper, giving her a kiss on the cheek. "You want me to braid your hair?" She swipes at her tears and nods her head. After grabbing a couple of rubber bands from Edie's dresser, I take a seat on her bed and tell Willow to kneel in front of me. I do the best I can at parting her hair down the center and pulling her hair into two braids at the nape of her neck. "There you go."

She feels the back of her head and starts crying again. "That's not right!"

"What do you mean?"

"They have to be *French* braids. Mama always did *French* braids!"

At the end of my rope, I start to get angry. "Willow—"

"Jon, I think Auggie wants his daddy," Emi says, the name cutting through my heart in a painful jab. "Let me worry about the French braids.

I taught Livvy. Edie?" she calls back into my bedroom, and my oldest eventually appears and follows her into her room. I take my son and trudge away to reflect on the absolute failure that this morning has become. When I return to the bathroom to get the bassinet, I realize Edie had gone back into the room and had gotten out Livvy's makeup from the cabinet under the sink.

"Please be a low maintenance child when you're older," I whisper to Luca.

After I put his bed back in its place, my brain processes what Edie had been doing and I return to her room where Emi's trying to teach her how to French braid. She's not paying any attention, though.

I put my hand under her chin and angle her face into the light. "Wash it off. Now." Although expertly applied, I can still see the darker rouge on her cheekbones. I follow her into the bathroom to make sure she does it. "Now you're gonna force me to throw away your mother's things?" I ask her, feeling my throat tighten as the words come out.

"No, don't," she pleads, her face lathered in soap.

I have to clear my throat before I can speak again. "If I can't trust you with her things, then we can't have them in this house," I threaten.

"I won't touch them again. I promise, Daddy."

"I will be very disappointed if you do, bunny." I shut the bathroom door, cradling Luca in my arms as I sit on the edge of the bathtub. "The last thing I want to do is lose parts of her." My eyes water, even though I will them not to.

"I'm sorry," she says, her apology sincere.

"Dry your face and come give me a hug."

After tossing the towel on the floor, she throws her arms around my neck and holds on tight. "I love you, Daddy." When she lets go, she kisses my cheek and Luca's forehead. This sets him off into another crying fit. Edie apologizes for that, too.

"He's a baby. He's going to cry sometimes, but you don't need to apologize. He's just ready for his nap. We have to figure out our new routine with you girls back in school."

She opens the door, revealing Emi and Willow standing in the hallway. My other daughter still looks like her world has fallen apart, but is wearing her backpack, ready to go. "Go grab your things," I tell Edie. After she runs back to her room, I thank my mother-in-law for her help, checking out the expert job she did on Willow's hair. "I need you to teach me that."

"We'll have a lesson. If you want company for dinner, Jack and I would love to hear how their first day went. We can get the girls bathed and we can use them both as hair models."

"Sure." I bounce lightly on the balls of my feet, trying to get my son to calm down.

"Maybe the walk will do Auggie some good," Emi suggests, leading us all downstairs. She can keep saying it, but I'll never accept the nickname.

I make note of the knee-high socks the girls wear. Both pairs have seen better days. Willow's left one actually has a hole in the calf. Livvy would never let them leave the house like this. I'm surprised Emi's allowing it. After checking my watch, I know we don't have time to fix anything.

"Luca, I swear, you can take a nap here, or after we get back," I tell him as I strap him into the stroller. "I promise you'll get your time, little man. Please stop crying for Daddy."

"Yes, shut up, Froggie," my youngest daughter says.

"Willow, don't talk to your brother that way," Emi speaks up before I have to. I catch the eye-roll response, but no one else does. I decide to let it go. Willow's having a bad enough day. We all are. No sense in making it worse.

When we get outside the building, I shake hands with Chance, the body guard we'd used the last few years for the girls. His only job for us is to walk to and from their school every day, keeping an eye on their surroundings and being ready in case something bad ever happens.

He's always been very professional, and even though both Edie and Willow like to tell him about their days and chat with him like he's their friend, he only extends his hand to them as a greeting when they were both expecting hugs. Emi holds Willow's hand and leads the way down the street to their private school. Edie offers to push Luca. I keep one hand on her back and one on the stroller handle, always in contact with both in case I need to stop her or the stroller.

Chance follows us, a couple feet behind, quiet and alert. When we reach the school, he stands at the metal gate while Emi and I take the girls inside to their classrooms.

In past years, their faces were alight with excitement at the prospects of a new schoolyear. Today, there's not a smile to be found.

I feel defeated. At least Luca has quieted down to a mellow whimper.

"I'll have new clothes for you this afternoon," I promise Willow. "No dresses. No skirts. Don't worry about it. Just make it through today." I flick at her pouty lip, trying to lighten the mood, but when she nods, a tear breaks free from her eye. "It's okay." I give her a big hug, trying to assure her that she'll be fine. "I love you." She steps to the side to let Emi tell her goodbye, too, but she doesn't say a word to either of us.

This really sucks.

In Edie's classroom, she finds her assigned seat and sets her backpack down. Hurriedly, she unzips it and starts unloading her supplies. "Daddy, where's my note?" she whispers.

"What note? Did you need a permission slip for something?" I ask her.

"No!" she says, her brows furrowed. "Mama always puts a little note in an envelope in my bag for the first day of school! Where's my note?"

I never knew she did that. She never told me, and my daughters never showed me any such letters. I shake my head, befuddled, then start to tug on my hair. "Bunny, I didn't know. But I promise there will be one in there tomorrow."

"Tomorrow doesn't matter. Tomorrow's not the first day of school," she informs me, her hands on her hips and her eyes narrowed.

"I understand... but..." I sigh, feeling like a gargantuan piece of shit. "I'm sorry." I hug her quickly, then stand up and push the stroller out of the classroom before she sees me fall apart.

I'm afraid it's about to happen. I'm not sure how to keep it together anymore.

Emi's talking to someone on her way out of the classroom but exits the room alone with a warm smile on her face. She puts her hand on my back, walking with me toward the exit.

"A bunch of parents were saying hi to you back there. Edie's teacher, too."

"Honestly, Em," I start, then sigh, "I never even saw anyone else in there. I saw my daughters, and that's about all I could focus on today, so." I bite my bottom lip and swallow, trying to maintain composure. "That's probably rude of me, but I'm overwhelmed today."

She opens the door for me and Luca and waits to respond until we're back on the sidewalk with Chance in tow again. "I'm sure they all understand. Don't beat yourself up."

It's far too late for that.

"Jon, would you like me to go get Willow's uniforms?" she asks.

"Nope. I'm going to do it. I'm her father. It's my responsibility to take care of these things."

"Okay, but I'm offering to help. It's not a big deal," she says.

"I'll just get her a size bigger, right?" I respond, ignoring her. "Or two?"

"Why don't you just get her Edie's size. Those clothes fit her nicely."

"That makes sense. Yeah."

"At least let me take Auggie off your hands–"

"Emi," I interrupt. "I've got this. You know? They're my kids. I have to be able to take care of them."

"Jon, you don't have to do it alone." Her eyes begin to tear up.

I stop walking and speak to her directly. "I appreciate you coming and being here with me this morning. I do. It meant a lot. I've got things to take care of, so... why don't we have Chance call the car service to get you a ride home? I'll call you soon. Chance, I'll see you this afternoon."

I hug my mother-in-law briefly, and without giving her any time to argue, I push the stroller away from them both. I can't stand seeing the pity in her eyes.

At home, I go upstairs, put a fresh diaper on Luca and grab a soft blanket in hopes that he'll fall asleep while I make the drive across town to the department store where they sell the girls' uniforms. I take a skirt and shirt from Edie's closet for reference, and then head down to where the car is already waiting.

As soon as I buckle myself in, the baby starts wailing. When I reach back, I discover he's somehow managed to throw the blanket I'd carefully tucked around him onto the floorboard. *I guess he's hot.*

"Luca..." I say to myself in frustration, pulling away from the drive.

It is warm today... is it too hot to put him under a blanket? How am I not mindful of that?

I shake my head, wondering how I'm going to make this work. The girls have to get to school right when he'd normally be napping, right after he eats. I mean, this is why it's optimal to have two parents, I suppose. The tear is falling from my eye before I even notice it, and I swipe it away angrily. I don't have time to get emotional. And then this morning, I didn't even have to account for my job. Sure, on most days I can work whenever from wherever, but there will be times when I have early meetings. Then what am I supposed to do?

Ask for help, Jon.

I get a text alert and press the button to let my car read it out loud.

"*Shea Scott sent a message. 'Send me the first day pics!' Would you like to respond?*"

My heart drops. "Fuck."

I quickly scan the street and pull over at the nearest curb, putting the car in park and setting my head against the steering wheel.

How could I forget pictures? We have an album. It's filled with pictures of every first day the girls have had. There are pictures of Edie. Pictures of Willow. Pictures of them together. Pictures of them with me.

Pictures of them with *her.*

I break down, and my crying rivals my son's. There will never be another picture like that in the album. There had been many times when I'd admired those pictures, noticing how the girls had grown by seeing how tall they stood next to their mother. It was one of the many reasons I loved those pictures. That, and seeing the subtle—and not so subtle—ways each of my daughters favored her. Edie looked so much like her, but in two of the pictures, Willow had mimicked Livvy's stance without even realizing it, putting her weight on her left leg, and putting her right hand on her hip.

How could I forget to take the fucking first day pictures to memorialize this day?

And then I remember the details of this hellish morning. I utterly ruined their first day, anyway. Who would want to remember it?

I should have ensured the uniforms fit last week, when I asked them both to try them on. I should have gotten them up early this morning to make sure they both had time to do their hair and look their best. I should have asked Emi to come over much sooner to help. I should have had Joel make them breakfast when he offered. Instead, I was tired, and I wanted to sleep in, and I needed to tend to Luca.

What about my girls? I remember their faces as I left them in their classrooms and wonder if they'll be scarred for life because I made them go to school today.

Putting the car in drive, I turn around and go north. When I reach Jack and Emi's brownstone, I take a few deep breaths before getting out of the car. They're on the front step waiting by the time I have Luca out of his car seat.

"Come here, Auggie." Emi takes him from me right away and goes inside. I must look like hell, because once the front door closes, Jack puts his arms around me and hugs me, not asking any questions as to why I'm here. I guess he knows.

"How do I do this without her?" I ask him through new tears. "Because every day can't be this way."

"It won't be, son," he says, patting me on the back and guiding me into the living room where Emi is already calming down Luca.

"I can't have another morning like this one, where I just see sheer disappointment on my daughter's face of how many ways I've let her down. I can't have that."

"Well, there will be days like that." Jack smiles at me. "They will be few and far between, but daughters will do that. If today was your first, consider yourself lucky."

I know he's trying to bring levity into the conversation to lighten the mood, but everything feels so heavy that I can't bring myself out of it. "How can I ever make up for the loss of the woman we loved? It's not possible. I can never be that to them."

"You're their father," Emi says, "and that's all they'll ever need you to be. You don't fill a void left by Liv, or by anyone you lose. The void is crucial to growth... to learning... to maturing. You learn to do things around the void; to shift it so that it's not the center of your being, like it feels like it is right now. But sometimes you'll want to revisit it. You'll feel comfort in the depth of emotions it brings. You'll remember the great love you shared with her. So, you don't want to lose touch with that. You don't fill it.

"I think of it as... setting it free."

I catch myself just before I ask the stupid question—how she became so wise so fast about loss.

Nate. She's been through this before, and suddenly, I feel a kindred spirit in her that I hadn't recognized before. I look upon her, feeling a little less lonely than I did when I arrived.

"Thank you, Emi." Although I continue to cry, I feel safe in their home and comforted by their support. Yet another reason to be thankful for Livvy.

CHAPTER 30

"Will and Shea moved their library of books to your house?" Emi asks me as she puts some paint on her small brush.

"Most of them. We had plenty of empty space on our shelves. We'd planned on expanding it as the kids grew up. I ended up donating a bunch of my old stuff, too." I study the drawing Livvy had done for Charlie's nursery and make sure I've got everything outlined onto the wall. "Kept all of Livvy's things, in case the girls want to read them someday," I add as an afterthought.

"Edie may like her design books."

"That's what I was thinking. And Willow's going to love having full access to Will's stuff." I laugh. "I had to put his more valuable books on the top shelf. We need to wait until she's a little older for some of them."

"Were you able to clean up the slushee stain?" Emi asks.

"The steam cleaner fixed the carpet, but the iPad was toast. We got her a new one yesterday with a waterproof case and a stern talking-to about respecting her things better."

"I know Willow felt bad about it."

"She did."

My mother-in-law joins me at the table we'd set up in the middle of the room. "So... just start painting dark blue around all the letters and illustrations?"

"That's the best way to tackle it... right?" I ask her for her opinion once more.

"I think that's what she would have done. And you can start at the outer perimeter with the broader strokes, and then fill in the gaps in between. We'll work on the details once the blue's done."

"Cool. I told Will we'd be done by Wednesday. Is that realistic?"

"Four days? We'll make it work. We have to let them back into their apartment before Shea has the baby," she reminds me.

"The due date's in a week." I take a deep breath and dip my brush into the paint. "I can't wait to meet Charlie. I can't wait to see him and Luca together."

"I know."

"Hard to believe Liv's original due date was just six days ago. And he's already seven weeks old."

"Auggie's doing so well."

It's just the two of us, and it's time to have the conversation I've wanted to have since the day he was born. I set down the brush and sit against the window pane, my arms crossed.

"Em, every time you call him that, I die inside." She pulls her brush away from the wall, surprised at the confrontation. "It takes me back to when she was here. I hear her." Tears threaten to stop me from speaking. "I hear her voice. I hear her tormenting me with that name, and I die."

"Jon," she says, walking over to me and putting her hand on my forearm, "that's what she wanted to call him. I want to honor that."

"I don't think she really would have called him that," I argue. "It was an ongoing joke. We talked about it, Emi. Together, we hadn't decided on a name. In fact, the only thing we had decided was to not name him after me.

"The way Auggie came about was when we were discussing using Augustus. I told her I didn't want to call him by that name, and she suggested Gus. I didn't like that, either. So, she mentioned Auggie, and I had such a visceral reaction to it. She latched onto it and laughed about it all night and she never let it go, but—"

"But, Jon, we love it, and I think Livvy fell in love with it. And... wherever she is, I want her to be able to find him... and know where he is."

I scoff at her logic. "Emi, she knows where her son is. She doesn't need a label for him." I take my phone out of my pocket and show my mother-in-law the background picture of him. "Look at this baby! How can you look at his face and not see Livvy? Look at those eyes! That nose. The ears and the smile! Everything about him is her. And that's why I wanted to name him after *her*. When I saw him in the nursery, I just knew she would live on in him.

"I thought I would honor her with the name forever. It just hurts so bad to hear the name *Auggie*."

"I don't want to hurt you, Jon, but he's Auggie to me. He's Froggie to the girls."

"I know he's Froggie to them. I've accepted that. I can't change that."

"But is it so bad to remember Livvy by that? To remember that night she wouldn't stop laughing? To remember *that* smile? Those are the memories you want to have of her, aren't they?" she asks. "Can't we try to associate the name with that night? With that beautiful smile of hers? With that memory? You don't have to call him Auggie, Jon, but don't take it away from me. To me, that's a connection I have to her."

After staring at the phone for a few more seconds, I tuck it back into my pocket and return to my paintbrush. I dip it into the paint once more and step on the ladder to reach the tall corner of the room. Eventually, Emi goes back to focusing on the other side of the wall.

As we work on the mural created by my wife–her daughter–I know I can't deprive her of something that makes her feel closer to the woman she loved. "I get it, Emi. I do." I sigh heavily and look down at her. "I can't call him that, but I don't want to take that from you."

She smiles graciously, continuing to paint. "Thank you."

*A*t the end of the day, Emi and I return to my apartment where Jack, Will, Shea, Joel and the girls are getting ready for dinner. After we both get cleaned up, we meet everyone else in the living area where the adults are strangely quiet as the girls both work on their homework.

"What's going on?" I ask the room, taking Luca from Jack on my way to the club chair in the corner. He's halfway through his bottle and continues eating while I settle in.

Jack, Will and Shea look between one another before my brother gets up and retrieves an envelope from the kitchen island.

"What is it?"

Will taps Joel on his shoulder from behind and signs for him to take the girls to their rooms for a few minutes.

"He's not a babysitter," I clarify aloud, not liking that my brother's asking Joel to do something like this. "Joel's not here to watch the girls."

"These are the autopsy results," my brother signs to the room, making sure Edie and Willow aren't watching.

"I don't mind," Joel says.

"Girls, clean up your things and go to Edie's room with Joel for a few minutes. He's going to have a signing lesson with you both."

"Now?" Willow asks. "We're about to eat."

"Yes, now. We won't start dinner without you."

"I'll watch the stove," Shea tells Joel, getting up from her seat with Will's help. We all move the conversation into the kitchen, just to make sure we're not overheard by the girls once they're upstairs. Luca continues to eat, unfazed.

Will pushes the envelope toward me and offers to take Luca. "You haven't opened them?" I ask, looking at Jack, since that's whose name is on the outside.

"I wanted to wait for you two to get back so we could read them together."

I nod my head. I had been so anxious to see what the final results were of the autopsy, but now I'm dreading the news inside. "I can't do it." I adjust the bottle as my son nears the end of his meal.

"I want to know," Emi says, taking the envelope. "I want to know if we need to have your kids tested for something genetic. Don't you want to know that?"

"I don't want to think about losing them, Emi."

"We would only think about *saving* them," she counters, sliding her finger under the paper seal. "Did you find Isaiah's results?"

"I never looked."

She looks at me disapprovingly before taking out the official paper. I watch her expression as she reads it over. "Sudden cardiac arrest caused by CHD."

"What's that mean?" I ask.

She nods her head. "Congenital heart disease."

"But..." I look between Jack and Emi. "How could you not know?"

"She never showed signs or symptoms," she says. "Doctors never said anything. I know these things can stay undetected for many years... obviously."

"We adopted her when she was four. Maybe when she was born, it was identified, but... we didn't know," Jack adds.

"And she could just go through life without anyone knowing?"

"Well, she did."

I set down Luca's bottle and hug him into my chest. "Don't they test for these things when babies are born?"

"With as many tests as Luca's been through, I bet you would know if he had any sort of defects. We can call the doctors."

"And the girls?"

"We get them tested," Jack says. "But we don't panic. And we don't do anything to scare them."

"You think Isaiah's results are in the studio?" Emi asks. I nod. "I'll go."

"I'll help," my father-in-law offers.

"If she has them, they'll be in one of the file cabinet drawers on the north side of the building. Most likely the bottom drawer."

While they're upstairs, I hand off the baby to Will and call the NICU doctor who'd been in charge of Luca's care while he was there. He'd given me his cell phone for emergencies, and while he may not consider this an emergency, I know I won't sleep without knowing.

"Dr. Williams," he answers.

"Good evening, Dr. Williams. This is Jon Scott, and I'm sorry for bothering you at this time of night, but we just got Livvy's autopsy results, and... her heart problem was caused by a congenital heart defect. I just have to know if you tested Luca for this when he was born. If you saw anything strange..."

"Jon," he says, sounding friendly and assuring. "Luca is... perfect. Yes, we ran the gamut of exams on him, and heart tests were a part of that. He has no arrhythmia, his heart is a good size, it's working just like it's supposed to. I'm very sorry to hear that about Livvy, but rest assured, Luca is fine."

"You wouldn't run any more tests... just to make sure?"

"There are no more tests to run. We did an EKG, an echocardiogram, a chest x-ray, pulse oximetry... nothing showed anything irregular."

"But Livvy never showed signs of a defect, either... that we know of."

"Listen, his pediatrician can run tests every year, if you'd like. Whatever will put your mind at ease."

"That... would, yes."

"Okay. But for now, please know that your little boy is doing very well... he was growing like he should and showing all signs of catching up to other babies his age."

"Okay. Thank you."

"Talk to the pediatrician at his next appointment."

Will and Shea are both waiting for me to say something. "He's okay?" Shea finally asks.

"So far, yeah." She hugs me, relieved.

I consider calling the girls' doctor, but I hear the internal elevator returning from the third floor. Jack and Emi step out, holding a file folder.

Jack shakes his head. "His was a heart attack. Not cardiac arrest."

"But does that mean he didn't have a defect?" I ask.

Emi looks at her husband. "I don't think we have any way of knowing that from this. It's not his cause of death, though, and that should bring you some peace."

"No. It really doesn't. Luca's okay," I tell them. "I need to call Dr. Avalon."

"Jon," she says, stepping toward me and taking the phone. "You would know if they had something wrong. She can't tell you anything more tonight. We can set up appointments tomorrow... but the office is closed right now. Let's try to have dinner, enjoy our time together and not worry the girls," she stresses again.

"Okay."

"Diaper," Will interrupts, heading upstairs with my son.

"You've got it?"

"Hell, yeah, I've got it," he says, slipping into baby talk. Shea and I look at each other and laugh.

"Get Joel and the girls on your way down!" I call out to him.

. . .

*A*fter dropping off Edie and Willow at school and before Emi and I start painting the following Tuesday, we swing by the girls' pediatrician for an appointment we'd set up. Dr. Avalon is waiting in her office with two folders laid in front of her on the desk. We both take the seats across from her, and I fold my hands in my lap, not knowing what else to do with them. I'd been fidgeting all weekend, nervous about what we'd hear today, and couldn't wait to know, one way or another.

Emi reaches over and takes my right hand, though, linking her fingers with mine. I meet her eyes and smile, appreciative of the support she's always so quick to give when I know she needs it just as much as I do.

"You two look worried."

I nod. Emi responds to her. "We want to be able to prepare and plan if the girls have any sort of genetic heart... things." She shakes her head and covers her mouth as her eyes tear up. I can see the fear in them.

Dr. Avalon stands up and gives my mother-in-law two tissues that she's pulled fresh from the box. "Let me put your minds at ease-both of you. Edie and Willow show no signs of a congenital heart defect of any kind. They were tested when they were born, and they've never exhibited any symptoms. I see no reason to make a special appointment for them now, Jon," she says, looking at me, "but we can do some extra tests at their next yearly exams. Again, I don't think they're necessary, but I know you may want more than that right now after everything you've been through."

"Thank you for understanding."

"I'm understanding about that," she says, "but I don't understand why I didn't get to see the newest member of the family today. I thought I'd get a special bonus visit with him."

"He was sound asleep with Granddaddy this morning, and we thought it was best to keep him on his routine," I tell her. "Emi and I are in the middle of a painting project for my brother and sister-in-law."

"Shea? Her baby's due this week, right?"

"This week," I confirm.

"I can't wait to meet him."

"We can't, either."

"Well, I'll make some notes in the girls' files, so next summer, we'll run extra tests. For now, don't worry about anything. Let the girls be kids. And most of all, don't let them know you're worried about anything like this. Don't scare them."

"Of course not."

"Good. Is there anything else?"

"That's it for us. Thank you for your time."

We both shake her hand and make our way out of her office and into the street where a car awaits us for what is hopefully our last day of painting.

CHAPTER 31

*W*ill bursts out of the maternity room into the hallway where we're waiting in the birthing unit of the hospital, his face red, his lashes matted with moisture and his hair a perfect mess. "It's a boy!" We all laugh at his announcement, since we all knew that already. "Charlie Hadley. He's perfect. Holy shit. He's just perfect. Eight pounds, six ounces, 19 and a half inches. Holy shit. Did I say he's perfect?"

"Three times now," Max says. "You've also cursed twice, so two bucks to his swear jar."

"He's in the other fucking room," Will argues, pointing behind him. "Shea did great. She was a rock star."

"She do that to your hair?"

"Maybe, but I deserved it. That's what she said, and I'm sure she's right, after what she just went through." He laughs, his smile full of wonder like I've never seen on him. It's a beautiful sight. "I should probably go back in there."

"Yeah," I agree. "But let us know as soon as we can see them. And tell Shea congratulations." I give my brother a big hug, so proud of him.

After he returns to the room, we all sit back down in chairs that line the wall.

"The girls didn't want to come?" Emi asks.

"They wouldn't come to the hospital," I tell her. "I couldn't bribe either of them. I don't know if they're sick of it, or scared of what might happen, but... they were both adamant, and I didn't want to push them. Steven said he and Kaydra didn't mind watching them for us. And Kayd couldn't keep her hands off Luca."

"I'm glad they could help out," Jack says. "They've been traveling so much recently."

"Yeah. Steven almost didn't recognize me with this," I say touching my beard.

"You ever going to get rid of that?" he asks.

"I don't know. It's not really... *grizzly* enough yet." Jack cringes and I laugh. "Once Luca starts pulling on it, I promise you, it'll come right off. It won't take much of that to convince me."

"I mean, if that's all it takes," he says, reaching over and tugging on the short hairs. I smack his hand away.

"You know, I don't get noticed in the street as much... and I like that," I admit. "If I put on my glasses, I may as well be someone else. No one bothers me at all. If you could go incognito sometimes, wouldn't you?"

"That doesn't sound so bad to me," Emi says, stroking her own chin. I smile. "Do you think Will and Shea have everything they need at home?"

"We did a run-through yesterday." I nod. "They need more diapers. They have plenty to get started, but they'll need more in... what, two weeks' time? They just have no idea yet."

"Jacks and I will stop and get them some more on our way home today and take them over tomorrow. Their concierge will let us in, right?"

"Of course. I'll let them know."

"I may take a few extra things. Clothes. I can't help myself."

"I'm aware. I see the new things appearing in Luca's closet all the time."

"So... Charlie's eight pounds six ounces." Callen comments.

"That's twice as much as Luca was. More than," I recall.

"How much is Luca up to now?" Max asks.

I smile and sigh. "Six pounds 10 ounces. But, hey, he's 18 and a half inches, so... that makes him sound like he's almost as tall, right?"

"We shouldn't compare them," Emi says. "I did that when Trey was little, and it drove me nuts. And then he caught up, and then he outgrew both of these guys," she explains, pointing to my youngest brother and his boyfriend. "So, don't compare. You just can't predict these things."

"I know. And hey, now Will can give me Charlie's hand-me-downs for Luca," I say with a laugh. "I think he'll love that, after having to wear my hand-me-downs all his life."

"He *is* gonna love that," Max agrees. "He *hated* you for that."

"And, yet, it had nothing to do with me."

"Yeah." Max swallows. "He hated Mom for that. But you by proxy. It was a loving-hate."

"Yep."

*A*fter a couple hours of waiting, Shea is ready for us to meet her newborn son. When I enter the room, it's such a stark difference from the experience Liv and I had just two months ago. In the birthing unit, labor, deliver and postpartum care all happen in one room, so all the comforts of home for Mom, Dad and Baby are available here. The room is warmly decorated with modern touches. It's a comforting place to be. Anyone in a room like this would feel cared for and well attended to.

I can't help but think of Livvy, her body on that cold, hard, metal operating table, where no attention was paid to her comfort in the final moments of her life. While everyone else surrounds Shea's bed, I take a deep breath, look up at the ceiling and turn on my heels, making my way back into the hallway before the tears fall. I will them not to, but I have no power over them at this point.

Such a stark difference. *Why couldn't my beautiful Olivia have had this fate, too? Why couldn't we have had the luxury of a cozy room and access to the gynecologist who had been with her throughout her pregnancy—the one who knew Livvy so well and may have been better equipped to recommend the right care for her that night? What would she have told us to do? Not get the shot? Don't do the C-section? Was there another decision that we could have made? Why weren't we offered that?*

All I know is that we made the wrong choice. I believe that there was a way for both of them to live—that some option was there that would have allowed them both to live. I've thought about this thousands of times since she left me.

"Hey."

I don't want to look up at Will. I don't want him to see me crying about Livvy on such a special day of his life. I keep my head in my hands, my hair threaded between my fingers.

"I know you're happy for me."

"I am," I choke out, then gasp in air, unable to mask my crying.

He puts his hand on my knee. "I wish, more than anything, Jon, that it could have been this way for you and Liv. You know how much of an effort went into Liv and Shea planning their pregnancies," he says with a laugh. "They practically planned the rest of our lives for us, you know?"

"Yeah."

"Yes, this is the best day of my life," he starts, "but it still isn't the way we envisioned this. It's not what we planned—what Shea planned. She wanted to do all of this with Liv by her side. I don't know if you had a chance to look at her, but the reason her eyes are puffy and her nose is red has nothing to do with giving birth a few hours ago. She's been crying about her best friend for the last 45 minutes... and I've been trying to assure her that she will be a perfect mother. That she will have her own natural instincts. That she didn't need to have her here to raise Charlie, but that she'd remember all the lessons Livvy taught her over the years—consciously or not. That you're still here and you have so much wisdom to share with us. That Jack and Emi, the people who taught Livvy all she knew, are willing to step in as grandparents to our son. That your girls will forever remind all of us 'that's not how Mama did it' as long as we're all alive, you know?"

"I do know that," I nod, finally lifting my head to look at him. I wipe my cheeks with the backs of my hands. "I've heard that more than I want to in a lifetime already."

"I know this isn't an easy day for you. I didn't think it would be."

"Thanks."

"But if you don't get your motherfucking ass in that room and meet your godson, I'm going to be so fucking offended that I might just give the honor to Callen. Poor kid is the only one who has no title now... I feel sorry for him."

"You're not giving him my title," I say as I stand up, smiling weakly. "But you know what? I can give Luca a third godfather. He can never have too many people looking after him."

"Sweet. That takes the burden off of me."

"So, I guess... Coley's his godmother?"

Will puts his arm around me and nods his head. "Yeah... if her sister lived in the States, it may have been her... but she couldn't even get time off for the birth. Coley's been there for her like a sister."

"She's a good choice," I tell him. "He'll get the straight and narrow from me and... a little bit of the wild side from her. Visual arts from me, literary arts from her. Man. You covered your bases, didn't you?"

"That was the exact train of thought we went through," he lies. "So, can we go see Charlie?"

"Let's go see this little boy. Who does he look like?"

He stands behind me with both hands on my shoulders and pushes me through the door. A crowd is around Coley, who's holding the baby. I go to Shea first, noticing the puffy eyes my brother mentioned, and give her a hug. She holds on for a long time, but neither of us says anything–nor do we need to.

I kiss her on the cheek as we break apart. "No more tears today, okay? Not from either of us. Let's make a pact."

She shakes her head. "My hormones are all over the place, Jon, so... no." She laughs at me. "No deal."

"Well, I'm going to try to hold up my end of the bargain then. I'm so happy for you guys."

"Thank you."

"Jon? Want to hold him?" Coley asks me as she walks to my side of the bed.

"Absolutely."

Charlie's wrapped tightly in a blanket and sleeping soundly when she hands him over to me. I know less than two pounds separates them, but it feels so different holding him than it does holding my son. His face is fuller than Luca's. He has more hair–a crazy amount of hair, actually– straight and all over the place. Picking up one of his tiny hands with my finger, I realize how pudgy his little digits are.

He's a beautiful baby boy and he looks like the picture of health.

"I thought babies were supposed to look like their fathers or something, Will. Where are you in this little guy?"

"You're one to talk. Two out of three of yours looked nothing like you."

"Hey!"

"The hair. Look at his hair..." my brother says.

"Oh, definitely that, poor thing... but... nothing else."

"Just because he's *my* color," Shea scoffs. "But give it time. He's just a few hours old. He just looks like a baby to me. Plus, I love Will's hair."

"Will's got plenty of it. Gets that from his dad, I think," I comment, because both of my brothers have incredibly thick, full hair. Max keeps his in control by keeping the sides cut short, but Will constantly misses hair appointments for weeks at a time. Shea has trimmed his hair at home more than once out of frustration with him. I think he just likes the extra attention from her.

Charlie will definitely have a unique look, with his mom's mocha skin and his dad's straight hair. As attractive as his parents are, I bet he's going to be the center of attention when he grows up. Watching him sleep, I wonder how it will be for Luca, standing next to him. Will my boy catch up to him? Will he fill out? Grow taller? Will he always be in Charlie's shadow? Will there be animosity between them?

Realizing I'm comparing them, I kill the thoughts immediately. They're newborns. We're going to be raising them together; they'll be as close as brothers–like Trey and Max.

I can only hope our boys' friendship can be as strong as theirs. I wonder if it's something we can foster, or if it's something that has to happen naturally. Trey and Max were never not friends. From the moment they met, they were the best of friends. I'm sure Trey had dozens of friends, but Max's social circle was limited. He never went on playdates. Didn't go to daycare when he was young, so when the two of them played catch with Jack for the first time, I remember that he didn't stop laughing the entire time. He'd catch a ball and giggle. He'd throw a ball and burst into a fit of laughter. He'd drop the ball and chuckle as he ran to chase it. And it was contagious–Trey was entertained by him, and he laughed until his stomach hurt.

Jack left them both in the yard with the ball. Their game of catch was over, but for Max and Trey, their lifetime of friendship was just starting. I'd watched them for a few minutes before Livvy and I stole some time for us, but Jack and Emi returned to the yard to revel in their joy.

I lift my head and look at the two of them now. Mid-twenties, both in love with amazing people, and still I don't think anyone or anything would come between Trey and Max as friends.

"Can I have my son back?" Will asks, taking him from me.

"Yeah." I shake my head, getting myself back into the present. "He's perfect, Will. I can't wait for him to meet Luca. We're on standby, starting now. You just tell me when I can bring him over."

"We just need to get settled at home," Shea says. "Then I want all of you to come—Luca and the girls. And all of you." She looks around the room. "The whole family. I want him to grow up knowing all of you."

"Well," Emi says, "it just so happens that on October seventh..." She looks at me in time to see my face fall, my head bow to the ground. "Jacks and I are hosting dinner at our house for anyone who can come."

I shake my head.

"It's mandatory for Jon, but optional for anyone else."

"No, I'll drop the girls off or something. Maybe Luca and I can... I don't know."

"You're coming, Jon," Jack says.

And I know there's no way I'll be able to get out of it.

CHAPTER 32

Three weeks later, Jack and Emi asked to take Luca on what we'd all decided to call Livvy Day from here on out—October 7, Livvy's birthday. It was a day that was significant to all of us—one that rotated around her while she was alive and the one we'll use to celebrate her life today. Not having Luca or the girls to care for on a weekday, and in a vain attempt to keep myself distracted, I went into work. I've been going for half-days three days a week and working from home as needed for a month, but this was my first day to be at the office for an entire day.

I had a few internal meetings, but none with clients. Regardless, I shaved this morning and wore a suit—I know I would have if she had still been here. When I was getting ready, I imagined her in some beautiful, faraway place watching me with her vibrant smile and wishing she could be with me today on our 10th wedding anniversary. Never in a million years would I have imagined that we wouldn't still be together to celebrate this milestone.

In the middle of the afternoon, I shut my door and pull all the blinds closed, feeling consumed by a flood of emotions and memories.

Tomorrow, it will be twenty years ago to the day that we went out on our first official date. I remember back to that night, frozen on the moment the night started when she opened the front door and I saw her in a dress for the first time. The words lingering on my tongue when I saw her were *'You look so sexy,'* but Jack and Emi were *right there* and if I uttered those words, they'd never have let her leave the house with me.

To prepare for the date, I'd asked teachers, shop owners, librarians—anyone I could find—what the most upscale restaurants were in the city. It was not a subject I was even remotely familiar with. I had many suggestions, but when someone mentioned the name One if by Land, Two if by Sea, I stopped asking. I remember going to the computer lab at school and looking it up, and it was everything I was going for. Expensive enough for a Holland and known to be romantic. The only thing I didn't know is if Liv had ever been there, so I had called her house to ask her parents. Emi was so kind when she answered my call, and I was relieved when it wasn't Jack, who terrified me back then. She encouraged me to take her somewhere less fancy and warned me how expensive it was, but when I assured her I had enough money and, more importantly, wanted to take Livvy to the best place I could choose, she didn't try to stop me.

When I selected the place, I didn't expect Livvy to dress up. She always looked cute—she'd wear shorts in the summer and jeans and pants in the winter. She always looked like she could have walked out of the pages of any fashion magazine. No girls at my school ever dressed like her, so I knew whatever she wore for our date, she would be stunning and perfect and look way out of my league.

So that dress was a wonderful surprise to the hormonal teenager that couldn't wait to hold her hand or, better yet, kiss her at the end of the night. And after that date, she wore dresses often. It was a turning point for her, and I always insisted she did it to drive me crazy. If she didn't purposefully do it, the action had that effect on me, nonetheless.

That date wasn't the best we would go on together, not by a long shot. It was awkward as we tested the boundaries of conversation and got to know each other's limits. She learned that I had already slept with someone before, and I learned—a week later—that she couldn't keep a secret—*that* secret—from her parents.

I will never forget that first confrontation with Jack. It would be the first of many, and it showed me what kind of man he was and what kind of man I'd have to learn how to communicate with—and he was never going to make it easy for me.

He was confident and had no difficulty making me feel uncomfortable, out of place and completely in the wrong, even when I wasn't. The first time, I wasn't prepared. I didn't talk back. I just let him speak his mind. He told me his daughter was too young to be in a serious relationship. *"You can erase every last one of those ideas you have flitting around in that 17-year-old head of yours, because they're never going to happen. Do you understand?"*

I told him I did.

Then he railed on me for taking her on a city bus at night.

I had no fear when I was younger and felt pretty damn invincible. That's just how it was, being brought up in the neighborhoods we'd lived in, spending so much time defending myself and my brothers in the streets of the city. The dangers Manhattan posed to his daughter were not obvious to me until I became better acquainted with their family, so when he brought this up, I was honestly offended, surprised and a little amused by his display of what I thought was ignorance, privilege and snobbery. It wasn't the Jack Holland everyone knew—and I'd soon learn that was a completely incorrect assessment of him, anyway. He closed the conversation by handing me a hundred-dollar bill. *"Take this and swear to me you will never put her on another city bus. I don't even like her on the subway. You need to be able to have more control over the situation when she's with you, do you understand?"*

I'd nodded my head, intimidated by the few inches he had on me. He'd used his height and stature, his clear and commanding voice, his piercing blue eyes—all of it—to his advantage. In hindsight, I knew it was all calculated and carefully orchestrated. He was making his claim on his daughter, letting me know he wasn't ready to let her go.

It had taken me about five minutes to cool off and break down what had happened. Five minutes to assess the situation. Five minutes to know that, if I could get Livvy on my side, I would do everything to let Jack know that I was there to take her away from him.

Those days are such a distant memory. The Jack I knew then is so different from the man I know now. There's no one I respect more. No one on this planet. He's the father I never had; mine couldn't show me love. He's the father my *brothers* never had, too. The most welcoming, most considerate, most compassionate person who has cared for me like no one else, with the exception of his wife, of course—unconditionally and with no prejudice whatsoever.

He did the same for Livvy. I feel like the love I had for her was all consuming and that no one could love her more than I did, but he and I competed for her attention for years—and I truly think that the love we had for her was equal. He loved her as a daughter every bit as much as I did as a wife.

Livvy Day is not only important because it's roughly the anniversary of our first date; we also got married on this day ten years ago. It was a surprise wedding on her birthday—we lured her parents down to Brazil from America under the guise of a surprise birthday party for her, but we turned the tables on them and gave them the surprise news of our nuptials—and told them a grandbaby was on the way.

To top it all off, this is the day that Jack and Emi finalized Livvy's adoption when she was four. Thirty-two years ago, she became a Holland.

I'm not, I hear her in my head.

But you very much are, Liv. Who else would have taught you to love me so fiercely—considerately, compassionately, and most importantly, so unconditionally—if not the Hollands?

My assistant knocks on my door. Typically, she comes in without waiting for me to grant her permission, but today, she waits.

"Come in, Angel."

She walks in with an arrangement of flowers. "These were left up front." She sets them down with the card facing me.

For Livvy... It's hand-written, not typed. I take the small paper and flip it over, but it's not signed. "You don't know who they're from?"

"They weren't signed."

I smile and nod, and she leaves the room.

Studying the arrangement, I ponder who they might be from. If I were to guess, I'd say a woman wrote the card, but it could have been the florist. There's no indication anywhere which florist these came from, either.

White roses, sprigs of lavender and a sparse mingling of another type of flower I'm not immediately able to name. Some sort of lily, and the insignificant blossom feels out of place in an arrangement like this. It's a small, delicate wildflower that would hardly catch my attention had I not been studying the bouquet.

There's really no point in studying it. It could have come from anyone. Any stranger, any minor acquaintance, an old friend—an old *enemy*? Hundreds of possibilities, really. It's a thoughtful gesture to remember her today, though, but I can't say they were thoughtful to remember the day. Even mainstream news had a brief tribute to her this morning to honor her life, which was nice, but hard to watch as I was getting ready for work.

After setting it aside, I dig back into a new sketch I'd begun earlier, getting used to the feel of my drafting table again and appreciating the return of at least some of my creativity. I was worried it had died with her, but it hasn't.

*T*hree hours later, I feel at peace in the Holland home with my son in my arms and one of my daughters sitting on either side of me on the couch, the two of them taking turns as they tell me about their days at school. They both had good days; they both have excellent grades to show off and cute stories to tell about how they were kind to a classmate. It was a new challenge that Trey had set forth for them a month ago, and they'd both taken it to heart: *come home every day with a story of how you were truly kind to a classmate or how you went out of your way to help someone.*

It was brilliant, and I'd already seen the positive changes in my daughters. I knew that he was the right choice to be a godfather for Luca. Having been raised by the Hollands, he would have ideas that would help my children grow up in the way Livvy would have wanted them to. The fact that he's stepping in and helping with the girls already makes me cherish the bond we have even more.

I'm surprised when Coley walks in the door with him a half hour after I arrive. They both encourage me to stay seated with Luca, who's now sleeping, while the girls shower them with hugs in the foyer. They come into the living room to talk to me after they've greeted Jack and Emi.

"Shouldn't you be in Boston?" I ask him.

"I skipped one class and took Dad's jet," he says. "I couldn't miss this."

"I'm so glad you're here." I don't know why I'm emotional, but I am. Coley somehow absconds with my youngest without waking him, but it allows me to embrace my brother-in-law tightly—a gesture I need, and it seems he does, too, although when he pulls back, he shows no evidence of sadness. I always thought I was the strong one, the stoic one, but it's Trey. As an adult, I've rarely seen him cry, although he's one of the most empathetic people I know.

Livvy's aunts, uncles and a few of her cousins are the next to show up.

There's so much laughter and chatter in the house, it's hard to feel sad among the people I've learned to call my own family. For many of them, it's the first time they've gotten to spend any *quality* time with Luca, so he's getting to see many new faces, and Jack, Emi and I are answering a lot of the same questions over and over again.

"*He's moving his head around on his own, yeah, and he's learning that he can make different sounds.*"

"*He just started smiling when he sees us about two weeks ago. So, it took him a little longer to recognize us, but he'll catch up.*"

"*We show him pictures of Livvy all the time. He'll definitely know all about his mama.*"

"*The girls are doing great with him. They know how to feed him and change his diaper. They don't volunteer, but they'll do it if we ask. They do try to play with him all the time. They'll speed his development along...*"

"*Yes, they still call him Froggie. No, the rest of us still call him Luca.*" Even Emi has been calling him that tonight. I guess it's to make sure no one else adopts the nickname she wants to use for him, and I appreciate it. I'm sure she knows how much I appreciate that.

My brothers and their "others" show up together and are attacked by my daughters, even though Will has his hands full with a diaper bag and a car seat carrying little Charlie. Quickly, I get up and take everything from him, freeing my nephew from his restraints.

He's awake but quiet, with his eyes barely open. "Look at you, little man!" I say quietly, holding him into my chest. "*Big* man!" I correct myself, again noticing the weight difference. Shea brings over a blanket and wraps it around him. "How's he been doing?"

"Pretty good. I hope he stays awake through this whole thing so we can all sleep a little tonight."

"Good luck with that." I smile at her, knowing exactly what she's going through. "Luca was sound asleep. Hopefully all the passing around has woken him up... although I'd probably know if it had. He would probably be crying after seeing people he didn't know."

"Is anyone sick?" she asks.

"Emi told anyone who was sick not to come," I tell her, "so if they're here, they're well."

"Okay." She scans the room. "And they have hand sanitizer out."

"It's all over," I laugh, showing her four different dispensers. "I've watched people use it on their own and I've watched both Jack and Emi point it out."

"Good. Does the worry ever go away?"

I nod. "Yes. With the second child."

"But..." She frowns playfully. "Oh, such a cute arrangement!" she says, taking a seat next to me and looking at the bouquet I'd brought with me to the party. "Did you buy that for her?"

"Someone sent it to the office. I don't know who. It wasn't signed."

"Hey, that's a sego lily," Will says, taking a seat in the club chair on the other side of me. Willow sits in his lap.

"Wils, come on. You're too big for that."

"It's fine," my brother says, trying to look over a book she's attempting to show him. "Did you know that's a sego lily?"

"No. Why is that significant to me?"

"It's not," he says.

"Why do you know that, babe?" Shea asks, touching the thick mop on Charlie's head.

"I picked a bunch of those for Laila because I didn't have the money to buy her flowers one time. They're the state flower of Utah."

"Huh." I find that curious.

"They only bloom in the summer, though, and I've never seen them in New York. Maybe they have a greenhouse here where they cultivate them."

"Who's Laila?" my youngest daughter asks.

"A witchy woman who lived in Utah when your uncles were there," Shea responds for my brother. "She took Uncle Will's delicate little heart and blasted it to pieces."

Will laughs at her answer, and at Willow's shocked expression.

"How'd you put it back together?" she asks her uncle curiously.

"I didn't." He shrugs, then points to his wife. "She did." When Willow looks at me for confirmation of their story, I simply nod.

"Wow. You must have magic powers..."

"All women do, Wils. Stick with me, and I'll show you how to use yours."

"Really?"

"Absolutely!"

"Today?"

"Not today. When you're a woman."

"So, when I get my period?" She's loud enough that at least ten people in the house stop what they're doing and look in her direction. My daughter doesn't seem fazed by this.

Shea nods. "Exactly." There's not a topic my sister-in-law won't discuss. "When you get your period."

"I can't wait," she says, giggling. "And Edie, too?"

"Of course!"

"I'm gonna go tell her!"

"Okay!"

After she runs off, the three of us laugh together. "I mean, if I can put a positive spin on that life event," Shea says, "I really do have magic powers."

I completely agree with her.

I hear Luca getting fussy in the other room and hand off Charlie to her so I can check on my son. When I look up, I see people looking at us. "Shea, they're coming for your baby," I tease her.

By the time I navigate through the crowd of relatives, my son is quiet again. Callen's holding him in the formal dining room where it's quieter.

"Your mom did that painting after visiting Paris. Yes, she went there often," he tells Luca as he stands in front of one of her more recent works. Liv and I did *not* go to Paris often, and Callen knows that. I listen from the doorway, watching as he goes to the next one. "This one was after a passionate night with your father." He pauses. "Not that one, no. You don't want to know about this one."

I smile, finding it humorous that Callen's making up stories for the paintings he's not familiar with. It's something Max would often do with Livvy.

"Oh, this one over here?" he says softly, still talking to Luca. "Nah, she didn't paint that one. I'm pretty sure Granddaddy and Memi bought that at a flea market. I bet the price tag's on the back. Should we check?" He touches my son's cheek, wiping a tear away. "Huh? Do you want to look?"

"I'd say you're good with him," I interrupt, "but then I'd be reinforcing the lying, so I'm torn."

Callen blushes. "I thought we were alone."

"I had to see what got him to calm down."

"Couple of Uncle Max's Klonopins did the trick, didn't they, Luca?" he teases in baby talk.

I look at him curiously, taking steps toward him. Putting my hand on his arm, I ask him, "My brother's not still taking those, is he?"

"He did one day, after she died, when the building was teeming with reporters and he had to get out to go to a doctor's appointment. It was the only way I could get him to go. I was worried we'd have to do that for the funeral, but Max was more... emotionally affected that day. He was less in his head and more in his... heart? I don't know how to describe it."

"I get it." I nod. "Have you talked to his doctor? Is that normal? It's almost been two years."

"A swelling crowd, or a scream... it makes it seem like he's in that moment again. And a car backfiring? Forget about it. I'm just glad I've been there the few times that happened."

"Yeah."

"But... it's normal for him. For what he's been through."

"He's just so different from the Max he used to be. Like, where is he, even now? It's a party, and... he's out of sight."

"Yes." He smiles, as if it's no surprise and no big deal for him. "He's out back on the patio swing, trying to maintain balance. You're welcome to go out there. I'm sure he'd like that... but don't try to talk to him about any of that—about PTSD. He won't do it."

I sigh. "I talked to him a few weeks ago about how he was doing. He didn't mention the Klonopin, though. We talked about pot... about California... about how he doesn't feel like he has a purpose."

"But not about PTSD?"

"I guess not exactly, no," I tell him. "He mentioned flashbacks offhandedly. I didn't press him."

"He wouldn't have talked about them anyway. But it's why he smokes. Why he wants to leave—well, I can't say *that*. He's wanted to leave New York for a long time, but... this just solidifies his reasoning. And I don't blame him. He needs more space than this city can give him."

"Is he still doing it? Smoking?" He hadn't wanted me to monitor him, so I hadn't. In fact, our last conversation was left unfinished, and I felt weird bringing it up again. All I knew is he didn't want to stop—and all he knew is that I'd hoped he would eventually.

"He does it in moderation, Jon. I'm keeping an eye on him. We have an arrangement... but it helps him. I know it disappoints you, but it really does help him. And Dr. Roberts is aware, and she supports it, illegal as it is *in this state.* There are plenty others where it's legal. But... if it bothers you, I encourage you to do a little research on pot and PTSD. That's all I'm saying. He's not high tonight. One of our conditions is that he can't smoke when we have plans to be around family.

"We just hadn't planned on seeing anyone the night that... we went to the hospital. But I'm truly sorry about that." I nod, looking at the floor. "And he hates lying to you. It's just one more reason that makes him want to leave. And he feels like he has to make a choice—lie to you or disappoint you. He doesn't like either."

That statement feels like a kick in the gut. "That sucks," I tell him.

"I know. For him, too. He has so much respect for you." Luca makes a soft cooing sound. "I know, isn't that sweet?" Callen smiles at him and touches his nose to my son's. Luca's eyes open wide.

"It looks like you have things under control in here with him."

"I'm great, actually," he says. "Go talk to him." He winks at me, knowing exactly what I was going to do, and what needs to be done.

"Hey, when are you guys ever getting married?" I ask him on the way to the back door.

"Not up to me," he says simply.

"Please don't ever leave him."

The look on his face is one I've never seen on him before—it's pure love and absolute defeat, all in one. "I couldn't if I tried."

I love hearing that from him, because he's left him before. He was a runner, just like I once was. Running away from adverse situations, not wanting to deal with the hard parts of relationships. But he's come around, finally, just like I had to—and that makes me happy and relieved for my youngest brother.

When I reach the bench in the back corner of the yard, I sit down on it, causing it to swing when it had been perfectly still for Max.

"Livvy and I had this horrible fear that she was pregnant after we'd had sex without protection once... when she was in high school... and we were on *this very swing* when we talked about our options." My brother's quiet. "Well, I bet they've replaced the swing a time or two, but... same place and shit. My point is, this swing is where you go for tough conversations."

"Then I'll go sit somewhere else," he says, but doesn't make a motion to move. "I just came out here for silence."

"I'm offended by that. I can be silent, too."

"But will you?" he asks.

"No," I tell him. "Not immediately... but I'll still be a hell of a lot quieter than all that ruckus in the house."

He puts his left hand on his shoulder and starts rotating it slowly, as if he's in pain. If I were to ask him if it hurt him, he'd say no. It's just a nervous habit for him now.

"You should be in there... for Livvy," he tells me.

"I'm holding it together for Livvy. I'm afraid if I go in there with Jack and Emi's 'celebration of life' attitude, I just may break down, so... I'd rather stick with my brothers. Maybe next year I'll be ready for this, but three months is too soon for me. I appreciate their gesture, though, and their support. And the free meal—which, by the way, I'm starving. You?"

"Not so much."

"Have you lost weight?"

He shrugs his left shoulder. "Maybe."

"You look... lean."

"I stopped eating meat."

"Yeah?"

"Just... trying to feel... better. Trying everything."

"How's that working for you?"

"Digestively, great," he says in an attempt to be funny.

"Mascot, I don't want you to feel like you have to lie to me about anything. I don't want that to be our relationship. We're brothers. I'm not your dad, even though I was more like a parent to you when you were little. That's not the role I play anymore. I don't *want* that role. I want to be someone you confide in. Share secrets with."

"But you're a judgmental little fuck sometimes, Jon."

"Starting today, no. So, you smoke..." I take a deep breath and exhale slowly. "Callen says it helps you. Can't we just be open about it from now on?"

"Callen talked to you about it?" he asks me, agitated. "It's not for him to talk about."

I could lie, but I just told him I didn't want us to lie to each other anymore. "Yes, because I want us all to have a relationship where we talk about things like this."

"Fuck," he says. "The *one person* I can trust, and—"

"No, Max," I interrupt. "It's not like that. He didn't tattle on you or anything. You're taking this out of context. He was... going to battle for you. That's all."

"I don't need that," he says stubbornly.

"Would you rather have a relationship with me where we have walls? Where there are some topics we simply can't talk about?"

"We were figuring that out, weren't we?" I notice he hasn't given me any eye contact all night. "We were doing just fine that way."

"I'm not disappointed in you. You haven't let me down."

"Did I ask if you were? Did I insinuate that I thought you were? Then why even say such a thing? If you have to tell me that, then I have to think two things—one, that you *are* disappointed in me, and two, that you're fucking doing the *one thing* you just asked me not to do—lie."

"Max, neither of those things are true. Why are you getting so defensive? I'm just trying to talk to you... to tell you... it's okay."

"Because nothing is that easy with you, Jon."

"Please, buddy, I don't want to fight."

"Then we don't have to. I'm out." He stands from the swing, leaving it wobbling with his absence.

"Max!" As I sit here pulling at my hair, I try to think of the moment when this conversation went south, but I can't pinpoint a word or phrase that I would have said differently. I feel like he's just overreacting.

When the back door opens again, I look up, hoping he's had a change of heart, but it's Callen, walking toward me with Luca.

"I've got to give him back to you. We're leaving."

"What happened?" I ask him. "I didn't say anything wrong."

He shakes his head. "You gave him an out. A reason to leave the party... which is what he wanted to do all along."

"Where is he? I don't want him to leave..."

"He's in the car. Don't worry about it. I'll calm him down. He'll be okay. I should have known that's how it would go, but... I didn't know he wanted to leave that badly." He looks at me apologetically. "Some days are worse than others. He *is* getting better..." Callen doesn't look me in the eye when he says it though, so I'm not sold on his line.

I follow him back into the house and watch as he quickly tells everyone goodbye, making excuses for Max—that he doesn't feel well. He hugs my in-laws, and by the looks on their faces, I can tell that they don't believe the lie he's feeding them, either. Still, they let him go without pressing him, just like I did.

When I open the front door, beating him there, a swarm of photographers is surrounding Callen's Tesla. "Trey?" I call back into the house. My brother-in-law is there quickly and takes Luca from me. With authority, I walk toward the car, hating what Max is going through.

"Get out!" I shout, having no patience. The cameras turn to me. Regardless of how they capture me—the image they portray of me—at least the focus is off my baby brother. "This is private property. Or have you forgotten? The Hollands own both houses on either side and all the property from here to the middle of the street. That's the deal they made with the city. The cops are two blocks away. You can spend a night in jail and pay the five-grand fine or you can get the hell out of here.

"We're having a private event... to celebrate my wife." My voice shakes as I speak through the lump in my throat. Callen stands behind me, his hand on my shoulder. "Please leave us alone."

Most of the photographers leave in cars that were parked down the block; a few of the more invasive ones stand at the property lines on the other sides of the houses next door. Still, they're away from Max, and that's all I wanted.

Callen and I walk to the car together. He gets in on the driver side as I tap on the glass of the passenger seat, squatting to its level. Max rolls down the window so I can see him.

"Buddy, I love you," I tell him softly. "That's all I wanted to say." I reach in and ruffle his hair. As I pull my hand out, he grasps for my fingers, then releases them and forms a fist with his left hand. I smile, bumping mine to his. "I'll call you tomorrow. Okay?"

He nods, a smile barely forming on his lips, but sadness is still the prominent expression on his face as it radiates from his eyes.

Once inside, everyone is waiting for me to say a prayer before dinner.

"Where are the girls?" I whisper to Emi.

"They're downstairs with Elizabeth and Lexi. They already fixed them plates."

I remember when Elizabeth was born, right around the same time

Lexi's son, Holland, was. Livvy was still a senior in high school... younger than Elizabeth is now. I shake my head, surprised at the quick passage of time.

I step out of the kitchen hastily to check on Trey and Coley with Luca, but they're doing great with him, so I rejoin Jack and Emi, and hold the hands they offer me while I bow my head. I'd never been one to pray, but I know they've found peace in their faith, and I'm still struggling, so I'll take whatever little bit of help I can get.

I glance up, looking for Will, and even he and Shea are taking part in grace. Shea's got Charlie strapped to her in a sling. Will winks at me before Jack begins speaking.

"Dear Lord. We are grateful that you brought Livvy into our lives. Thirty-six years ago, Olivia Sophia was born to Simone DeLuca, who loved her as much as any mother could while she was alive, and made sure she was cared for when she knew she would no longer be able to. Thirty-two years ago, the majority of the people in this room were witnesses to Livvy becoming an official member of this family. We had a party, not too different from this one, in this very house, celebrating the joy that she had brought to our lives—and that she would bring in the years to come. At the time, we didn't dream we'd have any biological children of our own, but Jackson surprised us a few years later, rounding out our small family, and showing us what a wonderful sister my Contessa would—eventually—become."

"Eventually," Trey echoes jokingly from the kitchen doorway. I look up at him as he continues to hold my baby into his chest, doing an excellent job at caring for his nephew.

"Then, twenty years ago, a brash and overly confident 17-year-old boy took her on her first date." Everyone laughs at this. "And ten years later, he would marry our Livvy.

"We couldn't be happier with the family that Jon brought with him: Will and Max, and then Callen, Shea, and now Charlie. Our lives are richer having you all in them. And not to leave out Coley—we've loved having her in our lives these past few years and can't wait for the wedding in a few months. I know we'll be a couple family members short," Jack says, his emotions audible, "but we'll be sure to include Martin and Liv as if they are with us. They definitely will be in spirit."

I can hear Coley sniffle from across the room. Out of the corner of my eye, I see someone move toward her. I look up again, curious, catching a glimpse of Matty taking her a tissue and putting his arms around her.

"We have so many unforgettable memories of my Contessa, and we hope to never let one slip away. We thank you, Lord, for giving us three grandchildren who will continue her legacy—who will deliver the joy that Emi and I always expected Livvy would bring for the length of our lives.

"We are blessed to know that our daughter, sister, wife and mother has a mom, a dad, a mother-in-law and Granna up in Heaven to keep her company. Thank you, God, for ensuring that she will never be lonely. For giving us peace of mind that she will always be loved and be happy. It would be so much harder imagining her up there alone.

"We also thank you for giving her a creative companion—a kindred spirit. None of us knows what awaits us, but if we get to do what we love, then Livvy will continue to paint. And there's another artist up there that I know she'd wanted to meet for a long time."

Emi lets go of my hand and switches places with me so she can be next to Jack. She'd been silent up until then, but she falls apart at this. I watch as she hugs her husband, putting all her strength into the embrace. He does the same and places his lips to the top of her head.

And then half the room is in need of those tissues.

It's something I hadn't thought of. The whole concept of Heaven still seems a little strange to me. I want to believe there's a beautiful afterlife, and I certainly want my children to think that's where she is, but logic is always a barrier that stands in the way of that kind of faith for me.

The idea of Livvy meeting Nate seems strange. He's someone we hadn't really discussed more than in passing in over 15 years. She was a teenager when she idolized him—painted him, cherished his sketchbooks. I think he was around 30 when he died.

And now she outlived him, but only by a few years. It's odd to think of them as contemporaries. As peers. It's even weirder to feel a tinge of jealousy about it, but I do. In the end, she and I inspired one another, pushed each other further, creatively. Our art was so different, and yet so closely intertwined. True art scholars could see the similarities. There had been a few articles about us before, and, of course, Liv and I could see them, but 99.9 percent of people had no clue. Even after reading the articles, they couldn't understand the intricate details. That's just how scrupulous we were.

Emi takes both of my hands once she's composed herself.

"Please watch over her. Watch over us. Watch over her husband, Jon, and her children, Edie, Willow and Luca, as they begin a new chapter of their lives where she may not be a physical presence anymore, but she will always be a part of them.

"In your name we pray. Amen."

Jack and Emi encourage me, Shea and Will to get our food first. After we prepare our plates, we go into the living room, where we're by ourselves for the moment.

"Do you believe that stuff?" I ask, my mind still stuck on Jack's fanciful ideas of where Livvy is now. "That she's with her biological parents, and being all chummy with Nate?"

My brother glares at me just before he takes a bite of lasagna, my absolute favorite dish of Jack's. "Dude. You're asking the wrong guy."

"Right, but..." I look to Shea, hoping for a more open mind. She squints at me, not really answering my question.

"What do you think?" she asks.

"It's a comforting thought, in a way, thinking she's not alone, right? But then, like..." I lean into them, talking more softly. "I don't want her hanging out with that guy. He was a player, you know?"

They both start laughing at me.

"Let's postulate that it *is* true," Will says, the laughter still evident in his eyes, "I don't think she goes on to date new people up there... have new relations, if you know what I mean. Nor do I think the magic man in the clouds is gonna allow for the player to seduce your married woman. See how this goes against all the shit they preach?"

"'til death do us part..." I mumble.

"You didn't say that. I distinctly remember your vows did not include that."

"But traditionally... is that why they're like that?"

"What is with you?" he asks, continuing to eat and dismissing any worries I may have.

"I've always... questioned..." I say, shrugging and taking a bite myself, beginning to think he's right.

"Yes, but nothing so specific. This is... weird. You can't be jealous of... a guy who's been dead for, what, 20 years?"

"Like, 30, I think. I've just never *ever* thought of anything like that. She idolized him when she was younger. Like, unhealthily so."

"And then she forgot about him because she got a life—with you—that included everything her heart desired. Out of all the things you have to focus on these days, this bullshit isn't one of them."

"Yeah, I know," I say, sighing. "It caught me off guard. I wish the idea had never been planted in my head."

"Why?" Shea asks. "Is it so bad to think she may have a friend up there?"

I think for a moment, then shake my head. "No. I've always wanted her to be happy. That will never change. If she... exists... in some way now... a way I may never understand or even fully believe, well... I still want her to be happy."

"That's right," my sister-in-law says. "Sometimes faith doesn't have to do with God. It just has to do with loving the people we care about unconditionally. This is what I try to sell Will on every day."

"And I do love you unconditionally," he tells her. "But when we're gone, baby... we return to the stuff of stars. And to me, that's a beautiful thing in itself. I don't need an afterlife for that. We're still a part of the greater universe. How incredible is that?"

She leans in to kiss him. "When you say it like that, it makes your way sound okay, too."

"I mean... I just think of Liv and... her of all people," my brother says. "Gravity couldn't keep her here." He shakes his head, tears in his eyes, and we both linger on that thought. *Gravity couldn't keep her here.*

Trey and Coley unwittingly break up the truly touching moment when they come into the room. She carries both plates as Trey continues to cradle my son. "Let me take him," I say, sniffling.

"Finish eating first," he encourages me.

"I can do both. I'm getting good at this." Even though Trey argues, I reach for Luca and hold him securely in the crook of my left arm. Before I return to my dinner, I look down at him and think about my brother's explanation. Luca opens his eyes, recognizing me and smiling wide. "Hey, little man. You've done such a good job tonight with all of these new people. I'm so proud of you. Your mama... I bet she's..." I sigh and shake my head, fighting with what I know as fact and what I want to believe for him and for my girls.

I look at everyone and push my food away, excusing myself with my boy tightly secured in my grasp. We make our way past guest after guest, finally going back outside to the swing where his mother and I first thought about the possibility of having a child.

"We were so scared then, Luca," I tell him. "You're not scary at all... are you?" His attention moves past me to the sky above us. I take his hand between my thumb and forefinger, believing that he's holding onto me, even though he's too young to consciously do that yet. I know he'd do it if he could because he needs me like no one else.

I lean my head back and stare upwards, too. It's why I wanted to come outside again in the first place. I wish the lights weren't so bright here. Wish I could see just *one damn star*, but I know they're up there, regardless. Few things are as constant as the stars, and that brings me comfort. Remembering what Will said, it brings me a lot of comfort.

"She's up there, kid," I tell him. "Somehow. In some way. We can look up and talk to her any time we want to. And she may never talk back to us, or hell, she may not ever see us again," I say, breaking down, "but she's with us. She's half of who you are. You know that? And because of that, I will always feel closer to her when I'm with you or Edie or Willow. I don't know what I would do without you.

"And it kills me that you will never know this amazing woman who sacrificed her life for yours. It was the most selfless thing she ever did... and I want you to know that... but I also *never* want you to know that... I hope that you somehow know that it was a pure act of love from your mother that brought you into this world. And... I could never resent you because I know you have more of her love and strength in you than anyone else... and when I need to feel that, I know you're my source... for now.

"It's too much to put on a little baby," I acknowledge. "But I promise I'll be stronger soon. I won't be so needy." I laugh and touch his cheek. "You're the needy one. Right? Say 'Daddy, I'm the needy one,'" I say for him in baby talk.

Luca starts squirming in my arms, and I realize it's his dinner time. I look up one more time, searching for that one star. A gust of wind comes out of nowhere, breezing over us, blowing my hair in all directions, and then I feel three quick, heavy raindrops on my face. Hurriedly, I get Luca to the porch, unaware that we were expecting any rain tonight. Before I go inside, I turn around; the yard is still, and no more drops have fallen. I wipe the three drops from my face and study the clear water. I check my clothes, then Luca's.

They're all completely dry.

I look up once more and realize there's not a cloud in the sky. There never was when I had gazed up before. But I do see something bright up there, far in the distance.

Whether it's a star or a planet or something completely unexplainable by anything other than faith, it's something, and it makes me feel closer to her.

CHAPTER 33

*O*n Thanksgiving morning, the girls and I are planted in front of the television downstairs, watching the Macy's parade in our pajamas and drinking hot cocoa. Recently fed and freshly changed, Luca is sound asleep in his playpen that's tucked under the east-facing window. The sun pours in, but aside from what we can see outside, the weather-proof windows give no sign that it's 28 degrees, windy and sleeting. It's toasty in the apartment, but we're all wearing fuzzy socks and find ourselves under a couple of soft blankets just because it feels cozy.

We've never spent a Thanksgiving morning like this, but I know I'd like to start a new tradition, enjoying the distinct lack of chaos and stress that normally accompanies this holiday. The girls would always want to watch the parade, but we always had to be somewhere for brunch, so it was a struggle to pull them away from the TV to get them ready and to make it to our destination on time... and when we got there, there was always some crisis. Someone couldn't make it for such and such reason, or so and so can't eat this dish because of some new fad diet... it was always something, more so on Liv's side of the family than mine, but my brothers and mom weren't immune from their own drama, too.

Jack took Emi to Europe for three weeks. As well as I thought she was doing on Livvy's birthday, when the holidays were mentioned, she fell apart. She couldn't face Thanksgiving without her daughter. The

December holidays would be different. With Trey and Coley's wedding five days before Christmas, their celebration would take up everyone's attention for most of the month. We were all in the wedding, and it was a huge affair. Because Liv and I got married in Brazil, New York hadn't seen the spectacle of a Holland wedding since Jack and Emi got married—and back then, the hysteria wasn't like it is today.

The whole city is buzzing with excitement for this event.

Despite Trey's tendency to shun the spotlight, he understood his position in the community and he and Coley had planned accordingly. This is as much a celebration for Manhattan as it is for the Holland family, and the fanfare of the day is going to rival the Royal Wedding. Streets will be shut down—and fully decorated—for a procession of limousines. Security officers will be everywhere. Coley and Trey will both make notable entrances into the church on white carpets. There will be screens outside of St. Patrick's Cathedral broadcasting the service.

Needless to say, there will be plenty of things going on in the coming weeks to keep anyone occupied who's involved in the wedding.

"Daddy, can I have some more pancakes?" Willow asks.

"No, sweetie. We'll be having lunch in..." I look at my wrist, but I haven't even put a watch on yet today. "Well, we'll start getting ready when the parade's over."

"Where's Joel?"

I huff. "He wouldn't give you any, either, if he were here," I tell her, "but he's at Matty's with Shea, prepping your lunch. Don't you want to be hungry for that? Turkey and sweet potatoes and—"

"Pumpkin pie?"

"Yes, Wils." She grins and cuddles back into me. "Are you girls going to help me cook when he leaves at the beginning of the year?"

"No," Edie says quickly.

"I will," Willow says. "I can pick what we eat if I help, right?"

"Not exactly. I'll be doing the meal planning."

"Then I don't want to help, either."

"What happened to that kindness thing Uncle Trey was teaching you?"

"That's for our classmates."

"Hmmm," I ponder. "I bet he would want you to make an exception here. Maybe extend a little kindness to Daddy and help him cook... or do dishes..."

"Why can't our maid do that?" Edie asks.

"Oh, no..." I say, shaking my head. "That did not just come out of your mouth, did it?" She shrugs. "Do you think I had a maid when I was your age? Do you think Mama did?"

"Yeah," she answers hesitantly. "Granddaddy and Memi are rich."

"That doesn't mean they didn't teach your mom responsibility. Neither of us had maids growing up. The only reason we have one now is that this place is... really big... and you two make more of a mess than either of us could clean. I certainly couldn't do it alone every week. But she only comes once a week, right? We have to cook and do dishes every day."

My oldest sighs like she's the most burdened child to ever live. I put my arm around her and hug her close. In truth, I'm grateful she doesn't know what I experienced as a child. The filth that I lived in because I couldn't possibly clean up after my drunk mother and her many men and my two messy little brothers. I was clean; my space was clean... but not much else was. It was embarrassing.

I still remember the thorough cleaning I did before Livvy came over to my apartment for the first time. I'd bribed Will and Max to help. It still looked like shit. I'm so amazed she picked me... that she loved me like she did. I'm so fortunate that she could see the things I could offer her—they weren't material things, but she was never looking for those anyway.

$\mathcal{I}$t was so much easier to get the girls motivated to get dressed once they had seen the parade; I'm surprised we didn't try to wait it out just once to see the difference it would have made. I feel like I've actually accomplished a small feat today when I show up to the lofts on 5th Avenue with three clean, fully dressed, adorable children—and *all* of them are in great moods.

The doors to both Matty and Nolan's loft and Max and Callen's loft are propped open, so everyone can flow in and out of each as they please today. There's a table set up in the hallway, too, with at least 10 desserts on them. Why they put desserts there, I don't know, because Willow's immediately drawn to a cupcake with blue frosting, and her little fingers are in it before I can tell her she has to wait until after lunch.

With wide eyes, she looks up at me, holding the decorated confection. "Go ahead. Just that one, though." She takes a bite. "You promise me?"

"I promise," she tells me with a mouthful of cupcake.

"Get in there and tell all your aunts and uncles hello. Both of you." They split up and go into different apartments–Willow into Matty's, where I'm sure she could hear Will, and Edie into Max and Callen's place.

"Matty's hogging Charlie," Nolan says, "so I'm going to have to take this one off your hands." He's tentative as he reaches for Luca, but when he sees my son isn't going to fuss, he swoops him into his arms and starts with the baby talk.

I follow my oldest daughter, wanting to check on my youngest brother, who hasn't been returning my calls. Max, Trey and Coley are all in the kitchen, sitting at the island. They're snacking on crudité and drinking what appears to be straight bourbon. I pick up Trey's glass and sniff it to check. The fumes are strong. I smile at my brother-in-law as I set it down in front of him.

"I'll pour you a glass," he offers.

"No, thanks. Maybe a beer?"

"Sure."

"Grab me one, T," Max says as he refills his glass halfway with more of the golden-brown liquid. Coley drops in two ice cubes for him. After Trey hands me a drink, I wander to the back of the apartment in search of Edie and Callen. I find them in one of the guest bedrooms, looking at an iPad.

"And what did you find in here, bunny?" Callen stands up to give me a hug, then sits back down beside her. I peek over the tablet to see what has her so enthralled. "YouTube again?"

"You know what she looks at?" he asks me.

I shake my head. "She's not allowed to get on YouTube on her iPad... that's why she does it on everyone else's."

He smiles at me. "She goes and looks at old paparazzo videos of you and Livvy... from when you were young."

I take a seat on the other side of her to see what she's found. "There are some I'd rather she not see," I mumble.

"I know," he says. "We don't watch those."

"Okay."

"I don't want to see you and Mama fight," Edie says. I look down at her and nod. "I know what they are, but I don't want to watch them."

"Good. I appreciate that. I was stupid–every time. Just know that."

"Okay. Oh, look! This one is of you and her shopping with Uncle Will and Uncle Max and Uncle Trey! Was this at Christmastime?"

"Oh, wow."

"Oh my god. Look at Max!" Callen says. "He was so little! And Trey!" He starts laughing. "I remember when he used to part his hair like that. He was such a dork."

"He was adorable," I tell him. "He just wanted to talk to *everyone*. He had no enemies."

"Well, does he now?" he asks.

"I guess not."

"What was Max like back then?"

"Rambunctious. Curious... too smart for his own good. He was going through a karate phase, if I remember correctly."

"Really? Karate?" Callen asks.

"It didn't last long. Couldn't afford the lessons."

"Am I rambunctious?" Edie asks.

"You can be," I tell her. "You're definitely too smart for your own good." I kiss her on the top of the head.

"I don't think that's a real thing," she says back to me.

"See? You just proved it."

"Daddy!" she says laughing. "Did you get Mama anything that Christmas?"

"I got her something *every* Christmas."

"Do you remember what you got her?"

"I think... maybe a purse that she liked?"

"Do you know what she got you?"

I think about it, but I can't remember. "No, I don't. I'm sure it was perfect, though."

"If it was, you would have remembered." She quits the app and hands the tablet back to Callen. "I'm gonna tell Will and Matty and everyone that I'm here."

"You do that," I tell her, feeling genuinely sad that I've forgotten a memory of Livvy... a memory that my daughter wanted to know about.

"It's a minor detail, Jon. You can't be expected to remember everything," Callen says. I look up, appreciative of his kind words to the worry I didn't even have to say aloud. My mind is still churning, though, trying to recall that day. I'd given her the small handbag immediately, and we dropped off our brothers so we could go back to my dorm and be alone. We'd made love, which I remember telling her that was enough of a gift for me, but she said she had something–

"A wallet. Some clothes and a wallet. I remember it was a cashmere sweater. I'd never worn cashmere before, and thought it was too nice to wear anywhere that I went. I remember telling her that. I wore it once, on New Years' Eve." I grin, proud of myself.

"Was she in college?"

"Yeah. That was her first year at Yale. We'd just gotten back together for good in October, so we were taking advantage of any and all time we had together."

"I get that," Callen says. "That was Max and me in college, too..."

"But you guys never had to sneak around in California."

"No, and it was nice," he admits. "It was never easy here until we moved back, and they let me move into the guest house."

"So... are you guys looking for a place in Manhattan?" I ask him. "Or do you just want to stay here in the loft? That's perfectly fine."

He shakes his head. "We won't stay here forever... but we're not looking here. *We're* not looking anywhere. *He's* looking..."

I question further, knowing, but fearing, the answer. "What do you mean?"

"Not here. He doesn't want to be here, Jon. He's made up his mind, and I don't know what to do. I'm afraid it's just a matter of time. It used to be that, like... he couldn't act without me. I had the money. It's not like that anymore. He's free to do what he wants. I can't stop him."

"But... you *have* to."

He shrugs his shoulders. "He's still here. Every day I tell myself that. Every day he is, I consider it a success."

"What a horrible way to live," I tell him.

"It's better than being without him." His eyes water. "I'll take any day with him, no matter how he is, than any day without him."

I give him a tight embrace. "Thank you for loving him like you do, man."

"Don't thank me. I've fucked up enough in our relationship that I owe him... patience... while he figures out shit."

"Uhhh," I start. "I don't think that's how relationships work, Cal, nor do I think he would agree that you owe him anything. And I sure as hell hope you're not doing things for him as a sort of debt repayment or something."

"I'm not. I don't mean it like that. I just mean that he's put up with me and my baggage since before we even got together. Since the day he told me he liked me. Before that, I'm sure. Watching me date girls, flaunting them in his face. The thing in St. Thomas." He looks away as he says this one; we never talk about it. "Disappearing anytime things got tough. My mom... and her unwillingness to accept who we are and how we live, no matter what we've been through and how many years of fucking therapy our family's been to. He shouldn't have to deal with that bullshit from her. Feeling pressure from me to make commitments he wasn't ready for. Waiting around while I went away to grad school in Philly when there was a perfectly good one here, just because it was a tradition in my family. I... regret that decision now."

"Callen, that's in the past, and you guys got through it just fine. You're fine."

"We're not fine. We try to look like we're fine. We'll be fine, but we both know we have a long way to go to get there."

"That tells me you're both willing to work at it."

He nods. "When it's good, it's good. No, it's great."

"And *that's* why he's still here," I comment.

"Yeah," he admits. "Those are the tethers that keep him here. I just have to keep tying them down, and it takes a lot of work and I don't know how long I can keep it up."

"If there's anything I can ever do to help, Cal, just let me know. I... don't know how to reach him right now. I had every intention of coming in here today to catch up with him, but... it's not even one and I can tell from his eyes and face that he's drunk... he's double-fisting bourbon and beer, for god's sake, and right in front of me... like it doesn't matter."

"He told me you wanted to be his brother—not a parent. You sound a little like a parent."

I bite the inside of my cheek and nod my head. "Am I not supposed to worry? What does Will think?"

"Will trusts me to know Max's limits. He knows I've been through rehab and we've talked about what to look for... with addiction. He's not an addict, Jon. He's a 25-year-old guy who's testing his limits with alcohol and marijuana. Max is honest with me about what he drinks or takes or uses and when. If he thinks he needs any prescription medication for his pain or PTSD, we talk about all of that before he pops any pills. An addict wouldn't do that. An addict would hide that shit from everyone..."

"How often is he taking pills? You acted like it was just that once."

"It's rare, and only when it's necessary."

"Do you report that back to Will?" He nods. "And Max knows?" Again, he silently answers in the affirmative.

"Max knows the only reason we're concerned is because we care and we're 100 percent on his side. He appreciates that we're willing to give him some space to make his own decisions, though. So far, he knows when to draw the line. There have only been a few times that he's been a little reckless, but that was a long time ago, and it scared the shit out of him, so..."

"What? When? And why don't I know about it?"

"It's not relevant anymore. He's past that point. He and I have dealt with it."

"Are you even equipped for that?" I ask him. "Isn't that too much responsibility for you?"

"He knows if he does it again, he crosses a line with serious consequences... a line I won't cross with him."

"But, Callen? That could be overdosing, right?" I'm truly concerned now, and don't care if I sound like a father.

"It was a year and a half ago in California when it happened, Jon. You don't need to worry. He was still adjusting to everything and was on higher doses of pain killers. We're past it. I promise."

I look him square in the eyes to see if they waver, but they don't. I finally nod. "But I want you to promise me you will tell me if anything happens to him that concerns you... the second you think you might be in over your head; I don't want you to just go to Will. I know the two of you are closer than we are, but I want to know, too. I won't jump in and act. I just want to help find solutions. I want to be here for him, too... as a brother."

He smiles and holds out his hand for me. "You have a deal... as long as you trust me now."

"Deal." I shake his hand and pull him in for another hug. "And thank you for screening the videos for Edie, too. She'll see the unfavorable ones when she's older. I won't be able to stop her... but I'd rather her not have any bad images of her mom or me for now."

"Neither of you ever did anything bad."

"We had stupid fights. Heated, passionate fights in front of audiences."

His laughter comes out in a snort. "Yeah, you're the only ones in the family who've done that."

"Yes, and that's why she has a higher opinion of me and Liv than she does of you and Max, who you kicked out of your car for *no fucking reason*," I tease him about the fight they had a couple of years ago that all the tabloid sites had picked up and overanalyzed for days.

"I had a reason," he mumbles. "It was a bad one, but... it was a reason."

"Hey, my brother did nothing wrong," I argue on Max's behalf, as I will until I'm blue in the face for this particular fight.

"I know. Yet another thing for me to regret."

"Hey, assholes, what are you two talkin' about in here?" my youngest brother interrupts us.

"*Assholes?*" I ask.

"It's a term of endearment. Trust me. I love... assholes." He takes a drink of his beer.

"I'm sure you do, buddy. I hope my girls aren't out there." I nod to the back living room, where Edie and Willow often hang out when they come over here.

"Maybe I want to fill their swear jars today, Jon, huh? Is that so bad that I wanna share my wealth with your little angels today?"

"Yes," I tell him. "Please... don't. They don't need your money, and they really don't need your style of vocabulary lessons."

"Yeah, yeah," he says, rolling his right wrist and popping it. "You didn't answer me, though. What were you talkin' about?"

"YouTube videos," Callen answers.

"Fuck YouTube," Max says. When he sees my severe look, he rolls his eyes. "They aren't out there, okay? They were eating sweets in the hallway."

"Awww, shit. Really?"

"Hypocrite," Max says with a smirk. "Cal, I need to talk to you about something that just came up... something private. Can we go on the roof?"

"Now?"

"You guys can have the room," I tell them, heading out. "It's freezing outside."

"Nah, we'll be fine up there. We'll be back down in... fifteen?" Max says. "It's more private than a closed door."

"Oh," I say, putting up my hands, not wanting to ask any more questions. "Don't let me get in the way... but I do have to stop the little cookie monsters in the hall, regardless."

I find both of my girls chewing on something, their cheeks puffed out in an obvious attempt to hide whatever they're eating from me. I stare at both of them as they look up at me innocently and wait until they've swallowed everything. Both of their mouths are covered in powdered sugar, so it's no secret they got into the special cookies that Shea's famous for.

"What were you eating?"

"Nothing," Edie tells me. Willow tries to sneak back into Matty's.

"Get back here, Wils." Slowly, she turns around and holds her hands behind her back. "What were you eating?"

"Fruit?" She tests out a lie on me.

I look down at the dark blue, long-sleeved tee she chose to wear today, seeing further evidence of her snack on her clothes—not only is there powdered sugar, though, but also two smudges of chocolate where she's wiped her fingers. "Edie, look at your sister's shirt and tell me what you see there."

They both look down. "I don't see anything," she says, then smiles at me as if she's outsmarted me.

"No?" I ask.

"No."

"Then switch shirts with her." Edie's far too concerned with her appearance to be seen in a shirt with food on it. "Let's go to Matty's bathroom right now and switch shirts."

"I don't want to wear her shirt. I don't like blue."

"I know that's not true. We just bought you a new sweater that is that exact color."

"But that style doesn't look right on me."

"Tees look good on everyone. Let's go." I put my hands on their backs and try to push them into Livvy's uncle's apartment.

"Daddy, no," Edie says. "Don't make me."

"Why?"

She looks up at me with the saddest eyes. "Please?" She folds her hands in front of her chest.

"Is that sugar and chocolate?" I ask her, point blank. She nods. "What were you two eating?"

"A cookie and... some fudge," she admits.

"I thought I told you not to eat any more," I say, looking at Willow. I can't get mad at Edie since I didn't explicitly have the conversation with her, although she should know better.

"You told me I could only have one *cupcake*."

"Dubskie's got you on a technicality," Will says, carrying both of our sons, but offering mine to me. "This one needs a diaper and I've only got one hand free."

I take Luca as my youngest daughter starts to walk away. "Hey." Willow turns back around. "Froggie needs a new diaper."

"I don't want to," she whines as I grab his diaper bag and lead her toward the back of the apartment.

"Let's go to Matty's bathroom and get started. I'll send Edie in to help. Do you have anything on under that?" I ask, pointing to her soiled tee. She nods. "Give that to me and I'll get it clean for you." She takes off her top revealing a tee from Malibu that Max and Callen had bought her last year. "No more sweets today. At all. If I catch you sneaking another, you don't get to go to Kelsey's slumber party on Saturday night. Got it?"

"Daddy..." she pleads.

"Nope. None of that." Her bottom lip juts out adorably as she pouts, and my heart melts just a little bit. "Hey, get the changing pad, okay?" She takes it out and puts it onto the bathmat in the middle of the large bathroom. I lay Luca down on it and kneel on the floor with Willow to kiss her on the head. "I love you," I tell her. "Thank you for your help."

"Where's Edie?" she asks.

"I'm going to send her in right now. Take care of your brother for me, okay?"

"I will."

After finding my oldest daughter and letting her know she's needed, I return to Max's apartment to use the washer and dryer I was intimately familiar with after using it for many years before we moved out. I find a mound of clothes that must be a couple weeks' worth of laundry, completely disorganized, in the room. I'm only surprised for a split second, because why wouldn't it be like this? I know for a fact that Coley did Max's laundry when he lived at Trey's. She would volunteer to do it because she was doing Trey's anyway, but she would always give Max hell for it, just to bust his chops for something. They always played around like that.

And, as for Callen, he'd always had a staff that did everything for him. Even when he was at grad school, I remember him saying he'd just swap out clothes from one week to the next. Every weekend, they'd magically be clean when he got back to his place.

It actually makes me wonder who has been doing their laundry up until now.

Wanting to help them out and knowing this is one small way that I can, I decide to put a dent in the pile and start sorting their clothes. Once that's done, I find the darks and put them in with my daughter's tee-shirt and start a load in the washer.

After setting a timer on my watch for 45 minutes to come back and check, I leave the laundry room, nearly running into Coley.

"Oh!" she exclaims, covering her mouth. "Did you just discover their dirty little secret?"

"If you mean their laundry situation, it's not a secret anymore. And it wasn't little." She nods. "Who normally does it?"

"Max is supposed to. I taught him how, but..." She shrugs. "He just... doesn't."

I frown. "I don't understand."

"He almost seems... paralyzed... when he's alone these days."

"Paralyzed?"

"Like he can't do much of anything by himself. Or won't."

"I'm obviously not doing enough for him. *With* him," I tell her. "I feel like I'm... failing him. How have I missed all of this?"

She smiles warmly and holds onto my arm. "Jon, you're doing such an amazing job right now with your family. Don't ever think you're failing anyone. Okay? We're all trying to help Max..."

"Am I the only one who doesn't know about all of this?"

"We didn't want to worry you. You have enough to worry about."

"Coles, you know what I want?" She shakes her head. "I want life to be... normal... again. I don't want people tiptoeing around me anymore, thinking I can't handle the truth about my own god-damned brother.

Because... you know what? It sounds like he's barely hanging on, and... fuck, Coley, I've lost my wife this year. I lost my mom last year. There's no way in hell I'm losing my brother in the next one."

"We won't let that happen, Jon." She hugs me. "He knows how much he's loved and cherished and appreciated by Callen as his loving partner, and by Trey as his devoted best friend, and by me as the pesky little sister he never knew he wanted but now he can't get rid of," she says with a laugh. "By you and Will as the most steadfast brothers, by Jack and Emi as surrogate parents that he's picked up along this crazy journey, and even by Matty and Nolan, the spooky glimpse of his future that lives right across the hall from him."

I chuckle with her. "He does have the best support system. I wish he'd use it more."

"With me and Callen, he doesn't have a choice," she says. "With Trey in Boston, I'm stepping in for him. I don't want you to worry. We spend a ton of time together. I try to keep him engaged... distracted... busy... entertained. And we have a lot of fun together." She looks up at me and nods her head. "*Clean* fun. I know you're worried about him. I could see it on your face when you walked in. He spends a good amount of his time sober. I want you to know that.

"I mean, he's clearly not right now... but that's what he needs to get through today, and we love him regardless."

"He used to really enjoy big gatherings like this. He was the life of the party; the center of attention."

"And then he got shot in a large crowd, and ever since then, he's had trouble when there are so many things happening around him that he doesn't have control over."

"But we're all family... and here, in this building, we're the only ones with access to this floor. He should feel safest here."

"He does, actually. But he *literally* can't help feeling anxiety when things get louder than he'd like them to... or if something feels too... *uncertain* for him."

"I feel so out of touch. I had no idea things were still that bad. I thought therapy had helped."

"It did, Jon. He just may never be the same." I look at her, possibly coming to terms with this for the first time. "He doesn't want to be a disappointment to everyone. He knows he's different. He feels it and he feels people looking at him differently. He sees what they say about him now in the tabloids. He doesn't like things not being 'normal' in his world, either... and he's having a hard time accepting that *this* is his normal now."

"Well, for one thing, fuck the tabloids."

"You know that's always been his mantra," she says, "but they love to analyze him more now that he's this national hero... you know, deep down, they're wanting that dark, fallen hero story. If they don't get it, they'll create it. You see them angling that way all the time."

"I try to avoid going to those sites as much as possible. I can't stand them."

"I wish Max would, too. But since he won't, I keep up with them, so I know where his head will be the next time I see him. It's helped me build defense mechanisms for him."

I pull her into me for a hug this time. "I cannot tell you how grateful I am to all of you today. I may be more worried about Max, hearing more about his problems, but at the same time, I know he has the best people around him to help. I feel awful that I haven't been more present lately."

"Again, Jon, you've had your own—"

"No," I argue. "He's been spiraling for nearly two years now. She's only been gone for four months. I haven't been there for him for quite some time. This is probably why he avoids my calls. Because I wasn't there when he really needed me."

"You're wrong. I promise, you're wrong. He just wants you to be proud of him, Jon... and he doesn't think you will be... right now."

Frowning, my eyes begin to water. "That hurts... a lot. I promise to be better. To show him in more ways how proud of him I truly am."

"I know he would like that." She smiles and pats my shoulder. "So that's why I'm telling you right now that you have to let me finish this laundry... don't tell him you had anything to do with this. He'd be mortified."

"It's just... laundry. You think I'd ever care that my brother didn't do his laundry?"

"It's the one thing Callen's tried to get him to do. One... small... task. And he hasn't been able to. It's a sore subject for him. He won't care if I did it, though. I used to do it all the time, and I talk to him all the time about his insecurities. But if he knew you did this, he'd be really ashamed of his inability to wash their clothes. Trust me."

I understand what she's saying. "That's fine. I had to put Willow's tee in there. That's what started this in the first place. She smudged it with chocolate."

"Perfect excuse for me to use," Coley says brightly. "I'll take it from here."

"Again, thank you."

I run into Max and Callen in the hallway. "How's the breeze up there?" I ask, pointing to the rooftop?

"Can't you tell?" Max asks, messing up Callen's already wind-blown hair as he quickly moves past me on his way into the loft.

"It's a little cold," his partner answers. "You want the key?"

"Yeah, if you don't mind. Is it still sleeting?"

"No, but it's slippery up there."

Before I head up, I return to Matty's to check on Luca and the girls. He's only in his diaper and his sweater, but it looks like Edie and Willow did a good job of changing him. Still, he's fussy—undoubtedly because he's cold.

"Bunny, where are his pants and socks?"

"That was Willow's job. I did the rest."

I see his clothes lying on Matty's bed and take him from his swing to finish dressing him. "Girls, come here," I say sternly, but quietly.

My youngest bounces too hard on the bed, forcing me to catch Luca before he goes flying in the air. My heart is racing as I hold him close.

"Willow!" Edie says.

"Sorry! I didn't mean to."

"Girls, you were both so good this morning, and I thought we were going to have a really great Thanksgiving day together, and so far, I've caught you both eating snacks before lunch, you watching YouTube," I tell Edie, "and you didn't finish putting clothes on your little brother... and then you tried to catapult him to god knows where... you have to be more cautious, Wils. He's a tiny baby..."

"I said I was sorry."

"Yeah, well sorry doesn't fix broken bones... or worse, right?" She shrugs her shoulders. "The answer is no."

"No," she says.

I swallow. "Your mom would be disappointed." I hate to say it and I don't mean to be manipulative. It's just a fact that they have to face. They never would have acted like this with her here. "I can't be everywhere at once, okay? I can't keep a constant eye on all three of you, so I expect you to act like the proper young ladies your mother raised you to be—especially you, Edie. You have to set the example for your sister. Do you understand?"

Willow's attention still seems to be elsewhere, as I'm sure she's on a sugar high from who knows how many treats she snuck in. Edie, on the other hand, looks somber.

"I'm sorry, Daddy." She gives me a hug. "I miss Mama."

"I know, sweetheart. I miss her, too."

"Sorry, Daddy," Willow says flippantly as she runs off to the kitchen where Will is trying to keep an eye on the food with Joel while Shea takes a break to feed Charlie.

Now that I know the bed is safe, I put Luca back down, finish dressing him and loosely wrap a light blanket around him. I return him to the swing next to Nolan, where he's snug and happy again. "I'm going up to the roof," I tell him.

"Daddy, can I go?" Edie asks me softly, tugging on my sweater.

"Bundle up—and put on your boots. Uncle Callen said it's slippery. Matty, can you make sure Willow stays inside your apartment and doesn't have any more sugar. No desserts, sodas... nothing."

"Buzzkill much?" he teases. "Consider it done."

I look at him seriously. "Don't be the cool uncle and do it anyway. I mean it."

"So, don't cave to her like I always did with Liv... even though she has the same genes and can tug on my heartstrings the same exact way... that's what you're saying?"

I look at Nolan. "Can I put you in charge instead?"

"Absolutely. Matty can keep an eye on Luca."

Matty switches seats with his husband.

"Give Luca whatever he wants," I instruct. "We need him to gain weight."

"Done and done."

After putting on own my coat and zipping up Edie's, we both borrow ski caps from the uncles to keep our heads warm. Once we've made it to the rooftop, I ask my daughter to hold my hand and walk slowly, realizing that the thin layer of snow is covering another layer of ice beneath it.

"Just follow in my footsteps," I tell her.

Past the waterfall, I forgo the rock walkway that leads to the tree that was given to Livvy and me for our wedding and step in the fresh snow that covers the dirt around it. I know the rocks will be too slick for us. Once my feet are firmly planted, I reach for Edie and help her find a place near the tree below me.

The trunk is much wider than it was when we received the young sapling nearly ten years ago. I remember that we had it planted before we bought furniture for ourselves once we moved back to Manhattan from Brazil.

"Mama was still pregnant with you when we planted this tree. Can you believe that?"

Edie shakes her head.

"Did you have something to say to her?"

"Like what?" she asks.

"You tell her why you love her."

"Out loud?"

"You're supposed to talk to the tree. The carbon dioxide is good for it."

"Can I whisper?"

I look at her and smile. "Sure. Go right ahead."

As she cups her hands around her mouth, I find the spot I'd carved into the tree last month for our 10th anniversary. We were supposed to do it together–it was always the plan–but as I've learned, plans change. Knocking away the snow, I trace the initials of her name. I'd fretted over how to carve them. *O* for Olivia? Or *L* for Livvy? I opted for the *O* because I remember how she used to melt in my arms when I'd speak that one word. If I added it to the phrase "I love you," she'd do anything I asked.

"Do you mind if I talk while you're telling your secrets?" I ask my daughter.

She shakes her head, looking up at me curiously.

"I'm sorry it's been awhile," I start. "I know Isaiah said to come daily, and when we moved, we vowed to come weekly... and we had stuck by that for the most part, on our own time. It's been harder without you here, Liv. Olivia. Don't think I love you any less, and I hope it has no negative effect on our tree. Maybe you can watch over it from... where you are." I look up and smile, feeling her everywhere right now. "The holidays are hard, baby.

Breaking traditions. Making new ones. I don't want to forget how we used to do things... but I can't keep up with our pace, either. We were rock star parents; did you know that?" I laugh. "Maybe it was all you. I'm sure it was all you. I realize now how much I relied on you to raise our girls while I was working. I know it felt natural for us. I know it was the way we wanted it without ever discussing it, but... I still feel like I should have done more for you. And I wonder if my absence in the everyday took a toll on your heart in some way.

"Your parents would tell me it wasn't my fault, but I will always bear some blame for this, no matter what they say, or doctors say... or what you would tell me if you were here to speak to me now. I loved every moment of my life with you, Liv. And right now, I intend to live it as if you were still here, as my wife... because it's the only way I can come to terms with who I am as a man. Jon Scott became the person he is today because of Livvy Holland. I owe my life to you.

"I love how you brought up our girls... even when they frustrate the hell out of me. I love that when I'm angry at them, I look in their eyes and see you... and immediately soften... and return to a giant puddle of mush that can only hope to remember what it was like to be the disciplinarian... the bad cop. I'm sucking at bad cop these days... because they miss their good cop, and I'm a sorry excuse for one. They'd be the first to tell you that.

"They probably *have* told you that."

"Daddy, you don't suck," Edie says, interrupting me. "And please don't cry."

"I'm sorry, sweetheart." Once I'm certain of my footing, I lean down to hug her tightly.

"Your tears might freeze."

I laugh and nod. "They might," I agree. I stand back up to finish, but Edie slips her hand in mine and doesn't let go. "And along with the girls, I love you for giving me Luca... I hope I make you proud with... how I raise them. I'll always do it the way we talked about. The way we planned. I won't stray from that. Everything I do will be in your honor, baby.

"Just like we said. Always. Everywhere. I meant it. I love you."

"I love you, Mama." I put my hand on Edie's shoulder, holding onto her as she carefully steps back onto the concrete. She turns back around before I'm on solid ground. "I love you, too, Daddy."

"I love you, bunny." I hug her again. "Thanks for being strong... so strong, like your mom. It helps me out more than you'll ever know."

"I'm glad," she says, her eyes wide. "But Daddy? I'm freezing."

"I am, too. Let's get inside and grab another cup of cocoa... okay—no, slowly!" I call after her as she slides on her boots toward the door.

"I'm fine!"

She's brave, just like her mom, too. As much as it scares me, I'm grateful she is.

CHAPTER 34

*P*acing back and forth through the foyer at the Holland brownstone, I try Callen's phone again. "Man, where are you guys? All the cars are here... I'm out of excuses for Trey. He's holding it together, but I'm not sure how. I guess he has other things on his mind, but you two have to get here, like... now. Seriously. Everyone else is waiting."

After checking my watch for the third time in less than two minutes, I head downstairs to the basement to check on the boys. Two of Livvy's cousins had agreed to keep an eye on Luca and Charlie today at the wedding, and they need to get going. It's just hard to let my son go, even if I've known these women, their husbands *and* their families for years.

"Lex, Jackie... Kyle's waiting." I take Luca into my arms one last time and walk back up the stairs with him. Will follows us, carrying Charlie in his car seat.

"You be good today, Champ," I tell him. "Daddy will see you at the church."

"He'll be fine, Jon," Lexi assures me.

"I know." I secure him in his seat, and the four of us venture outdoors to meet their husbands, who are waiting in an SUV with darkened windows—a rental for the day. As soon as we step out the front door, we're greeted with gasps and squeals, as if they don't see us every day on the streets of Manhattan.

"You look so hot, Will!" a woman yells.

After a few seconds, someone else adds that I do, too.

"A pity compliment," my brother teases me as we both secure our children into the backseat of the SUV.

"You don't have to tell me."

"At least you shaved," he says, shrugging at me. "I think you look hot," he assures me with a smirk.

"Screw you," I mutter, just before kissing my son goodbye.

Another commotion outside the car begins to bubble up. After I shut the door, I see Max and Callen emerging from the Tesla down the street.

"Finally," I sigh.

Callen's fully dressed; Max has his pants and dress shirt on. He's wearing his trademark Vans and is holding his jacket over his head, as if he's hiding from the crowd. His partner guides him through the closed-off street toward me as people cheer at the sight of the two of them. Livvy was the city's favorite, but Max and Callen, as a pair, have always been a close second.

When Max reaches me, I put my arm around him and take over for Callen, leading my little brother into the house. He tosses his jacket onto the back of the couch as soon as the door closes, and he shuts his eyes, digging the base of his palms into the sockets of them. I can tell he's stressed out.

"Hey, buddy, just tell me what you need, and I'll get it for you. Anything."

"I'm good," he says, his breathing uneven. He pulls his hands away suddenly. "Where's T?"

"He's in the study."

He nods and walks there quickly. Callen, Will and I follow him in, where Nyall and Joel are quietly playing on their phones and Jack is talking to Trey, making his son laugh.

"Fuck, I am so sorry, T." Max barges in.

"Mascot, don't worry," he says, shaking his head and removing his hand from his pocket. They start to do the handshake they'd been doing since they were kids, but my brother stops, mid-arm-bump, and throws his arm around his best friend.

"I should have been here earlier. All day. I fucked up, Trey. Like... Jon should be your best man. Or... Joel... or..." We all stand back, watching the exchange between the two of them.

"What? No!" Trey scoffs. "Did you think I needed you here to help me dress?" he asks. "Or to keep me from backing out of this wedding?" He shakes his head. "I'm good. I'm set, man. I'm just glad you're here now, and I'm happy you'll be standing next to me at the church, as a witness to our vows. I mean, no one's closer to us than you are." Trey pats Max's good shoulder. "No one."

My brother sighs and looks down at the floor, but Trey picks his chin up, forcing Max's attention back to him. I can see him studying his eyes.

"You okay?" Trey asks, his gaze drifting to Callen momentarily for *his* response.

"I'm... I'm... yeah," Max answers.

"He's fine, T," Callen says.

"I promise you, Trey. The crowds were..." I don't have to guess what's going on, but it doesn't make me any less sad. He's *somehow* medicated. Will puts his hand on my shoulder.

"I get it, Mascot. Don't even..." He hugs him again. "You're here. You made it here. That means the world to me and Coley. I know this isn't easy."

"But I'm perfectly... capable... of everything. I've even got the rings." He pats his shirt. "Oh, fuck."

"I have them," Callen says. "I got them out of his jacket when he took it off earlier. I'll pass them off when we make it to the church."

Max's face blossoms into a bright red when he turns around, and I do notice a strange look to his eyes. *He's definitely high.* I make sure to keep my face unchanged, not wanting him to feel judged in any way. "Callen would be a great best man," he offers, clearly disappointed in himself.

"You're not shirking your duties. Never in my life was there another choice for my best man. You're it. Sorry. And, look, I don't care how you get to the church... to the front of the aisle, even. Just make sure you're there with me, and we're good. Cal, if you guys want to go separa—"

"We're fine," Callen interjects, and Max agrees. "Let's do it—the way we've planned."

"All right, then. Dad, can you show everyone else to the stretch?" Jack nods, giving his son one last hug. As we follow my father-in-law out the door, Trey puts his arm around Max, and I hear him declare, "It's just me and you, then."

"Don't forget your jacket on the couch, babe!" Callen yells to him from the doorway.

"Thanks!" my brother responds.

As we all settle into the long limousine, Jack and I sit across from each other. Nyall and Joel are deeply entrenched in their own ASL conversation, and Callen reaches across to adjust Will's crooked tie, so I engage in some small talk with my father-in-law. "I thought Emi would be here with you."

"She wanted to be with the girls," he tells me. "Thought she'd be too emotional with Jackson and embarrass him. She had breakfast with him, though. We all had a good morning together."

"Good. I hope my daughters have been behaving. I haven't heard a word from anyone."

"I'm sure they're doing fine—both of them having their hair and nails and makeup done?"

"Willow's not supposed to have any makeup done," I say. "I only agreed on Edie."

"You'll have to take that up with the women," he says. "I just know what I've been told."

"Great..."

"I'm sure it will be tasteful," Will says. "Shea and Coley are there, remember? It's not like the clown college was hired to do the job."

"I guess. We'll see when we get there. Where's the ring bearer? I thought Hampton was riding with us."

"Peron was running late," my brother tells me. "He's meeting us there."

"I'm so glad we didn't do a big wedding like this," I admit. Jack smiles at me; it's bittersweet. "There's just too much to coordinate. Liv and I just had to hide everything from you and Em."

"That was a great day, too. A beautiful wedding. She was so lovely."

"Absolutely, she was."

Jack reaches across the limo and takes my hand in his. It's such an unexpected move that it kind of chokes me up. "She should have been here to see her brother get married."

"I know," I tell him, "but she's watching. I believe that now. She wouldn't miss this, Jack."

He wipes away a lone tear with his handkerchief and nods. "You're right. I just wish... you know... I just think about the pictures. The wedding pictures, with the family, and... why didn't we take more photos as a family, Jon? Do you know we don't have *any* with all of us—with your brothers and Shea and Callen... and the girls, and now the babies? How could there be such an oversight?"

"Because we've spent so much time living our lives... and not looking at them through lenses. Everyone else seems to capture us through the eyes of their cameras. It's... it's something we've come to loathe, I think." I hadn't even thought to look out the window all this while, but when I finally do, I see crowds of people lined up behind the roped-off streets. No wonder Max is so shaken today. This must bring back memories of the inaugural parade in DC, and of the chaos of the day when he got shot.

"It stops today," he declares. "Everyone in this car is a part of our family, and I want *our* photos lining the walls of *my* house, celebrating all the moments of our lives."

"I agree. We'll make more of an attempt. I certainly will with my kids... for all of us." I look around the car, and everyone agrees to make the same effort. "And we need to do more things as a family. I worry that... we won't all be here this close forever.

"Careers or, you know, anything could take any one of us away from Manhattan... at any time."

He points at me. "You're not taking my grandkids from me."

I shake my head. "No."

He looks at Will, too. "Don't take that little boy of yours, either. I'm planning a baseball league, and I've got my pitcher and designated hitter lined up with your sons, so... don't ruin my dream," he jokes.

"I'm staying where Jon is. He fucking moved down the street to be closer to me. What kind of an asshole would I be to pick up and leave, right?" he asks. "Sorry about the language."

"Will, I don't give a shit," Jack says, causing us all to laugh. "There are so many bigger things in life to worry about. We're all adults here. Right now, anyway."

When we finally get to the church, I offer to let Jack get out first. "I'll go last... maybe gauge who gets the most screams—Callen or Will," he teases.

"My money's on Callen," I tell him.

"I'll take that bet." I'm intrigued by Jack's playful offer. "I'll put twenty on Will," he says.

Joel taps me on the shoulder and signs, "Twenty on Callen."

Nyall disagrees. "Twenty on Will."

"A hundred on myself," Callen says.

"Yeah. A hundred on Cal, and I don't gamble, but... still. A hundred on Cal," my brother agrees. I laugh at his self-deprecating bet.

Before I get out, I summarize everything. "That's 240 on Callen and 40 on Will. Winners split the pot?" Everyone agrees.

*O*nce we get inside, Ja'nese, Trey and Coley's wedding coordinator, leads us to a back room where we're out of the way of arriving guests. Callen's still in shock that Will got more attention than he did, but I don't think he took into account his new hair style, which is really short and a darker color–so, not *trademark Callen McNare*. Maybe people didn't recognize him.

"You guys just give your money to Nyall," Jack says, taking out his phone. "I'm good."

Coley's oldest brother looks pretty happy with that arrangement.

"Men," Jack announces after clearing his throat.

Will's bandmate, Peron, shows up with Hampton just as we're organizing ourselves for a picture. The little boy stands in between my brother and me. I flip his collar down and smooth out his windblown hair.

"Get in the picture, Mr. Holland," Ja'nese says, taking his phone from him. He walks around behind us, finding a spot where he can be seen. Peron grabs his phone, too, and snaps a few photos of his own. "Such a handsome group."

"Thanks to this one," Will says as he messes up the hair I'd just fixed.

"Where's Willow?" Hampton asks. "Don't I get to walk down the aisle with her?"

I smile and laugh as I look at his father. "She's with the bridal party in another room."

"He's right," Ja'nese says. "He needs to be with them. Let's go, stud."

"Hampton, remember what we talked about!" Peron yells while his son gleefully follows the coordinator down the hall. He looks at me. "He wanted to kiss her at the end of the aisle."

I shake my head. "Oh, no. That is not a good idea."

"I've told him..."

I remember back to our sexual assault conversation and laugh out loud, then immediately worry that my youngest daughter will react as her uncles taught her after dinner that night if he tries to make a move on her.

"Max taught her a self-defense move, and, uh... I'll apologize in advance if your son ends up with a broken arm in the middle of church."

Will laughs, too.

"Shit," Peron says, smiling. "What can I say? I warned him. He just likes her so much and got it stuck in his head that a kiss is how you show a girl how much you like her."

"*You* put that thought in his head," Will says.

Peron explains. "Three years ago, he asked me why I kissed Finola so much, and yeah. That's how I answered. *It's how you show a girl how much you like her.* I did not expect that to stick with him like it did... and I can't undo it."

"Well, leave it to Willow, then. She'll undo it," I assure him. "Just one kiss, because she's not ready."

"I don't blame her. Not one bit."

"Okay, guys." Ja'nese looks down at her clipboard. "Let's line up like we did last night. Jack? Emi's waiting for you at the entrance down the hall."

"Noted. Guys, good luck. Do my boy proud."

"We will," I tell him as I stand directly in front of the wedding planner. Everyone files in behind me: Callen, Joel, Nyall and then Will. She does one final check of all of us, fixing flowers and ties and coats and hair, and then tells us to go stand in the back of the church at the grand St. Patrick's Cathedral and wait for our best man and groom to show up, which they will do—ceremoniously—in a few minutes.

Once we're settled in our spots, the guests notice and quiet down, finding their places and facing the front of the church. I see where Luca and Charlie are seated toward the back, safely with the cousins. Will's son seems to be sleeping at the moment; mine is awake and taking in his surroundings, but currently content with things. I'm comforted just knowing he's close by.

With the church doors open, and a few people still making their way inside, I see my brother and Trey walking up the steps to a cacophony of applause. I'm proud to see Max standing tall, keeping pace with his best friend, and pulling off a look of confidence that I haven't seen in months. At the back of the church, Ja'nese meets up with them, putting everything in place.

Both of them look incredibly handsome. Max's eyes are still glassy, but they don't affect his good looks in the slightest. I smile at both of them, and pat Max on his good shoulder after he retrieves the rings from Callen and exchanges a brief kiss with him. The tender moment is met with a few swoons from the pews from curious people who are now watching.

"Why am I nervous?" Trey whispers to me. "Were you nervous?"

"I drank. Did you drink?"

He holds up his fingers to motion that he had a little.

"I drank more." I wink at him. "You're going to be fine. You've been in front of larger crowds. And she was it for you—from the moment you met her," I remind him. "She's amazing."

His shoulders relax as he nods his head.

I watch as Max hands Ja'nese the rings for her to give to the ring bearer, and as he does, I see him tell her to guard them with her life. She slides them both on her pinky and swears that she will, then tells him that he and Trey should head up to the front of the church. Heads turn as my brother-in-law makes his entrance, and Max follows closely behind him, still walking with his shoulders back and his head held high.

"He looks okay," I tell Callen.

"He will be."

Finally, the church doors close, and silence settles over the building as the street noise is blocked out. It feels like a private moment, although the church is still packed with hundreds of friends of Trey, Coley and their families.

The women—and girls, and Hampton—come in through a side door, joining us in the narthex. Everyone looks absolutely beautiful, my daughters especially, both with minimal makeup. Edie's hair is long, thick and curled, and she looks so much like her mother did when she would dress up for occasions just like this one.

She glances up at me, smiling as if she knows exactly how lovely she looks.

I signal for them to come to me, taking a knee so they can hear me speak in a whisper. I hug each of them, careful not to mess up their dresses or hair. "You girls are stunning. I'm so proud of you both."

"Thanks, Daddy," they say in unison.

"Are you ready?"

Edie nods her head, but Willow rolls her eyes at me. "Do I have to do this with him?" she asks, giving Hampton the side-eye.

"Yes, Wils. He's a sweet boy who has a crush on you. He can't help it, okay? What boy wouldn't like a smart girl like you, huh?"

"I just feel like... we're too old for this."

I nod. "Yeah, you're not little kids, but... they wanted you both to be a part of this, so... you're doing this for Trey and Coles, okay? And then you get cake after."

"Look, she gave us necklaces, Daddy," Edie says. "Like Mama's."

"Girls, we need to line up," Ja'nese says, taking Willow and placing her next to Hampton. I check out my oldest daughter's necklace, though. It's the same style as the pendant I gave Liv when she was 16–her *Choisie* necklace. But Edie's name is engraved in this one, and I assume Willow's in etched in hers.

"It's beautiful," I say, looking around for Coley to thank her, but I guess she'll make the grand entrance from outside, just like Trey did. "You ready?" I offer her my arm as music begins to play and we head to the back of the line behind Callen and one of Coley's college friends, Pryana.

"You'll do great, Wils!" she says to her sister, possibly a little too loudly, as I hear a few people in the back of the church laughing. Unfazed, though, Willow and Hampton begin their walk up the aisle toward Trey and Max. I see my brother signaling for her to slow down as she tries to get away from her partner, who's attempting to hold her hand. This results in a clump of petals toward the front of the church, rather than an even distribution, but her job was done.

Max takes the rings from Hampton and slips them inside his jacket pocket, and I watch as Emi and Peron get the kids settled into the front row–separated by Jack and Emi. No kiss was exchanged or even attempted.

After watching the rest of the coupled bridesmaids and groomsmen, Edie and I begin to walk down the aisle. At last glance, she was all smiles, but as I hear the reaction from the guests, and know what's going through their minds, I can't help but feel the same way. Livvy should be walking on my arm right now. *How can it be that she's not?*

I keep my focus to the front, on the cross hanging on the wall, asking the man questions there are no answers for. *Why did you take her? Why leave my girls with no mother? Why didn't you let her see her son, even once? If she had to go, why didn't you let me say goodbye? Why couldn't I tell her I love her just once more? Why couldn't I hear the same from her?*

The statue's purpose is not there to shield my questions or take blame, but today, I feel unburdened, casting off this culpability onto someone else—someone who doesn't *look* like a faceless deity, but one who looks *human*. I realize many believe Jesus Christ is so much more than that. From what I've read, he was a great man. But that's just it, he was a man, just like I am. Like Trey is. Like Jack is. A human being, like Livvy was. And in that sense, I can believe in him more than many things religions teach, more than many things in the Bible. It's not the way Christians want me to see him, but, to me, it's not a bad way to look upon him.

I'm on autopilot but am aware enough of my surroundings to stop before I reach the steps where the rest of the bridal party is. I give my daughter a kiss on the cheek and guide her to her place next to Pryana. Stella, the maid of honor, is already coming toward us by the time I step between Max and Callen. When she assumes her position, the church gets silent, and the organ begins to play the wedding march, causing all the guests to stand.

The back doors open, and Coley walks in wearing a slender, strapless gown that subtly flares out toward the bottom. It looks lacy from here—she looks beautiful, and I'd love to turn around to see what Trey thinks, but I know that I can see it on video later, as there's a cameraman just a few feet from me, capturing the moment. It must be a good response, though, judging from the expressions on the bridesmaids' faces.

In the absence of her father, Coley's mom walks her down the aisle. Again, a tinge of sadness dampens the celebration, but it's only momentary. Trey steps down to meet her, to take his bride's hand from her mother, and smiles enliven the church again. Carefully, he helps her to the top of the stairs, and I can finally see his face, rosy in color, but beaming with excitement. He doesn't look nervous at all anymore now that Coley's at his side.

"You look lovely," I mouth to her. She nods to thank me.

As writers, I was surprised to hear that the two of them wouldn't be reading their own vows, but discovered it was because it wasn't allowed in the Catholic church.

"We wrote things for the reception," Trey assured me.

"There will be a poem," Coley had added.

I had been to a few Catholic weddings in my life—all of them with Liv—and as lengthy as they were, we'd always gotten through them together with little inside jokes, laughter about songs, and sweet, intimate moments of hand-holding, or even a stolen kiss every now and then. She is noticeably absent from this service in so many ways today, but they do request prayers for her in one part of the service. While she's not here, she wasn't forgotten. I knew there was no threat of that, but it was comforting to hear her name, nonetheless.

Toward the end of the ceremony, while the rings are being exchanged, I find myself in the middle of Callen and Max sneaking in their own private moment of hand-holding behind my back. I don't even care that my ass cheek is getting bumped periodically. The fact that they're doing this in St. Patrick's makes me proud that they're in my family, and I wouldn't do anything to stop them.

After the pronouncement of man and wife has been made, and a conservative kiss has been exchanged, Trey and Coley walk down the aisle as a married couple for the first time. It's been a long time coming, but I'm so happy I was a witness to it. I feel like I've been a part of their life together from the beginning, when it wasn't easy for them at all.

Stella taps Pryana on the arm when she makes her way down the steps, and the two of them link arms and walk out together. Confused, I look around, but realize their mode of exit is to let Max and Callen walk out together. I turn around and hug them both quickly before taking Edie back down toward the back of the church. She relishes the attention, but I think she would have much rather made the trek alone, like a runway model or something.

As I get to the back of the church, I hear a familiar squeal and look in its direction. Lexi's bouncing Luca, but he seems very much upset by the loud organ and the restlessness of the crowd around him.

"Wait here for your uncles," I tell Edie, veering to the side to take my son in an effort to stop his tears. He wails loudly, his expression so heartbreaking it makes me want to cry with him. "Luca, baby, what is it?" I ask him, trying to find the quietest place in the back. When I realize there is no such place, I step just outside the doors, even though I know we're going to draw attention there, too. Even with the shouting there, the open air allows for the noise to escape. I reach inside the diaper bag and find a pacifier, which he takes right away. His sweet little eyes meet mine. "I got you, kid. Don't you worry about anything. I've always got you."

He reaches his fist up toward me. Whether it's an intentional move or not—because *of course*, it's not—I take it as one, and bump it with my own. This is one time I'll check the tabloid sites—I wouldn't mind having a picture of this moment.

Will opens the door and summons me back inside for photos with the bride and groom as some of the guests begin streaming out. Now calm again, I hand off Luca to Lexi and follow Will up the north aisle to the front of the church, where everyone in the bridal party, except Trey and Coley, are waiting.

Ten minutes later, they show up with the photographer, and we make quick work of the requisite photos. I notice Jack snapping quite a few candids of his own in between takes.

When we're finished, Shea, Will and I say goodbye to our sons for the evening. I'll be picking up Luca after the reception, but Will and Shea have opted to take their first night away from the baby today.

*B*ay Room is impressive at night. I'd been here once for a conference during the daytime last year, but it was a rainy day and the view was wasted on us. Tonight, the sky is clear, and the city is beautiful from the 60th floor.

Coley had a third of the space transformed into a bridesmaid's lounge, where she and the other ladies could change clothes and touch up their makeup after the wedding. Before the rest of the women arrive, I go behind the *BRIDAL PARTY ONLY* sign and peek inside with my daughters to see what luxuries await them. There are healthy snacks and drinks—champagne for the women and sparkling juice for the girls—and embroidered pink robes, along with three plush couches. Music is already playing through speakers strategically placed throughout. There's a huge mirror behind four individual vanities, each with beauty products and ample lighting for any primping necessary. In the back, I see a rack with clothes, and behind that must be a separate changing area for them.

Coley's thought of everything.

"Do you see your clothes back there? What you're changing into?" I ask my girls.

They both run along the rug to the clothing. "That's mine!" Edie says, pointing to a short, white dress that's even less suited for winter than the one she's been wearing all day.

"These are mine!" Willow yanks a navy-blue jumpsuit off its hanger and starts to lift her gown over her head.

"Wils! Not yet!"

"Daddy, I'm cold and I'm sick of this scratchy thing!"

"Can't you wait for Aunt Shea to help you? Their car hasn't even arrived yet."

She pouts. "Daddy, I'll wait," Edie says, "but I'll take Willow into the dressing room and help her... but you're not supposed to be in here." She crosses her arms and nods her head, her lips pursed. "Girls only."

"That's why—I know, bunny," I say with a chuckle. "Thank you for helping your sister. Do one more favor for me, okay?"

"Anything you ask," she says, smiling.

"Don't ruin your appetite with those snacks. Don't eat the dessert stuff. Have some fruit. Okay?"

"I promise." Willow takes her outfit to the back. "And I promise for her, too."

"Thank you for taking care of your sister. I'll be right out here if you need anything."

"We'll be good, Daddy."

I smile, thinking of how much Edie has matured in the past six months. She used to be our handful, and while Willow seems to be going through a phase, it's to be expected. So much has changed in our lives. But my oldest daughter impresses me more every day. Am I sad she has to grow up faster than I'd like her to? Sure; but I'm proud of her, nonetheless.

Max and Callen are among the next wave of guests to show up. They keep me company, looking out the grand windows at the Statue of Liberty, as I wait for the girls. Their fingers are still linked together, as they were during the ceremony and through most of the pictures that were taken. Max seems to be the one holding on, and it's not like him—not to be affectionate, but to be needy.

"How are you doing?" I ask him, patting him on the back.

He simply nods and sighs.

"There'll be much fewer people here than at the church," I assure him. "I think they got down the guest list to 160?" I look to Callen for confirmation.

"Yeah, I think that's right."

"And it's a big space. Huge ceilings," I comment on the architectural details. "There's also a big dance floor around the corner there—lots of space—with an open bar."

"Open bar, you say?" Max asks.

"That's what I said."

"I'll be back." He releases his partner. "Want anything?"

"I'll take... whatever craft beer they have," I tell him.

"Club soda. Can you carry all that?"

"Not a problem."

"So," Callen says. "How much do you want to bet I'll get him out on the dance floor tonight?"

"Dude, you ready to lose another bet?" I ask him. "Our luck isn't so good today... and you're asking me to bet on you... again. Seems like a dumb move."

"We're dancing," he assures me, "on that dance floor. Fifty bucks."

"Are you hard up for cash, Callen McNare?" I tease him. He laughs. "Fifty bucks says the only reason his sneakers hit that dance floor is to make his way to and from the bar."

We shake on it. "This won't even be a challenge."

"I know my brother likes to dance," I concede, "but that was the Max I knew before the shooting. The outgoing one. The life of the party one. I haven't seen him in a while."

"He's coming back."

"You keep saying that," I respond.

He pats me on the back. "I believe in him."

I don't know what it is about this kid these days, but he just keeps saying things to me that... that move me. I turn to him and pull him into a hug, surprising him.

"Whoa, whoa, whoa, what the fuck?" Max calls out, his voice echoing in the cavernous room and turning more than a few heads. Luckily, most of the guests are familiar with my brother and his lack of a filter.

"Fraternal," I say, putting my hands up. He sticks the beer he got me into my left one.

"Sorry, just... I never know when you'll be on the market again, and... this guy's taken."

Smiling, I answer him. "Not anytime soon... and not my type. I wasn't born that way."

"Laaaadies and gentlemen," a deep voice says over a sound system. "Mr. and Mrs. Trey and Coley Holland!" In front of us, from the elevator lobby, my brother-in-law and his wife emerge, stepping in between the designated East and South rooms of the building and kissing to raucous applause. I spy Edie and Willow rushing out of the dressing area at the last minute, clapping, jumping up and down, and shouting for their aunt and uncle. Willow's in her jumpsuit, her hair tucked under a blue beanie with silver-sequined stripes. The tresses look shorter than normal, no doubt because of the curls that linger from her afternoon style. She looks adorable, but I can tell she has a freshly applied layer of gloss to her lips. I let it go. She runs over to me while Edie follows Coley into the room again, where Trey leaves her with another kiss.

As soon as she disappears behind the temporary curtains, he removes the tie that's been undoubtedly driving him crazy all day and unfastens the top button of his shirt. While Trey is inundated by congratulations from family members and old friends, Max adds the dark gray neckwear to the lighter gray one that's been hanging around his neck all day. Even though Ja'nese had nagged him multiple times to actually *knot* his tie, he refused, preferring to stick with his signature look that had been accepted by all of us long ago.

Max walks over to Callen, holding one end of each tie in his hands. "One for each wrist later."

Callen nods, blushing, clearly embarrassed by the suggestion. As much as I don't want to think about my brother and his partner in the bedroom, I seriously doubt that bondage is something they do—not with Max's arm, wrist and hand being as messed up as they are... but I know my brother likes to portray this illusion of mystery and have an element of shock in what they do, so I take every insinuation of his sex life with a grain of salt.

"Can I have one of your ties, Uncle Max?" Willow asks him.

He cocks his head and scratches his chin, not quite expecting that question from my little girl. "It's a little selfish of me to keep them both," he tells her, bending over and removing the one he'd had on all day. "This one will contrast more with your outfit. Love it, by the way."

"Shea and Coley bought it for me."

He ties the tie perfectly around her neck but loosens it to hang more casually. "This looks fucking chill, Wils." She puts her hand over her mouth in shock. "You're gonna turn heads in that."

Callen hands her a dollar bill. I'm sure I'm going to get a note from one of their teachers any day now that they've used that word. It's just a *word*. I know this, but their teachers aren't going to go for that. Most of their classmates' parents won't, either.

"Where'd you learn how to tie a tie like that?" I ask Max, making the conscious decision to not be critical of him tonight.

"Who do you think dresses Callen?"

"It's true."

"Look at her shoes!" Max exclaims as my youngest daughter runs toward the front of the South Room to Jack and Emi. "Vans." He swipes at a non-existent tear. "Raising her right, Jon."

"She idolizes her uncles," I tell him. "You, Will, Cal... don't be surprised if she emulates your every move."

He licks his lips nervously and starts rubbing on his bad shoulder. I honestly didn't mean anything by it.

"The skateboard being the perfect example," I add. "Have you seen her on it lately? She can do a small... jump... whatever, on it."

"Yeah?" he asks.

"Yeah. You need to go with her again. When it's warmer, of course. Show her the next trick."

"Definitely."

Max and Callen see Will and Shea at our table and decide to sit down. I wait at the back for Edie, and eventually, it's just Trey and me lingering there.

"Congratulations." I shake his hand again. "How many years did you guys date?"

"Nearly six," he says. "I can't believe it took us this long."

"Me, neither. You've been engaged forever."

"Yeah. I wish we had done it earlier. Obviously. But even now, sometimes it feels like we're too young to be married. We're younger than you and Liv were."

"True. When you know, you know, though. No point in putting it off because you didn't hit some milestone, or some age, right?"

"Definitely." He plays with the ring on his finger. "We'll always have some goal we haven't reached yet. We'll always be working toward something. There have to be rewards along the way. This is a big one."

"Possibly the biggest."

A few of the bridesmaids file out of the changing room, looking elegant in colorful cocktail dresses. Edie finally skips out, her long locks bouncing, her white, knee-length dress billowing from her waist. There are six bright, multi-colored butterflies attached to it—one on the shoulder and the rest on the skirt. They look real, the way their wings extend from the fabric. It's a beautiful dress, one that somehow reminds me of Liv's free spirit.

Coley steps out from behind her and flips the long hair that had been hanging loosely down Edie's back over the shoulder without the butterfly. "Isn't she gorgeous?" she asks me.

Trey puts his arm around his bride and kisses her again.

"Breathtaking. I feel like her mom's in the room with us."

"There's something about it, right?" Coley says.

"Absolutely." I reach for Edie's hand, and we leave Trey and Coley behind as I guide my daughter to her seat at the kids' table. Hampton has snagged a prime spot, right in between my girls. I squeeze his shoulders and speak quietly in his right ear. "Behave."

"Yes, sir. I will, sir," he says nervously. I laugh, though, patting him on the back, hoping that he knows I was teasing him. He's always been a sweet kid with good intentions. Willow even looks to be in good spirits sitting next to him. She has one of her books about space opened up toward him; I guess she was trying to teach him something.

As I'd walked through the tables, I noticed eight place settings at each one—except for two tables. There are only seven at the one in which I'm seated, and the same is true for the one in which Coley's mom is seated. It's a thoughtful and bittersweet gesture by both Trey and Coley to not replace their loved ones at these wedding party tables, but also not to leave a stark reminder that they aren't here tonight.

My place card is right in between my brothers, and I can't imagine a more perfect place to sit tonight. The girls are one table away and within my eyeline, and my in-laws are at the table beside me. The bride and groom have their own table, where they can enjoy a modicum of peace and quiet during dinner in between receiving guests and dancing and doing toasts and more dancing... all the things that exhausted Liv and me on our wedding day.

"How are you holding up?" Will asks me.

"I'm good," I tell him honestly. "It's been a beautiful day. She would have loved to have been here to see Trey and Coley and the girls... but I feel her here," I tell him, blushing, because I know he's staunch in his beliefs. "I know she's with us."

"I think so, too." I look at him with suspicion. "Just look at the stars," he adds, glancing over the Hudson, where we're high and far enough out to actually see hundreds of them.

I smile. "Thanks, Will."

Before dinner begins, a sea of servers floods the tables to pour champagne. Jack stands up, taking a few paces toward the head table and taps his fork to his glass a couple of times to get the guests' attention.

He clears his throat. "I'll make this short and sweet to follow tradition. I've apparently been giving toasts wrong at weddings, but these literary geniuses who just tied the knot have done their research and given me my orders."

"That's not true, Dad!" Trey argues. Coley is shaking her head, too.

"Stella, Pryana, Kamiesha, Lucy, Shea... and especially Edie... thank you, ladies, for assisting Coley as she prepared for the big day. Since she got engaged, her life has vastly changed," he says as his eyes water. "Since they set a date, our world has, too. But somehow, you were able to make sure the light that this woman has brought into my son's life never dulled, never lost its shine or sparkle, in the most difficult of days. And today, she is more radiant than ever. To me, you've achieved what I thought was impossible. For tradition's sake, here's a toast to the lovely bridesmaids." He raises his glass, and we all toast with him. I make sure to look at all six of the bridesmaids, crediting each of them with the important role they played in the ceremony today.

"And bucking tradition," my father-in-law adds, "to our little—not-so-little—miracle, Jackson, and the wonder that wandered into his life one unexpected day at Columbia, Coley. We're all grateful for that moment of fate, surprising as it was to all of us. Once we met you, we knew you would someday be a Holland, not only in getting to know the gracious woman you are, but also in understanding the love our son had for you then, and the love that has continued to grow between you two ever since. Welcome to the family, Coley, and congratulations to both of you. To Jackson and Coley!"

"To Trey and Coley!" most of us respond.

"Ladies first?" Trey asks his new wife.

She nods and stands. "See, Jack? I'm bucking tradition, too... so thank you for doing so. And thank you for the kind words. Mom, I love you so much. Thank you for supporting all of my crazy dreams, even when they seemed unattainable. I am forever grateful that you let me and Joel journey off to see what New York had to offer, because I found everything I ever wanted here. I wish Dad could have seen me today," she says, maintaining her composure, "but I know he was happy with the choices I made—especially with this one." She reaches for Trey's hand.

"Emi and Jack, not only have I always felt a part of your family, but you've always warmly welcomed my brothers and parents into your lives, too. No one has bigger hearts than the Hollands, and I hope that I can live up to the name." Unexpectedly, she breaks down. "To live up to the expectations of a... a daughter."

My eyes drip tears with hers, and I use my napkin to wipe them away.

Jack walks across the room and hands her his handkerchief. "Have I taught you nothing?" he says jokingly to Trey. We all appreciate the laugh in an otherwise particularly sad moment.

Coley wipes her face and takes a few breaths. "In Trey's defense, I used his handkerchief in the limo over here. My emotions got the best of me—happy tears—so... you've taught him so much, Jack. Be proud of him."

"I am," he says, his voice caught in his throat.

"I, too, want to thank Stella and the bridesmaids for all of their help... and Edie, for stepping in and doing such a wonderful job. You may not know the importance of your role today, but someday, you will.

"But most of all, I have... something to say to Trey... it is a poem. Our vows that we couldn't exchange in church, so if you don't mind, we'd like you all to be witnesses to an extension of our ceremony here.

"Fair warning, it is a *love poem*. Expect an ombré of red over here," she says, pointing to her groom.

> *"My lungs never gasped without your air*
> *My lips never swelled without the touch of yours*
> *My blood never rushed without the beat of your heart*

My skin never dampened without your cover
And I swear, they never will, without you

"I never heard sound until you called my name
I never tasted sweetness before your kiss
I never saw beauty before I stared into your eyes
I never felt safe until your hands touched me
And I swear, I never will, without you

"And as I walk through my life—
The days, months, years
As I walked down the aisle today—
The seconds, the anticipation of hours, minutes
I know I have never loved until you showed me love
And I swear, I never will, without you"

*C*oley's delivery is smooth and confident, as I would expect it to
be. I've seen her do readings of her poetry in bookshops before.
What I don't expect is Trey's response—he's barely a shade of light pink...
and that poem was *all about their sex life.*

Our little Trey is growing up. Will and I exchange a look with one
another, so I know he's thinking the same thing.

Trey stands up to give her a kiss—a real one—one that might be
prompted by the exact poem she just read to him. There's a lot of cat-
calling in the room, and I make it a point *not* to look at Jack and Emi. I'm
sure Trey's making that same effort, and that's likely why he's remained
cool and collected so far.

"To my husband," Coley says, one arm still around him, the other
reaching for her champagne glass, "and to never being without you."

They both drink and he kisses her again before he begins to speak.

"I..." He sighs as she settles into her seat and folds her hands under her chin. She blinks up at him innocently. "I don't know how I can compete with that, but..." He bites his lip and admires her again. "Wow, am I lucky..."

The room laughs and cheers in agreement.

"Fortunately, I don't have to compete. She's my teammate. She's on my side... for life. She has been from the start.

"First, thank you to Stella, Shea, Pree, Kamiesha, Lucy and Eeds... I mean, Coley is the farthest thing from Bridezilla, but I know you had some days when you had to delegate things to yourself because she didn't want to burden anyone, so I appreciate you taking control and helping her out... because she's too nice sometimes."

He grins and nods to the ladies who helped out his bride. "So, thank you.

"I also have to thank my groomsmen—and I hope it's okay for me to do that—but you're all brothers to me, and most of you have been here with me all my adult life and most of my childhood, too. With the help of my parents... my sister... you got me here. You helped me become the man I am today, and I'm grateful. And Max? I can't say this enough, but... thank you... for today."

I pat my brother on the back.

Trey takes a deep breath and swallows. "Now the real stuff. The serious stuff." He looks at Coley.

"I think we're probably in the minority—being this young and knowing exactly what we want out of our lives. We both have our dreams. You've known for years what you've wanted to do, and I love that I've been able to support that dream. I had a vague idea before of what I wanted to do, but it became very clear about two years ago... and it's a big, scary dream. It got even scarier after what we witnessed in DC, but... I know that I was put on this planet—and in this city—to serve the people, and that's what I intend to do—relentlessly, fearlessly and with integrity.

"Knowing the battle we have ahead of us, the scrutiny we both will face, I gave you the option to weigh in. I was afraid you'd say no. I was afraid your concerns would convince me to change my mind.

"I was afraid for nothing. Because, with you, Coley, I've never been afraid. I've never had reason to be. And what I vow to you—what I wish for you—is that I never give you reason to be afraid, either.

"I will always be open-minded and listen to the people around me. I will never think that I know more than an expert in their field.

"I will always be aware of potential threats that may put you or the people we love in danger.

"I will take the necessary steps to protect our family and friends.

"I won't take careless or uncalculated risks.

"I will put you first, knowing that we're working together toward the same goals, and in time, we'll get there. I will understand that it may take longer than the timeframe I have set for myself.

"I will be patient.

"I will cherish you every day for the sacrifices you've already made for me, and the ones you'll make in the future. I know there will be late nights, and missed dinners, but there will never be a missed anniversary... or a missed birthday..." He clears his throat. "Or a missed birth. Period.

"And if you ever become afraid, or if I ever break one of these promises, I swear to you right now, we will reevaluate everything—our plans, our goals—and come up with something that will work better for you and me.

"My first dream was to be your husband. It was the critical one, and it came true today. All the rest of them build on that dream, so I'm not messing that one up. I promise you that tonight, in front of our parents, our brothers and Shea, our friends, and the rest of our families.

"I promise to love you most. To listen to you first. To make you the priority. Above all else. I wouldn't have it any other way.

"To my wife." He raises his glass and drinks, and we all follow suit. When he sits down, they kiss again.

My youngest brother stands up but doesn't leave the safety of our table. "Fuck tradition," Max starts into his microphone. I shake and bow my head simultaneously.

"Earmuffs!" Matty yells.

"Too late!" Will counters.

"I doubt it," Livvy's uncle follows up. I'm sure he's not wrong; I'm sure there will be more. I look over at my girls, who are both giggling at their table. *I so dread that day when their teachers call me in for this.*

"What was I supposed to do? Like, accept thanks on behalf of the bridesmaids? How outdated is that rule, right?" He walks around our table to Stella, putting the mic in her hand. "Here, would you like to say something? Accept thanks or... you know?"

She laughs. "You're all very welcome," she says, nodding. "I love Coley and I'd do it again—wait! No! I don't mean—"

"Wrong answer, Stel," Max says after stealing the microphone back. Everyone laughs. "Shea? You want to try?"

"Just a simple, 'you're welcome.' Love you, Sister Holland!"

"Love you, Sister Scott!" Coley responds.

Max wanders to the other table. "Pryana? Lucy? Kameisha?" They all shake their heads, but Edie is raising her hand. "Look how polite this one is. Edie? What would you like to say?"

"Thank you for inviting me to be a junior bridesmaid, Coley."

"You're welcome, sweetie!"

"And you owe me and Willow swear money, Uncle Max."

"Does Uncle Max *ever* carry cash?" he responds quickly, making everyone laugh again as he returns to his spot at the front of the room. "You know where the deep pockets are." He pauses once again, reading his audience well. "So... I really want to talk about Coley... and I want to talk about Trey... because I don't think anyone knows these two as a couple better than I do. They probably wish I didn't know them as well as I do sometimes, but, I mean, I lived with them for about two and a half years. I definitely wore out my welcome," he adds with a sheepish grin, his voice trailing off.

"I don't know how many of you know about the night I first met Coley. It was right after they started dating. I lived in California at the time, but I had flown back to the city one Saturday with a friend, and my return flight wasn't until the next morning. Naturally, I went to hit up Trey for a place to crash.

"Now, I know what you're all thinking—you had family that lived here, even then, right? Yeah, well." He points to me. "Rugrats." Then he walks to Will and Shea and draws a big heart over their heads with his fingers. "Newlyweds. Like, of the *worst* kind. It was embarrassing to be a guest in their apartment."

"Shut up, Mascot," Shea says, putting her hands over her face.

"Yeah, you weren't shy back then."

"TMI, buddy," Will adds, his cheeks red. "Cut it. This is for Trey."

"I'm building up to the story. That's the background. So, I went to

Trey's apartment, knowing that Coley would be there. I also was ready to give her a piece of my mind because the friend that I had flown with to New York was... Trey's ex... who was my other best friend.

"And I was pissed, because the breakup was still fresh, and I had spent the past week or so consoling my friend—my friend who I was *certain* was perfect for Trey.

"And what did Coley do?" He shakes his head. "This girl answered every awkward question head-on. She never missed a beat when I tried to shake her confidence. She went toe-to-toe with me and kept up with my banter, dishing back what I gave her. She was my perfect foil.

"And fuck—10 bucks, girls, whatever—see Uncle Cal—I'd found a new friend. I literally went to sleep that night thinking Trey found the straight, female version of me."

Trey and Coley both start laughing. "I'm not as vulgar as you," Coley shouts.

"Oh, yes, you are," he argues. "You just use prettier words—that *don't rhyme.*"

Her jaw drops and she looks at her new husband, who shrugs his shoulders and nods. "He's not wrong, laureate," Trey says. "I love you for it. But I don't agree that she's the straight, female you, Mascot. She's... very different."

"You keep telling yourself that... and now that I put that in your head, you're always going to think about it. It's a good thing, though. I'm your lifelong friend. That only means good things for her, right?"

Trey nods. "I guess so." He holds her hand on the table, then picks it up to kiss it. "She's much tidier than you, though."

"I'm tidy; I just know you and Coley and Callen can do a better job, so..."

"We can leave the arguing for... after dinner," Trey suggests.

"You're right. I wasn't expecting the two of you to talk back. This is my speech, right? So... now I turn to Trey. Whoa. There is so much I could say about T... but it all starts with Livvy, so I want to mention her briefly. If my brother, Jon, hadn't met Trey's sister, Livvy, I never would have had this life... and it's been rough lately," he says, his eyes watering, "but I will never take a day of it for granted. Because Livvy and Jon became an item, Trey and I became best friends. Not simply friends, but the best of friends. My brothers taught me a lot, they did, but it was so nice to have a friend my age. Someone to teach me things he was learning in his fancy school, someone who was going through similar things as I was at the same time. Someone who liked the same sports I did. Someone who watched the same shows I watched, laughed at the same jokes I thought were funny. A kid really needs that. It's something I didn't have at home.

"Now, Trey, he had dozens of friends. I mean, look at this room. You're all here. But he was so gracious and kind that he shared them all with me. When he was invited to outings or parties, he'd politely ask if he could bring a friend. I remember him telling some of you that we were a package deal." He laughs. "What eight-year-old kid does that? Especially when the other part of the package is a kid whose clothes were older than he was, and who wasn't always able to shower every day because the water kept getting cut off at his apartment?

"Trey Holland was that kid. He was never embarrassed of me. Not ever. Well, not until we were teenagers, maybe, and I got a little lippy in public. Then maybe I embarrassed him. But he tolerated it all, and still called me not only his friend, but his best friend."

Max walks over to Callen. "And if it wasn't for Trey, I wouldn't have Callen, my... cornerstone. Trey has always been supportive of us, and I love you for being so persistent in leading me back to him when I was so stubborn. You always know what's right. Always.

"But..." He looks around the room. "If you're wishing I wasn't here right now... wasn't keeping you from your dinners... you only have Trey to blame." Facing the head table again, he speaks from the heart. "He risked his life to save mine on those steps in DC." He bows his head to the floor. "And trust me, twenty Maxes aren't worth one Trey. I've done the math." His voice is shaky, and the room is silent. "I'm grateful for what he did, but if that opportunity ever presents itself again..." He looks up. "Don't do it again."

"Max," Callen pleads audibly from his seat. I put my hand on his shoulder, feeling the same pain he must feel at that directive.

Coley can't contain her tears, and Trey gets out of his seat, taking the mic from Max and shutting it off. He holds him tightly, and they exchange words that none of us can hear. They're both crying—I can tell—and I can't stay in my seat any longer, feeling the lump in my throat.

I join in their embrace. Before I know it, Will and Callen have joined in, and soon after, Coley and Shea throw their arms around us, too. No longer quiet, the room is filled with sniffles and muffled weeping.

"If only Liv were here," Trey says, "it'd be the perfect circle." He looks directly at me, and I nod, wiping my eyes.

"It's pretty damn close, though," I admit. "I love all of you so much."

Everyone repeats my sentiment, and Coley's giggle sets us all off in bittersweet laughter.

Trey switches on the microphone again. "Were you finished?"

"Almost," Max says, clearing his throat and taking his place again. He waits until they both sit down before continuing. "You're gonna be a perfect husband to Coney—sorry, Coley." He winks at her, the mistake on purpose. "And I know you have huge dreams, but I hope you have some normal ones, too... like, have some kids, because you helped to raise me right. I can't give Jon and Will all the credit. You had your work cut out for you, too, and it was harder for you, because you were a kid, just like I was. But you would be such a good dad, following in the footsteps of your own.

"And I promise I'll be the uncle to make sure their swear jars send them to college, just like I'm doing for Jon's and Will's kids." The guests laugh again. "And you guys didn't know there was a reason behind all the cursing. I'm not selfish."

A waiter brings out three tumblers, putting a pair in front of the bride and groom and handing the other to Max.

"To the female me, Coley, and the guy everyone should want as a best friend, but somehow, I'm the lucky one, because he's mine—Trey Holland. I hope you guys are nothing but happy... and healthy... for the rest of your lives."

"Here, here!" Will shouts, standing up with his water.

Max walks over to them and taps the rim of his glass to theirs. He and Trey finish their drinks quickly, but Coley only takes a few sips, setting the glass next to her champagne.

"To Trey and Coley!"

"Now... you can all eat," Max says before shutting off the microphone. Instead of taking a seat, he walks down the middle of the aisle toward the back of the room. Callen follows him, weaving through the stream of the waitstaff who are now pouring in, delivering plates to tables.

"Is he okay?" Shea asks.

I shrug my shoulders, deciding to send Callen a text to ask him the same question. I expect his standard "*he will be*" response, but I don't hear anything right away, and decide to eat dinner with the rest of the table, assuming that he will be.

"Was there something with the drinks they had?" Will asks us.

"I think it was bourbon and coke," Stella says. "If it was, that was what they had the night Max met Coley. I think they all kind of consider it their... drink."

"Ohhh," I say. "That makes more sense. Yeah, I knew Trey drank it... I was his supplier for a while before he could buy it."

"You?" Will says, surprised. "Like, before he was 21?"

"Guilty."

"I don't believe it. He's such a by-the-book kind of guy... and you're pretty strait-laced yourself."

"I made him follow rules to stay in my good graces. He was really good about it," I say, blushing.

"Did Liv know?"

"Hell, no."

"So, you *did* keep secrets from her..."

"No," I say, shaking my head. "No. That can't count. I told her everything that mattered. We never hid anything from one another. That... that doesn't count."

"I'm just kidding," Will says, putting his hand on my arm. "Of course, it doesn't count. It's inconsequential. She knew her brother was a good kid. A responsible kid."

"Yeah."

"She knew you'd never do anything to hurt him, either," Shea adds.

"Never. He's my brother." I look up at him as he talks to his bride. I wish Liv could be here to see how happy they both are. I wish she could be here to wish him well. To give Coley guidance. I wish she could see how proud her parents are to see their son marry this woman who lights up any room—and in so doing, shines a light on him. I *do* rest easy knowing that she saw the perfect match that they were for many years. She knew they would make one another happy for the rest of their lives long before a ceremony was even planned.

And tonight—that gives me peace. Being in the presence of my family and her family—that gives me peace. Having her daughters here to take part in the service—that gives me peace. Knowing that we'll be picking up Luca on the way to our dream home and spending the night together—that gives me peace.

After dinner, I look over at the other table and notice Edie and Willow aren't there. Peron lets me know that they went to the dressing room after my oldest suggested they reapply their lip gloss. It doesn't look like they ate much of their dinner, but it doesn't surprise me. It was a pretty sophisticated meal for their taste. I'll make them something if they're hungry when we get home.

"Is it clear?" I speak into the dressing room before going in, not wanting to barge in on any of the bridesmaids who may be lounging inside.

"Come in, Daddy!" Willow yells, then laughs hysterically. I brace myself for what I'm about to find, but even then, I wasn't prepared for the sight in front of me.

Willow's tucked into Max's side as he flips through one of her books. He's squinting, clearly unable to read because he's not wearing his glasses. Callen has pulled over one of the vanity stools to sit near him, and he's holding a tray of makeup. Edie is standing in front of my brother and appears to be putting the finishing touches of eye makeup on to him—and not just a small amount to highlight features. It's a smoky eye if the eye had been through a seven-alarm fire and burned down to soot and ashes.

Edie has already finished with his lips and cheeks. They're very similar in color to each other—sort of a deep coral red.

"Oh, lord. Bunny, what have you done?"

"I'm just practicing," she says, matter of fact.

"Was your uncle awake for this, or..."

"Yes... he said it was fine."

He blinks up at me, and I notice the clumps of mascara on his lashes.

"Looks great," I tell him.

"I trust you're being honest with me. I haven't seen yet—but we're not lying to each other anymore..."

"Yeah, I'm lying," I admit, shaking my head. "Not sure what look you're going for."

"Whatever look makes your daughter happy."

I smile, appreciative of his response.

"That's sweet of you. Liv would let her do this on occasion..."

"That's what she said." He looks back at the book. "What am I looking at here, Wils? Is that an octopus?"

"No! It's a woman in a spacesuit!"

"How many limbs does she have?" he exclaims, trying to move closer to the page before Edie pushes him back into the sofa to apply powder to his forehead.

"Let me have it." Willow takes the book from him and slides it into her lap. "That's Sally Ride, you dummy," she mumbles.

"Wils."

"Sorry."

"She's right. She's lightyears ahead of me in science. I won't argue with her there."

"She's not allowed to call you *dummy*. It's not nice."

"Gimme five bucks." Max holds out his hand but doesn't turn away from Edie's steady application of makeup. "I know you have it. I saw Callen give it to you. You owe me."

"You don't need that money," she states.

"You don't either, sweetheart," he argues. "You're gonna be a billionaire before I am."

"Really? Am I, Daddy?"

"No." I glare at Max, but it's wasted on him since he can't see. "Hey, you guys didn't eat anything. Do you want me to get you some plates? I'm sure they can put something together for you in the kitchen."

"We're good," Callen says. "We're staying down here, and there's a restaurant nearby that he likes... we'll just go there in a bit."

"Like *that*? Are you sure?"

"Maybe after a shower, but yeah. We ate just before we left."

"That was hours ago. What's the restaurant?"

"It's a... a vegan place," he says.

"Wow, you really went through with that, huh?" Max nods. "You, too?" I ask Callen.

"For the most part. He's hardcore. I'm about 90 percent there."

"Oh, Trey didn't offer a vegan plate, did he?"

"He had vegetarian," Max said. "And the salad was vegan. He offered to go out of his way for me, but I told him it was dumb. Not to worry about it."

"I can't believe he didn't do it anyway."

"I'm sure he did..." Max says, making a face. "But... I just... I don't know if I trust the preparation when everything else here isn't vegan, right?"

"I guess I can see that."

"Finished!" Edie finally exclaims.

Callen sets the tray of makeup aside and hands Max his glasses.

"I don't know, babe. I don't think it's your look."

"I could go drag," he argues. "Gimme a dress and heels. I could pull it off."

"There are some dresses back here, Uncle Max!" Edie suggests.

"Nooo..." Callen and I both say in unison as my brother stands up to study himself in a mirror.

He grins. "You don't think I make a pretty girl?" he asks Callen.

"You *do*, but..." He stands up and puts his hands over Edie's ears. "She was way too heavy-handed. It's way too much. You could do light contouring, some concealer under the eyes, maybe a little highlighting on the lids, just some gloss on the lips, and your lashes, babe, they don't need mascara. You have gorgeous lashes."

Max turns quickly and grabs Callen around the waist, holding him there so he can kiss him and smear some of the lipstick on his partner's mouth. They both look a mess now.

"I hope you have a plan to take all that off," I say.

"I hope he does, too," Callen says, looking only slightly annoyed.

"For you," Edie says, handing a small packet of makeup-removing cloths to him. "But don't give it to Uncle Max, please?"

Callen hears something outside the makeshift room. "I think I hear... cake?"

Of course, my girls try to take off in a sprint, but I stop them at the door. "Let's walk together, okay? Like proper young adults..."

"You're not young, Daddy," Willow says, taking the hand I offer her. I look at her sideways, but follow them both as I'm dragged out, one daughter on each arm.

CHAPTER 35

$\mathcal{A}$t the end of the night, I swing by Lexi's apartment to pick up my
son. Thankfully, she meets me at my car, so I don't have to wake
up the girls quite yet.

"He was perfect," she whispers. "He just ate, so he should go right
down for you."

"Oh, great. Thank you." I give her gift cards to her two favorite
restaurants.

"I told you I wanted to do this."

"And I appreciate that, but I also want you and Kyle to have a few
nights out on me, okay?"

She gives me a hug. "Livvy was so lucky to have you, Jon."

"I was the lucky one."

"Don't deflect the compliment. You were both lucky, but... you're
doing an amazing job with them and I know she's so proud of you and... at
peace with the way you're continuing to raise them."

I smile at her. "Thanks for saying that. It means a lot. I really hope
she is."

"I have no doubt in my mind. I pray for you every day... and when I see
these kids, I know you're going to be fine."

"Really?" I ask, teasing. "When you see Edie mouthing off, or Willow
running around like a banshee..."

"I see you raising extraordinary little girls... normally. They have a childhood; they're going through adolescence. They aren't privileged little brats... a lot of the kids I teach private lessons to are... horrible. They're Edie and Willow's age and they're entitled little brats and... yours could be just like them. But they're not. They're smart and funny and talented and caring and, yes, they can be a handful sometimes... but that's how tweens are. You just haven't raised them before."

"I kind of have..." I think of my brother, Will.

"Not in this decade, Jon... and it gets harder and harder with each one."

"I'm sure you're right."

"Go home and tuck them all in under their warm blankets... and then you do the same. Get a good night's sleep. Dream of her. I know she's watching over you tonight. I feel her."

"Thanks, sweetie. I'm sure you'll rest well tonight, too. Good night."

*E*die wakes up just enough to help push Luca's stroller into the building while I guide a sleepy Willow, and carry the bags containing the formal dresses and shoes they wore earlier in the day. Our new night doorman greets us and pushes the elevator button, seeing I've got my hands full.

Had I a third hand, I'd tip him right now, but I don't, so I'll make it a point to come downstairs tomorrow night, when I think he'll be on duty again.

The door to my apartment is cracked when we get off the elevator. "Edie, stop." I grab her shoulder and leave Willow with her, my heart immediately racing. I know I locked up this morning. Just as I reach the door, it swings open, revealing Will and Shea.

"Shit," I breathe, pulling at my hair. "What the hell, you guys?"

"I thought the after party was here," Will says. Shea hugs me quickly, then moves past me to wrangle my kids into the apartment.

"No party, no. I'm exhausted... plus, this was your night off! No baby, right?" I nod.

"Yeah, but... why not spend it here, with my favorite brothers?"

"Broth*ers?*" I check to make sure Luca's okay; he's sound asleep in his stroller.

"Max and Cal are getting changed in the other guest room." He nods across the way.

"No, they got a hotel downtown..."

"They changed their minds," he says. "You've got space. We won't be bothersome. I promise."

"I really... I really just want to sleep." I smile at him.

"And we want to support you in your endeavor. Callen and Max are going to sleep on the pull-out couch–"

I snort.

"Right? We laughed about it earlier, too. But, yeah. Callen's committed to being on godfather duty tonight. He wants to do it. I told him Shea and I would be on standby downstairs for help... so you could get a good night's sleep. How long's it been?"

I think about his question as I watch Shea lead my daughters upstairs. Biting the inside of my cheek, staving off tears, I answer. "The night before she died."

He hugs me before I break down, but tears are dripping onto the dress shirt he wore to Trey's wedding, and I hesitate to let him go right away.

"It's okay, Jon," he says softly. "Let us take care of you tonight, okay?"

I nod my head against his, knowing he can feel my response.

"Jon?" Shea calls down. "Do we need to do baths tonight?"

"Oh," I say, wiping my eyes and sniffling, then looking up at her. "No, they're wiped out. We'll do showers in the morning. If we can get them into pajamas, I'll call it a win."

"I've got this," she says.

"What're you drinking?" Max asks, breezing past me in purple yoga pants and a tank top that's not befitting for the cold, winter night we're predicted to have. There's no trace of makeup left on his face, but I'm wondering if he got this clean at the venue, or here, in my guest bathroom. "Beer... or that fancy scotch you have with Jack sometimes... whaddya want?"

"Are you drinking with me?" I ask him, knowing the pot has worn off by the vibrant look in his eyes.

"Nope. This is to help you sleep better."

"Then pour a glass of scotch. A little goes a long way," I tell him. "But help yourself..."

Callen greets me in a Bruins sweatshirt, matching flannel pants and light blue fuzzy socks—not a look I'm used to seeing Callen wearing, but I like that he's made himself at home here.

"Did you guys eat?" I ask him.

"Nah."

"Eat. Raid my fridge. There's plenty. Lots of healthy stuff..."

"You hear that, babe? Your brother's feeding us."

"Fuck, yes, I'm starving," Max says as he hands over the scotch. "First, though, should we put the baby to bed? Take him upstairs?" he asks me.

"I'll do it."

"No." Callen puts his hand on my chest. "Sit down. We can do this. Does he need to be changed?"

Holding my drink away from the stroller, I stick my head in and sniff. "No, seems good right now. But he'll need to be at some point tonight."

I watch as Callen carefully tucks his hands under my son's body and lifts him, supporting his head like he was taught, and brings him into his chest. "Tell your daddy good night, pal," he whispers, bouncing lightly.

Luca's still sound asleep, proving that Callen might be perfectly suited for caring for my son. Not many people can get him out of the stroller without waking him. I gently press my lips to Luca's head. "Good night, son. I'll see you... in a few hours?" I look at Callen, and he shakes his head.

"In the morning," he confirms. "We're taking the baby monitor."

"No, you're not."

"We are," Will confirms. "Shea and I will have one, and Max and Cal will have the other. That's four people looking after him to your *one*. I *promise* you he'll be in good hands."

"I don't know that I'll be able to sleep well without that," I admit.

"Then Max didn't pour enough," Callen says, looking at his partner, and then back at my glass.

"On it," my youngest brother says as Cal starts up the stairs. My gaze follows him until he makes it to the top, nervous of the precious cargo he has in his arms.

"No, not yet," I laugh. "Let me drink this first, and then I'll let you know if I need more."

"We've got better stuff," Max says. "Not here, but it's a cab ride away."

"No, Mascot. I'm not doing *that*."

"No! They're sleep aids, you dolt." He leers at me, then chuckles.

"I don't know why you have sleep aids, too."

"Perhaps they're not mine," he says. "When are you gonna sit down?"

I sigh, then finally take a seat on the couch. My brothers join me. "Why's Cal taking sleeping pills?" I ask him casually.

"Stress. His job. His brain just churns and churns and doesn't shut the fuck off."

"Boy, do I know that feeling?" Will says. "But that woman upstairs saved me..."

I smile at Will, but look back at Max, curious. "And the other *stuff*... doesn't... help?"

"He doesn't do that. That's just me."

"Oh." I take a sip of the Glenlivet. "Okay. Hey, do you want me to make something for you to eat?"

"I'll get it," Will says, getting off the couch. "Is everything fair game?"

"Whatever you want," I tell him.

"Vegan," Max states his preference.

"Wow... how things have changed. I remember you nearly gagging at my place over an eggplant dish," Will teases him. "What do you think of it now?"

"I liked it after I ate it then," Max says, "and I love it now."

"I've got some... in that bowl on the counter."

"And I know how to cook it. What does Callen like?"

"He likes it, too."

"Perfect. I get to cook one of Shea's new recipes. She'll be so impressed with me," Will says, almost giddy.

"I wanna watch," Max says, relocating to one of the barstools.

"Daddy? We're going to bed," Edie says, her exhaustion evident in her pronouncement.

I set my drink aside. "Do you want me to tuck you in, Wils?" Edie had recently informed me she was *too old* for this.

"Aunt Shea's going to, but will you check on me when you go to bed?" she asks.

"Of course, I will. I love you girls. You were great today."

"Love you, Daddy," they both tell me.

I decide to follow Max to the island, where I can look up and see the doorway to Luca's room. The baby isn't crying, so things must be going well with him.

"Your partner appears to be a natural at this baby thing." I bump Max on his left shoulder.

"Right? I had no idea." He shrugs. "Good thing that kid got the third godfather," he teases me as he watches our brother add seasoning to a slab of eggplant. "Let me see those spices."

When Shea joins us, she fixes glasses of ice water for everyone else in the apartment. Subconsciously, I took the "they'll take care of me" idea to heart, because it never occurred to me to offer them anything. I don't apologize for my inhospitableness. I just take another sip of my scotch, relaxing, reveling in the way it's making me feel. It was a long day, and I feel unburdened right now, having my brothers, Shea and Callen here. The absence of Trey and Coley is noticeable, but I'm too happy for them to miss them.

The absence of Livvy is... becoming something I'm used to. The fact that I thought of her brother and sister-in-law before her is significant. I drink the rest of the scotch to rid my throat of the lump residing there. Before my glass hits the countertop, Max has it in hand and is returning to the bar. He pours double the amount. I don't stop him.

"Luca's sound asleep," Callen says, squeezing one of my shoulders and putting a baby monitor on the countertop, equidistant from all of us. "I ended up changing him, and he got a little fussy, so I rocked him back to sleep."

"Shut up, no you didn't."

"I did," he says, smiling.

"I saw him." Shea validates his story.

"He always cries when someone else changes him."

"Then they don't know how to do it right," he challenges. "With confidence, speed and grace. Just how I played ball." He's cocky when he says it. "It works in so many aspects of my life."

"It's true," Max says. "Sometimes, we ditch the grace."

"Mascot," Shea says, throwing a dishtowel at his head and laughing. Callen's quick in his reflexes, though, just as he bragged he was, and catches the makeshift weapon mid-toss.

"He's not wrong, though." Before he's finished with his sentence, he's done a jump-shot, hurling the balled-up towel into the far side of the sink across the kitchen. "Still got it. Hey, Jon, do you have any avocados?"

I nod to them on the counter, not far from the dishtowel's final destination.

"I'm making your dinner, *Grace*," my brother says as Callen grabs a knife and a piece of fruit.

"This is an appetizer. Anyone want some avo toast?"

I plug my ears. "You sound like California. Get out."

"We plan to," Max says, pulling one of my hands from my ear. "Give us time. I want some."

"I was kidding. I don't want you to leave."

Shea pulls herself up on the counter, watching how Callen prepares the dish and, I suspect, monitoring how Will is cooking the eggplant, too.

Once a plate is set in front of my youngest brother, I grab a wedge and take a bite, wondering what's so special about this delicacy. I'm surprised to actually like it. I nod, placing the rest back on Max's plate. "Guys," I start, looking between him and Callen, "really... you aren't seriously... thinking of moving all the way to the other side of the country, are you?"

"We are," my brother says quickly. Callen's biting his lip and lets Max answer for him.

"But with everything that's happened—"

"No," he shuts me up. "I'm not gonna feel responsible, or guilty, or whatever. Jon, sometimes we have to take care of ourselves, and this is what I have to do."

"But tonight, right? It feels right, all of us together, doesn't it? And with Trey and Coley, it would be perfect. Don't you feel like that's how it's supposed to be?"

"I'm not denying that you guys and Trey and Coney are... the people I'd want around me all my life. No question. But the rest of this city is slowly suffocating me, man. It's sucking the life out of me, and that shouldn't be okay with you. It should concern you, and it should be reason enough for you to support this decision."

My eyes plead with Callen, who hasn't said a word. I gather he's still reluctant to move to the West Coast, too. His *career* is here—the company he and his father currently run—the one he's set to take over next year. He looks away from me, but I call him on it.

"Callen, come on. What about McNare Holdings?"

"That's why we haven't gone yet," he responds. "There are details to iron out."

"And he's got to do it soon," Max adds, not looking at him. "But he will." I notice he doesn't talk *to* Callen when he says it, but *about* him, as if it's something unresolved between them. To me, that means there's still room to talk him out of the idea. There have to be reasons for him to stay in Manhattan, or at least closer to New York than California. I just have to work harder to find them.

But if the people he loves most aren't reason enough, I realize I have my work cut out for me.

"Will, Shea, what do you think?"

They look at one another, then at Max, then at me. "We support him," Will says. "He swears he'll come to visit us often, and I believe him."

"The food options here are much more diverse," Shea says, "and I know they're used to that." She winks at Max, and he grins.

"We still gotta find a way for you to ship stuff on dry ice to us."

"I'm working on it. It's a whole new business model."

"Wow," I say in disbelief. "Well, Trey can't support this, right?"

"Trey and Coley are moving to Boston until he graduates from law school," Callen informs me, and I'm shocked no one has told me this already. "Then he's floated the idea that they may go to DC after that for a little bit."

"No way. There's just... no way. What about Jack and Emi?" *What about Max?*

"They get it. They support him," Max says. "That's where everything happens. It's where he'll get the most experience. He'll come back, though. But, see, Jon, this is what I'm talking about. We all have places we need to be. Will went to fucking Abu Dhabi and you supported him."

"He came back. It was part of his program. I knew he had a plan, and he came back. It's obvious you don't want that... and what's your plan?"

"Not everyone has a fucking plan, man!"

"Guys, guys," Will says. "Jon, we're not doing this tonight. This isn't why we came over. We came over to take away all your cares, right? Isn't that why we did this, Max? Cal?" They both nod their heads.

"I didn't bring it up," Max says.

"Don't argue," Will tells him. "Let's drop it for tonight." He looks at my glass and shakes his head. "Keep drinking, okay? I'm sorry it went there. Just... know that we're all truly here for you. In the ways you need us, when you need us. Okay?"

In an effort to forget what's stressing me out, I quickly drink the rest of my scotch, knowing that Max will replace it with more. I haven't been drunk in a long time, and if that's what it takes to forget about Livvy not being here, and Max and Callen moving 3,000 miles away, then so be it.

A deafening whirr awakens me sometime later. Alert, I sit up and blink, feeling my dry contacts still in my eyes. Finally, they allow me to survey my surroundings. It's snowing heavily outside–I can see it from nearly every angle, and it's beautiful in the moonlight, but I can feel it, too. It's cold in here. I pull the comforter tighter around me, and realize I'm lying on the polished concrete floor of the studio. The noise was the heater, set to come on when the temperature hits 55 degrees. I know this because I set it that way last spring, knowing I'd change it when winter came, and we would come up here to work.

My head pounds and I stumble when I attempt to get up, feeling the effects of the far too many glasses of Glenlivet I had. Finding myself in only boxers and an undershirt, I don't leave the comfort of the blanket. Wandering to the thermostat, I bump it up to 80, then realize it will take hours to heat the cavernous room. My feet are like icicles on the floor, and I should probably just go downstairs to go back to sleep. I'm too tired to trudge all the way down there, though. The logical–and economical–side of me turns it back down to 70. It'll still feel vastly warmer than it does now.

On my way back to the spot in the middle of the room, I see a painting, and it hits me.

I'm in the studio. *Her studio*. That restricted space I haven't allowed myself to go since she herself stopped coming here after she got pregnant. Slowly, I turn in a full circle to see how she left it, and it's like time stopped one day–or over a few days–as there are multiple paintings on easels that await their artist's adept hand to complete them. There's her steel water bottle, which she'd looked for and asked me about many times, placed on a stool next to one of the canvases, likely the last one she had worked on.

I step in front of it and study it, noticing first the fine layer of dust that lines the top of the canvas and wondering why I didn't at least come up here and cover her work. After finding a small, clean brush, I gently begin to sweep it away, hoping she doesn't think I've mistreated her art in some way.

"I never would, baby," I whisper aloud. "I hope you know that."

A thicker brush lays at the base of the canvas. After picking it up, I mimic her strokes, wondering which was the final one, studying the streaks closely, assuring myself that if the lights were on, I could figure it out.

"Was it this one?" I touch a curved, light blue line, the only one if its color. "Why this one? Huh? Where were you going with this painting?" Taking a few steps back, I squint my eyes in an effort to see her vision, but I can't. My heart sinks in a feeling of loss, but she was never predictable in that way. It's not like I ever could have come up here and known what she would have painted. I could have tried. I would have been wrong.

Or, had I been right, she would have changed her plans.

"Right?" I laugh to myself. "You totally would have." I start to cry through my laughter. "As much as I think I don't know you... by your art... I know every move you'd make, baby.

"That says something about me, doesn't it?" I wipe my face with the blanket and move on to another one that looks nearly finished, but is still incomplete. "See? Like I know this isn't ready. I know you still wanted to do more with this. At the time, I'd say... you'd add some cadmium yellow... lemon... to the red and put it up here." I make the strokes with the brush. "But today, I think you would mix in some deep ochre, maybe with a wider brush, too, because you'd want it to be more like the earth on a fall day.

"And tomorrow, you'd have a different take on it. But whichever day you ended on, you would have created a masterpiece."

When I replay those words in my head, they come back at me, hard, to my gut... to my *heart*.

"Fuck..." Now in a pile on the floor, shivering, I stare at the gray wall across from me. "Oh, but those masterpieces you've left me," I'm barely able to choke out the words. "They are *beautiful*. Our girls are... the best of us. I'm grateful they knew you, but I hate that they know this pain and loss. Our girls shouldn't be without their mother. Who will teach them all the things I don't know? The whole other half of our life—our *world* together? I'm inept. Ineffective. I can't teach them the beauty of the world—as you envisioned it. As you put it on each of these canvases. Each building and wall. What a thing to deprive them of! *All* of us!

"Will it ever not hurt, baby? Will it ever not feel like a part of myself died the day you did?"

I struggle to compose myself. To catch my breath.

"What's it like where you are? What are you doing with that extra love you took of mine? Half of my heart? What use is it to you up there? Wherever you may be?

"Will you slowly give it back? Does it come back in... memories of you? Are they my own? Ones that others share with me? Or will this love come back entirely new?

"Or is my love with you for good? Always. Everywhere. That is what we promised. But god, baby, it hurts, having it ripped from me like this." I hold my hand over my heart. "You can keep it," I tell her, "but at least sew up the wound somehow. I'm bleeding out here."

I think about her again and realize how selfish I am to complain. I'm here with our children, her family, our friends. "I'll take care of them all, Olivia. I promise you. And please." The tears seem endless on this winter night. "Find a way to know your son. He's so sweet and good and everything you would want him to be, Liv. He gets stronger every day. He looks more and more like you. Had they let you hold him once, would that have been enough to keep you here with us?" The blanket is soaked with my tears. "Why didn't they try? Had they let me see you, I would have held him against you. Held your hand. Reminded you how much I needed you.

"God damn it, Liv, where are you?" Standing up, I go to the center of the room and shout it. "Where are you, Liv?!" Another 360-degree turn proves that she's not here.

And why did I come up here, anyway? To be closer to her through *her paintings*? To be closer to her through some... *god*... in the *sky*?

I kick the legs out from one of her paintings and watch it crash to the floor—not angry but frustrated at the lack of response. At the relative silence. I find an unopened box of tissues in the corner and go through half a box of them in an effort to get out all of my emotions. I watch the snow fall. *Blizzard conditions*. I can barely see the Flatiron from here.

When I turn around, I see her artwork on the floor. From this angle, it yields an entirely new perspective. I think I like it even better this way. "Is this how you intended it?" I ask her as I pick it up. Instead of setting up the easel again, I simply prop it up on the ledge of the window, its frame only slightly bent from falling to the ground. *And after I just promised I'd never mistreat her art.*

Drained, I return to the floor with the comforter, curl up in it, and, staring at her unfinished masterpiece, my eyes drift closed.

*T*he sunlight naturally wakes me up in the morning. It must be around 7:30, because the golden orb is barely over the horizon. Warmer than I was when I woke up last night, but still cold, I stand up and stretch, then return the blanket to my shoulders and walk to the windows. The snow has stopped, but it's left its mark over the city below me. Scant cars brave the streets, indistinguishable from sidewalks, and even fewer people appear to be walking in the wonderland left by last night's storm.

The whole city is white or gray; it's not a common sight, and it's not one we've seen since we moved into this building. It's pretty awe-inspiring. If Liv were here, she'd probably be exactly where I stand, a mug of hot chai in her hand as ideas whirled through her magnificent mind. Deciding to take the path I know she'd walk, I slide along the perimeter, wishing I had socks, but forgetting about my cold feet as I see the city from another view. It's gorgeous. It makes me want to draw again—something I haven't done creatively in ages.

On the north side, color jumps out at me. It's a familiar pop of colors, but I haven't seen it in a while, and I'm used to seeing it on a much smaller scale—on paper; in pictures. I'd seen her sketches and her studio mockup as she planned it, and only a handful of times had walked past the actual site. I'd avoided it since her death. This one's 26-stories tall, nearly half the size of my building. It's the wall Liv painted last winter for the Lexington Park Art Society to kick off their year-long, city-wide campaign for public art. It's as vibrant as it was the day she painted it.

She had signed a three-year contract with the society to paint the building every year. No one has mentioned what will happen to this piece come January, when this campaign has run its course.

Leaning against the window, the bottom few inches coated in a layer of ice, I take in this particular masterpiece, hoping to remember all the details just as I see them now. If she could see it at this moment, she would appreciate the impact it truly has—the only spot of color on an otherwise white and gray day. She always loved it when nature played in her favor. Nature was loving her today.

Turquoise and coral and red and deep blue—the only four colors on the whole sign—arranged in such a way, in different gradations that the depth played tricks on the eyes. It was powerful. Art in its finest. They even used her design in their brochures for the year—something Liv wasn't used to seeing.

And the *LPAS* logo, in a typeface I actually designed with her—*for* them. They'd wanted to rebrand and let us go carte blanche, but Livvy couldn't pick a letterset that felt right with her art. I listened to her complaints and worked with her until we got it right. It's humble, yet entirely unique, with spacing that gives it its own sense of harmony and understated strength.

"Holy shit, Olivia. Do you see it?" I smile, standing up and walking to the farthest corner of the building—the closest I can get to her graphic artwork without going downstairs and walking there myself in the blustery weather, which I'm tempted to do. "*LPAS*. Holy shit." I feel the stubble on my chin and smile. "I... I... I didn't mean to, but... holy shit!

"Baby... look..." I point as if she's standing next to me. "You painted your little boy's initials on the building! Luca. Paxton. Augustus. Scott."

I know it's a coincidence. She didn't pick the letters to paint, and she certainly didn't pick his name, but... even still, I swear I'm sharing a moment with her right now. It's like she's reminding me of the beauty she left me to care for. And the colors, being so vibrant and lively, only lift my spirits. It's why she put them together in the first place.

"I guess I don't need to second guess the name," I say aloud, still grinning and feeling hopeful. "That was the one, right? That was what you were thinking, too?" I look upwards, wishing she could talk back, but feeling oddly comforted anyway. "What am I saying? You got Auggie. That's all you wanted."

I'm sure Luca's awake by now, and I should relieve my brothers, Callen and Shea. The girls will want to see the beautiful sight outside, too.

I return downstairs the way I'd obviously come up—by the private stairway we'd built as a part of our bedroom, thinking we'd be going up to the studio a lot more than either of us had. I'll go up later today and clean off her paintings, though, and cover them up for storage. Perhaps I'll tidy up the rest of her space while the kids are out of school for Christmas. I know one daughter who'd get a lot more use out of her skateboard with those polished concrete floors.

After putting on some jogging pants and a Yale sweatshirt, I leave my bedroom only to find silence in the rest of the apartment. The girls are both asleep in Edie's room. Max's arm is draped over his partner, but it's literally the only thing keeping Cal warm, since Max has all the blankets and Callen apparently sleeps in his briefs. He must be freezing—the library isn't the warmest spot in the place. I take a blanket from the back of an armchair and drape it over Callen, careful not to wake them up.

I hear Luca stirring—in stereo over the monitor as well as from the next room. Before he awakens anyone else, I hurry in there and shut off the electronics in his room and close his door.

"Little man," I say, happy to be reunited with my son after a night without him. "It's been too long, hasn't it? Did you miss Daddy?"

He starts to cry.

"No, Luca, sweetie, I'm here now... let's get you a new diaper..." By the mess that's still on the changing table, I know someone was in here doing the job at some point overnight. "Who took care of you, huh? Was it Callen? Callen wouldn't leave things in disarray like this, would he? He would?" I tickle the soft skin of his belly, getting him to smile for me. "There's my happy baby."

After changing him, I look through his closet for something warm to wear. I find an outfit I've never seen before—long pants, a long-sleeved shirt that buttons down the front, soft as can be, and the best part is that it looks like a little baseball uniform. It's a pin-stripe print with a big "3" on the back under the word "SCOTT" in bold, arced block letters. On the front, it says "Auggie" in cursive. *I know where this came from.*

Smiling, I put it on my son, even though it's clearly too big for him. I fold up the sleeves and pant legs a few times. The drawstring at the waist keeps the pants over the diaper; otherwise, they'd fall right off if I held him upright. There's a cap to go with it, but it swallows his tiny head, and he squeals when I put it on him. Instead, I find a little red beanie in his sock drawer to keep his head warm.

He looks adorable. I hold him up, earning myself another gorgeous smile, seeing Livvy in the way his mouth curls up and his nose crinkles. "Olivia, doesn't he look like you?"

I keep holding him up, making sure she gets a good look. "She thinks you're so handsome, Luca. *Auggie*," I whisper, just for Livvy's sake. "Do you want to see something? We have to go wake up your aunt and uncle... let's go do that."

Because of the angle of the building and the placement of our bedroom closet, Livvy's mural can't be seen from our second floor, so I take my son down the stairs and knock softly on the north guest room door, where the entire outer wall is a window.

"Come in," Shea says. She responds quickly but sounds tired.

She's typing on her phone.

"Where's Will?"

"He went to pick up Charlie."

"What? How? Have you seen the streets?"

"My baby's taking the subway."

"It's so cold!"

"Charlie's got arctic wear, trust me. Will borrowed some of your clothes and your ski jacket... he said you were gone, too."

"No... not gone. Do you want to see something cool?"

"Sure," she says, getting out of bed and following me to the window.

"What do you see out there?"

"Snow... a lot of snow."

"And?"

"Well... Liv's art, of course."

"Notice anything... interesting about it?"

"Is something different?" she asks. I shake my head. "It's the only colorful thing out there today."

"I know," I say with a sigh. "It's also the only thing advertising my little boy's initials."

She looks, then gasps playfully. "Wow!" She takes hold of Luca's hand and leans over to his level, now speaking in baby talk. "Do you see that? Your mama painted *LPAS* on that building just for you!"

"Isn't that weird?"

"That's... incredible."

"Yeah."

"How did you just now notice that?"

"Can't see it from my floor, and I don't come in here... but I apparently made it up to the studio in a drunk stupor last night... and that's what I woke up to this morning."

"You went to the studio?" she asks, her hand over her mouth. I nod. "You haven't gone since... she..."

"Since she got pregnant and told me it made her sick. No."

"Oh, Jon," she says, giving both me and Luca a hug. "How was it? How are you?"

"I had a talk with her. Or, rather, I talked *at* her. She didn't say much back, but... I felt closer to her anyway. Seeing her artwork up there was great. It felt... cathartic. Maybe it's something I should have done a lot sooner," I suggest. "Seeing that acronym, though, and realizing they're Luca's initials... that felt good. Maybe it's a sign or something. Maybe she's saying she approves of the name... or approves of the job I'm doing."

"God, of course she does, Jon," she assures me.

"Sometimes it takes... something out of this world to convince people of things, though. I'm not the most stubborn one of us, but... I am pretty hard-headed."

"Oh, you're stubborn," she agrees, laughing.

"I'll leave you to whatever you were doing. Little man needs a little bottle. Should I get breakfast started?'

"I stayed up late. We've got a casserole in the fridge and you have plenty of things on hand to make some pumpkin muffins... which I know you like. Just go put the top oven on 350 and the bottom on 375. I'll go shower and we can divide and conquer."

"Sounds like a plan."

Will and Charlie come in while Luca's taking his bottle and the coffee just finishes brewing. I heard them coming from the moment they stepped off the elevator because his son is wailing, very unhappy about something. "I'm sorry I'm sorry I'm sorry," my brother says as he comes in. "He's hungry. We didn't pack enough milk. Where's Shea?"

I cringe. "Shower."

Luca is not bothered by the noise, though, and continues to happily suck on his breakfast, fighting off the milk coma while I feed him.

"What the fuck?" Max says, rubbing his eyes as he comes down the stairs in his underwear.

"Get back up there and put on some clothes. I have little girls, you know, and they don't need to be asking what that is." I nod to his bulge, annoyed.

"They've never seen you in your underwear?" he asks me, filling a mug with coffee.

"Not... casually, walking around the apartment. If they did, I was rushing to cover up because they walked into something they weren't supposed to see."

"Ahhh. Sexy time," he says.

"Since when do you drink coffee?"

"I do nice things for that guy upstairs sometimes, you know? Especially when I know he didn't sleep well because some little poop monster kept wanting a clean butt."

"So, Callen left that mess in his room?" I ask, not as an accusation, but just because I'm surprised.

My brother glares at me before opening the refrigerator door. "Don't give me shit about the mess."

"So, *you* did that," I say, nodding. "No shit given... it just wasn't in Callen's character."

"It wasn't in Callen's character," he mocks me in a voice that doesn't sound anything like mine.

"What can I help you find?"

"Got it," he says, pulling out a beer.

"No," I tell him. "It's barely eight in the morning."

"Pain doesn't follow a *schedge*, Jon. I left my meds at home."

"I've got some ibuprofen."

"This is numbing *and* calming, though. Why kill one bird when you can kill two? Tweet tweet... am I right?" He opens it before I can protest any longer. "Want me to put it in a cup so the girls can't see? I can hold it over my junk, too. That'll kill three birds." He grins his charming smile and picks up the coffee, then leans in closer to me. "I'll go put clothes on," he whispers loudly in my face.

"Good god, brush your teeth."

"Left my toothbrush at home, too."

"Seriously? There are some extra ones in the guest bathroom down here."

"I'll grab one after my beer," he calls out to me, opting to take the elevator up one floor instead of the steps.

Charlie's latched onto Shea's breast when she makes it into the kitchen. It takes me a moment to realize she plans to carry on as normal with breakfast preparations, even though her little one's trying to eat.

"Sit down, Mom," I tell her, kicking out the chair beside me. "Breakfast for everyone else can wait, but your son needs your attention now."

The doorbell chimes, and I do a quick mental calculation to make sure everyone's here; I'm pretty sure we're all accounted for.

The front door opens on its own, though, startling me only momentarily until I see Trey holding the door for his newlywed wife.

"What the hell are you guys doing here?" I ask, standing and setting Luca's empty bottle aside. On my way to greet them, I grab a dishtowel and flip it over my shoulder.

"Teterboro is shut down," Coley says. "So are most of the roads to get there... so the honeymoon's off for a few days, I guess. We checked the app, saw that everyone was here and thought we'd take the train over."

"We felt left out," Trey says. "May I?" He reaches for Luca, so I secure the towel over his shirt instead.

"Can I help with breakfast?" Coley asks.

"No," I tell her as I make my way to the kitchen. "Go sit down and put up your feet. Just because you're not on a tropical island somewhere doesn't mean we're putting you to work. I've got breakfast under control."

"Coley?" Edie shouts from the second floor. "Coley and Trey?"

"Well, I guess Callen's really awake now," I mumble, now hearing the familiar patter of my daughters' footsteps as they run down the stairs. "Girls," I say to them as they hug their aunt, "don't run down the staircase."

"Sorry, Daddy," Willow says.

"But Coley and Trey are here!" Edie argues.

"I know, I know!" I say, trying to meet her level of excitement.

"Casserole in the top?" I ask Shea.

"Yes, but we need to get the muffins started first."

"I've got it," Will says, wearing one of my Columbia sweatshirts as he glides into the room.

"Did no one bring their own stuff over here?" I tease him, yanking on the hood.

"I didn't pack for a blizzard, I'll put it that way."

"We can start a fire," I suggest.

"If someone wants to take Luca, I'll do that," Trey offers.

"Give me that baby," Coley says. "The girls and I want to play with Luca, don't we?" She turns around. "Shea, they've got things under control. Come in here and let's have some girl time."

"With our sons..." Will and I both say at the same time.

"Is this when they put dresses on them?" my brother asks me.

"Possibly," I tell him. "It was always a matter of time... it's the makeup you need to worry about. Ask Max."

"What?"

"I should have taken a picture. Not sure why I didn't," I say, scratching my head. "Edie gave him a makeover at the wedding last night." I lean in so my comments don't make it to my sensitive daughter's ears. "It was awful."

"Surely Callen got a picture..."

"I don't think Cal wants to remember that."

"You don't think he likes a little kink? A little roleplay?" I backhand him before getting out some eggs for him. "I think he does."

"Why do you insist on making me uncomfortable like that?"

"It's just sex."

"It's our brother." I close my eyes and shake my head.

"It's easy for me to separate the two," Will tells me. "Coconut oil?"

"In the pantry."

"Right."

"Do you have this recipe memorized?"

"I've been helping to make these for the restaurant every weekend this winter," he tells me. "Gives Shea more time with the baby. Cloves?"

"Right next to the cinnamon on the spice rack."

"Cool. Want to cut up some fresh fruit? I saw you had a bunch."

"Yeah, I can do that."

"Hey, Jon?" Coley calls out.

"Does he need a new diaper?"

"No, Luca's fine. I wanted to know if you had some chai. It seems like a good morning for chai..."

"I do... I'll get some started. How many do we need?" I take a count of hands around the room, and know that Max will probably drink a cup, too. Emi has made addicts out of all of them.

My daughters relocate to the hearth once Trey's started the fire, and he joins my brother and me in the kitchen, taking over tea duty. "Where are Max and Cal?"

"Upstairs. I think I heard the water going," I tell him. "Taking a shower, maybe."

"Why the slumber party?"

I smile at him. "They wanted to give me a night off... Callen and Max took care of Luca during the night; Shea put the girls to bed last night. I got drunk."

"Drunk? You?"

"They got me drunk, I should say. There was obvious intent."

"I'm ashamed to say it," Will speaks up, "but it's true. It was the only way we were gonna get him to stop being a responsible adult for a night."

"Yeah, there's really no other way, with Jon." I punch Trey's arm playfully. "So, did you pass out?"

"After I climbed up the back stairs to the studio, I did."

Their eyes get wide. "Is that where you were this morning?" Will asks me. I nod. "Oh. Oh, wow. I... I never would have checked there. I assumed you went to the store to get something. I guess I should have looked at the app."

"I was fine. Freezing, but fine."

"Was the heat not on?" Trey asks.

"It came on when it hit 55. I turned it up to 70 at that point, but... I wasn't dressed for that. Thankfully, I had our down comforter."

"I stripped you down to your boxers and t-shirt," my brother says, laughing. "Shit, you must have been an icicle."

"You took my socks, too, asshole."

"You can't go to bed with underwear and socks. That's such a dad move."

"I'm a dad. Newsflash, so are you."

"We don't have to look like them." He pats my stomach. "Some sit-ups should help."

"What are you saying?"

"You've got a gut," Max says from across the room. I feel my face flush. "It's manageable. Sit-ups... less of those muffins they're making you, for sure..." he mumbles when he gets into the kitchen.

"Hey!" I look around, shocked, and feel the ab muscles—or feel around *for* them. "Holy shit... when did this happen?"

Callen finally joins the rest of us and puts his arm across my shoulders. "Gradually, man. But we've got you. There's a gym downstairs, right?"

"Yeah," I say with a sigh. I've *never* had a problem staying fit, but I realize I haven't been taking care of myself like I did when Livvy was here. I used to run daily. Together, she and I were much more active. Now, when I'm not taking care of the kids, I typically sit or lie down in an attempt to get a moment's rest.

"We'll start running again," Will suggests. "You can bring the kids over in the evenings for an hour—"

"Shea has a newborn baby; I'm not quadrupling her workload!"

"Max offered to help her out," Callen says, pulling me into him, "and I'll go running with you guys, too. We're family, dude. We're gonna help while we can."

"On the weekends, I'll come over and do weights with you," my youngest brother offers. "It's part of my strength training anyway."

"Wait a second," I say, looking around at all the guys. "Is this... is this an *intervention?*"

"Nope," Max says too eagerly.

"You assholes," I say. "The girls in there with their girl time, and all you standing around telling me I'm fat, in the nicest way possible."

"We never said you were fat," Callen laughs.

"You know what we're doing, man?" Will says. "We're taking care of you." His expression is sweet as he shrugs his shoulders. "You've taken care of us all our lives. We just want to return the favor."

"I don't need to—"

"I don't need to be taken care of," Max mouths off, again in some unrecognizable voice that makes us all laugh this time. "Just shut the fuck up and let us do this for you, okay?"

"Did Uncle Max just say *fuck?*" Willow loudly asks.

The entire apartment goes silent.

"What?" my daughter asks meekly, knowing she said something wrong.

"Hey, Wils?"

"Yeah, Daddy?"

"Go get your swear jar."

"Okay!" she says, the smile evident in her voice. Callen pulls some cash out of his pocket.

"Nope," I tell him. "New lesson. *Hard* lesson... but this is how it was always going to be..." It was Livvy's idea, and a good one, I'd thought.

"Oh, don't do it," Will says. "Not to my goddaughter."

"I have good people like you and Max to thank for this..."

"Shit," he whispers as she comes back into the room, proudly holding a mason jar stuffed full of bills, big and small. I bet she has a few hundred dollars in there. I'm sure she knows exactly how much she's amassed over the years, and it's been her choice to save most of it and not spend it.

If it were Edie's swear jar, we'd be looking at about 10 bucks.

"Put it on the counter," I tell her. She sets it there but doesn't release it. "Let go."

"Daddy..."

"What did Mama and I tell you would happen if you ever said that word?"

"I don't know..."

"You *do* know."

She sighs. "You would take some of my swear money."

"How much of your swear money?"

"All of it." Tears form in her eyes.

Max, Callen and Trey leave the kitchen at that point; Will turns his back, going back to mixing the muffin batter.

Willow climbs up onto a bar seat and puts her head onto her crossed arms. She watches as I take the jar and put it high up into the pantry, out of her reach. "I'll be taking that upstairs after breakfast."

She nods; her fat bottom lip makes me want to give the jar back to her, but I can't.

"Daddy, are you gonna spend all my money?"

"No, sweetie, I'm not going to touch the money, but it's not yours anymore. Not now. Do you understand?" I ask her. She blinks, and the tears fall down her cheeks. "I'm going to count it, and I'm going to work with Aunt Shea... and together we're going to come up with ways that you can earn most of it back. But you're putting five dollars in a jar for Luca, and five dollars in a jar for Charlie because you said that word in front of them. Is that fair?"

She nods.

"What about me, Daddy?" Edie says. "Don't I get five dollars, too?"

"And a dollar to Edie, too."

"Doesn't Uncle Callen have to pay for Uncle Max, though?" Willow asks.

"Uncle Max has a different punishment this time. He has to see his niece cry, and that's worse," I explain to her.

"I'm sorry, Wils," he says to her with more sincerity than I've seen from him in a long time. He gives her a big hug, too, and she chokes out some forced sobs to amp up the drama. I know it's fake, but Max can't tell, and I know he feels terrible seeing her go through this punishment.

"Willow, go see if Aunt Shea needs anything right now. You can start earning it back today. Okay?"

"Okay, Daddy. I'm sorry."

"Okay. Good girl. Thank you, Wils."

The guys come back into the kitchen. "See, one good thing about us moving to the West Coast—you'll have one less bad influence on your kids."

"Max," I tell him, stopping what I'm doing and looking right at him, "I'd take Coley's stance on curse words any day of the week if that meant you'd stay here. Call me a hypocrite, but I would." He doesn't say anything, and in fact picks up the knife laying in front of me and begins cutting the fruit I'd been working on. "You're not a bad influence. Nobody in this apartment is a bad influence.

"Built a business from scratch and owns her own restaurant and catering company," I say, pointing to Shea. My attention moves to Coley. "Has written and published three poetry books—no, three *successful* poetry books." I focus on the guys now. "Graduated from business school and is set to take over one of the most reputable companies in the country. World-renowned physicist and rock god. Helped get the first gay, single man elected president and at the top of his class at law school. Paved the way for other single gay teens, and then *risked his life* to save the president-elect, his best friends and hundreds of other strangers.

"I'm standing in the room with... *fucking legends!*" I'm loud enough that everyone can hear me, but it's a point I have to drive home. "I'd be happy if my kids do a fraction of what any of you guys have done with your lives."

"Your kids are on their way," Shea says, carrying a sleeping Charlie with her into the kitchen. Coley follows her. Edie's on the couch with one arm around Willow. Luca's bundled in a blanket, spread across both of their laps. "Look where they got their start, Jon. Pulled himself and his brothers out of poverty. Excelled at Columbia. Partner at one of the top architecture firms on this planet... and who was their mom? Only Livvy Holland Scott. Her name is more recognizable than most world leaders. Her work has been called the art of our generation. Like... Edie and Willow and Luca were given the greatest of parents, Jon." I look down at the floor, acknowledging the loss of one of them, but Shea–astute as always–knows exactly where my mind has gone. "Her absence will never be a disadvantage to them, because we will live our lives lifting her up. She was the best of all of us–for all of us. She brought us all together. Without her, this room full of people simply wouldn't have happened. The friendships. The relationships. The kids. None of us would be here without her.

"So, we won't go a day without her, either. She is a constant in our lives. In our existence, whether she's a physical presence or not. She's not something that disappears. She's not someone who is ever forgotten, not even for a moment. You know why? Because when I look at my son, I see her. When I look at Will, I see her."

"When I look at Cal, I see her," Max says. "I thank her every day. I know it's the bond you two had that brought us all together."

"Even for me," Trey says. "I never would have gone to Columbia had you not talked it up like you did... and I never would have met Coley."

I look around at all of them, grateful. *Thankful*. "And really, let's be real. Don't we owe a lot of this to Jack and Emi? It was their art school; their scholarship that let me in... that allowed me to meet her in the first place."

"Jack and Emi and a little thing called fate," Callen says. "Let's go with that."

"A little thing called fate," I repeat as I look out the window, trying to wrap my head around that. If there's one thing fate is not, it's small. It's the inextinguishable unknown that forces itself upon you like a tornado in the dead of night. Whether it strips you from your roots or leaves you standing in one piece–sometimes you don't discover the outcome until it's come and gone, and the sun begins to shine again.

"Granddaddy and Memi sent a picture," Edie says, slipping in through the crowded kitchen and handing me my phone. I take a look at it and see the two of them smiling, wrapped in a blanket we'd given them as a gift last year, holding up mugs of what I am certain are filled with chai latte.

Cheers from us to you on this blustery winter morning! Jack has typed.

"I think Jack Holland took a selfie," I say with a laugh, handing the phone to Trey.

"Holy crap, he did!" he giggles, giving the phone to Coley. I take my son from her, gently waking him.

"That's so cute!"

"You have to remember, my dad was a tech genius in his day," he reminds us.

"And then he sold off everything and relied on us," Will says.

"And we happily helped him," Callen adds.

"Because we're family." I can't help but get a little emotional, looking around the room again at all the people I love the most. "Thanks to Livvy, I have this family... and it's an entirely different one than I had when I met her, but I love it all the same, and the best part is that I've never felt more secure in the love and the friends I have. And I know we're going to be okay."

Callen has poured lattes for all of us—even my daughters. "Everyone, go sit around the couch with your mugs." I leave mine on the counter, holding my baby close instead.

"Here's Jon's phone," Shea says, giving it to Max's boyfriend.

"I want to be in the front!" Edie says, putting her drink down to fluff her long hair, still curly from last night.

"I'll take the picture," Max offers, sitting next to Edie.

I make sure Luca's outfit can be seen, knowing Jack and Emi would want to see him in uniform. A little tickle to his belly gets a smile out of him, too. After seven attempts, we can't take a photo where someone isn't laughing or purposefully trying to make someone else laugh. In the end, when they hand the phone back to me, I decide to send the entire series.

Wish you were here! is the message I type, but before I hit reply to Jack's text, I add one more person to the message: Livvy Holland Scott.

Wish you were here...

ABOUT THE AUTHOR

Inspired by popular fiction and encouraged by close friends, Lori L. Otto returned to writing in the winter of 2008. After a sixteen-year hiatus, she rediscovered her passion for fiction and began writing what would soon become her first series, **Emi Lost & Found**. Although the books of Nate, Emi and Jack have concluded, other characters from the books continued their own journeys, demanding their stories be told.

For more information:
   www.loriotto.com
   writer@loriotto.com

ALSO BY LORI L. OTTO

Lost and Found

Time Stands Still

Never Look Back

Not Today, But Someday

Number Seven

Contessa

Olivia

Dear Jon

Livvy

Hollandtown Extras

Crossroads

Love Like We Do (side a)

Love Like We Do (side b)

Love Will

In the Wake of Wanting

(It Happened) One Friday

Make Waves

Made in United States
Troutdale, OR
01/16/2024

16967424R00229